Adam Fitzroy

Stage Whispers

Manifold Press

Published by Manifold Press

ISBN: 978–1–908312–93–8

Proof–reading and line editing: F.M. Parkinson
Any remaining errors are the sole responsibility of the author.

Editor: Fiona Pickles

For further details of Manifold Press titles both in print and forthcoming: manifoldpress.co.uk

Other titles by Adam Fitzroy:
    Between Now and Then
    Dear Mister President
    Ghost Station
    Make Do and Mend

Dedicated to Laertes and Rosencrantz –
only a fraction late!

Acknowledgements

The author wishes to thank
Louise and Pamela,
who read the manuscript and kindly
offered suggestions and amendments.

To Louise – Happy Christmas 2013!

Act 1

Scene i
(An attic bedroom somewhere in central England. It is an early morning in the spring of 1996. JON is alone in a double bed, apparently asleep. The telephone rings on his bedside table.)

◆

No actor likes to be startled awake by the telephone ringing before eight o'clock on a Sunday morning, especially if – as is sometimes the case – he happens to be the conscientious type and to have endured a punishing schedule of rehearsal and performance on the previous day. If Jonathan Stapleton was already showing signs of a return to consciousness, and even if by fortunate chance he was also an habitual early riser, the wretched thing was still an intrusion on what until that point had been a leisurely awakening. A moment beforehand he had been drowsily at his ease and basking in the luxury of some well-deserved relaxation, but this unpleasant timing boded either lack of courtesy in the caller, a wrong number or – worse and infinitely more probable – a genuine emergency.

"Jon?"

"Yes?"

"It's Ewen. I'm looking for Callum. Is he with you?"

Astonished, Jon sat up quickly. "I don't keep him in my bedroom, Ewen; he lives downstairs, and that's on a separate number. Let me ... "

But Ewen was still talking.

"He's got to come in." There was more than an edge of panic to his voice. "Sober him up, get him dressed, pour him into a taxi, do whatever you have to do but get him to me as soon as you can; he's going to have to spend the day rehearsing."

1

"What?"

"I'm at the hospital." Ewen sounded like a man who had drunk too much coffee, smoked too many cigarettes, and was hanging close to the brink of exhaustion. "Douggie Pirie, silly bastard, had one too many in the White Horse last night, fell up a flight of stone steps and smashed his bloody knee to smithereens. It's going to be weeks before he can walk properly; nobody can play the Scottish King on crutches, so the boy will have to go on tomorrow night – and for the foreseeable future until we can get somebody in to take over. Never played the part yourself, I suppose?"

"Never! I'd be completely wrong for it."

"Of course you would," acknowledged Ewen, limply. "You're really one of nature's Banquos, aren't you? Well, dig him out, will you, Jon, and point him in my direction? I'll take him through the fights and run lines with him, and I'm calling a full rehearsal for two o'clock. Make sure the others know – and I'll expect you to be there, as well."

"Of course."

"The rehearsal room will be open at nine," Ewen continued, relentlessly. "Maisie's coming at half past to have a look at Callum's costume. I don't want to keep her any longer than necessary – these people have a better union than we do."

"All right. But he can't be there in less than an hour, and probably more like two."

"Understood. I'll get some breakfast, then. Make sure he eats something, for God's sake; it may be a while before he has the chance again, and I don't want him fainting in mid–soliloquy. He knows the part, I suppose?"

"I'm sure he does." But why Jon had been expected to have this information he was uncertain; being the senior man in the house did not exactly put him in the position of either parent or teacher, although heaven knew some of the younger ones over the years had shown a tendency to treat him as such. He was merely a lodger like themselves – of longer standing and with additional privileges, it was true, but with no greater status than their own.

"Then I'll leave it in your hands – and see you at two o'clock." The line clicked abruptly, filling the sunlit bedroom with the disconnection tone.

Jon sat for a moment trying to collect his thoughts. Callum Henley was one of this year's new intake: four or five years out of LAMDA, with a bit of telly and regional rep. behind him, he was supposedly destined for super–stardom by the quickest route – at least, so gossip had it. Not that gossip was infallible, but Jon had seen the boy work. Callum certainly knew what he was doing, and when his fruity light baritone had matured a bit he would be natural casting for the great theatrical roles. The Scottish King at twenty–six, however, would be a stretch even for him. If he was to have any hope of doing it well, he would need someone sensible and grounded to shepherd him through these first chaotic hours.

So much for his quiet Sunday. With a sigh of resignation, wondering which of the several million things he ought to be doing should be first, Jon reluctantly hauled himself out of bed and began to dress.

Ten minutes later he was knocking on the door of Callum's ground–floor bedroom and hoping the young man had not brought company home the night before. Callum was going to need to concentrate without distractions, and being flustered by the presence of some dizzy female would probably not be the best way of starting a difficult day.

"Who the fuck is that?" Some of the provincial vowels that drama school had supposedly smoothed out were evident in the half–awake bellow from behind the closed door. Judging by the direction from which it came, Callum was obviously still in bed.

"It's Jon. There's a problem." Then, when there was no sound of movement from within, he added, "Callum, I'm serious; open the door."

An incoherent sound followed, the creaking of bedsprings, and a fumbling with latches before a sleepy fair head and unshaven jaw appeared around the corner of the door.

"What's up?"

Jon drew a breath. He did not quite know how to deliver what could be either the best or the worst news of Callum's life. "Douggie's broken his leg," he said, gently. "You're going on, at least for the week."

Callum blinked, blue eyes struggling to focus, and then he stood back. "You'd better come in," he said, holding the door open. "What happened?"

Standing in the gloom of the ground–floor bedroom, its extra–thick curtains cutting out a glorious spring morning, Jon related what little information he had. The room looked as if a bomb had hit it: stale clothing was piled on one chair, with several pairs of shoes scattered on the floor. It was obvious that Callum's nights here had been solitary, at least recently; no girl in her right mind would have spent more than half an hour in this turmoil of her own free will.

"Christ, I'd better find some clothes." Callum, wearing only a pair of faded blue boxers, was glancing around despairingly as if expecting a valet to waltz up with a freshly–pressed shirt and pair of trousers. "I'm sorry the place is such a mess."

They were always like this in the beginning, the first–timers who lodged at the Old Crown. They could never get it into their heads that Jon wasn't the landlord, only his representative, and that he didn't care if their rooms were untidy or their bedding was never washed. He handed over the keys at the start of the season and took them back at the end, and if there was any damage he dealt with it; beyond that, whatever they did behind locked doors was their own business.

"It's not important." He was trying to sound reassuring. "Why don't you have a shower and get dressed? I'll make you some breakfast, if you like."

"Good God, really?"

"Yes, really. Bacon, tomatoes and fried bread?"

"Fine. I mean, that's extraordinarily kind." Callum still looked stunned. "I'm going to need a taxi, aren't I?"

"I'll take care of it."

"Thank you."

Jon was moving towards the door, about to abandon Callum to his own devices, when on impulse he paused and turned back.

"This is only happening because you're ready for it," he said. "Concentrate on doing one thing at a time, and let people help you if they want to – although you don't have to listen to every piece of advice you're given. Nobody's jealous; we all like to think it could happen to us one day, too."

"You're telling me I haven't got time to fall apart, aren't you?"

"Absolutely. And to grab your chance with both hands because it may not come again."

"Got it. Thanks. Promise I won't let you down."

"I know."

But Jon had left the room and was back in the kitchen taking the bacon out of the fridge before it occurred to him to wonder why it was his business whether Callum Henley succeeded or not. They hardly knew one another: they had lived under the same roof for a couple of weeks, rehearsed on the same stage, and gone out for drinks with the rest of the company; that was the extent of their acquaintance, and it was all he had ever expected. Callum was lively and formidably energetic – not to mention much younger than Jon, who could scarcely have been described as either of those things. Indeed, he had studied most of his life to be self–effacing and to adopt the colouration of his background; it was one of his reasons for having been attracted to acting as a profession in the first place, that it gave him such a variety of places and ways in which to hide.

Some twenty minutes later, when Callum found his way to the large communal kitchen, they ate in almost total silence. Callum made distracted attempts to be polite; Jon refilled his coffee cup without being asked. The room was quiet and sunny and the house still, with no sign of movement from their fellow inmates.

"The girls are probably still asleep," Jon said, in answer to Callum's enquiring look. "I've left a note for Izzy; she'll make sure they get there on time."

Callum nodded and returned to his breakfast. "What time's my taxi coming?"

"There's no taxi. I'll take you in. It's the best way to stop Ewen panicking." Jon was absently piling plates into the sink.

"You've got a car? I didn't realise."

"More or less. The finance company still owns most of it. I've booked a cab for the others for twelve thirty. Are you ready?"

Callum checked himself over. "Coat, keys, money," he said. "What else?"

"Script?"

"Oh God." Quickly he retrieved it from his room, and a moment later they were crossing the road outside the house. "You're really settled in here, aren't you?" Callum watched Jon unlock one of a line of concrete garages which flanked the pub car park. "Is this your permanent home?"

Jon shrugged. "Not exactly. I've got a flat in London, but there are tenants living in it. Roy lets me stay here more or less rent–free in exchange for keeping an eye on the place."

"Roy?"

"Roy Arbour. This is his house. He and his family own a lot of property in the area. They've been living here for generations."

"Roy Arbour the actor, you mean?"

Jon stared at him. "Of course. We're old friends – we were at drama school together – 'When Roscius was an actor in Rome'." He reversed the car out of its narrow space, flung open the passenger door, got out to lock the garage.

"Roy Arbour," Callum repeated, in awe. "God, he's one of my all–time heroes. I saw him play Tybalt when I was about … "

"For heaven's sake, don't remind him! You'll get a lecture about pink nylon tights and swords that fell apart whenever we tried to use them." A deft turn across the empty car park, and they emerged onto the silent road. "Roy hated everything about that production, but I agree with you – he was very good in it."

Callum nodded. "I haven't heard anything of him for ages. Is he still working? I don't suppose he needs to, does he, if he's got all this property?"

"Only when he feels like it – if he gets a chance to travel somewhere interesting, or meet somebody he admires. He went all the way to

Malaysia once, just to get shot by Sean Connery. He was only on screen for about thirty seconds."

"Hmmm. I would probably have done the same."

"Me too. Unfortunately all I get offered are cuckolded husbands and bewildered doctors, and I never go anywhere more exotic than Newcastle for any of them. Still, it's a living – of sorts." Jon looked up through the windscreen, waiting for the lights outside the church to change. They took their sweet time, but eventually the car pulled away smoothly and began to leave the village behind. "Do you want to run lines on the way?" he asked, diffidently.

"In the car? Are you joking?"

"Only if you want to. If there's anything bothering you."

"What, you'll do it from memory, will you?"

"I'll try. I had thirty–six performances as Young Siward and Second Murderer," Jon told him, smiling out of the corner of his mouth. "Not to mention going on as Malcolm when Bryan Aven sprained his ankle. It was almost my first professional engagement. I wouldn't say I was word–perfect but I'll have a go. Throw me a line and see what I come up with."

Callum seemed to regard this as a challenge. "All right, then, how about this:

> *Methought I heard a voice cry, 'Sleep no more!*
> *Macbeth doth murder sleep.' – the innocent*
> *Sleep that knits up the ravell'd sleave of care,*
> *The death of each day's life, sore labour's bath,*
> *Balm for hurt minds, great nature's second course,*
> *Chief nourisher in life's feast."*

Jon smiled at him. "Too easy," he commented wryly. "'What do you mean?'"

"Hey, concentrate on the road!

> *Still it cried, 'Sleep no more!' to all the house*
> *Glamis hath murder'd sleep: and therefore*
> *Sleep no more, – Macbeth shall sleep no more!"*

Carefully Jon negotiated the mini–roundabout by the industrial estate.

"'Who was it that thus cried?'" he continued. "*Why, worthy thane,*
You do unbend your noble strength to think
So brainsickly of things. – Go get some water,
And wash this filthy witness from your hands. –
Why did you bring these daggers from the place?
They must lie there; go carry them; and smear
The sleepy grooms with blood."

"Hand," corrected Callum, brandishing the script. "Not 'hands'."

"Hand," repeated Jon. "We're not rehearsing me," he added.

"No, but I wish we were. I bet you could play Lady Mac standing on your head. You'd be brilliant."

"Unfortunately I lack a couple of necessary attributes." One hand indicated a particularly flat bosom.

"You could wear padding," laughed Callum. "In true Elizabethan tradition. But I suppose you'd have to lose the beard, which would be a shame."

"Thank you. Are we going to continue rehearsing?"

Callum's mood sobered instantly. "Yes, we are. How can I possibly pass up a chance like this?
I'll go no more;
I am afraid to think what I have done;
Look on't again I dare not."

"'Infirm of purpose!'" rejoined Jon.
"*Give me the daggers, the sleeping and the dead*
Are but as pictures: 'tis the eye of childhood
That fears a painted devil."

"You know, you sound just like Margaret Rutherford."

"I do not!" But it was impossible to be serious with Callum in this mood.

"Jon, would you mind sticking around for the day to help me rehearse?" he asked, almost tentatively. "I think I'd feel a lot more comfortable if you could."

"Of course, as long as Ewen doesn't mind. I can always do with a bit of extra fight practice, anyway."

"But you're not … " Callum stopped in mid–sentence, as if it would be ungenerous somehow to point out that Jon had little or no fighting to do in this production. "I'd really appreciate that," he said, quietly.

"Part of the service.

> *If he do bleed,*
> *I'll gild the faces of the grooms withal,*
> *For it must seem their guilt."*

"'Whence is that knocking?'" continued Callum, smoothly.

> *"How is't with me, when every noise appals me?*
> *What hands are here? Ha! They pluck out mine eyes!*
> *Will all Neptune's ocean wash this blood*
> *Clean from my hands?"*

"Hand."

"Hand.

> *No: this my hand* ('these my hands'?) *would rather*
> *The multitudinous seas incarnadine,*
> *Making the green one red."*

They were slowing again, to a pedestrian crossing outside a school. "It would be more use," said Jon, indicating the signal, "if you could learn to make the red one green."

"I'll work on that for next time." The tension had almost completely drained out of Callum's square frame, his body relaxing, the look on his face calmer now if not entirely optimistic. "You know, I might end up not hating this whole experience after all."

"I'm certain of it. You can do whatever you put your mind to, Callum. Remember that. And look behind you occasionally, because there will always be people who aren't quite as brilliant as you are who may need you to encourage them. They'll appreciate it if you take the time."

"Christ," whispered Callum. "You really think I'm headed straight for the top, don't you?"

"I know you are. I've never doubted it for a minute."

And in the silence that followed this remark Callum murmured something under his breath which Jon, had he felt so inclined, might have interpreted as "God, Jon, I really wish I wasn't."

◆

Ewen Snow, who was anxiously pacing back and forth outside the entrance to the rehearsal room – an unpleasantly industrial–looking facility near the railway line, half a mile from the craggy Victorian theatre – was almost comical in his relief and gratitude at their arrival. Small and stringy, with grey hair and the sort of sinister wire–framed glasses beloved of movie Nazis, he appeared to have been steadily wearing himself away to a frazzle since the day he was born. As Callum and Jon approached, he came within an inch of throwing his arms around them and covering their necks with kisses.

"My God I'm glad to see you!" he exclaimed, crushing his cigarette under one heel. Its limp carcass joined a great many others on the tarmac. "I'm sorry about your weekend, Callum."

"It's hardly your fault," Callum told him. "How's Douglas?"

"Fast asleep when I left him, the stupid sod, piled up on pillows and surrounded by nurses – completely oblivious to all the bloody chaos he's causing. Did you have other plans for today?"

"Nothing that couldn't be postponed." But the idea that anything could be more important than rehearsing for an unexpected lead in so prestigious a production amused them all.

"Jon – are you staying?"

"If I can help, of course I'd be glad to stay."

"Oh yes, please. I'll need a shoulder to cry on long before the day's over, I assure you. Well, come along, young man, let's have a look at your costume first, shall we?" And he took hold of Callum like a jailer escorting a prisoner, and steered him into the ugly but functional building.

The next twenty minutes or so were simply confusing. The form–fitting black leather ensemble which had been designed for Douglas Pirie was a good enough match for Callum's shorter but equally stocky frame, although the boots were nothing like a fit. An extra pair of socks would suffice if he was only going to play the part for a week, however; Ewen's jaded manner seemed to indicate that he was hoping not to have to order a new pair, although what the consequences would be of bringing in a completely new actor he did not enumerate. Perhaps the call would go out for someone of sufficient theatrical stature who could fit seamlessly into Douglas's discarded costume. It occurred to Jon that Roy would have been a good candidate, if only he hadn't been carrying a little extra weight around the mid–section these days. Roy had played this part a time or two before.

"So what are you doing here?" Maisie, the wardrobe assistant, asked as Callum and Ewen moved to the other end of the room to take up their swords. She was chubbily domestic in a sweatshirt and jeans and looked as if she had only been extracted with difficulty from a gruelling session with a muffin pan.

Jon perched on the edge of the table and watched Maisie packing away her wares. "I gave Callum a lift. I thought he might appreciate the moral support."

There was a strong hint of South Wales in her vowel sounds when she relaxed enough to let them out. "One of yours, then, is he – at the Old Crown? How many have you got this year?"

"Four. Well, three and a half: Bill Wildman's only staying every other week – he's filming, part of the time – but I've got Izzy and Jacinta on the first floor."

"Full house, then?"

"Yes."

"How long have you been living there now?" asked Maisie. "Ten years?"

"Nine. *Coriolanus*, just after my daughter was born – she's nearly ten now."

"Oh yes, I always forget you have a daughter. Do you see anything of her?"

Jon shrugged. He was not sure whether it was supposed to hurt or not. He had heard other divorced and separated fathers complaining about how they missed their kids, but he had never had much of a chance to bond with Justine. They had only lived together for the first few months of her life and she had never really felt like his, only her mother's. Perhaps the fact that she had never borne his surname had something to do with it.

"I see her two or three times a year," he said. "Birthdays and

Christmas, of course. Her mother sends me lists of things to buy her. I think she thinks I'm a millionaire."

"She writes books, doesn't she, your ex–wife?"

It was a subject that always came up, sooner or later. Rosemary Pacifico's witty, waspish books about the theatrical profession had something of a cult following, especially with insiders who had little trouble decoding the pseudonyms she'd given her characters. Within a fifty mile radius of Stratford – or Oxford, or Bristol, or wherever there was live theatre in the UK, which was everywhere large enough to throw a plank across a couple of trestles and rig a curtain – it was an open secret that Finn, the hapless hero of Rosemary's comic masterpieces, was a fictionalised version of Jon himself. To those who knew him the only puzzle was what on earth a gentle man like him could possibly have done to merit such extreme, vitriolic and bitterly exaggerated retribution.

"She does," he said. "I read the first three. They were very funny. I think she's started to repeat herself a bit, though."

Maisie chortled. "The way those things sell, she should be paying you maintenance," she suggested, "rather than the other way around."

"I've often thought that," he smiled. "Ouch!" For down at the far end of the hall Callum had lunged a little too enthusiastically and almost taken Ewen's ear off with his sword.

"God, I'm too old for this!" the director groaned. "Jon? Can you take over?"

He scrambled to his feet. "No rest for the wicked."

"How can you?" Maisie asked. "You haven't rehearsed it, have you?"

"Not for this play," Jon admitted. "But this is an off–the–peg fight; I've been on both ends of it in different productions. The details vary, but basically this is the same fight that's been handed down from one generation to another since Irving's day – and he probably stole it from somebody else." He pulled off his chunky green sweater, threw it over a chair, and advanced up the room to where a sweating Ewen was retiring gracelessly from the field.

"Have to give up the coffin–nails," Jon teased, as they passed. He took Ewen's sword and swished it in the air experimentally.

"Have to give up sitting all night in hospitals with plonkers who are too pissed to recognise a flight of steps when they see one," came the grim response. "You realise the stupid bugger's contract will probably be cancelled, don't you? Management are absolutely ruthless about that sort of thing." Ewen stopped, then turned to where Callum waited, every inch the scruffy young actor in deplorable jeans, trainers, and a hideous pink tee–shirt. "Look after the boy wonder," he said. "Don't damage him, or I'll make you play the bloody part."

"Don't be unkind," retorted Callum, his words thrown at Ewen's retreating back. "Besides, he'd make a far better Lady Mac. 'This is a sorry sight'," he teased.

"'A foolish thought to say a sorry sight'," replied Jon, smiling. "You don't seriously intend to rehearse two scenes at once, Callum, do you?"

"D'you think I couldn't?"

"I'm absolutely sure you could," was the confident response. "But one of these days you'll realise that, unlike you, most of the people around you are only mortal."

"Mortal? Am I not mortal?"

"I have no idea what you are," said Jon, taking the first position for the fight, "and I don't think you have, either. It's frightening to contemplate."

"Hah, old man, just see if you can keep up with me!
I will not yield,
To kiss the ground before young Malcolm's feet,
And to be baited with the rabble's curse.
Though Birnam Wood be come to Dunsinane,
And thou opposed, being of no woman born,
Yet I will try the last. Before my body
I throw my warlike shield. Lay on, Macduff,
And damn'd be him that first cries, 'Hold, enough!'"

They closed, and the clash of steel echoed through the largely empty room. Maisie looked up in appreciation over the top rim of her half–moon spectacles, and Ewen wearily pushed open the fire door and lit another cigarette. Jon caught a flash of amusement and delight in Callum's eyes and realised that the boy's nervousness had gone; he was now wholly committed to the task at hand. His enthusiasm was infectious, too; Jon determined to give back as good as he got, throwing himself into the fight with every scrap of energy at his command, and as he did so he felt the years beginning to fall away. He was deeply absorbed in the process, backing and advancing, stepping smoothly from foot to foot, and he was laughing, and Callum was laughing too, and Jon could not remember the last time he had enjoyed himself quite as much as this.

The rest of the morning was just as productive, if less kinetic. They ran lines, with Jon standing in for virtually everyone with whom the king had any interaction, and playing his own scenes as Banquo with only slightly less than the intensity he brought to the role in performance. Ewen, too, stood in, with a version of Duncan which prompted Callum to remark that if Duncan had really been like that Banquo would have been delighted to join the conspiracy to knock him off. At one o'clock a tray of sandwiches was delivered from the White Horse, and the three of them – Maisie had returned to her baking – sat on the floor of the rehearsal room leaning against a side wall and ate their way through soggy supermarket white bread and fish–paste, washed down with the swill the theatre management was pleased to call coffee. It should have been awful but somehow it was not and, when Ewen trudged away doggedly to push another cigarette between his lips and contemplate the infinite iniquities of life, Jon was left propped against the wall with Callum's shoulder brushing his own, their legs stretched in front of them, and no ready topic of conversation.

"How d'you think it's going?" Callum asked at last.

Jon considered. "Rather well. You're going to look a bit too young, I think, but apart from that … "

"Well, Shakespeare never tells us how old he is, of course, and Gruoch must be of child–bearing age, so she'd be under thirty or thereabouts."

"Izzy's a few years older than you," Jon pointed out, "and looks more; you have a baby face. Nobody ever suggested Lady Mac had married her toy–boy."

"I know. It's always difficult to get people to take me seriously." Callum thought for a moment. "I'd look stupid if I dyed my hair or grew a moustache and in either case, I doubt I could find time to do it before tomorrow night. I'll have to see what I can do with make–up – draw in a few veins and wrinkles and go for a grey stubbly look."

"Don't go over the top; we don't want you looking like Duncan's grandfather."

"True."

"And you'd better talk to Ewen; he may need to change the lighting if you're changing your slap."

"Good point. I'll brave the smog and see what he thinks about it." Without a word of warning he put a hand firmly onto Jon's shoulder and used it to lever himself upright, hitching the back of his jeans absent–mindedly as he walked away. "Thanks, Jon."

"You're welcome." It was polite and instinctive, but Callum was already outside and enveloped in the permanent cloud that seemed to follow Ewen from place to place. Jon watched the door swing back until it reached the fire extinguisher Ewen had used to jam it open, and then thoughtfully began to clear away the remnants of their extempore repast.

The rest of the cast arrived in dribs and drabs ahead of their two o'clock call. Izzy – who appeared in playbills and listings magazines as Isabella Thorpe – was, despite being the child of parents named Jolyon and Prunella, a down–to–earth young woman of rational outlook none the worse for having endured childhood in an ivory tower. Jon had felt secure in leaving her to shepherd her less sensible room–mate, Jacinta – a fluffy blonde of the newly–hatched–chick variety – to the rendezvous on time. Jax might well be capable of forgetting appointments, door–keys or even knickers if her little bubble brain had too much to deal with; Izzy, on the other hand, would have been capable of organising a substantial and ultimately successful military campaign. Izzy was a woman very much after Jon's own heart.

She sidled towards him while Callum and Ewen had their heads together over the script. Jax was making enough noise for six people, greeting her dearest and bestest friends in all the world, all of whom she had seen during the previous evening's performance. If she hadn't been known to turn in a perfectly respectable combination of Third Witch and Lady Macduff night after night, she would scarcely have been tolerable even for a moment.

"How's he doing?" No preamble, just the question. Jon respected that. Izzy was as professional as they came.

"Very well. Almost word perfect, and the fight's coming together nicely. Maisie's getting the costume sorted out; he'll have it for tomorrow morning."

"How about make–up?"

"He's going to age a little."

"Good," she smiled. "I'll go a bit younger, then, and meet him in the middle. I must say I think he'll be more fun to play against than Douggie." She paused. "I suppose I should go and see him in the hospital, shouldn't I? I am supposed to be his wife, after all."

"He'd probably appreciate that. I expect he's been feeling like a leper since he woke up."

Elegantly, Izzy sniffed. "Well, so he bloody well should," she said. "He's let us all down." Then she stopped again, her eyes fixed on the figures at the far end of the room. "Is this the start of it for Callum, do you think? Does he knock this one out of the park and never look back?"

"Honestly?" But it was a redundancy; nobody ever expected anything but honesty from Jon, and Izzy's scornful look was the only answer he received. "Yes, I think he does. He's too good an actor to let this opportunity pass him by."

"That's what I thought. Well, we'd better appreciate him while we've got him, then, hadn't we? Twelve months from now, he'll be too posh to talk to either of us." And she patted him on the shoulder and turned away to try to calm Jax's over–excited babbling and introduce a note of sanity into the proceedings.

Ewen kept them busy until eight that evening, by which time there were rumblings of discontent among the cast. Ewen himself was apparently running on empty, and Callum, too, was obviously tired; some of the bounce had gone from his step and the sparkle from his eyes, although he still put himself loyally and energetically through every hoop demanded of him by Ewen. In the end, however, he glanced at Jon and rolled his eyes towards the ceiling, and that was the moment when Jon knew he had to do something. At the next opportunity, he drew Ewen aside discreetly.

"You're exhausted," he said, "and you've been going round in circles for the past two hours. Why don't you let everyone go home now, and get some sleep yourself? You can always pick it up again tomorrow."

Ewen stared at him, his eyes sunken and red–rimmed. "Have we done anything useful here at all?" he asked. "Is this boy going to be as good as Douggie?"

Jon smiled. "If you weren't so tired, Ewen, you'd be able to see that he's twice as good as Douggie ever was. Let him do it his way; he'll rip up the stage."

Ewen's expression turned suspicious. It was his default response to anything he did not immediately understand. "What's the matter? Do you fancy him or something?"

"Certainly not. All I'm saying is that he can do this and do it well, if only you'll stop micro–managing and let him get on with it. He's never going to be Douglas Pirie – but a week from now you'll be telling me Douggie's no Callum Henley. If you don't trust him, Ewen, trust me; this will be a better play with Callum in the lead."

"You mean that, don't you?"

"I do."

Ewen's coat–hanger shoulders slumped in defeat. "All right," he said. "All right, people, thank you. Get a good night's sleep, and we'll start an hour late in the morning. Callum – well done."

There was a muttering of assent around the room. Nobody liked to heap too much praise at such a delicate stage in the proceedings, and anyway most of them were too tired from putting in an unexpectedly vigorous rehearsal to raise much enthusiasm, but agreement seemed to be pretty general. Izzy, however, went over and kissed her new–found husband swiftly on the cheek.

"Nice," she said, briskly. "I'm going to enjoy being married to you. Jax and I are going to see Douglas in the hospital. Any message?"

"No." Callum looked stunned. "Except maybe – 'thanks'."

"I'll tell him. Make sure you get something to eat; you'll have burned off a lot of calories today."

"I will." But he was glancing at Jon as though not quite sure of himself. "All right for a lift home?" he asked.

"Of course. And Charlie's Chipper should be open when we get back, unless you want to stop somewhere along the way."

"Nowhere with people," was the weary response. "I'm peopled–out for the time being. Goodnight, Izzy; give Douglas my regards."

"'Night, luv." And she was gone almost before the words had left her mouth, collecting up a flirtatious Jax on the way out.

"She's never called me 'luv' before." Callum was wriggling into the thin jacket he'd thrown on first thing in the morning; it did not seem nearly warm enough now that he'd expended so much energy.

"You've never been married to her before," was Jon's easy reply. He had pulled his sweater back on over his head and was smoothing down his hair.

"True. I always thought she only ever called me 'Callum' to prove she'd remembered who I was. She's a bit jolly–hockey–sticks, isn't she?"

"Not really. More 'Bohemian'. Her father's an artist. Jolyon Thorpe."

"Oh. Orange blobs making love to blue blobs?"

"That's the one. Are you ready?"

"Are they frightfully intellectual, her family?"

"Frightfully," confirmed Jon, steering him out of the hall with only a cursory glance in the direction of Ewen and the last few stragglers. "And so's she. But one of the nicest girls we've ever had in the company, in my opinion."

"Hmmm," murmured Callum, lost in thought. "This is going to be quite an adventure, Jon, isn't it?"

"Yes. Make sure you leave yourself time to enjoy it," said Jon, as they opened the door and passed out into the night.

◆

Callum fell asleep in the car on the way home. Almost unconsciously, Jon found that he was slowing a little, driving more smoothly to avoid upsetting him, the way he had when Justine was a baby and her carry–cot had been on the back seat. He and Rosemary had never had much to say to one another anyway, so long periods of silence had never bothered them. Come to think of it, perhaps even then she had been planning the first of her comic masterworks, parodying every little thing that had ever gone wrong in his career, holding his ambitions up to ridicule. It was an unpleasant recollection, of a time in his life when he had attempted to fit into the template his parents had planned for him. The acting profession hadn't merited their approval, but a pretty wife and lovely baby daughter – even though they had been acquired in the wrong order – met their specifications nicely. Unfortunately, however, they had both lived to see the edifice crumbling and Jon retreating to a lonely life between an ex–council flat in Hackney and a series of unimpressive theatrical digs. Rosemary had taken every penny, had asked for more, and then had taken that too. Jon, cruelly aware of his failings as husband and father, had simply stood still and let her do so.

The silence in the car tonight, however, was of a different quality, with Callum slumped easily in the passenger seat. There was no spiky air of menace emanating from him, and it was not a case of wondering what on earth Jon had done wrong this time. In fact, for once, he was not conscious of having failed to measure up at all. He could honestly say that he had done his best for the boy, and in chauffeuring him back to the house in Shapley and making sure he got something to eat and a reasonably early night he would have delivered faithfully on his promise to look after him. The minibus would pick them both up in the morning as usual, and it would be back to the old routine from then on.

But this – this was pleasant, and the fact that Callum trusted him enough to fall asleep was something of a compliment. It made him feel useful again, however temporarily. He hadn't realised, he supposed, how much he missed having someone to take care of. Callum was not Justine, of course, and would never be an adequate substitute, but if there was a nurturing instinct in him that lacked a focus he supposed it might as well be directed towards Callum as anybody else.

The boy was young and vulnerable and in need of a mentor. Jon could do that. He could provide moral support.

He could, in short, be the kind of friend to Callum that he'd always wished he might have had himself.

An hour later they stowed the car back in the lock–up and walked towards Charlie's Chipper, which straddled an awkward corner at the intersection of Market Place, Sharp Street and River Lane. Even on a Sunday Charlie stayed open late; he had long ago calculated to a nicety the distances people were prepared to travel for really good fish and chips and was never short of business. For weary theatricals who crawled through his doors at godforsaken hours, Charlie was a very present help in time of trouble.

Back in the kitchen of the Old Crown they sat at opposite sides of the table waiting for the kettle to boil. Something other than tea had been offered and declined – there was brandy in the house somewhere, although Jon was not completely sure where he had left it, but Callum refused to offer such an insult to a decent brandy.

"Not that I'm a wine snob or anything," he said, picking through his chips with greasy fingers.

"Perish the thought."

"I mean, I didn't grow up knowing good from bad. It's not as if I came from a wealthy family like you or Izzy."

"I'm not sure I'd call my family 'wealthy', exactly. My father was a barrister; his income depended on his fees. But I did," Jon conceded, "go to public school."

"Have you got any brothers and sisters?"

"A sister. She's a professional musician. A harpist."

"Is she married?"

Jon shrugged. "Actually, I've never been quite sure. She lives with someone – in New York – but I've never really known … " He stopped, aware of Callum's very blue eyes observing his discomfort.

"Not a man, then. If it was a man, you'd assume they were a

couple."

"A woman. Her name's Alice. My sister's name is Diana."

"Hmmm. Alice and Diana. Both musicians?"

"Yes."

Callum was nodding. "Sounds lovely, doesn't it?" he asked, wistfully. "Peaceful. I've got a sister – Katy. Younger, of course. Doesn't like me much. She thinks mum and dad gave me all the advantages and didn't leave anything for her. Unfortunately she's never shown any talent for anything but making trouble. She expects me to provide them all with a millionaire lifestyle when I'm a star." The expression on his face illustrated how preposterous he considered this notion to be. "It would almost be worth not being one, so that she'd have to make her own way in the world and not cling to my coat–tails all the time. I'd like to be allowed to fail just once in a while, you know."

Jon got up and made the tea, pushing a mug across the table in front of Callum. "I'm afraid you'll be out of luck this time," he said, soothingly. "Failure isn't really on the cards."

"No. I know."

"You're just going to have to be brave and take it on the chin," continued Jon, smiling at him as his raised his tea–mug in a toast. "I'm sorry to have to break it to you, Callum, but you probably have a roaring success on your hands."

And so, in fact, it proved to be. There were uncertainties, of course; at the first performance, with printed understudy slips falling out of every programme and littering the floor of the auditorium, the atmosphere was decidedly tense.

"Owing to the indisposition of
MR DOUGLAS PIRIE
the role of Macbeth will be taken by
MR CALLUM HENLEY.
The role of Malcolm will be taken by
MR RORY COOPER."

Nobody had given Rory a great deal of thought in all of this, Jon realised as he buckled himself into the graphite–coloured doublet the wardrobe department had chosen to bring out the grey in his hair and beard as well as his grey eyes. Nevertheless, Rory – one of those eternal juveniles who had grown up in the company, working his way up from a fairy in the *Dream* to the Boy in *Henry V* – could take care of himself. Rory did his job, drew his pay and went for a drink afterwards – usually, these days, in company with Jax.

Rory, predictably enough, took it in his stride. Callum, however, looked nervous. His make–up was good: a suggestion of five o'clock shadow to indicate villainy, some crow's–feet around the eyes to age him, and a stretched line at the corners of his mouth which took away its cherubic shape and made it a crueller and less reliable instrument. There was something deeply untrustworthy about this character, although when he smiled he displayed more than enough charm to deceive the wariest opponent. With a quiet chuckle, Jon realised that he was looking at the Shakespearean equivalent of the polished modern politician, all shiny surface image and arrant treachery beneath. It should match the spirit of the present times nicely.

"Break a leg," he whispered, as they watched the witches stir their cauldron.

Callum turned to him, something like abject terror in his eyes. "Jon … ?"

Jon squeezed his shoulder. "You're on. Go out there and amaze them."

Callum took a deep breath, tightened his grip on the pommel of his sword, and proceeded to do just that.

Celebrations at the end of the evening were muted. It was not, after all, an opening night, and nor had any firm decision been made yet about replacing Douglas; Callum was still on trial. Nevertheless a scattering of people in the audience had risen to their feet when he took his bow – the usual suspects, the cognoscenti who had been frequenting the place since it opened in 1857 – and let him know, to the astonishment of the bored school parties and the pensioners on reduced–price tickets, exactly what they thought of him.

"Oh God." He slumped in front of the mirror in his corner of the dressing–room and scowled at his reflection. "I have to do that seven more times this week."

"It will get easier." Jon had played the occasional leading role himself in his time, albeit not at such prestigious venues. There had been one tour of the *Tale* with him as a grief–numbed Leontes soon after the divorce when he had felt as if he was carrying the weight of the world on his shoulders. If ever a role had been suited to an actor's mood, it was that one.

"Yes." Callum seemed uncomfortable amid the general elation, and not inclined to glory in his personal triumph. "I don't feel like going for a drink tonight," he said, quietly. "I think I'll just get a taxi and go home."

Jon glanced over his shoulder. Jax and Rory were inclined to be loud enough even without a drink inside them, and once they started imbibing they could get uninhibited very quickly. Izzy, too, for all her refined ways, was known to be a bit of a party animal when the mood took her.

"I must admit," he said, "I don't much fancy it myself. I'll share the taxi with you, unless you'd rather be alone."

"No, that's okay," Callum told him. "Being with you is almost as good as being alone." Then, realising how bad that sounded, he said, "Shit. What I mean is, I can relax with you around. You don't get on my nerves the way the others do."

"Thank you."

"I'm a royal pain in the backside, aren't I? You probably have much better things to do with your time than look after me."

"None I can think of at the moment," said Jon, as he turned away. "But I'll let you know if I come up with any."

"Will your parents be coming to see it?" Jon asked, later, in the back of the taxi. They were out on country roads, and the darkness seemed to encourage confidences.

"I doubt it." Callum sounded deflated. "They won't want to spring for the cost of a hotel."

"Well, they could stay at the house if you like. At the Old Crown."

Callum turned to him, puzzled. "Where?"

"My flat, in the attic. There's a double bed your parents can have, and I could put a camp–bed in my living–room for your sister if she came with them. They'd have plenty of privacy – there's a proper bathroom and kitchen up there too."

Callum laughed softly. "Where would you sleep if they did that?"

"Downstairs in the lounge, if it was only for one night. If they wanted to stay longer, I could always beg a bed from Karen and Tim next door."

"You'd be willing to do that?"

"Of course. Why not?"

"It's incredibly generous of you," was the quiet response, "and I'll certainly make the offer, but I doubt if they'll want to come. They'll probably decide it's too far to drive."

"Why, how far is it?"

"Swindon? Fifty miles. But it's not physical distance we're talking about, is it? It's the distance between my world and theirs. My dad's waiting for me to get tired of poncing about like a poof and find myself a proper job."

"Which would be what, in his opinion?"

Callum shrugged. "Engineering. Construction. Something with machinery and overalls and a hard hat and safety boots. It embarrasses the hell out of him that I go to work in tights and make–up every day. If ever I'm on the telly, he feels he can't show his face in the pub again for weeks afterwards."

"Fathers," Jon mused. "We never do enough for them. What about your mother, though? I'm sure she's proud of you."

"She was, when I first got into drama school. Then she decided I was getting above myself and started accusing me of looking down on her. I don't know what it is I've done to upset her, but try as I may I just can't seem to put it right."

"I'm sorry, I didn't mean to rake up unpleasant memories for you."

Consolingly, Callum patted his arm. "Of course you didn't, you're much too straightforward to do anything like that. You treat people well, and you expect them to treat you well. It just isn't the same for everybody, I'm afraid. Some of us are battling things we don't really understand."

Jon looked away. He was thinking of Rosemary, and the vices she had accused him of. "I'm not sure it's true that I'm completely straightforward," he countered, mildly, "but it's a very sweet thing to say. I promise I won't intrude further; this is obviously private territory."

"You weren't intruding. I like having someone to talk to who doesn't think they can fix things for me in half an hour. I like talking to you."

"I like listening to you talk." Jon hadn't realised it before, but as he said it he knew it to be true.

A contented silence fell. After a while, Callum said, "Jon, could I ask you something?"

"Of course. What?"

He drew a deep breath. "As long as I'm playing this bloody part, do you think we could travel backwards and forwards in your car – just the two of us? I'll pay for the petrol, if you like, as long as you don't mind doing the driving."

"No," said Jon. "I mean, of course I'll drive, but I'd rather go shares on the petrol if you don't mind. If the girls continue to go in the minibus – and Bill, when he's around – we won't have to wait for them after the show. Or we can stay on in town after they've left. It isn't a problem, if that's what you'd like us to do."

"I would," said Callum, from the heart. "I'd like to be able to start and end the day as gently as I can. I don't mind disembowelling myself in public eight times a week as long as I get a chance to sew myself back together again afterwards. I need a bit of space, that's all. Last night, when you brought me back in the car and I fell asleep … that was just about perfect."

"All right, then. I'll tell Ewen in the morning that's what we're planning to do."

"Good. He listens to you, I've noticed."

Jon smiled. "He'll be listening to you, too, Callum, from now on," he vouchsafed. "And so will a lot of other people, mark my words."

The invitation to Callum's family was issued and refused precisely as expected. Eric Henley had to go to work, it seemed; he could not ask for time off just like that, even for something as out of the ordinary as his only son's début in a challenging Shakespearean role. In fact, as Callum suggested when he relayed the news to Jon shortly before they were due on stage on the Wednesday evening, it was doubtful whether he had even bothered to ask; he probably had no intention of coming to see the play in the first place.

"Your mother wouldn't come on her own?" asked Jon, hopelessly.

Callum shrugged. "If he says 'jump', she says 'how high?' If he says 'no', she pretends she'd never consider it even for a moment."

"Your sister?" But he already knew it was a vain enquiry.

"Only if I send her the train fare," was the dispirited response. "It's all so petty: 'You're earning good money, now, Cal, you can afford to help us out a bit.' It's not that I begrudge them a share of my earnings – God knows, they kept me long enough and they didn't have to – but I get tired of constantly being reminded of everything they've done for me and how I should be starting to pay them back."

"I can't understand why anyone would behave like that," Jon told him. "It seems so … completely foreign to me."

"I know. Is it selfish of me to wish they'd be a little less grudging from time to time?"

"No. You want to be appreciated for yourself rather than as a source of income, that's all. My mother used to call that 'cupboard love'."

"So did mine, when she was accusing me of it. Now that she's doing it herself, she seems to think it's perfectly all right." And Callum grimaced ruefully, waved away the subject as if it were of no importance, and went out and made the Scottish King, if anything, an even more dangerous tyrant than he had been the night before.

By the end of the week, indeed, he had inhabited the character so thoroughly that discussions about re-casting had been discontinued and Ewen's thoughts had turned instead to reinforcing the understudy contingent.

"Can he really carry on like this?" he asked Jon, when they met again at the half for the Friday evening performance. "If we're going to keep him I'll have to renegotiate his contract with his agent – and get new inserts for the programmes printed. Not that that will be expensive," he continued, thinking aloud. "They only do so many at a time: they've been caught out like this before – actors dropping out or dying in mid–season."

"You know he can," said Jon. "I've told you, he's told you, and you've seen it for yourself. He can play it as well as Douggie ever could. Better, in fact."

"Much better," acknowledged Ewen. It had been a long and difficult week for all of them but they were gradually beginning to realise that they'd survived it after all. "He's fresher than Douggie. With Douggie you get the sense that he's seen it all before. With Callum … sometimes I think he's saying the words for the first time. It makes him seem a lot more menacing, somehow. And that baby face: you'd never take him for a villain at all, would you?"

"He isn't," was the quiet reply. "Just selfish and arrogant. He's not a cruel king; he just doesn't think anybody matters but himself."

Ewen nodded. "You were right all along," he said. "How is he at home, Jon? Coping?"

"Quiet," supplied Jon. "Still adjusting, I think. But he'll bounce back eventually. We'll need to keep an eye on him, but I really don't imagine he'll give us any trouble. In fact I'm more concerned about Jax and Rory at the moment."

Ewen snorted. "I can buy a dozen Jacinta Burroughses and Rory Coopers," he said, dismissively. "She's good, but she's not that good, and he … he's just

an attendant lord, one that will do
To swell a progress, start a scene or two.

His agent wants to put him up for a long–term part in *The Bill* anyway. Let's concentrate on Callum for now, shall we?"

"If you like."

"All right, then, I'll tell him tomorrow that he's got the job.

Permanently. I'll order a new pair of boots, too, to convince him I mean what I say. What about you, Jon? Can you keep doing what you're doing? Wrap him in cotton wool, hold his hand, get him to me safely every evening in time for the show?"

"Yes," responded Jon. "If that's what you want me to do."

"I do. Stick to him like glue. Make him your project. For the next few months, he's going to be this company's most valuable asset – and I'm making him your personal responsibility from now on. Do the best you can with him. Love him like your only child."

From anyone else this was a remark which would have had enormous potential to give him pain, but from Ewen it was a simple if graphic description of exactly what he required in the circumstances. Jon braced himself, his thin shoulders squaring, the expression on his face becoming still more serious than before.

"All right, Ewen," he said, quietly. "I'll do everything I can."

◆

(The kitchen of the same house, a few weeks later. IZZY is sitting comfortably at the large scrubbed-pine table, fully absorbed in reading _The Tenant of Wildfell Hall_.)

◆

Jon got home late on the first Saturday afternoon of the mid–season break. For other companies a two–week hiatus at the end of June would no doubt have been considered luxurious if not positively suicidal, but with this one it was a necessity by virtue of a clause imposed in the terms of their tenancy at the theatre; the Midsummer Literary Festival, which had started out in a tent in the river meadows way back in the early nineteenth century, took absolute priority. Shakespeare, Marlowe, Beckett and their ilk could all take a running jump for two weeks; in came performance poets, celebrity chefs, and a large number of occasional punters who wouldn't be caught dead in the place at any other time.

For Jon the timing was fortunate: his daughter's birthday fell on the sixteenth, and it gave him the opportunity of spending a few days with her. This year had been the usual exhausting round of child–friendly trips within reach of London – Chessington, Windsor Castle, Hampton Court – and he now returned to the Old Crown feeling severely depleted in both energy and pocket. Izzy was in the kitchen when he arrived, looking as comfortably settled as any woman ever had in this house for the whole of the time Jon had known it.

"Ah," she said with evident satisfaction. "Tea?"

"Yes please." He dropped his luggage in the hall and sat down gratefully. "On your own?"

"Thank goodness. It's been bliss."

He grimaced. "Sorry."

"Idiot, I don't mean you." She sighed. "It's just a relief to have a break from Jax – she's gone to Italy with Rory. They got some last–minute package holiday deal – it sounded ghastly, but at least it was cheap. Bill's in Hampshire finishing his film, and Callum's gone to see his mum and dad. He had a phone call on Monday and decided he'd better go right away. It's a shame; we were getting on quite well. He can be good company, can't he, when he isn't under pressure to perform?"

"Yes, he can. Did he take the car?"

"He did, and it was very brave of you to lend it to him. Anyway, I've had a wonderful time – mostly re–reading the Brontës, as you see. Tim and Karen asked me to dinner on Wednesday, and this morning we went to the Craft Fair at Gostrey and ran into Roy and his partner; they're renting a house and having a party and it seems we're all invited. I told him you'd be home today and he promised to phone."

"Really? I had no idea they were back in England."

"They weren't, apparently, until last weekend; Pete's been doing some hospital soap–opera in Canada. I'm surprised Roy remembered me, I haven't seen him in ... well, it's been a while. And of course I didn't know Pete at all."

"Ah," Jon smiled. "He's not the sort of person I ever imagined Roy settling down with – but they've been together seven or eight years now, so they must be doing something right."

"So they said. It was the Connery film, wasn't it, by all accounts?"

"It was. The flight out, anyway. The way Roy tells it, they met in the Departure Lounge at Heathrow and jumped straight into bed the minute they landed in Kuala Lumpur."

Izzy laughed indulgently. "I wonder if it ever really happens like that?" she mused. "A bolt from the blue. Somebody you've never seen before, and suddenly you want to throw yourself at them and rip their knickers off. Lust at first sight. It must be desperately exciting."

"I can't say it's ever happened to me," Jon admitted. "I met my wife when we were both working on *The Archers*; I was an architect who came in to discuss alterations to The Bull, she was playing a barmaid. We had a lot of very short scenes together. It was a process of attrition."

"Oh dear, that sounds rather pedestrian, doesn't it? But of course:
Some must watch, while some must sleep:
Thus runs the world away."

"I'm obviously one of the sleeping ones," Jon told her, ruefully.

"I know," she grimaced. "I'd keep it like that if I were you, luv. Probably more peaceful in the long run. Somehow I don't think instantaneous attraction would work for either of us; maybe one of these days we should just settle down and marry each other."

It was light–hearted and he knew it for a joke, yet there was more than a grain of truth in it. He and Izzy would have been ideally suited, if only the circumstances were favourable; they could have a calm, ordered existence; they could be domesticated in a way other people would find boring. If he had met her instead of Rosemary, they would no doubt have had three or four children by now and never wanted any other life. His parents would have loved her; her parents would surely have smiled on him.

"It does sound fun," he admitted. "If only we'd met sooner. I'm too set in my ways to change now, I'm afraid."

"Shame. But I'm sure you're right. I'm not all that keen to get married myself, as it happens, but my mother keeps reminding me about my biological clock. Whenever I see her, she ticks and tocks like the crocodile in Peter Pan."

Jon had met Izzy's mother, and struggled to process that image. Dynamic and white–haired, Izzy's mother was formidable even without the sound–effects.

"I suppose," concluded Izzy, smiling, "I'll have to do what Captain Hook did when the crocodile went after him. Keep running away."

"Yes. Of course, it did catch up with him in the end."

"I know, luv. That's precisely what I'm afraid of."

Callum returned before lunch on Sunday looking tired and washed–out. He made no attempt to tuck the car into the garage but left it in the pub car park and crossed the road with a large holdall over his shoulder to hand the keys to Jon.

"The state I'm in," he said, "if I tried to put my head in my hands I'd miss. Seriously, I don't want to risk scratching it. But you've got a full tank of petrol and I took it through the car wash this morning."

Jon smiled. "I'll sort it out later," he said. "How did the visit go?"

"The usual. Unremitting guilt. I did manage to escape long enough to see my agent, though; he's got some fascinating projects lined up. There's a film in Australia he thinks I'd be right for – *Leichhardt the Visionary* – starting in November. It would be a tough shoot, incredibly hot, but I really fancy it. Could get my name out there a bit."

"It sounds interesting."

"I thought so. But many a slip, you know."

"Of course. Are you hungry?"

Callum's shoulders slumped. "Aren't I always?"

"Now that I think about it, yes, you are. Izzy's done a roast; she thought you'd be back in time. Make the most of it – she's going to Paris on Tuesday and we'll have to fend for ourselves after that."

"Paris?" Callum sounded envious.

"Her parents live there."

"Yes, she did say. Very glamorous."

"Not without its drawbacks," Jon reminded him. "Family's a mixed blessing, don't you think?"

"Not only do I think it," replied Callum, following him through to the kitchen where Izzy was bustling about happily, "I know it for an absolute fact."

Early on Tuesday, Jon drove Izzy to the station to catch a train for Birmingham and her flight to Paris. He returned to find Callum sitting at the kitchen table with a mug of coffee and a plate of toast.

"Roy rang," he said, the moment Jon walked in. "Can you believe he introduced himself to me over the phone? As if I wouldn't recognise the voice?"

Amused, Jon made himself a drink and sat down. "For goodness' sake, I hope you'll be a bit calmer when you meet him."

Callum's eyeballs revolved like those of a cartoon character. "I'm trying not to think about that. He gave me the address of the house they're renting and he's invited you to visit tomorrow. He says you can bring me with you if you think I'm interesting enough. He also wants to know how his doves are getting on."

Jon grinned. "Did you tell him I'd eaten them?"

"No. You mean the ones in the dovecote in the garden, I presume?"

"Yes. They've been here ever since this was a pub. When Roy moved out, I took over looking after them. They're not much trouble, really."

"It was a pub?"

"For about fifty years. Roy's grandmother was born here – in Izzy's bedroom, as a matter of fact." With the air of one returning to a well–rehearsed story, Jon pushed aside his mug and explained. "The house on the corner, which is now the Templar Building Society, used to be a pub called the Bear. This house was called the Crown. Roy's grandfather inherited the Bear, and his grandmother inherited this place, and when they got married they closed them both and built the New Crown on the other side of the road. It was a merger of two great local families, you see. 'Two households both alike in dignity'."

"Hence the property empire?"

"Hence the property empire. Hence Tim and Karen living next door – you know Karen's Roy's sister, don't you? – the garages beside the pub, and the doves in the dovecote. This is Shapley; you can't move in Shapley without falling over the Arbour and Westall families, they built just about everything and they've owned most of the town at one time or another. Once you get used to it, it's really quite reassuring. The good side of family, I suppose," he added, with a smile.

"The side that isn't emotionally manipulative?"

"Exactly."

Callum thought about it for a while. "You're telling me this house is your safe place, aren't you? It's where you feel comfortable."

"I suppose so. That's why I've stayed so long. I feel as if I belong here."

"I'm sure you do. It seems to suit you."

"It does. The truth is, I'm not particularly ambitious. I like my work, I like my friends and I like my home. I've forgotten what it felt like ever to want more."

"So you'd call yourself a happy man, then, would you, Jon?"

"Moderately so, I think," was the considered response.

Callum was watching him with amusement. "That's what I like about you," he said. "You're calm and peaceful, and you make everyone around you calm and peaceful too. You just don't let anything worry you, do you?"

"Not these days. I've been through enough, Callum; I try to make sure it doesn't happen now – to me, or to anybody else. You understand, don't you, that if there's ever anything you need from me, you only have to ask?"

Callum coughed awkwardly, as if the conversation was becoming a little too personal for his liking.

"Actually, Jon," he said, "I do, and I'm grateful." Then, after a taut little silence, he added briskly, "So, what exactly is involved in looking after doves anyway?" and the conversation wandered off into more practical avenues, the atmosphere in the kitchen eased, and they were soon perfectly comfortable with one another once again.

Late the next morning they left Shapley, in its workaday guise, quickly behind and turned north–east towards the smarter and more ambitious settlement of Gostrey, some fifteen miles away. Gostrey fancied itself more than a little; it had a museum, and New Age shops full of incense and hand–made soap and bright knitwear from Peru. It also had a fancy–pants executive housing section built on what had once been a pig farm, which was where Roy and Pete had temporarily established themselves – in a vulgar strawberry pink house with shutters and chandeliers and six bedrooms and a pool.

"Jonathan!" Roy Arbour's famous mellow baritone had distinct overtones of Edith Evans. "And this must be the blond boy we've been hearing so much about."

"Callum," said Callum, and held out his hand. Roy shook it enthusiastically, then swooped in and kissed him on the cheek into the bargain.

"'Ill–met by moonlight'," he said, laughing. "Come and have a drink." He slung a familiar arm around Jon's narrow shoulders. "Pete's sunbathing," he said. "It's like a beached whale. I'm glad to see you never get any bigger round the middle."

Jon laughed. "I wish I could," he said. "I keep getting cast as weeds and cowards; heroes just aren't this shape."

"Oh, I don't know. You could come to South Africa with us next year and do Antonio in *The Merchant*; you've got the build for it, and we could put in a word. I'm trying my hand at Shylock and Pete's going to play the Duke."

"It's tempting," smiled Jon, "but who'd look after the house for you in my absence – not to mention the doves?"

They were out by the pool now, and Jon was being embraced by a bulky man in a pair of denim shorts and plastic sandals. Pete Pascal, known as 'Pierre' in his homeland, was Québécois and could fairly be described as larger–than–life. He had a tumble of grey curly hair and the scruffy beginnings of what would soon be a luxuriant beard. Roy, by contrast, was a little shorter, urbane and manicured, given to extravagant hand–gestures and body language veering between mildly camp and outrageously gay. He had made a good living playing suavely sinister authority figures like the drugs king–pin liquidated on the silver screen by Sean Connery so many years before.

"Well," he said now, "Pete Callum, Callum Pete. What are you drinking, blond boy?"

Callum seated himself under the shade of an extravagant umbrella. "Fruit juice, please," he said. "I'm thirsty."

"Oh dear. I see Jon's abstemious ways have rubbed off on you already. But as it's the middle of the day I'll forgive you this time. I hope you'll do rather better at the party, though. You do know how to have a good time at a party, I hope?"

"I'm not sure." Callum glanced nervously in Jon's direction. "What sort of party is it?"

"Oh God, you're no fool, are you?" chortled Roy. "It's a perfectly straight party, for heaven's sake. Well, you know what I mean. An ordinary party–party." He pushed a glass of juice into Callum's hand; ice floated on the top, and he'd stuck a twist of lemon on the rim. "Orange and pineapple. We're celebrating," he went on. "A long–term project of ours. We're going to build ourselves a house."

Over lunch, the plan was inspected and discussed. In fact it was not to be a new house at all but a barn conversion, which had recently been the subject of a complicated planning application. At long last this had been resolved in favour of the proposal to demolish an asbestos–riddled concrete 1920s farmhouse and replace it with a new dwelling inside the envelope of an old barn some fifty metres away. As both the farm and the house on it had been in the same family for most of the century, and the cold–hearted demolition of the original house could be laid to the charge of an earlier generation of Arbours, the committee had been sympathetic to the notion of an Arbour belatedly redressing the balance.

"Of course there have always been tenants in it," Roy said, easily. "When the last one died we took on a manager – a guy named Tony, very good–looking – and we'll keep him for the time being. He's got a nice cottage to live in, it won't make any difference to him. But I've been itching to get my hands on that barn; every time I went up to visit old Wilkins it broke my heart to see that another bit of it had fallen off."

"Where exactly is the farm?" Callum asked. The address on the plans meant nothing to him.

"Ah, that's the good part. It's on Worthy Moor. Let me see, now – you know where the Banbury Road crosses the Fosse Way?"

Callum looked blank.

"We'll show you, dear boy. And of course you'll have to come and visit when it's finished. Any friend of Jonathan's is a friend of ours."

"But it's gonna take a while," boomed Pete, who had been fetching out another bottle of wine from the kitchen and now placed it conveniently within Roy's reach. "Coupla years at least, which is why we're in this Pink Palace. Guy that owns it is working in Dubai. He's a banker," he said, with a shrug.

"Banker," repeated Roy delicately. "With a 'B'."

"Although … ?" suggested Callum, recognising a feed line when he heard one.

"Hmmm," said Roy. "Very much 'although'."

There was, of course, little chance that the pool, blue and tempting in the sunshine, would remain untenanted throughout a brilliant afternoon in high summer. Pete was first in, dressed just as he was, and a few minutes later Callum had stripped to his boxers and followed him. Roy and Jon shrank back into the shelter of the umbrella and watched them in bewilderment.

"Much too active," Roy said. "Where do they get their energy?"

"I have no idea," Jon told him, amused, "but I can assure you – keeping up with Callum is a full–time job."

"Yes, I can see that." Roy paused, watching the two figures thrashing about in the sparkling depths. "He's a hairy little beast, isn't he, your blond boy? He'll give Pete a run for his money in a year or two's time."

Jon laughed. "He is, and he probably will, but you know as well as I do that he's not my blond boy."

"Shame," said Roy. "You look rather good together. I take it he's not that way inclined?"

"I honestly have no idea, and no interest in finding out."

"Indeed?"

"Indeed. For heaven's sake, Roy, he's got enough problems in his life – he doesn't need any more. And I'm not looking, anyway."

"You should be. You haven't had anyone since Rosemary, have you?"

It wasn't easy to respond politely to this remark. Nevertheless Jon drew a deep breath, quelled the annoyance which had bubbled to the surface – a constant danger when dealing with Roy's well–intentioned but clumsy exuberance – and made an effort so to do.

"Whether I should or not, I won't be looking in his direction."

"All right, dear boy, I understand. No more on that subject, then. So, is he as good at his job as everybody seems to think?"

This was safer ground at last, and Jon had no hesitation in answering. "Absolutely."

"Ah." Roy's gaze on Callum was thoughtful and had turned distant, as if he could only dimly perceive the heights of their profession to which Callum was expected to rise. They all started out with that aim, and some of them worked all their lives towards it, and now here came some fair–haired lout from the wrong end of Swindon – was there even a right end? – who would move past them as easily as a man running up an escalator. "Well, that explains it, doesn't it?" he asked, idly.

"Explains what?"

Roy's mouth furled. "You," he said. "If he's heading for the top, he isn't going to be staying here. Not much point losing your heart to someone who won't still be around in a year's time, is there?"

"None at all."

"Wouldn't be sensible, would it?"

"No."

"And whatever else you are, Jon, you are always the most sensible of men."

"I try to be," Jon told him quietly. "I find it a lot less painful that way."

"Not going in the water, then?" Callum slumped, dripping, onto the steamer chair next to Jon a few minutes later. Roy and Pete were inside the house now, and the sound of a toilet being flushed was followed by indistinct raised voices from an open window somewhere above.

"If you'd ever seen me without my shirt you wouldn't ask that question. It's not a pretty sight."

Callum had taken up one of several towels that were dotted about the place and was scrubbing the water out of his hair. Jon smiled at him, but made sure his gaze did not stray below the neck.

"Really?" To Jon's surprise, Callum treated the remark with more respect than it deserved. "Well, you're probably wise. Too many of us take every opportunity to flash a bit of skin; there's nothing wrong with preserving the mystery, is there?"

"That's what I've always thought."

"Hmmm." Callum fell silent for a while, then said, almost impulsively, "Listen, while those two are busy indoors, there's something I need to talk to you about. Something that's been preying on my mind."

Jon turned with an enquiring expression; he had rarely seen Callum looking quite so troubled.

"Let me tell you the whole story. Don't beat me up about it till afterwards."

"You know perfectly well I'm not going to beat you up, whatever it is – but I'm listening."

"All right. It was something that happened last weekend, while you were away seeing your daughter."

"What sort of something?"

Callum grimaced. "I suppose it was an indirect result of you lending me your car – which, by the way, was incredibly generous of you."

"So you've said," Jon reminded him. "More than once. I hope you didn't get pulled over by the police or anything?"

"No, nothing like that – sober as a judge, milord. It was a bit more complicated than that, actually. After the show, when you went off to catch your train, Ewen invited me for a curry at the Blue Rajah so that we could talk about next year. Well, since I had my own transport for a while, I thought 'fair enough', you know? Anyway, we had our curry and our talk, and we got quite a few things sorted out, but after a while I noticed that there was a girl at one of the other tables who kept looking my way … And, anyway, to cut a long story short … "

"You picked her up?" Jon surmised, smiling.

Callum laughed, but there was absolutely no humour in it. "It would be more accurate to say she picked me up – but that's essentially what happened. We got talking, and after Ewen left I offered her a lift." He stopped. "I'm not sure exactly how it happened," he said, "but I took her back to the Old Crown and she ended up staying the night."

Jon's brow creased. "That's not a problem," he said. "What you do in your room is entirely up to you. You can have all the guests you like, Callum, as long as they don't disturb the other residents."

"I know. That isn't the point. The point is, I had trouble getting rid of her afterwards."

"Oh?" Jon's expression was puzzled, but there was no hint of criticism or mockery in his voice. "How do you mean?"

"Well, in the morning … which was Sunday, of course … I asked if I could drop her somewhere in the car, but she said she didn't have to be anywhere in a hurry and she'd like to stay. Now, that was awkward because Izzy was in the house as well. They bumped into one another in the kitchen and they both got quite a shock – Thea was wearing nothing but her knickers."

"Ah."

"Well, they circled round each other for a while like a pair of cats, and then Izzy decided to be gracious. She cooked us a huge breakfast and wouldn't let me apologise. She's a class act, Jon."

"I'd noticed."

"And the day went on," continued Callum wearily, "and Thea didn't show any sign of leaving, and in the end she decided she'd stop another night and get the bus home on Monday. Naturally I said I'd drive her but she didn't seem to be interested, so I took her over to the pub and bought her dinner in the place upstairs, and she stayed the night in my room again."

Jon was watching him in some confusion now. It was unusual to find someone so professionally confident as Callum at a loss in dealing with what amounted to a casual pick–up. Most actors learned to deliver the brush–off with style even before they had given their first big speech. "So what happened on Monday?" he asked.

"Well, as luck would have it my mother rang up, doing one of her tragic arias about how ungrateful I am and how I never want to spend time with her any more. Apparently she'd been expecting me to go down there on Sunday and stay the week, although I'm sure I never promised anything of the sort. Then she started in with the emotional blackmail about how dad's working much too hard and how worried she is about him, and in the end I thought … 'I've got the car, I should just go'. I must admit, it looked like a good opportunity of getting rid of Thea, too – I dash off to deal with a family emergency and leave her to find her own way home."

"And did you?"

"More or less. Izzy offered to help, so the two of us played it up a bit … pretended my dad was really ill and my mother was panicking … and I packed a bag and got ready to go. Thea didn't like it, of course – accused me of running out on her – which obviously I was. But between us we managed to convince her it was all above–board, and in the end I drove off and left Izzy to mop up. She walked Thea to the bus stop and waved her away and we thought that was the end of it, but it wasn't. Thea's phoned the theatre several times since, trying to get hold of me, and I've seen her hanging about at the stage door. Managed to avoid her so far, but there's no telling how long that'll last. Two nights together and she seems to think I'm her exclusive personal property."

"A bunny boiler," Jon murmured, sympathetically.

"Classic," admitted Callum. "And she knows where I live and how to get there, so sooner or later she's quite likely to turn up on the doorstep again."

"You'd better tell me who it is I'm watching out for. What does she look like?"

Callum sighed. "Her name's Dorothea Dawson. She's little, not much over five foot. Masses of red hair – a real Pre–Raphaelite look, Lizzie Siddall reincarnated – and skinny as a rail. Quite a strident voice; I thought she was just vivacious at first, but it's actually fairly manic when you get to know her."

"Where does she live?"

"I don't know. She was staying in a B&B in Woodstock Road, but she said her family came from Croydon. Plenty of money, I think; she doesn't seem to work."

Jon was silent for a moment, then said, "Exactly how worried are you?"

"What?"

"I mean, do you think she'd try to hurt you? Because, if so, maybe you should tell the police."

"I couldn't! God, Jon, look at me! I'm not exactly a wilting little violet, am I? I used to play rugby at school; I should be able to take care of myself against somebody who looks about as dangerous as a strawberry milkshake."

"Hurt doesn't have to be physical," Jon reminded him.

"I know. And you're right. But how stupid would I look, eh, playing this ruthless bloody king every night and in real life running away from a twenty–one–year–old girl?"

"All right. So who else knows?"

"You. Izzy. That's all. I feel a complete fool."

"You needn't." Jon thought about it for a moment. "Look, tell

Ewen. Or I'll tell him, on your behalf. He can warn theatre security about her, at least, and have them keep an eye out. And if he leaked it to the local paper that you've been the victim of an obsessive fan it might embarrass her enough to leave you alone."

"We can only hope," replied Callum, fervently.

"It's worth a try. If you're worried about going places on your own, I'm available for moral support – and I'm sure Izzy will be, too."

"You don't have to, either of you. It's my mess, I ought to clear it up."

"Not necessarily. It seems to me she caught you at a vulnerable moment. I can't turn my back on you even for a weekend, can I?"

"Obviously not." Callum sounded rueful, but more comfortable than when the conversation started. An easy silence lapsed between them, and when Jon spoke again it was in a brighter tone.

"What was Ewen chatting you up about, anyway? Did he make you an offer for next year?"

"Hmmm. Subject to the usual … Bosola in *The Duchess of Malfi*."

"Bosola? You'd be excellent casting for that. Not a play I'm fond of, though; I prefer *The White Devil*. I played the idiot husband in that once."

"Oh. Actually I was hoping you'd be available to do it. Ewen was talking about you for Antonio."

"Really?"

"Really. I'm serious, Jon – would you fancy working with me again next year?"

Jon let the words sink in before answering. "That's two different Antonios I've been offered for the same season. How odd."

"I know. Maybe you'd rather go to South Africa with Pete and Roy?"

"Not especially. I've never been, but it isn't high on my list of priorities either. And I don't fancy being a third wheel on another one of their extended honeymoons." He nodded his head towards the source of the two voices audible from inside. "Anyway, I'm not certain how serious Roy was; you can never be sure until you have the contract on the table."

"Well, suppose he hadn't suggested it? Could you overcome your perfectly natural prejudice against Webster, do you think?"

"To be honest," Jon smiled, "it's not Webster I'm prejudiced against at all. It's you."

"I'd noticed, from the hostile way you always treat me. Well?"

"Well, if Ewen does offer, of course I'll accept – although I can't imagine I'd be anything like his first choice."

"That's where you'd be wrong," was the surprising response. "I have it on very good authority that he thinks we make a remarkable team."

Jon spluttered with laughter. "What, like Morecambe and Wise?"

"Exactly," grinned Callum conspiratorially. "Are you by any chance making some allusion to my short fat hairy legs there, Jonathan?"

"It never crossed my mind," replied Jon, "but now that I come to think about it, Callum – maybe I should!"

It would not be strictly accurate to suggest that it was the cream of theatrical talent which assembled at the Pink Palace the following Saturday evening. It might, however, be reasonable to describe it as the cream of theatrical talent within a fifty mile radius not presently occupied elsewhere. In simple terms, it comprised those of the local company who had returned from their mid–season break and were in a party frame of mind, a handful of Birmingham–based television actors, a couple of the more enthusiastic or predatory agents and a few people famous simply for being famous. Including the hired caterers and some ineffectual spotty boys engaged to provide security, sixty or so people swarmed about under the banker's honeysuckle drinking, talking, eating things they could not identify and moving to very ordinary music as though divinely inspired.

The contingent from the Old Crown travelled together, Jon having taken the precaution of booking the minibus and its driver for the occasion. Jax was inclined to be tiresome; although she and Rory had been home more than twenty–four hours from their Italian trip, she had not yet exhausted her fund of anecdotes about language difficulties, amorous waiters, or the British tourists who recognised her at the airport. Izzy was tired and irritable: Paris had been hell, her parents hell too, the flight hell and the train back from Birmingham sheer unmitigated purgatory – overcrowded, expensive and just about the last bloody straw. Bill, by contrast, was sallow, spare, and still in possession of the dignity and sense of humour without which he was rarely seen. He managed to find a wry word to deflect any incipient unpleasantness, and benevolently made it his business to keep Jon entertained on the journey.

They had been established in the general milieu an hour and a half or two hours, and had gone the rounds of the company at least once, before Callum – in jeans and a white silk shirt but barefoot – succeeded in detaching himself from Roy and headed over to the quiet corner Jon had staked out for himself.

"Does he never stop talking?" he asked, sinking onto the other half of the bench beside the pool and clutching a bottle of beer as if his life depended on it – which probably it did.

Jon blinked. "I couldn't tell you," he said, "I've only known him seventeen years. He does sleep occasionally, though."

"Not nearly enough," grumbled Callum. "So, do you know everybody here?"

Jon looked around. "Just about."

"Good. Then for heaven's sake tell me – who is that awful woman in green?"

Jon did not need to follow Callum's pointed glance. He had been well aware all evening of someone looking like a cheap knock–off Elizabeth Taylor, buttonholing people into intense and in most cases unwanted conversations.

"That's Roy's agent, Caro Llewellyn. She set up that South African trip he's so keen on – it's some kind of British Council thing, I think."

"Is that what he meant by 'putting in a word'? That he'd talk to her?"

"Probably. He seems to forget that she's also my agent."

"Good lord, really?" Callum looked from one of them to the other in astonishment.

"Afraid so. Roy introduced us years ago."

"Oh. Well, in that case I won't say any more about her."

"Indeed?" Jon glanced up at him sideways. "You've got that 'butter–wouldn't–melt' look again," he remarked. "You're thinking, I suppose, that she's a hardened old battle–axe, and wondering what on earth we could possibly have in common?"

Callum's expression blossomed into a rueful grin. "You read me so well," he said, taking a swig from his bottle. Jon watched the movement appreciatively; this boy could make the most ordinary gesture interesting, and he wished he understood how. Or why. "I'll admit," Callum continued a moment later, "she seems a bit ground–glass–and–acid to appeal to you, but I'd guess she's a ruthless negotiator and she's found you a lot of good work. Am I right?"

"You are. Let's face it, I'm a tough sell: I can get plenty of radio and voice–over jobs but I'm difficult to cast visually. Too tall, too thin – and getting too old now, too." He batted aside Callum's boilerplate demurral almost without noticing it. "Plus, nobody's ever going to cast me as a football hooligan or a member of a motorcycle gang – I have a rather limited range. Caro scours the country for vicars, bank managers and so forth. She knows I need to keep on working; I have financial responsibilities to maintain."

"Your ex–wife and daughter?"

"Exactly. I want Justine to have the best. Caro gets me some quite lucrative engagements, as long as I'm not too choosy about what I do."

Callum was quiet for a moment. "Then I like her," he said, at last, "even though she does look like a shark in a frock."

Jon chortled. "Pete says she's got all the compassion of a concrete cow," he remarked, good–humouredly.

"Don't tell me … ?"

" … she's his agent, too? In this country, yes, she is."

"So what should I do if she approaches me, then?"

"What you usually do, I suppose," was the absent–minded response. The bench was a narrow one, and unthinkingly Callum had slumped against Jon's shoulder. It was certainly warmer that way, and personally Jon was inclined to let it continue for a little while, but knowledge of the suspicions that would pass through Roy's mind if he saw them like that was enough to discompose him and he edged away a fraction.

Callum, too, moved, as if registering Jon's unease. "If you're happy with your representation, just tell her. I forget who you're with?"

"Lenny Simonson at MTI. He grabbed me straight out of LAMDA. I owe him a hell of a lot."

"I've heard good things about him," acknowledged Jon.

"Well, he suits me. He comes up with strange stuff like this *Leichhardt* movie. He's pretty keen for me to do the *Duchess* next year, too. Have you mentioned that to Caro yet?"

"Not yet. But I've got automatic first refusal on anything local, so if Ewen means what he says I'm sure I'll be getting the offer eventually."

"And what happens in between? What will you be doing while I'm in Australia?"

Jon laughed. "Provincial tour of *Educating Rita*," he said. "Do you think I can be cynical and disillusioned enough?"

"Oh, definitely." The beer bottle was upended, the last dregs tipped down Callum's throat. "Let me get you another drink."

"I don't think so, thank you. I try to keep my wits about me at these affairs – especially where there's a pool. Sooner or later somebody's going to end up in the water and – since I'm not exactly the type to go around pushing people into pools – I could, if I'm not careful, end up being the pushee."

"I suppose you could."

"I'm a boring old fart," continued Jon. "I see people letting their hair down all around me and sometimes I wonder if I know how to enjoy myself any more."

"Oh, I bet you do," laughed Callum. "You probably just need to be with people you trust. And you don't trust this lot, do you? Not one little bit."

"To be honest, excluding Izzy and Bill – and yourself, of course – there's not a soul here that I'd trust any further than I could throw them."

"Which, as we've established, wouldn't be far," completed Callum, grinning. "I'm just pooped enough to take that as a compliment, Jon, if you don't mind too much."

"Please do. That's the way I meant it."

"Good." Callum put one hand on the arm of the bench and the other on Jon's leg, pushing himself upright without the least self–consciousness. "I'm going to see if I can find another bottle of this stuff," he said. "Are you sure I can't bring you anything?"

"Not a thing, thank you. And if Caro approaches you, you have my full permission to be absolutely as rude to her as you feel inclined."

"All right. I'll see how creative I can be – on your behalf, of course."

Callum sauntered away, and Jon tried to interest himself in whatever Pete and Rory might be talking about over by the barbecue. Anything, rather than think about the imaginary hand–shaped weal even now developing on his thigh. It had been unintentional, he knew that; with a drink or two inside him Callum was as ungainly as a Labrador puppy, all hands and feet and blond goodwill, and there was no accounting for whatever he did in those circumstances. It would be a big mistake to take anything he said or did too seriously; Jon was far too mature to let himself get caught out by that kind of random stupidity. Besides, he had meant what he said to Roy: he was not looking, and he was most especially not looking in Callum's direction.

That would be the end of it, then.

He sighed in relief. Not something he would ever have to worry about again, thank goodness, which meant that he was free to appreciate the casual warmth of the touch for as long as it lasted.

And it lasted, he found, a surprisingly long time.

Only when the most surreal part of the evening arrived did Jon realise that his iron resolution to stay sober had wavered. He had remained detached from the worst excesses of the fray, though, which at one point had involved a rather impressed–looking police officer asking for the music to be turned down, and he had been conspicuously elsewhere – inside, waiting to use the facilities – when the sound of a mighty splash followed by hysterical shrieking indicated that Jax had been the one to end up, fully clothed, in the pool. He was a charitable and compassionate man ninety–nine per cent of the time, but it would be false to deny that there was a part of his soul in which he was perfectly comfortable enjoying her distress.

Not that it was distress, exactly. He returned to the pool side a few minutes later to find her huddling damp–haired under a massive beach–towel, wearing a suspiciously well–chosen set of underwear which exhibited her tan to its best advantage, and suitably delighted to be the centre of attention.

"Did you do that?" Jon crouched beside Callum, who had rolled up his trouser legs and was dabbling his feet in the corner of the pool furthest from where Jax held court.

"Chuck her in? No. I may have mentioned something to somebody who thought it would be appropriate, though."

"Somebody?"

"Somebody with an alibi almost as good as yours." Yet, for one who had apparently engineered a considerable coup, Callum sounded surprisingly deflated.

Jon was concerned. "Is everything all right?" he asked, quietly.

"Yes," sighed the younger man. "No. Actually, I don't know."

"Hmmm. Helpful."

Jax and her coterie were moving indoors. A fresh batch of something had apparently been mixed up in the kitchen, the flames on the barbecue had died to a sullen glow, and a cool night breeze was cutting sharply through the garden. From outside on the road there were the sounds of car doors opening and closing, of people trying to be quiet and failing.

On impulse Jon pulled off his shoes and socks, rolled his trousers to the knees, and swung around to join Callum. They were shoulder to shoulder, and he was never certain afterwards whether that had been accidental or deliberate.

"So?" he asked.

Callum shrugged. "I honestly don't know," he said again. "I feel good. I feel great. I should, shouldn't I? Everybody thinks I'm shit–hot, and they all want to be in on the action. You'd be astonished how many new best friends I seem to have acquired."

"Oh. I'm sorry."

"I don't mean you. You're just … " Callum trailed off, obviously lost in thought. Then, after a long pause, he said, quite irrelevantly,

"Nice feet."

"Hmmm?"

"Elegant. Like the rest of you."

It was such an unlikely thing to say that for a moment Jon was completely taken aback. "Skinny," was the best rejoinder he could come up with, when his brain started working again.

"Slender," corrected Callum. "Not like me. I'm just a lump. One of these days I'm going to be exactly like Pete – all big and butch and hairy."

"I doubt it." The words were out before Jon had a proper chance to think, but he did not entirely regret them. He would have said almost anything to try to reverse this awful mood of negativity. He wished he understood what it was that made Callum seem at such a disadvantage in dealing with the rest of the world. "Are you tired?" he asked, for want of anything more sensible to say.

"Desperately." A weary acknowledgement, which somehow Jon knew was not so much to do with the present evening as with a deeper and greater tiredness; the burden of expectation was pressing down too firmly on this boy, and he didn't immediately know what he could do to lighten it.

"Let's go home, then," he said. "We could all do with our sleep, couldn't we, even Jax? How about I start rounding people up?"

"Oh, Jon, would you? I'd be so grateful."

"Of course. It's going to take at least half an hour to get everybody out of the door and into the minibus anyway. Don't fall asleep on me, now, will you?" he added, attempting to make a joke out of it.

"I won't do that," smiled Callum. "I'd never do that, Jon."

Unthinkingly Jon grabbed Callum's shoulder and scrambled upright, marching off barefoot to start assembling his party, leaving Callum at the edge of the pool looking smaller and lonelier than anyone in his position in life had the right to look. He could not help thinking that there was something he ought to be doing about that, although he wasn't sure exactly what it might have been.

It was the end of the season long before they ever got to the theatre on the final day. Bill, whose one–man show about Alexander Selkirk had closed the evening before at The Venue, the town's experimental theatre space, had already packed and gone; he was going straight into another film and was off to Cornwall to be taught to sail. Although he had only been an intermittent presence at the Old Crown, his departure left quite a gap; he was more missed than any of them expected, which would have astonished him had he known.

For Jon in particular, Bill's dry personality had provided a bulwark against some of the insanity which prevailed during the latter weeks of the run; when Callum, Rory and Jax had insisted on haring off to Gostrey one memorable Sunday to go paintballing, for example, Bill had been content to sit with his feet up in the garden and listen to the cooing of the doves and a Test Match on the radio. Jon, much relieved not to be the odd one out, had cheerfully provided an alfresco lunch for the two of them – and for Izzy, who had staggered down towards noon without her contact lenses, having for once in her life had almost enough sleep.

The return of the paintballers, bruised and riotous at teatime, had disturbed an idyll which would stay in Jon's mind for a long time as one of the calmest days of the summer; Izzy and Bill were the ones with whom he really seemed to have made a connection, and either of them would be welcome back here at any time. He would think long and hard, however, before he opened his doors to any of the younger ones again.

But even Callum, notoriously sloppy about the house, had done his part in getting ready to move out. Unable to use the washing machine, which was constantly in occupation by Izzy and Jax and which Jon suspected was too advanced for him anyway, Callum had taken himself off to the launderette and returned to hang his jeans and tee–shirts in the garden. The ghastly heliotrope tee–shirt hung too close to the straggling crimson roses for comfort; Jon did not look out of the window again until it had gone.

Then all too soon everything was packed and they were ready to leave. Izzy and Jax were to depart on Sunday, Callum's plan was to set off on Monday; Jon had promised to drive him to the station. There would, of course, be an after–show party on Saturday night – a networking–with–the–patrons shindig at the White Horse where cast members could swear eternal fealty and then go their separate ways praying they never saw one another again in their lives.

Such was not to be Jon's fate, however; although he had made little of it so far, and had heard even less from the other party concerned, it was looking very much as if his partner for *Educating Rita* would be none other than the irrepressible Jax herself. Eight weeks of closer acquaintance with her was not a prospect to be relished, and he had scarcely dared mention it to Callum for fear of the teasing he suspected would ensue.

Or perhaps not. Callum had settled down a little, becoming steadier by degrees, maturing into the role he was playing. Step by step, night by night, a considerable actor had begun to emerge from beneath the winsome smiles and puppy fat; Callum had grown up almost before his eyes, and although he had plenty still to learn before he could be the commanding stage presence everybody seemed to expect – almost to insist on – he was establishing himself as a force to be reckoned with.

At the last matinee there was the traditional end–of–term mayhem and customary practical joking: the Second Witch, for example, wore a moustache, the Third a star–shaped blue beauty mark below her left eye, and there was tomato soup in the cauldron. By the time they reached 'Fail not our feast' the spirit of merry–making had infected even Callum; he gripped Jon's hand as though to shake it warmly, and simultaneously crushed something sticky in between his fingers. Jon stared at him, seeing the way the blue eyes rolled, a spark of outrageous mirth leaping from them challengingly. Slowly he shook his head in gentle reproof.

"'My lord, I will not'," he said, taking a subtle revenge by putting into the words all his own extensive knowledge of parting, grief and loss, and to his satisfaction heard Callum deliver his next speech with a kind of stunned distraction dawning on his face. He had meant only to quell the over–boisterous hi–jinks, but somehow in that wordless exchange he seemed to have communicated more than he intended. He made his exit a moment later, lurching into the wings to discover what appeared to be the remnant of a yellow jelly–baby stuck into his palm.

Jon glanced back. Callum's eyes were on him, and that was surely not a good thing. He escaped into the backstage darkness with increasing turmoil in his heart.

Between shows he pleaded a headache and hid himself away in the scenery dock. There were refuges concealed all over the theatre for those who knew where to look: a room in the roof where tables and chairs were stored, a small First Aid room among the offices, a luggage room near the stage door – and this corner between the hoist and the stairs, where long ago someone had shoved a ratty old sofa that people used occasionally to snatch sleep, study lines, or indulge in illicit liaisons if there was really nowhere else. Jon had put it to all three uses over the years, and had rarely felt as uncomfortable there as he did now.

He tried to tell himself that finding Callum attractive was not a problem. Callum was supposed to be attractive, dammit! He had a good face – sweet, rather than handsome – a nice body, and a manner which could be utterly charming. These were an actor's assets, the tools of his trade, to be parleyed into anything the profession required; he could indeed be a murdering Scottish tyrant one week and a bumbling German explorer the next, all without ever giving himself away in the slightest.

Yet Jon was too experienced to be taken in by surfaces; he knew how these effects were achieved. He knew, too, that he had startled Callum, out there on the stage, into revealing something else. Something deeper. Something Jon was not expecting, nor equipped to cope with. He still did not know for certain what Callum's sexual preference might be – the Thea incident, for a while, had convinced him that the boy was straight – and nor did he have any better idea about his own. He had adventured on both sides of the tracks and had never yet made a definitive choice between them; two disastrous failed relationships, one with either sex, had left him with a distrust of the whole business. But there had been a connection of some sort with Callum, although he reminded himself savagely that he could have misinterpreted it to a quite ridiculous extent.

He did not want to take the risk. By remaining out of sight before the evening show he could avoid any possibility of coming face to face with Callum and having to deal with whatever it was. There would be time to talk tomorrow, if they were going to, but he was convinced that they would not. The last thing Callum wanted along on his express elevator ride to super–stardom was an unambitious man a dozen or more years his senior who had nothing to offer but affection. Even if, by some miracle, the feeling should be mutual, there would be no reason for it to last longer than the time it took to satisfy their curiosity, and Jon had long ago abandoned that kind of casual experimentation. He was better off without it, Callum or no Callum.

He emerged at the last possible moment to be told that Callum had been looking for him earlier, but Callum was nowhere to be seen now and that was a relief. They did not meet, in fact, until they found themselves shoulder to shoulder again in the wings, watching the witches stir their pot, and Callum took hold of his arm and said, "Jon?"

But it was too late. "'Peace! – The charm's wound up'." And they were on.

Even at the interval they somehow managed to avoid each other; the place was heaving with visitors, people who had come for the party and just dropped in to say 'hello'. Douglas Pirie, on crutches and trying to body forth 'gallant wounded warrior' bravado, established himself in the corridor outside the dressing–rooms and posed a good–natured but irritating obstruction, a misdemeanour compounded by his annexation of Callum into whose ear he poured a bibulous description of exactly how much better he would have played the part himself. Jon was privileged to hear the response, which hit like a punch in the solar plexus.

"Yes, Douggie. But you see … you weren't there. You'd have been great, mate, but the first secret of acting is to actually show up for work. If you can't even manage that, none of the rest of it matters a shit."

Jon stood in the shadows, cheering silently and feeling unaccountably proud of Callum whether he had a right to or not. The next time he glanced out of his refuge, Callum and Douggie had both gone.

On the whole he was successful in avoiding Callum's gaze for the rest of the play. It was not difficult: he was blood–bolter'd Banquo, staring out balefully from his unquiet grave, frightening the king and bringing to Callum's face a look of horror that he hoped he never saw for real. At the curtain he finally let himself relax, let the weary triumph of the season wash though him with gratitude, but between the bowing and the congratulations and the flowers thrown from the audience – really, what did people imagine they were going to do with them? – and the stomping and cheering which threatened to shake the theatre to its venerable foundations, there was a moment when the king threw both arms around Banquo's neck, hugged him impulsively and said, clearly but incomprehensibly, "I'm sorry, Jon. I'm sorry."

Jon almost lost it then, but made up his mind to extract an explanation from him during the party. He changed afterwards in a fog, single–minded, having conversations but forgetting them before they were over. He was in the pub ahead even of Jax and Rory, appropriating one of the wooden benches with their sad squab cushions, trying not to let his eyes stray every time the door opened.

After an hour, Izzy came to sit beside him.

"It's just not the same without Callum, is it?" she observed. "He always brought a party to life somehow."

"Without?" Some numb part of himself had been clinging stupidly to the notion that Callum was here somewhere, unseen and unheard but present in the room nonetheless.

Izzy turned. "You did hear what happened?"

"No. What? Was it something to do with Douggie?" A momentary nightmare assailed him, of an aggrieved Douglas bashing Callum with his crutch. But no, surely even Douggie's stupidity did not extend that far.

"Douggie? No. Callum's mum rang the theatre … his dad's had a stroke. They wanted him to come home right away."

"Oh." Then he said, "He's supposed to be flying to Australia on

Tuesday."

"I know. He'll only go if his dad's well enough, though. But he says he's all ready, and he can get to Heathrow from Swindon quite easily on the train." She paused. "He dashed home in a taxi between shows to collect his stuff. He was looking for you, Jon, but there wasn't a lot of time."

Jon smiled at her wanly. "I had a headache," he said. "I wanted to be by myself for a while. It's been a long season."

"It has," Izzy concurred. "And it's gone on quite long enough for my liking, too. Jax is going to be dancing on the tables any moment now; how about you and I crawl off and find a cab, before people really start embarrassing themselves?"

"Good idea," he said, vaguely. He was still searching for that unmistakeable mop of fair hair, even though he would not see it. He wanted Izzy to be wrong, but he knew that she was not. Izzy did not get things wrong; not things that were important, anyway.

When they left the pub, side by side, they walked up the steps where Douggie had fallen at the start of the summer.

"There ought to be a plaque," Izzy said. "'Here, on this spot, Callum Henley began his meteoric rise to fame.'"

Jon did not answer her, but he took extra care on the steps.

By lunchtime on Sunday he was alone again. Rory had come for Jax in a van and she had gone off blowing kisses and promising to see him soon; Izzy had departed an hour later in the direction of a little place in Bayswater belonging to her parents. Jon waited a couple of hours, and when the house felt quiet again he went round and unlocked all the doors of the rented rooms, threw open all the windows, and inspected for damage. Bill had spilt coffee on his carpet, Jax had scratched her wardrobe door, but otherwise there was little that needed to be put right. It was as if they had all walked through his life and out again leaving very few discernible traces.

In Callum's room he opened the doors to the garden. He didn't think they had been open since the day Callum moved in. There was a scent in the room, musty and close, which cool garden air and mellow impending autumn served to drive away almost immediately. Just as well, too; there would be someone else in here next year. He would offer this room to Izzy, if she wanted to stay again. By then, with luck, Callum would be nothing but a memory – and maybe not even that.

He left the internal doors standing open all night, although he closed the windows. It didn't matter to him; when he had the house to himself he rarely strayed from his attic flat except to do laundry or use the better cooking facilities in the ground–floor kitchen. Or, of course, to wander down the garden and feed the doves.

He happened to be in the downstairs kitchen when the florist's van pulled up outside the New Crown and the driver crossed the road and rang the bell, and he realised at once exactly what he could expect when he opened the door.

They were roses, of course. Roses of every conceivable colour: white, cream, shades of yellow, three or four different pinks, coral, scarlet and burgundy. Two dozen of them, in a dozen hues; whoever put them together certainly had some imagination, and so did whoever ordered them.

Jon shut the door and leaned against the wall inside. He almost didn't want to look at the card, because he knew that either it would be bad or it would be very much worse.

It was worse, of course. Infinitely, inevitably worse.

This have I thought good to deliver thee, my dearest partner of greatness, read the card. *Lay it to thy heart, and farewell.* It was not signed.

For a moment he stood there, holding the bouquet in his arms.

"He is not *my* blond boy," he said aloud, but it didn't sound convincing even to himself.

He went into the kitchen, dug out a couple of vases, and spent the next few minutes putting Callum's flowers carefully in water.

◆

(The same kitchen on a late afternoon in winter. JON is sitting hunched close over the dual-fuel Rayburn, methodically opening and reading his way through a considerable number of Christmas cards.)

◆

Rita was educated, to general satisfaction, at Bath, Oxford, Nottingham and York over the next few weeks. She relinquished the last of her dressing–rooms only when it became necessary to make space for Widow Twankey, who promptly moved in to get the pantomime season under way. Jon returned to the Old Crown to prepare for his usual semi–solitary Christmas. Justine, predictably, was occupied elsewhere, although he would have a brief opportunity of seeing her; Roy and Pete, also predictably, were on their travels once again.

Among the cards waiting when he got home was one postmarked Darwin. The picture was of a blue wren with a magnificent wedge–shaped tail; the handwriting was unmistakeably awful.

This is what we do for robins out here. Sorry, no doves.

Thrown together in a couple of minutes spared from filming, unsigned, it was precisely the kind of generic remembrance he had been hoping for. Similar had arrived from forty or fifty other people already; only Izzy had troubled to write a letter, brief but newsy, mentioning the reviews he'd garnered for _Rita_. There and then Jon sat and responded to her, in his meticulous script, offering the garden room for the summer; there was mercifully little danger of Callum ever requiring to live in it again.

Jon's schedule for the early part of the following year was looking depressing. There was an engagement to record an audio book of Randall Garrett's _Lord Darcy_ stories – about an alternate reality detective solving crimes with the aid of magic – a part in a BBC Radio version of _Emma_ which was still casting, and Caro was juggling guest roles in a couple of long–running television shows. Little, however, had been confirmed before the March start date for _The Duchess of Malfi_.

He had not troubled to ask whether Callum's name was still attached to that particular project; he would have accepted the engagement in any case, as being the more convenient of the two on offer.

In the absence of work commitments, therefore, he could devote himself to his subsidiary role as Roy's business manager. There was nothing to be done at the barn conversion – christened, with Shakespearean insouciance, Fardels – until better weather, but there were always renovations to be carried out at the Old Crown. The garden room could stand a lick of paint, so could the antique wainscotting in the hall, and there had been talk of turning the coal–store into a downstairs bathroom. Roy had also suggested new kitchen units, and had provided for them in the house's budget. If these things were to be done they must be fitted in when Jon was not required elsewhere, otherwise the responsibility for them would fall on Karen. The first stage of the kitchen renovation, therefore, was arranged for early in the New Year. It would clash with the *Darcy* tapings, but Jon could be present for at least part of every day and Karen could stand in when required. So far so good, until his telephone rang late on the first Sunday in January.

"Jon?"

Something in his chest gave a leaden thud. "Callum? Where are you?" Surely he couldn't be calling from Australia? What time would it be in Darwin, anyway?

"Swindon," was the downbeat response. "My dad died. Listen, Jon … " Callum went on, determinedly overriding whatever expression of sympathy he might have been about to utter, "is there any chance you could put me up for a few nights? I need to pull myself together a bit before I go back to Oz. Have you got anybody staying with you at the moment?"

"No." He thought about it. "We're in a state, I'm afraid; the place is going to be full of workmen. But if you'd like to … " He stopped short of issuing any kind of welcome; somehow it did not seem appropriate.

"God, I don't care what state you're in as long as you've got somewhere to put me. I just need a place to stay where people aren't shouting at me all the time. You won't shout at me, will you?"

"I'll try not to. When are you coming? Will you need a lift?"

"Tomorrow," said Callum. "After the funeral. I've got a hire car."

"All right. I'm in Birmingham tomorrow, I won't be home until about seven thirty. Karen can let you in if you get here before that, though."

"That won't be a problem; I can't set off until late afternoon anyway, so I'll have something to eat and make sure I don't get to you before eight."

"Fine." A short, unhappy silence. "Callum, are you all right?"

"No," was the reply, "I'm not. My dad's dead. It's messed everything up, and for some reason it seems to be my fault. Tell you about it when I see you, okay?"

"Of course," said Jon, and the call ended in empty platitudes.

Driving from the station the following night, Jon tried not to think about anything but the progress of the kitchen renovations. He had spent the weekend emptying cupboards and transferring things into the small front room where Bill had lodged in the summer; the garden room he had been leaving strictly alone, but following Callum's call he made the bed and ensured that the place was at least habitable. Now he was expecting to find the kitchen a wasteland except for the Rayburn, but – assuming Callum had eaten as he had said he would – they should be able to manage. If all else failed, they could always adjourn to the pub.

By the time he had put the car away and got to the front door, Jon was aware of no longer being alone. Someone small and shabby had got out of a vehicle tucked into one of the darker corners of the car park, lugged a holdall across the road and lined up beside him on the doorstep like a hungry cat. When at last he turned to look at Callum, he scarcely recognised him.

"Good heavens," he said. "You've changed!" It was not the most welcoming remark, but had the virtue of blistering honesty.

"You should see the diet they've got me on. I'm supposed to be starving to death, so it's all lettuce leaves and vitamin pills at the moment."

Jon opened the door and ushered him in; Karen had left the lights on.

"You look older with that beard." Jon was more concerned with the alteration to Callum's appearance than with the devastation visited on his kitchen, which had effectively been stripped to its bones.

"And you look younger without yours," was the response. "Whatever made you get rid of it?"

"New pictures for Spotlight. One with and one without."

"Of course."

"Well, take your coat off. I can make some tea, if you like, or there's plenty of booze."

"Did you ever find the brandy?" Callum hung up his coat and brought two kitchen chairs over to the front of the Rayburn.

"I did, and I even know where it is now. Anything to go with it?"

"A glass."

"Good choice." A moment later, they were facing one another across the range and warmth from it was starting to creep back into their bodies. "Here."

Callum took the drink with a smile. "Appreciate this, Jon. I had to get out of there. I told everybody I was going straight back to Darwin."

"Your family?"

"Such as it is. Mum, Katy, Auntie Ada, assorted cousins. They didn't dare argue, they're too hung up on the 'movie star' thing."

"You're escaping them, then?"

"Yes. Ever since I got home ... three weeks ago, after Dad had his second stroke ... I've had my mother issuing instructions night and day. It didn't help that I was sleeping on the couch to let Auntie Ada have my bed; they wouldn't let me go to a hotel."

"Sounds as if you've had a rough time," Jon sympathised. "Would it help to tell me? How is any of it supposed to be your fault, for example?"

The shoulders slumped further. "I've never been quite sure," Callum admitted. "Something to do with being in Australia when I ought to be at home, I think. The whole acting thing was my mother's idea in the first place, she's pushed me every step of the way, but I suppose she thought I'd be living with her and just doing the occasional bit of telly. As soon as I started having to go away, especially out of the country, she began to resent it. She was never keen on me going to Australia in the first place, but my dad's doctors were sure he'd make a good recovery after the first stroke so I thought it would be safe enough. I talked to him on the phone and he seemed to be making good progress – even got enthusiastic about the film, which surprised me a bit. Then he had the second stroke and Mum said if I didn't come home I wouldn't see him alive again, so I dropped everything and flew back home just to sit around and wait for him to die. They put the film on hiatus for me; they didn't have to do that." The line of his mouth distorted as though trying to avoid the words it was uttering. "But it wasn't enough. Mum felt I should have been there all the time, and if I had Dad wouldn't have been ill. She said I was going to go away and leave her again the moment he was dead, and of course that's exactly what I did. I've got two weeks left on this bloody film, there's a contract I have to fulfil, but all I've been getting at home is stuff about my obligation to the mother who sacrificed everything for my career. The goalposts have moved again, and I can't quite work out where they are now."

"I'm sorry," Jon said. "You shouldn't have had to deal with that on your own. Why on earth didn't you call me?"

"How could I? I couldn't involve you in my family's crap. Besides, I thought you'd be busy with your daughter. And I was coping right up until he died … Christmas Eve, of all shitty times … but all I wanted after that was to be somewhere else. Somewhere I wouldn't have to choose coffins and flowers and hymns and make speeches. Believe me, those people can take all the 'fun' out of 'funerals'. Anyway, I'm supposed to fly out to Australia again on Saturday and I'm so tired I don't know where to put myself. I thought I could hang out here and have hot baths and watch telly until I start to feel normal again."

"It's going to be noisy," Jon warned him. "And if you want a bath you'll have to go next door – the plumber and electrician will be here tomorrow, and I'll be out all day. You could spend the day with Karen, if you like, or drive over to the Pink Palace – I can give you the key."

"No, that's okay, I'll head for the pub if it gets too bad here, or go for a walk by the river. I just need a couple of ordinary days, Jon, if that's okay?"

"By all means. You're always welcome."

It would have been impossible to say for which of them this remark was the more astonishing: Callum, who was surprised but gratified, or Jon, who had never had any intention of saying anything of the sort and was staring into the depths of his brandy glass as if expecting to find some miniature demon sporting there.

"I do know." There was nothing insincere about the smile Callum directed at him, but it looked as if it had been tested almost to destruction. Then, without apology, he yawned. "God, I want to fall asleep and not wake up until it's time for my flight."

"Not a good idea," Jon told him, smoothly. "But your room's ready. I'll be leaving early tomorrow, so you'll have to sort out your own breakfast and lunch, but we can have something out of the freezer for tea – it's running on an extension from Karen's kitchen."

"I'll be fine," Callum said. "Don't worry, I'm a big boy now."

"If you say so."

"I do. Thanks."

"Any time," Jon responded automatically, then wished he'd kept his mouth shut. It was just like encouraging a stray cat: you let them in out of pity, made them comfortable, and suddenly you realised that while your back was turned they'd taken over your life and heart and you weren't at all prepared for the consequences.

As if, he thought ironically, it had ever been possible to prepare for the consequences of knowing Callum Henley.

Throughout the second day of the *Darcy* taping Jon was understandably preoccupied. Geraldine Bland, the efficient young producer he was working with, remarked on it more than once, even asking if there was anything wrong at home. He managed to shrug it off with something about the perils of having workmen in the house, which provoked a torrent of cowboy–builder anecdotes from everyone with whom he came into contact. It was tedious, but served to disguise the true source of his concern – that, at the end of the day, he would be going home to Callum.

When he reached Shapley and returned the car to the garage, it was with some trepidation that he crossed the road and let himself in. The house was in darkness; there was no immediate sign of life.

"Callum?"

"Here." A shape emerged from the gloom carrying a torch. "There's no electricity."

Jon was taking his coat off. "What happened?"

"I think it was a breakdown in communication between the plumber and the electrician; Derek started cutting pipes in the bathroom before everything was switched off and managed to blow the main fuse. Gerry says he's not allowed to touch that – it has to be done by the electricity company, and they can't get here until tomorrow. Karen's given us a couple of torches and a box of candles and she says if you can't rustle up something to eat we can go next door." They were in the kitchen now, where candles were flickering merrily in holders, wine bottles and saucers on every surface; Callum had apparently decided to use the entire box all at once.

Jon laughed. "I'm sure we can cope. What time did it happen?"

"About four. I was keeping out of the way in my room, when suddenly there was a bang and all the lights went out – followed by an ominous silence. Then Derek came wandering downstairs looking stunned. Gerry was really calm, though, just sighed and got on with it, and we spent the rest of the afternoon drying out the cupboard under the stairs. The guys haven't been gone long."

"We? All three of you?"

"Of course. You don't think I'd just sit here and watch them, do you? It made a change to do something practical – and I bought them a pint afterwards. It's a pain the arse, Jon, but these things happen."

"All right. Thank you for dealing with it."

"No worries. I must admit I'm getting hungry, though; I was quite fancying the steak and kidney pie over the road."

"Do you still want to do that? Only there's frozen lasagne if you'd rather."

Callum's mouth wavered. "Garlic bread?"

"Of course."

"And can we get pissed?"

"Not so pissed that I can't drive in the morning but yes, we can if you like. You'll find the wine in Bill's room – why don't you go and choose something?"

"Italian wine to go with Italian food, I presume?"

"Why not?"

"I go, I go," grinned Callum, *"look how I go,*
Swifter than arrow from the Tartar's bow."

Jon sighed tolerantly and went out to retrieve the lasagne from the freezer.

An hour and a half later they had eaten and drunk well and, with music from a battery radio Jon kept on the kitchen windowsill, the situation had become not so much demanding as entertaining. One glass of wine had relaxed them, the second added lustre to the proceedings. There had been no mention of the practicalities of doing without electricity and having only limited plumbing – there would be cold washes in the morning for example, unless they cared to wait for a kettle to boil on the Rayburn – and they were still disposed to find the novelty amusing.

"I thought you meant frozen lasagne out of a packet," Callum said, "but that was home–made, wasn't it? Did Karen make it?"

"No. I did."

"What, you actually cook? Properly, I mean, not just heating things up?"

"It has been known."

"Bloody well, too, if that was any guide!"

"I expect you were just hungry," was the self–deprecating response. "It always makes food taste better. Like fresh air."

Callum considered the remark thoughtfully. "Food's definitely nicer when you eat it out of doors," he admitted. "From a barbie or a camp–fire."

Jon was watching him over the rim of his wineglass. "Have you ever actually been camping?" he asked.

"Only in the back garden, but we had beach cook–outs in Australia. What about you? Were you a Boy Scout?"

"Not a chance. I like my comfort far too much."

"Me too. But there's no harm in making the best of what we've got, is there?"

"None whatever," Jon agreed. He was pouring more wine; somehow they had already started on the second bottle.

"Look what I found in Bill's room." Callum produced a box which he had been concealing under the table. "Isn't this what Jax and Rory brought you from their holiday?"

"What? Oh, I'd forgotten all about that."

"An Italian Monopoly set. What a mad present. Do you even speak Italian?"

"Not a word."

Callum grinned. "Me neither, but there's a dictionary. Want to try it?"

This made quite as much sense as anything else, and Jon was not really surprised to find himself agreeing – after which it was the work of moments to set the board out on the rag rug. Then they transferred themselves, their wine and candles wholesale to warmer locations closer to the Rayburn.

"*Lo Spirito del Gioco*," Callum read from the instructions.

"We know all about the *spirito* of the *gioco*," Jon teased. "What character do you want to be?"

"The dog."

"There isn't a dog. There's a Chianti bottle, a candlestick, pepper, salt, oil and Parmesan."

"I'll be the Chianti bottle, then."

"Of course."

Thereafter, for the next half–hour or so, it was all good–natured confusion and the cold–blooded murder of the Italian tongue. Having a grasp of the game in one language was more than sufficient to begin playing it in another, and there was the dictionary whenever anything became too complicated. There was also the wine, however, which added to their appreciation of the ridiculous, and as the levels in their glasses declined the whole proceeding became steadily sillier and sillier.

"It's a lyrical language," declared Callum. "You could say anything in it and still sound fabulous. Can't you imagine going up to some beautiful Italian girl and whispering, *Andante in prigione direttamente e senze passare dal <<Via!>>*?"

"'Go directly to jail, do not pass "Go"?'"

"It's sexier in Italian."

"It wouldn't be, to an Italian."

"It would if I said it." Callum was inclined to be giggly. "*Avete vinto il secondo premio in un concorso di bellezza,* Jon," he breathed, seductively. "*Ritirate* a thousand *lire.*'"

"Only second prize? Who won the first?"

"I did."

"Naturally. Have you lost interest in the game?"

"Only as a game," replied Callum. "Not as a cultural artefact." He scooped a double–handful of *Monòpoli* money, threw it into the air and watched as it fluttered down languidly like multicoloured paper snow, miraculously avoiding the candle flames around them, more carefree than he had been in months.

A 50,000 lire note landed on Jon's shoulder. In reaching to remove it Callum over–stretched, fell across the game board and rolled onto his back chuckling.

"Idiot." Jon pushed the wine safely out of the way, then glanced down to find the cherubic face, wreathed in the softest of smiles, grinning back up at him, and his heart stopped beating. This was the moment he had both longed for and dreaded, he realised in alarm, the moment he had known would come and for which he had tried so hard to prepare, when his care for Callum would be tested to the limit. It was so long since he had felt like this about anyone; indeed, he was not certain he had ever felt anything this intense before, but with Callum it had always been there – the subtle hint of friendship shading over into desire. No matter how inappropriate or impossible he had tried to tell himself it was, he had been running away from Callum since that first wonderful, awful day – and now he no longer had the strength to flee. Let whatever would happen happen, then; Jon would do his best to be equal to it.

Callum reached up lazily to ruffle the short hair at the back of Jon's neck. It was the most affectionate of touches, the absent–minded smoothing one would give a beloved dog, or cat, or child.

"Jon?" he whispered, "would you ever consider … ?"

Jon leaned closer. Just a fraction, so that they could find the truth in one another's eyes. So that he could, if he felt the need, bend and kiss the boy into sweet oblivion. He hesitated there, needing the decision to be taken in full consciousness of what he was doing rather than falling into it almost by accident.

"You?" he asked. The fingers in his hair were drawing him nearer.

"Well … would you?"

The answer must have been obvious to them both. "God, Callum … of course I would! You didn't need to ask."

"Yes I did," said Callum, but now his mouth was open beneath Jon's and they were kissing with the kind of avidity Jon had always thought must exist somewhere in the world but had never encountered before. His arms tightened on Callum as their tongues dipped, touched and stroked, and they rolled together across the *Monòpoli* board scattering little green houses in their wake. Jon's hands were in Callum's hair, Callum's fingers in Jon's clothing, and nothing and nobody had ever been quite so perfect before.

Callum was breathless against him. "I want this, Jon. I want it so much. Tell me you do, too!"

"Of course." Yet he halted Callum's searching lips, and awkwardly his body drew away. "I always have. But it's too soon, you're too vulnerable, and we've both had far too much to drink. Besides, I've got an early start in the morning." It sounded disappointingly adult and sensible and Jon could have died on the spot for even mentioning it. He reminded himself sometimes of his own father, of the repressive voice which had driven any thought of enjoyment out of his head all those years before. What would he not have given, when he was younger, to be able to see the world as fresh and challenging and, in spite of all its faults, tremendous fun? Why should he have been cursed with this awful burden of common sense? "If it's right today," he heard himself continuing, apologetically, "it'll still be right tomorrow, and we'll have more time to enjoy it then."

Callum was watching him, eyes full of something Jon could not put a name to. "Are you scared?" he asked.

It would be ridiculous to deny. "Actually, yes – a bit. I'm afraid it'll be an absolute disaster and we'll wake up in the morning wishing we hadn't done it. I don't want that for either of us – especially not for you. I couldn't bear it if this went wrong, Callum, it's far too important; I'd rather it didn't happen at all."

Callum's eyelids fell, the slow movement of clouds across the sun, then rose again in acquiescence. "If you think that's best. It's sweet of you to care so much."

"I can't help it."

"I know." And, with a delicacy the more unexpected for being heartfelt, Callum extracted himself from Jon's arms and wriggled upright. "I suppose you're going to send me to bed like a naughty boy, are you?"

"Not exactly. But I am going to send you there alone. Let's not rush into anything we might regret, shall we? We've got the rest of the week to think about this, and to do whatever we want to do."

"I know what I want to do."

"Do you?" Jon looked away. Callum's forthright gaze was almost too much; he had little experience of being desired, and he was struggling with his own feelings. It was all very well to admit to wanting Callum, but he had been so sure Callum could have no possible interest in him that he had omitted to think the rest of it through. Admiring the boy from a distance had been simple enough; wanting him but never being able to have him had become a way of life. Now he was prepared for the whole illusion to dissolve into mockery, humiliation and scorn. "If you still do tomorrow … if I still do … there's nothing to prevent it. But if you change your mind you'll be grateful to me for having stopped it now."

"I'm grateful anyway," was the soft response. "You've always worried more about me than I have about myself." A pause, then, "How about I buy you dinner at the pub tomorrow night?"

"If … If you'd like to." He had almost said, 'If you're still here' – but Callum seemed to have heard it anyway.

"I promise not to leave without talking to you first. Is that fair?"

"Yes." Jon was aware of staring into Callum's eyes the way a child stares into birthday candles – as if all delight and wonder lay within.

"You know this could be right, don't you?" asked Callum. "I mean, it could really be right for both of us." But there seemed little more to say, if they were not to tempt one another beyond endurance. "I'll crawl off to bed."

"That's probably a good idea," Jon admitted. "Sleep well." He did not try to keep emotion out of his tone; the words embodied endearments he would have liked to add but had somehow not quite managed to voice.

"You too, love." Callum pulled him close, kissed him, scrambled to his feet and left the room before Jon had reconciled himself to his going. He could hear him after that, moving about by torchlight, while he extinguished candles and made an attempt to tidy the kitchen. He left the *Monòpoli* board as it was, its scattered houses and paper money a reminder that the business of the day was not concluded. He could not bring himself to pack it away; in the morning, if Callum succumbed to sanity, it might be all that was left of tonight's interlude.

Callum's kisses burned on his lips. He had wanted more, of course he had, but he had never wanted it to be scrambled and indecent and quickly forgotten; he wanted it to be sweet and tender and as close to permanent as could possibly be imagined.

"'His rash fierce blaze of riot cannot last'," he told himself, sternly.

"For violent fires soon burn out themselves;
Small showers last long, but sudden storms are short;
He tires betimes that spurs too fast betimes."

He closed the kitchen door behind him and went to bed equally prepared, he hoped, for delight or disappointment to greet him on the following day.

Jon did not manage a great deal of sleep that night, and left for work in such a bedraggled condition that he was glad to have the excuse of domestic chaos to fall back on – as well as an audience, in the audio–book–buying public, who could never guess at the hollow–eyed and exhausted condition he had been in during the recordings. Fortunately he was actor enough to keep such turmoil out of his voice, and he made Darcy urbane, knowledgeable and highly–strung, the Sherlock Holmes of an alternate universe. Nevertheless it was a punishing day, and with the equivocal promise of Callum at the end of it he could scarcely greet the journey home with enthusiasm. He was weary when he reached the Old Crown again, and did not feel equal to coping with Callum – or, indeed, with anything or anybody else.

All that changed, however, the moment he got in through the door. Callum, who – curse him! – would have looked good in virtually any outfit, was waiting, wearing denims and a sweater the colour of his eyes, relaxed and glorious and in his arms between one heartbeat and the next.

"Jon, can we? Please?" A child's wheedling, although not with a child's purpose; Callum against him was adult and muscular, his solid frame wrapped tight around Jon, his expression all eager affection. It was clear that a few hours had not altered his opinion, and there was to be no denying him even for his own sake – and when all was said and done Jon was not made of stone; he could no longer resist such delectable temptation. If this was to be some kind of apocalyptic disaster, he reasoned, they would just have to deal with it together.

"Yes," he said, scarcely aware what he was agreeing to but kissing Callum anyway, deeply and dementedly and with no thought but him. "All right."

"I knew it!" triumphed Callum. "I knew we were meant to be together!"

"You knew I couldn't resist you, that's what you mean. You knew I'd be a helpless pushover."

"Darling," came the affectionate response, "whatever you are, you're not helpless and you're certainly no pushover – and you can take that from one who's tried."

Shortly thereafter, without Jon ever understanding the precise mechanism, they were in the warm, bright upstairs room at the New Crown, whose window lined up with the one which had been Jax's during the summer. They were at a corner table, partly hidden from the room by a column supporting the top floor. Jon, who had been expecting to be hauled into the Public Bar and regaled with something–and–chips amid an atmosphere of smoke and noise, was relieved to be in more decorous surroundings where they were almost the only customers.

"I thought you meant ... " Confused, he shook his head.

Callum shrugged. "You're not a cheap date," he said, in a breathy undertone. "The only reason we haven't gone somewhere more upmarket is so that we can stagger home from here under our own steam. You said you wanted to take this slowly, Jon – well, so do I. I want us to be sure. Let's stick with what we know, shall we, for now?"

"All right. Thank you."

"Besides, I can have steak and kidney pie up here just as easily as downstairs. It won't be a patch on your cooking, but it saves on the washing–up."

Reassured, Jon drew a shaky breath. "You're such a romantic," he teased. "I'm out of practice at this. I can't remember the last time I went out with someone for anything other than work. Except my daughter, of course."

"It seems to me you don't have nearly enough fun," whispered Callum. "Maybe I can take care of that for you."

"You could, but I'm not sure why you'd want to." It was ridiculous, but even after more than twenty years in the profession Jon was still capable of blushing.

Callum's fingers flickered affectionately across the back of his hand. "Honestly," he admitted, "neither am I. Only it's like iron filings to a magnet; when you're around, I just can't look away. The first time we met, I thought you were a nice, straightforward guy, someone I could really enjoy being friends with. But that weekend ... "

There was no need to say which weekend.

"I know."

"Was that when it changed for you, too?"

"Yes." And then, slowly and reluctantly, dragging the words out in defiance of every instinct for discretion, "You opened the door that morning, and you were such a mess ... "

Callum sighed deeply. "You're about three hours ahead of me, then. It didn't hit me until the sword–fight. I don't really ... I mean, blokes in general ... " He grimaced, grinding to an inarticulate halt. "Help me out here, Jon, what am I trying to say?"

"That you don't make a habit of seducing your male co–stars?"

These words were greeted by the gentlest of laughs. "Darling," said Callum, scarcely audibly, "before I met you I was a spear–carrier; I didn't have co–stars of any sort, male or female. But I don't sleep with the people I work with. At least, I never have before. I don't know why you should be different – but you are."

"We'd better not have this conversation here," Jon reminded him. "We might be better not having it at all."

"I understand what you're saying. It's going to have to be a great big deep dark secret, isn't it?"

"Yes. Apart from anything else, my ex–wife would love an excuse to stop me seeing my daughter. She doesn't really like me associating with Roy and Pete, and I'm not allowed to take Justine anywhere near them, but if she tried to stop me having any contact with gay men at all she'd be robbing me of the chance to earn a living – and she does rather like it when I'm working and there's plenty of money."

"You'll forgive me, Jon, but you don't live like a man with plenty of money. Does that mean that your ex gets most of it?"

"Yes. But it's worth every penny, of course; I love my daughter."

"I'm sure you do. Got a picture of her?"

By the time their food arrived they were discussing families, and nothing but the tangled confusion of their feet and ankles, concealed by the floor–length tablecloth, would have given even the keenest observer any indication of the more intimate nature of their connection.

They sat talking in the restaurant longer than either had expected, getting used to the newly familiar pleasure of one another's company and the notion that suddenly there were no barriers between them.

Nothing about it felt rushed or pressured, and they did not notice the evening slipping steadily away as they relaxed together. Callum, who had earlier been making an obvious effort not to be overwhelming, now settled into a mellow frame of mind which was a good match for Jon's quiet temperament, and when the initial flood of conversation eased they found they were spending longer and longer periods in refreshing silence. Eventually, after the second cup of coffee, when the restaurant was beginning to empty and the staff were starting to check their watches, Callum said, "Well, love, should we go?"

"I think so."

They had paid up and were crossing the road to the Old Crown less than five minutes later. In the hallway, Callum's face took on a serious expression. "You're not going to make me sleep downstairs again, are you?" he asked, concerned.

Mutely, Jon shook his head.

"All right. Give me a moment." Callum slipped into his room and returned clutching a sponge–bag. "Something for the weekend," he explained wryly.

"I've got those."

"Can never have too many." An arm slid around Jon's waist. "Still scared?"

"Of course."

"Me too. One step at a time, all right?"

Jon was staring at him in confusion. "But you seem so comfortable with this," he said.

"Comfortable? Not exactly – and absolutely not blasé. This is pretty special for me, Jon; if I act as if I know what I'm doing, it's probably because I'd like to believe it myself. You'll find I'm not the most experienced guy you've ever been to bed with, I'm afraid."

"I haven't had what you might call an extensive repertoire either," Jon told him, softly. "I had a very good teacher, but that was a long time ago."

"I'm sure we'll muddle through somehow. I mean, it's not something you forget – is it?"

Jon's eyebrows lifted. "Famous last words," he said, sceptically, taking Callum's hand and beginning to lead him up the stairs.

Jon's apartment at the top of the house seemed smaller and shabbier than ever when he ushered Callum into it, and he was embarrassed to have offered it to the Henley family earlier in the year; they would have been unbearably cramped up here and probably better off sleeping in their car. He supposed it didn't matter since they hadn't come anyway and would never know whether the place was poky or palatial, but what had seemed hospitable back then was starting to look rather pathetic now.

"It's a bit basic," he apologised. This was the first time Callum had ever been up here; no invitation had been issued before tonight.

Callum smiled. "I shouldn't have thought you'd need a lot of space," he said, soothingly. "You strike me as being a pretty self–contained sort of man."

"I suppose so. But there are always books, of course."

"Yes." Callum was looking around the sitting–room in astonishment. There were, indeed, books: on shelves, on chairs, piled on the floor and on the windowsill. There was a saggy old couch, an archaic television, a threadbare rug and a hearth with a gas heater installed in it. Everything was ten years out of date, shabby, comfortable and without pretension. A big rooflight dominated one side of the room; under it was a table flanked by two chairs.

"Kitchen's through there," Jon said. "Bathroom next door, bedroom the other side of that."

"Okay." But Callum seemed in no hurry. He was peering at the oil painting above the fireplace. "This is Justine, isn't it?"

"Yes. A friend of Roy's did that when she was six. From a photo. She's still got the same cheeky smile, though."

"I bet. Does she take after you?"

"Not really. She's always been her mother's child. If I didn't know better … " He stopped. "Well, never mind. Come on through." And, with this businesslike invitation, he ushered Callum into the bedroom.

It was dark except for a few stars idling above a rooflight the twin of the one in the other room. Beneath it was a desk, and next to that an antique wrought–iron bedstead deep with pillows; a wardrobe occupied most of the remaining space, but once again there were books everywhere.

"Oh," said Callum. "This is lovely. Peaceful."

"Thank you. The furniture belongs to Roy; he's been very generous to me."

Callum was leaning on the rail at the foot of the bed staring across it like a man on shipboard contemplating the ocean. "This room is totally you," he said, relaxed and calm. "Comfortable, but not fussy." Without turning, he added, "I haven't stopped thinking about you all day, Jon. Hoping you'd let me get close. Hoping you wouldn't be afraid of me."

Jon moved to stand behind him, his hands on Callum's waist. "I'm not afraid of you," he said, with careful emphasis. "But I've made mistakes in the past that took a long time to recover from. It's made me cautious." His lips came to rest on the side of Callum's neck. "And no doubt I'm a bit rusty," he added, with a laugh.

"Well, that makes two of us. I'm more nervous now than I've ever been going out on stage; an audience of one is always the toughest kind."

"Stage fright?" Jon mused. His hands slid under Callum's sweater and stroked across the tee–shirt he wore beneath.

"Paralysing. Such a discriminating gallery." Callum's hands covered Jon's, and moved with them for a moment. Then he took over, guiding Jon's touch, at the same time pressing back against him in a gesture scarcely open to interpretation.

"So, what do you … I mean, how do you … ?" Jon's lips brushed Callum's ear. "I don't want to assume anything."

"That's okay." The voice which had held theatre crowds mesmerised was now a shuddering whisper. "Whatever you want; I'm happy to go either way."

"Yes," replied Jon. "So am I."

A remnant of tension drained from Callum's shoulders. "Oh God, I'm so glad. I'll do anything, Jon. Any damned thing you like."

"Well, maybe we should get to know one another properly before we start worrying about things like that, what do you say?"

"Absolutely." With a determined movement Callum shrugged out of his grip, hauled off his sweater and tee–shirt and threw them anywhere. Still without turning he slid back into Jon's embrace and carefully placed the other man's hands on his chest. "Here," he said, pushing into slightly cupped palms.

"Of course." Jon was not slow to catch on, his fingertips immediately attentive to Callum's nipples. "This?"

"Yes." Callum was wriggling against him. "You could have me right now, if you wanted. From behind, standing up."

"I will if you like, but there's a perfectly good bed over there which would probably be more comfortable." Jon's hands were on Callum's waist again, making short work of his belt, unfastening his jeans, pushing them out of the way. There was nothing underneath but Callum, hot and hard, and Jon's long fingers captured him tenderly. "Pretty boy." His mouth caught at Callum's ear; his free hand savagely pinched the nearest nipple. "You're so thin, I can feel your ribs."

A moment of incoherence, and Callum was out of his arms again and turning towards him.

"You need to be naked," he growled. "Now." And immediately he began on Jon's trousers while Jon divested himself of his sweater and shirt. By the time they had kicked themselves free of legwear and shoes there was a dangerous excitement in the room, and they fell onto the bed desperately determined to touch one another everywhere at once.

"You are a hairy little beast," Jon rasped, his mouth on Callum's chest with its soft coat of golden fur. The contrast with his own narrow, pale, almost hairless form was utterly bewildering. "Roy called you that, the day you went swimming at the Pink Palace."

"You wanted me then," Callum accused, arching to him. "I know you did."

"I did."

"Tell me what you wanted."

But there was no brain matter left over for articulacy; every nerve and cell of Jon's body was dedicated to feeling, to enjoying, to consuming Callum by any means available.

"You," he confessed. "I wanted you, any way I could get you."

"You can have me every way," was the impassioned response. "Every way you can think of. You can't imagine how much I've wanted this ... all summer, all the time I was in Australia, ever since I got home. All I've been able to think about for months is how wonderful you and I would be together." His hand was cool on Jon's overheated flesh, stroking, caressing his skin like a gentle breeze. "We've waited long enough, Jon."

"Yes." A sharp bite to an upraised nipple, then Jon exerted his strength and rolled Callum onto his back and was between his thighs with the speed of thought, but it was Callum's hand which captured their parts, brought them close and made a place where they could thrust together into sweat and mingled juices. Heat pulsed, half–words and kisses fell from matching mouths, and Callum crushed up as Jon crushed down, trying to climb into one another, to get closer than anatomy allowed. It was like that for an age, riding the cusp of pleasure until without warning Callum gave a cry and his body shuddered, letting go of control, and Jon was quick to follow into Callum's tight–slick hand. His heart raced, his brain faded, his arms shook with the effort of supporting him. Slowly, with the best grace he could muster, he subsided onto Callum's chest, his face mashed hot against Callum's neck.

"Darling?"

"Yes?" One strong arm wrapped around Jon's shoulders. Callum's other hand was between them, tangled in lax and soaking flesh. He made an effort at coherence. "Wonderful."

Jon found a nipple, sucked it softly.

"If I had anything left," said Callum, "that would start me off again."

"Next time ... " Jon bestowed a regretful kiss on the pap and turned his attention to the mouth that lifted to his " ... perhaps we won't be in such a hurry."

"Hmmm, darling, I can't guarantee that," Callum told him, yielding to the pressure of his mouth. "I'm going back to Australia at the end of the week, and you and I have a hell of a lot of lost time to make up before then."

Moonlight was pouring in at an oblique angle when Jon got out of bed a couple of hours later. As he returned from the bathroom, he found himself halting in mid–stride as a sense of unreality overtook him. His bed, which had been empty for so many years, was occupied at last: Callum, all loose limbs and tangled hair, had one arm outflung across Jon's pillow, and seemed perfectly at home. Jon felt a vague unease, as if he could not quite comprehend the spectacle before him. Indeed, the way the moon was sprinkling silver onto Callum's hair and eyelashes like the glitter on a Christmas card was almost enough to convince him he had wandered by accident into an enchanted dream.

"What's the matter, love?" There had been no indication that Callum was awake until he lifted his head and spoke clearly. When Jon still did not move, he threw back the bed–covers. "Jon? Come back to bed, it's bloody January out there."

Released from his momentary paralysis, Jon slid in beside him and let himself be folded into a reassuring embrace.

"Tell me what's wrong." But Jon shook his head and pulled closer into his arms; his skin was chilled, and Callum offered the kind of rough warmth and uncritical welcome which must inevitably overwhelm his reservations.

"This wasn't supposed to happen. I'm much too old and sensible."

"Too old and sensible for what?"

"For anything with you. You must realise how I feel."

"Yes." Silence, then, "It's the same for me. This is the most awkward bloody thing that could possibly have happened, but I want it desperately and I wouldn't change it for the world."

"I don't see how we can expect it to work."

"Nor do I," admitted Callum. "But people do have long–distance affairs – secret ones, too, if it comes to that. By the law of averages some of them must work out eventually."

"Very few of them, I suspect."

"All right, so the odds are stacked against us. Does that have to mean that we don't even try?"

"No. Not if you really want to."

"I do. I thought you did, too."

"Yes. But I've got such a lot to lose. My daughter, to be specific."

Callum digested the words carefully, stroking Jon's hair as he did so. "That's fair," he conceded, after a while. "I promise never to forget it. Nothing public, not a word to a soul, but we'll get together whenever we can." A hand stroked sensuously down Jon's flank by way of punctuation. "I've got such plans for you, my boy," he added, in an altered tone. "Do you know what I've got with me? Flavoured condoms, that's what. I was hoping you might let me put one on you so that I can find out if they really do taste of anything."

Jon was not sure whether to be shocked or fascinated by the suggestion; he would have had to be dead for Callum's lascivious tone not to make some impression on him, yet he had the sensation that his life was already spinning out of control.

"What are they supposed to taste of?" he asked, intrigued despite himself.

"Banana," laughed Callum. "It seemed appropriate."

"Oh God." Jon's whole body was suffused with two entirely conflicting impulses, lust and terror. It was not as if he had never looked at Callum's mouth and thought, somewhere in the back of an otherwise wholly respectable mind, how sweet and wet it must be inside; indeed, he had even, sometimes, been able to acknowledge to himself that he harboured this particular fantasy. No, it was more a matter of performance anxiety, the suspicion that somehow one is likely either to disappoint abjectly or to be abjectly disappointed. Whatever he wanted most, that was bound to be where he would fail the most – and he had dreamed of the intimacy in such graphic detail that he was half–afraid to test the reality; how could it possibly match up to his expectations? "You mean you really want to … ?"

"Absolutely. If you trust me."

When Callum put it like that, there was no possibility of debate. Besides, the look of hope on his boyish face was so appealing that only a tyrant could have refused him – and Jon was far from being a tyrant.

"Don't expect ... too much," he warned, although he had the feeling he was being ignored. Square fingers moved competently on the little foil packet; a tearing sound followed, then a moment of awkwardness before cool latex engulfed him. Callum was astonishingly good at this; he must have done it before. Jon's hands would have been shaking far too much by this stage for it to be anything but a total humiliation, yet when the thing was smoothed down onto him he was aware of being very much aroused and ready to oblige simply because it was Callum who asked it of him.

"Wait a moment," came the husky whisper, "we should both have them. We ought to have used them before, if we hadn't been in such a hurry." And Jon was grateful that Callum seemed to be in control now, to be making the decisions, to be guiding him through the maze; it was not that he himself was entirely without experience, but the world had been a safer place back then. Or, at least, so they had believed at the time.

"Ready?" Callum whispered eventually, kissing him. "I've been looking forward to this." Then, without ceremony, he wriggled around in the bed and, with more enthusiasm than skill, took Jon into his mouth.

If he had been completely naked it would all have been over at the first touch but, armoured as he was, Jon felt only a fraction of the sensation he vaguely remembered – and that had been rare enough, Lord knew, even then. The absence of direct contact seemed to have removed any sense of urgency, and he was able to luxuriate in the sweet pull of lips, tongue and teeth in sensitive areas which for far too many years had received no attention but his own. As he watched, through half–lidded eyes, the fair head bobbing enthusiastically, and took in the sounds of delight Callum was making, he wondered whether there wasn't something he ought to be doing in reciprocation. However Callum had chosen – deliberately, it seemed – a position which would make that impossible. Therefore he sat, propped amongst the pillows, his thighs spread and Callum moving between them, and all he could do with his hands was stroke the boy's head and shoulders, run his thumb along the line of Callum's mouth where it encircled him and have it sucked in, too, and licked and nipped in its turn.

He lasted longer than he would ever have believed possible, in a sweet haze of sensation where all he needed to do was feel, react, and from time to time moan in soft appreciation – although softness was by now the furthest thing from his mind. He was vividly aroused, all response centred in the shifting interface of skin and latex, latex and skin, in the play of air and fingers and in the obscene soundtrack of gluttony as Callum devoured him over and over again. He felt anchored to the bed, pressed beneath an insurmountable weight, wanting to reach for Callum and return the pleasure but being denied even that. And Callum, trembling, obviously at war within himself, wanted this as much as he did but was determined to choreograph it his way for reasons of his own. Well, Jon was used to taking direction. An actor's body was never wholly his own property; he had learned that years ago, yet he had never been aware of surrendering it so completely before. And it was this knowledge, perhaps, combined with the ministrations of the prentice mouth, which brought him at last to his moment of quiet culmination.

"Oh," he exclaimed in surprise, as if it had not been what they were both striving towards. And then, almost as an afterthought, " … my God … " He did not know whether or not it was intended as a warning, but there was no alteration in Callum's movements except that he opened his throat that impossible fraction further and swallowed him a little more deeply, so that it felt like releasing himself directly into the young man's heart. The look on Callum's face, when he could see it, beneath sweat and matted hair and the sheen of moonlight, was transfigured, blissful, and in a quiet way triumphant, as if it had been his own climax and not Jon's he had so assiduously been seeking.

"Are you all right?" Jon whispered, when he could summon breath to voice the thought. "Is there something I can do for you?"

Slowly Callum relinquished him, unwinding from what appeared to have become an incredibly uncomfortable posture. "No," he said, with a grimace. "Embarrassingly enough, I came when you did … and about twice as hard, I think. Not what I had in mind, just the way it worked out. I've always wanted to find somebody who'd let me do that, it's been a dream of mine for years." His lips and tongue were swollen; the words were not entirely clear. "When the moment finally arrived, I just couldn't help myself. It was the first time, as if you hadn't guessed."

Jon shook his head slowly, easing the boy into his arms. "I wouldn't have known if you hadn't told me," he said. "Why was it so important?"

"I don't know." Callum was heavy against him. "Perhaps I just wanted to find out whether banana–flavoured condoms really taste of banana. Or perhaps I wanted to work out once and for all whether I'm gay or not. I've never been completely sure, but I thought … if I could do that, and we both enjoyed it … "

"Well, it's one way of finding out. I take it you've never gone all the way with a man before, then?"

Callum pulled the covers around them both, snuggled further into Jon's embrace. "Until tonight, I'd never been to bed with a man at all. I've had the occasional hand–job, but it isn't quite the same – although I never wanted much more until I met you. You're the first guy I've been with where it's been emotion first and sex last. In fact, the emotion wasn't there at all with anybody else. I've never known what it feels like to be in love, but if this thing with you continues the way it's starting I have an idea I may be well on the way to finding out."

"Thank you."

"I could never have done any of this while my dad was still alive," Callum went on, earnestly. "He was so anti–gay, he wouldn't even use a public toilet in case somebody propositioned him."

"Mine was the same," mused Jon. "He said it was better to pee in the street and get fined for it than to risk ending up in prison because some bugger said you'd smiled at him. He prosecuted a lot of men for indecency in his time. He'd have hated having a gay son."

"What about your sister? Did he know about her?"

"I doubt it. He wouldn't have believed it anyway; he didn't think lesbians really existed. He was old–fashioned like that: men were supposed to be tough and make the decisions, women were empty–headed and needed to be protected. Very gallant, bless him, but …

misguided. Wrong, in fact."

Callum sighed. "Mine was more of the beating–up variety," he admitted, bleakly. "He might not have got involved himself, but he'd have sent his workmates to teach me the error of my ways – and there wouldn't have been a safe place anywhere in Swindon if he'd ever found out about me. I couldn't have gone home again. He wasn't a bully in the physical sense, but he did like to impose his will on everybody – and that included the way people thought. The only time my mum ever stood up to him was when she wanted me to start drama lessons, and I think she talked him into it by persuading him I'd go into politics and end up as prime minister one day. Which would have been all right with him, as long as I was a good union man first. Anyway, while he lived I could never have done this – with you or anybody else. Not," he concluded, soothingly, "that I was in danger of doing it with anybody else."

Jon kissed him softly. "Poor little straight boy," he said.

"I'm not."

"I know. But you had to pretend to be, didn't you? So did I, for a time. That's what marrying Rosemary was all about. It was largely her idea, as I expect you've gathered. I never really matched up to her specification for a husband."

"But you were good enough as a meal–ticket, is that it?"

"I assume so. I haven't tried arguing it out with her; she holds all the aces. Or, at least, the only one I care about."

"Justine."

"Yes."

"So we're forced into being straight," concluded Callum, "for our fathers' sakes – and our children's?"

"And against our personal inclinations?" mused Jon. "Yes."

"Family love: twisting people into what they're not supposed to be since the dawn of time."

"Yes. It's one of the reasons we're actors, isn't it? Because from the day we're old enough to walk, we're never allowed to be ourselves – we're always meeting someone's expectations."

"True." Callum sounded sleepy. "But we're good, aren't we, at pretending to be what we're not?"

"We're excellent. Both of us." It was so easy to lie there and hold Callum, to listen to his heartbeat, to enjoy the luxury of looking at him without hindrance, to touch him anywhere he chose, to say whatever strange or silly thing entered his head and never be criticised for it. Jon felt he had been given the keys to the world and offered the chance to take it out for spin, yet all he wanted was to stay here and enjoy this moment, and the next, and the next. "'Your face, my thane'," he teased, "'is as a book, wherein men May read strange matters'."

"Gruoch, my lovely lady wife," laughed Callum, "I've missed you! Say on, sweetheart."

It was hardly the most appropriate of lullabies, but these characters had been their companions throughout the summer and they slipped into them easily. It was a truism of their trade that sometimes words were of only minor importance compared to the tone in which they were uttered. How else, for example, to account for the popularity of the late–night shipping forecast, a catalogue of names and weather conditions which had resonated with the national consciousness to become a beloved institution? Nothing mattered but the way the words were spoken, and Jon felt he could have turned the fatstock prices into poetry given Callum as his inspiration.

"'To beguile the time'," he continued, tenderly,

"Look like the time; bear welcome in your eye,
Your hand, your tongue: look like the innocent flower,
But be the serpent under't. He that's coming
Must be provided for: and you shall put
This night's great business into my dispatch;
Which shall to all our nights and days to come
Give solely sovereign sway and masterdom."

"'We will speak further'," said Callum, but Jon was certain he was already asleep.

"'Only look up clear'," he concluded in a husky fond whisper. "'To alter favour ever is to fear: Leave all the rest to me.'" And then, sinking down beside him, no more energy for further thought, "Sleep well, darling boy."

"Hmmm," responded Callum, incoherently, and nestled against him, and made a point of obeying his instructions to the letter.

◆

(The upstairs living-room of a holiday
cottage on a cold, dark evening in
February the following year. Despite the
date, JON is kneeling to arrange
decorations on a Christmas tree and the
room is generally in festive trim.)

◆

Jon was trying to decide between a fuzzy plastic reindeer and a
pregnant–looking Santa when he heard a car creeping stealthily over
gravel and jumped to the window to look outside. The private road,
effectively disguised as a farm entrance, was rutted and full of holes and
difficult enough to navigate in full daylight – which it had been when
he arrived himself. Now that it had fallen dark, however, it became
even more obvious that this place was some distance from any centres
of civilisation; there was no ambient light anywhere, and the car's
headlights jounced about so crazily that they couldn't be a great deal of
use either. Crawling at snail's–pace was therefore the sensible approach,
but it was always going to be a nightmare. For Callum – having flown
from Los Angeles, where he had been taking meetings about future
projects, and with an eighteen–hour journey behind him already – a
slow–motion roller–coaster ride up a narrow Welsh sheep track was
probably exactly what he didn't need.

It was a little less than four weeks since Jon had driven him to the
airport and said 'goodbye' to him in a car park under a silvery dawn;
even then they were being careful. Since that time there had been a
couple of telephone calls but – as they could never work out the time
difference – it was always the middle of the night for one of them and
the middle of the day for the other, and anyway they had no idea what
to say and were both afraid of saying too much. Indeed, in the interim,
it had all seemed to dissolve into the realm of unreality somehow, and
Jon was struggling to believe that Callum had ever been with him at all,
let alone that he had spent three long and gloriously satisfying nights in
Jon's bed.

Looking back, in fact, the days had seemed far more real than the nights, right from the first morning's panicked scrambling to cover up evidence of their activities before the builders arrived – which consisted largely of dispatching Callum naked through the house while the van was being unloaded, so that he could emerge tousled and sleepy from the garden room some time later and hopefully not give himself away by a misplaced look or giggle. But they were not actors for nothing; the habit of dissembling was not new, and they could lie with brazen faces when they needed to. They had carried it off with aplomb, and only one deeply meaningful glance exchanged behind Derek's back had ever signified that there was more to this relationship than that of indulgent landlord with favoured lodger; yet it had confirmed that it absolutely would not do for Callum to stay at the Old Crown again in the summer if they were to have any hope of keeping their relationship secret, and he had reluctantly been persuaded to look around for other quarters for the season.

So it had been with the knowledge that there was something unfinished between them that they had parted on that cold January morning, and with trepidation mixed with delight that Jon now prepared to welcome him home – although this was in fact nobody's home, but an Italianate folly on the Welsh coast which Roy and Pete had bought in the first flush of their own great romance, and which they now used as an occasional bolt hole and tranquil retreat from their otherwise frantic globe trotting existence. Roy had always intended to write here at Portofino, but somehow he had never managed to find the time. It seemed, indeed, very much like a place where the best–laid plans would always come to nothing when set against the distractions of the sea, the sky, the sheltering woodland – and a well–appointed bedroom with a panoramic view of all three.

Jon abandoned his decorating and went outside to meet Callum; even with the lights from the house it was difficult to see anything except that the vehicle which had brought him was small and red and drawn up at the most peculiar angle. The engine noise died away and the door was flung open, and as Jon made his way down the steps from the front door he was virtually assaulted by a flying figure erupting out of the darkness. He was grabbed, embraced, and kissed within an inch of his life by someone who had far more energy than he would ever have imagined possible.

"God, I've missed you," gasped Callum, stretching up on tiptoe, his arms looping around Jon's neck and pulling Jon down to kiss him thoroughly. "I don't remember you being quite as tall as this before."

"Twit." Jon descended the last step of the flight. "Is that better?"

"Much." But it was only the occasion for more concentrated kissing, and a serious attempt to crush him to death in the manner of a boa constrictor.

"How … was your … flight?" The conventional remark was somehow blurted out in the intervals when he was actually allowed to breathe.

"There were two of them," said Callum, "and they were both too long." A pause, during which they were peering at one another solemnly without a single word to say. "Jon … "

"I know. Come on inside, it's too cold to hang about here. Have you got much luggage?"

"Have I ever got much luggage?" demanded Callum reasonably.

"I suppose not."

"Well, then, let's assume I haven't this time, either."

"All right. Are you planning to lock the car? Or just close the door, perhaps?"

"Hmmm. I should, shouldn't I?" Callum turned back and slammed the front door viciously, opening the back to extract the holdall he had brought to the Old Crown at the beginning of the year, and a couple of bags from airport stores. A moment later he had locked the car and was following Jon up the steps into the house. "Not so much 'parked'," he observed, "as 'abandoned'. You might have warned me I'd need a 4x4."

"I had no idea the road was still that bad," commented Jon. "I haven't been here since Roy and Pete first bought the place, and I took it for granted they'd have done something about it by now."

Callum dumped his bags in the hallway and stared around himself. There was a black and white checked floor, and the walls were sugar–almond pink. "Tell me it isn't this colour everywhere," he asked, anxiously.

Jon grinned. "'Sicilian Lemon' in the kitchen," he said. "Spare bedroom's there, downstairs cloakroom, kitchen–diner. The sitting room and master bedroom are upstairs."

"Master bedroom. I like the sound of that. It sounds … " he smiled tiredly, " … masterful."

"It is, to the point of butchness. Come and have a drink; dinner will be about half an hour."

"Timed to a nicety as usual. I don't deserve you, Jon, do I?"

"Probably not," was the response, "but it looks as if you're stuck with me anyway."

Minutes later Callum was sitting on the couch in the living room with a glass of wine. The room was decorated with streamers, plastic holly and snowmen; a half–dressed artificial tree stood on a table in the corner just as Jon had left it.

"I nearly said 'I can't believe you went to all this trouble'," Callum said, looking round. "But it's you, so of course I can. Attention to detail, that's your thing, isn't it?"

Jon shrugged. "You obviously didn't have much of a Christmas," he explained. "Anyway, it gave me an excuse to get you a present."

"Bless you, love – Christmas was complete crap and I hated every minute of it, and I really wouldn't mind giving it another go. And I got you a present, too, by the way; it's nearly Valentine's, after all." He paused. "I suppose we're the soppy type who care about things like that, are we? Perhaps we're secretly girls."

"Maybe." Jon was watching him carefully. "How were your meetings? Any interesting offers?"

"Not bad. I didn't fancy the TV part in the end – they were looking for a seven–year commitment, and I don't want to sign up for anything that long–term. But it looks like I might get a couple of movies out of it though – the *Fall of Man* series by Dylan Judd: *Planetfall, Deadfall* and *Firefall*. They want me to play Rossi."

"I haven't read the books," Jon told him. "I'm not a fan of science fiction. Is that a good part?"

"Depends on the final script – but it certainly should be. Rossi's the sidekick; Bryce Gullory's playing the Commander – it's his project. They wanted to see if there was any chemistry between us."

"And was there?"

Callum grimaced. "Some," he admitted. "He's a nice enough bloke, I'm sure we can make it work. But how about you, any projects worth talking about?"

"Not to the same extent. I did the Austen for Radio 4; that goes out in May. Bill Wildman was in it, and I met Edgar Treece. For some reason our paths had never crossed before, but of course Bill knew him. Bill knows everyone."

"Edgar?" Despite himself, Callum was impressed. "My God, he's a legend! Didn't he work with Anthony Quayle at one time?"

"So he says. According to Edgar, they played the Ugly Sisters at Frinton in about 1958."

"Mad old bugger, I bet they did! I take it you got on well with him?"

"Like a house on fire; he's a walking talking theatrical encyclopaedia and I loved him to bits. If there's anybody in the business he hasn't worked with, they're just not worth knowing."

"He hasn't worked with me," was the plaintive response.

"QED, then, I'd say, wouldn't you?" asked Jon, elbowing him conspiratorially.

"Bitch," returned Callum with a laugh. "I'm glad you had a good time, love. I can imagine you, Bill and Edgar terrorising the rest of the cast – in a thoroughly gentlemanly way, of course. What else? Was there a reason for that brutal haircut, for example?"

Jon grimaced, running a self–conscious hand over the fierce military crop which made the grey in his hair more prominent than ever. "I know – it's not quite me, is it? I had a walk–on as an army officer in a TV thing about a court martial, and they wanted me to look severe. Well, the money was good – and it shouldn't take long to grow it back."

"I hope not. I prefer you a bit softer around the edges." And then the immediate demurral. "No, that's a lie – I don't like you soft at all, I prefer you as hard as you can possibly be. Do you reckon that if we put our minds to it we might actually manage to spend the entire week in bed?"

"I suspect we could, if that's really what you want. But maybe we could fit in the occasional meal break as well?"

"If you insist."

"I do. I wouldn't want you fading away on me."

"So you're going to feed me up, are you? In the intervals when you're not screwing me through the mattress, that is?"

"The very brief intervals."

"Exceptionally brief, I hope."

"Almost imperceptible," countered Jon, smiling at him reassuringly. "In fact, you'll hardly notice them at all."

They talked about ordinary things over dinner: about Roy and Pete's activities, the schedule of works at Fardels, the renovations at the Old Crown.

"Izzy's having the garden room this year," Jon said, without preamble. "And Catherine Senior's coming; she's got a one–woman show at The Venue – about Flora Sandes, an Englishwoman who was a sergeant in the Serbian Army in the First World War. I expect there'll be a couple of younger ones looking for lodgings nearer the time, too; they always leave it to the last minute before booking anything."

"Not Jax again?" asked Callum, worriedly.

"No. She's not in the company this year. I think she's doing something on TV instead."

"Good. I'll never understand how you managed to put up with her all the time you were working on *Rita* together. A little of Jax Burroughs goes a very long way indeed."

"Oh, that was easy enough. I just arranged to be in different hotels and then accidentally forgot to tell her where I was staying. She had Rory in tow most of the time, anyway, and she couldn't have cared less about me. And, as you know, professionally she's not much more than mildly irritating; it's only in social situations that she really becomes a pain."

"Was she any good in the part?"

"Well, she's no Julie Walters ... but in fact she pulled it off rather nicely. I'd say she ought to concentrate on comedy a bit more, actually; it seems to come naturally to her. It doesn't to me," he added, "but then I was playing a miserable sod anyway, and I didn't have to act a great deal."

"You're not a miserable sod," came the answer, right on cue.

"Oh yes I am, but only when you're not about."

Callum laughed. "Sweetheart. You say the nicest things." He paused, and then dug into one of his airport bags. "Here. I couldn't wrap it in case Customs wanted to have a look. I bought it in LA." He was looking very young and uncertain as he added, "Hope you like it."

"Oh. Wait a moment." Rifling through the box of Christmas decorations, Jon produced a small wrapped package to which was tied a sprig of plastic mistletoe. "You can't get the real stuff at this time of year," he explained. "I don't know where it all goes."

"They have red mistletoe in Australia," said Callum, inconsequentially, chattering to cover up what appeared to be a sudden attack of nervousness. "But it doesn't look much like the stuff we get here. They're not condoms, are they?" he asked, indicating the parcel. "Only I've brought enough with me for an army."

"So have I," replied Jon, "and they're not condoms."

"Okay." Callum's stubby fingers plucked at the green ribbon and the gold paper. Inside the box, in a nest of shredded toy paper money, was a set of enamelled cufflinks made in the shape of little green houses. "Oh, they're ... " The word eluded him for a moment, and when he glanced up he was blinking furiously. "You know, this is one of the sweetest presents I've ever been given. Means I'll have to start wearing better shirts, though, if I'm going to show them off properly."

"I expect you'll be going to a lot of occasions from now on," Jon told him. "You know how Americans like to party."

"I'm not going to live over there permanently, you know," was the concerned response. "They'll be doing most of the filming in England, like with *Star Wars*."

"Good. But 'the money' will want you to show your face on the West Coast from time to time, and you'll have to dress like a movie star there or they'll never take you seriously. I suppose in the circumstances I should probably say 'wear them in good health' or something, shouldn't I?"

"Thank you, darling. Are you going to open yours?"

Jon had been trying to postpone the moment, but now he took a breath and pushed open the hinged lid of the jeweller's box. The shape seemed to indicate that what he found inside would be a wristwatch, and this surmise turned out to have been correct. It was an expensive one, too, of a brand he had never hoped to be able to afford on his own account; the design was classic and understated and mercifully the thing did not come with a dozen dials and an attachment for getting Boy Scouts out of horses' hooves.

"I hope it's the sort of thing you like," Callum was saying, apparently from a vast distance. "I asked the guy for something classy and this was what he suggested. There's something on the back," he added, almost humbly.

Jon turned it over. In small, discreet characters on the reverse of the watch he saw a line of capital letters: JILUC.

It took a moment. The 'J' was obviously for his own name, and the 'C' for Callum's. The initials in the middle, however, gave him a moment's pause. Then he looked up, mouth open in surprise.

"You … ?"

"Don't act all shocked," was the uncomfortable response. "Make it 'I Like You', if you'd rather."

"But we've never … "

"Honestly, Jon, do you really think I'd make the beast with two backs with somebody I didn't care about at least a bit? No, scratch that, I probably would. What I mean is … This is … You're … somebody I feel I want to get sentimental with, and that hasn't happened to me before. Like I said before, maybe I'm a girl."

"I've had convincing evidence that you're not," Jon told him, recovering slightly. "Callum, I don't know if I can … "

"No, that's all right, I understand. I shouldn't have, either, should I? It's too soon, and it's not as if I had any idea what love is anyway. But it isn't easy to find an acronym that means 'I feel great around you and

I wish it could go on for ever and ever even though I know it can't possibly'."

Jon smiled. "We'll have the summer," he soothed, running his fingertip affectionately over the engraving. "As long as you find somewhere to stay where I can visit you, of course. We can use Fardels as soon as it's habitable, which will probably be about July. From then on we can go there sometimes at weekends."

"Good. I think I have found a place, actually, although it's self–catering so you'll have to come and cook for me from time to time. I'm terrible, I bet I could burn salad if I tried."

The jump to defensive blokishness was typical of Callum; it was like him indeed to follow up a moment of vulnerability with a bit of macho pantomime.

"I'm sure that's not true, but of course I'll cook for you whenever I can. Where will you be?"

"The Old Coal Wharf at White Elm. Do you know it? They've got permission to have residential narrowboats there now. It's going to be a bit of a long drive every day, but think of all the peace and quiet there'll be at night."

"Oh. Yes, I'd heard about that; I had no idea they were opening yet, though."

"Well, I'm in luck; there's still only one boat, so I should have the place virtually to myself. Believe me, though, I'm paying through the nose for it."

"It sounds idyllic," mused Jon.

"It does, doesn't it? But it could hardly be more idyllic than this place; I mean, a tower by the sea … "

"A rich man's folly," was the amiable correction. "People have always paid through the nose, as you say, for their privacy."

"True. Which reminds me that we ought to be making better use of it. I presume we've got a shower or a bath or something upstairs?"

"Both, in fact, and pretty sensational examples at that."

"Good. Then I need to wash the journey off, if you don't mind. I'd invite you to come and scrub my back, but I was hoping we could save that sort of thing for later."

"Of course. Let me show you where everything is, then I'll tidy up a bit before I come to bed."

Callum sighed deeply. "I like that idea," he said. "Sharing a bed with you, I mean. I've missed it. Not just the sex, but everything else as well. The comfort. Having somebody there. I got a bit lonely on the other side of the world without you. Maybe next time … "

"Oh yes. I can just see you explaining that. 'I'm bringing my boyfriend with me and we'll want a double room.'"

"Boyfriend," Callum repeated. "Doesn't sound quite right, does it?"

"No, it doesn't."

"So, what are we, then? Lovers? Mentor and pupil? 'Friends With Benefits'?"

"None of the above," replied Jon, quietly. "Just two people who make each other happy. Let's not look deeper into it than that for now, shall we? Life's much too uncertain."

"Amen. All right, then, person–who–makes–me–happy, I have an overwhelming desire to throw off all my clothes and step into a nice hot shower before I'll be fit for any other sort of activity, whether in polite company or only with you – so why don't you come and show me the way to this legendary masterful bedroom of ours?"

The bedroom was indeed somewhat butch. It had a dark wood floor, a Welsh slate feature wall, a picture window the exact size and shape of a movie screen – in front of which was the room's only concession to old–fashioned luxury, a white–upholstered antique chaise longue of heroic proportions – and a deep white bed that looked as smooth and inviting as an enormous slab of iced cake. The bathroom was equally uncompromising, featuring a bath large enough for a whole family and an extravagant frosted glass shower.

"This looks like Pete's taste," mused Callum, as he glanced around.

"Yes. Roy's tends to be a bit more delicate. I suspect Pete pulled rank when they got to the bedroom." There was a pause, and then, "I'm not sure I meant that quite the way it sounded."

"No. Probably pretty accurate, though."

"I try not to think about it," admitted Jon. "I mean, one knows one's friends have sex, but I'd rather not dwell on the gory details."

"So if I asked you what they use the chaise longue for … ?"

"I'd say 'looking at the view'," was the disingenuous response. "But I notice that it's Scotchgarded, which might give you some indication … Anyway, if you've got everything you need, I'll leave you in peace to freshen up."

"I'll be fine, love. I'll just unpack a few bits and pieces first and have a shower. It shouldn't take me long."

"All right, then. I'll be back soon."

"I promise not to start without you," Callum told him mischievously as he headed into the bathroom.

When Jon returned a few minutes later, it was to find Callum sitting in darkness on the chaise longue wearing nothing but a bathrobe. In his hand he held the remote control for the curtains; the long muslin drapes were swept out to the extremities of their track, and he was staring in fascination at a rectangle of black sky, black hills and black water. There were a few tiny twinkling lights on the far shore of the inlet, but there was nothing else out there except the occasional farm and a couple of holiday cottages on a rather more modest scale than their own.

"It's beautiful," he said, quietly. "Perfect peace in all directions. Exactly what I've been dreaming of since you first told me about the place. Of course I should have guessed there'd be a balcony – I didn't see it when I arrived, but there's a sea view so naturally there's a balcony!"

"Naturally. It must be wonderful in summer."

"'Must be'? You mean you haven't seen it in the summer?"

"No. Roy's pretty possessive; this is his private retreat, he doesn't often lend it to people."

"Not even you?"

"I've never asked before. Look at the place, Callum; it's all set up for lovers, and I've never … "

"I understand." Callum smiled at him. "Well, plenty of opportunity for balcony scenes, anyway:

The orchard walls are high and hard to climb,
And the place death, considering who thou art.

I was a lousy Romeo. Absolute rubbish, I was really embarrassed. Couldn't even make myself believe it."

Jon sat beside him and they leaned together and stared out at the night, balm to their weary and over–attenuated senses.

"Perhaps there was a reason for that. Who was your Juliet?"

"Grete Sanger. Visually we made a wonderful couple, but there was no kind of spark at all. The people you end up playing love scenes with are always the people you can't actually stand at any price. And the people you really have something with … " Callum stopped. "You and I could play a love scene that would burn the theatre down, but the audience would hate it. It'd be far too honest for them."

"Among other things. We're still supposed to pretend to be raging heterosexuals, aren't we? Even if we did end up playing a love scene, we'd have to make a big fuss about how it was just a job and we weren't really enjoying it. You can never let anybody see what it is you're truly feeling."

"The best thing is to stop feeling altogether," was the downbeat response. "Build a wall round your heart. Everybody says they want truth in acting, but the moment you let real emotion in they carve you up and throw away the pieces. I could never say I loved you, on stage or in front of a camera, because the world would know I meant it – and I could never say it to anybody else again afterwards and have a hope of being convincing. It would shatter the illusion for ever."

"I know. I assume you won't be asking me to play Juliet, then?"

"No, and for God's sake hit me on the head with a brick if I ever look like trying Romeo again. Not that you and I wouldn't be great in it, mind you; we could certainly give the world something new to think about."

"Logistical difficulties notwithstanding?"

"Gender–blind casting," laughed Callum. "It's all the rage these days."

"Age–blind, too," Jon reminded him. "I'm twenty–five years too old for Juliet, at a conservative estimate, and no amount of make–up is ever going to change that."

"True, alas. So once again the world is robbed of your definitive performance – as if losing your Lady Mac wasn't bad enough already. But I'd have liked to hear you say the lines just once – especially the bit about the stars."

"The stars?" Momentarily Jon was confused. "I don't … "

"'And when he shall die' …" prompted Callum.

"Ah, yes, of course, I know the bit you mean.

And, when he shall die,
Take him and cut him out in little stars,
And he will make the face of heaven so fine
That all the world will be in love with night
And pay no worship to the garish sun."

"That's it. Go on. More."

Jon's brow furrowed. "'Oh, I have … ' bought? built? ' … the mansion of a love and not possess'd it, and though I am … ' something ' … not yet … '" He stopped in confusion. "I'm sorry. Drama school was just too long ago. I haven't touched the play since then."

"You have bought the mansion of a love and not possessed it," Callum paraphrased, quietly. "Well, I think it's about time – don't you?"

"Time?" Jon was genuinely bewildered. "What time?"

"Time I lost my virginity. Time you took possession of your mansion. Here and now would work for me," he added, matter-of-factly.

The concept was more than slightly shocking. "Right here? Right now?"

"Right here, on this very chaise, Pete and Roy notwithstanding. Can you honestly think of a sexier piece of furniture to be deflowered on, Jon? Because I can't. Let's just get on and do it, shall we, before we chicken out altogether and both die wondering?"

"Are you sure you're ready?"

"Absolutely. I'm more than ready; I've been thinking about nothing else ever since the first time you kissed me. It was the only thing that got me through wrapping the movie and having all those interminable bloody meetings on the way home. Christ, I would have agreed to just about anything if only they'd let me leave." Then, sensing still a further hesitation, he lowered his voice to a husky whisper. "I mean it, I want you in me. Think you can do that for me, love?"

Jon's breath hitched sharply. "Of course. We'll have to take it slowly, though; I wouldn't want to hurt you."

"I know. Take your time, make it work for you; however you want it is fine with me."

"We'll need … "

"Got 'em here." The deep pockets of the bathrobe yielded a handful of little foil squares and a tube of gel.

"This is an ambush," Jon complained, softly.

"It is, darling. I knew you'd never get around to asking, so I thought I'd better take the initiative. And what better setting could there be for a couple of exhibitionists like you and me?" he asked, gesturing extravagantly towards the window. "It's just like being on stage; everybody can see us, but nobody can!"

"All right. Promise you'll tell me if you need to stop."

"I will. I'm not the noble, self–sacrificing type, love; I leave all that sort of thing to you."

"Very well." The words sounded as if Jon was only reluctantly being persuaded to agree, but his tone said otherwise. There are few men so altruistic that they can refuse something they have been dreaming of in exquisite detail for months, particularly when it's offered to them with as sincere a promise of no recriminations as can be imagined, and Jon Stapleton could never have been numbered among them. "So," he added quietly, slipping loose the tie on Callum's bathrobe, "let me have a good look at you."

Callum stood up, dropping the robe behind him on the chaise. He stood there naked, hands on hips, and in the muted light from the bathroom it was possible to see that he was smiling softly. Outside there were few stars and no moon, just a tumble of inky clouds.

"So, like what you see?" he asked, half–teasingly but with an eager catch in his voice.

"Yes." Jon's fingers whispered across his ribcage. "You're looking a lot healthier now you've started to put some of that weight back on."

"I've been eating like a horse," Callum confessed. "You know how they feed you in LA when they're trying to impress you: all those big steaks and things in cream sauces. Everybody wanted to wine and dine me while I was there."

"At least you got some offers out of it."

"I did, but I'm damned if I'm going to talk about those now; haven't we got better things to do?" Jon was still exploring delicately, making no move to close the arm's length gap between them. This continued for some considerable time, and there was no further dialogue until Callum said, almost nervously, "Shouldn't you be naked too?"

"Probably. But I thought we were going to do this my way?"

"We are. Does your way include slow death by sexual torture?"

"It might. I haven't decided yet."

"Oh God, you tyrant, you know exactly which buttons to press, don't you?"

"Hmmm," agreed Jon, thoughtfully. Then he leaned down to the floor and handed Callum a wrapped condom. "Let me watch you put it on."

He heard, rather than saw, the shudder which ran through Callum's body; observed the fingers moving about their task; followed them as they smoothed the thin sheath carefully into place.

"Does that feel good?" he asked, hoarsely, even more affected by the spectacle than he had expected. "Was that how you learned, by putting them on yourself?"

"Over and over again," Callum admitted, trembling. "And thinking of you all the time. Closing my eyes and imagining it was you and me putting them on each other. Want me to put one on you now, love?"

"No, I can manage." Jon was beginning to climb out of his clothes, his sweater, tee–shirt, cord trousers and underwear being thrown in the approximate direction of the floor. "What flavour are these supposed to be, anyway?"

"Milk chocolate. That's why they're ... brown, I suppose. I picked them up in ... the States." Jon eased Callum back onto the chaise and, naked himself now, knelt between Callum's knees and drew an experimental tongue slowly up the length of the tightly–filled condom. Callum's hands were in his hair almost immediately, neither holding nor guiding but simply caressing him affectionately. "They make … " he went on " … all kinds … spearmint … grape … cola … I got everything I could lay my hands on, and flavoured … stuff … too … "

"Very considerate." Jon detached himself from Callum's hands, rose to his feet again, and made a slow, elaborate performance out of caressing a matching condom onto his own superheated flesh. It was very necessary indeed to try to gain some respite from one another; they had been apart so long that emotion and desire had built almost to fever–pitch, and although they were both aiming for control and intent on making this lasting and enjoyable rather than some frantic, functional encounter, the limitations of self–discipline were becoming more apparent by the minute. "Tell me what you think of the taste," he said, guiding himself gently between Callum's lips, which opened to receive him with alacrity. Callum inhaled, all but swallowing his entire length in one open–throated manoeuvre, held his thin hips with aggressive fingers and dined on him with obvious enthusiasm.

"God, I want this so much," he said, freeing himself after only a short while. "You are going to do me, aren't you?"

"I promised, didn't I?" Jon bent and kissed him, deeply and thoroughly, exchanging flavours between their mouths. "So, milk chocolate?" he teased.

"Just about, don't you think?"

"Better than the banana, certainly." Then, very softly, "Turn over, darling, and let me kiss you properly." And he heard Callum's indrawn breath of anticipation, and watched him rearrange himself on the chaise, and knelt again, and stroked, and pressed his lips lovingly into the sweet, dark place.

"Oh fuck. I never thought you'd do that." Callum was almost whimpering as he was sounded, tongued, kissed again, slobbered on and made very, very wet. He wriggled back into it, pushing against Jon's mouth. "It's so good. So good." His fingers had closed over the elaborate scrollwork on the back and armrest of the chaise. His legs shifted, his knees drawing further apart as he abandoned himself to Jon's attentions. "You can do that all night as far as I'm concerned."

"Thank you. Perhaps I will. I'm sure it would be more satisfactory than actually … " He paused, put his mouth close to Callum's ear, and said, with his most precise actorly diction, " … fucking you."

"No, no, it wouldn't. You should absolutely do that."

"Should I?" One long, elegant finger, rich with lubricating gel, pushed into the heat of Callum's body and was caught immediately by spasming muscle. "If you can still talk, the chances are I'm doing something wrong."

"No, you're not. Not at all. But you could go deeper."

"All right. Relax."

"Cue for a song?"

"Hush." And Jon reached up further into the long darkness, and felt Callum open to him like a flower. "There," he soothed, tenderly, "you like that, don't you?"

An inarticulate sound of pleasure was the only response; Callum's knuckles whitened on the dark mahogany and his body seemed to tense and relax all at once, centring on the probing fingers as they spread inside him. He writhed shamelessly, emitting tortured little gasps of need, and some detached part of Jon's brain revelled in being able to reduce him to a quivering mass of desire, mindless and purposeless except as he directed. It was a strange power to wield, but one he was just as ready to surrender to in turn; the giving and receiving of pleasure on such a scale was the embodiment of trust, and in Callum's moaning inarticulacy were all the poems of the world.

He took his fingers out slowly; memory suggested that it would sting if not done with caution, but Callum seemed to have no consciousness of his surroundings whatsoever.

"Last chance to change your mind." Curse his honourable streak, his gentlemanly nature; how much he would have liked, for once, to play the villain, to take without permission, to use and throw away without having to care! But there was no such matter in him, and he had long ago acknowledged it to himself.

"Do it," said Callum, soberly and sensibly, his tone one of gratifying comprehension. He was not so smitten by lust that he did not understand what he was agreeing to, and understand it fully. "Do it, love, please." Awkwardly, he offered himself again. "Now."

Jon wiped his fingers on the bathrobe beneath them, eased his body into a less twisted position, uttered some inconsequential reassurance, and went inside Callum in one long, deep movement to the hilt, to be greeted by a heartfelt sigh.

Thereafter there was neither time nor space for memory; it simply did not form; all was blind sensation, all animal–brained rutting as stroke after stroke was met with gasps and cries of delight, and where words were discernible they were invariably demands for more. In straining to meet them Jon became less tender, less considerate, rougher than he had believed himself capable of, but Callum absorbed everything and begged again, until at last on a high and wondering note he suddenly said "Yes, yes" and his body shook and seemed to fold in on itself, and Jon found sudden release amidst juddering flesh that gripped, tightened and threatened to mangle him to oblivion. He was aware of Callum swearing reflexively, mouth and body venting uncontrollably in the quiet room, the powerful orgasm apparently both physical and verbal.

"Oh God, oh fuck, yes, yes … yessss … " And a cry like the high lost wail of a seabird echoed in the stillness and faded slowly away to heart–thumping silence.

"Precious boy." Jon held him close, overwhelmed by affection for him.

"Oh, Jon, thank you … thank you." A brief, exhausted pause, and then: "That was beautiful. You're beautiful. Thank you."

"Fool." He slipped, wet and diminished, out of Callum's body, and could have cried for the loss. "If anyone round here is beautiful … " he added, sentimentally.

"Only in your eyes."

"Then perhaps we've both been blinded by our feelings." But practical considerations were beginning to intrude: the room was cooler than they could have wished, and the chaise longue stylish rather than comfortable; nobody but a cat would have considered it a suitable place to pass the night. "Shall we go to bed?" he offered.

"I think we'd better, love, I'm exhausted. But when I wake up, I'm going to want to do that again. Or maybe the other way round, if you don't mind?"

"I don't."

"Good. Then let's make ourselves comfortable and get our strength back, shall we?" After which came the unromantic business of disengaging from one another and disposing of used condoms before sliding together between fresh–scented sheets, limbs entangling readily, Callum's head falling to rest on Jon's shoulder and his voice saying, distinctly, on the edge of sleep, "You know, sweetheart, I'm really going to enjoy being made happy by you."

They had not had enough time to become used to sleeping in the same bed before Callum returned to Australia and, although in theory it should have been blissful, in practice it was not. Callum was restless, and too warm, and only seemed to drop into and out of the occasional light doze. It was apparent to Jon that he was not at all comfortable, and when at last he could stand it no longer he ran a hand over Callum's shoulder and asked sympathetically, "What's the matter, darling?"

Callum let out a long sigh. "I was hoping not to wake you," he said. "Bloody jet lag; my insides are still on LA time – I'm getting hungry again."

"Oh. What would you like? A snack, or a proper breakfast?"

A dry, exhausted little laugh. "You would, wouldn't you? You'd really get out of bed at fart o'clock in the morning and start cooking breakfast for me."

"Of course. There's eggs and bacon, if you like."

"No, thanks, love – but I could probably chew my way through a couple of pieces of toast, if that's okay?"

"So could I." Jon slid out of bed and reached for a burgundy silk dressing–gown. "Are you coming downstairs, or shall I bring it up to you?"

"Up all those bloody stairs?" Callum sounded incredulous. "Don't be daft, I'll come down. Maybe I can make the tea, eh?" He was clambering into his bathrobe even as he spoke, stuffing his hands into the pockets to encounter one last forgotten condom. "Hmmm, that'll come in useful later," he grinned cheekily.

They pattered down the stairs together barefoot and a moment later they were in the acid yellow kitchen, two hollow–eyed and stubble–chinned men moving about with all the co–ordination of a pair of drunken ice–dancers.

"God, we're really not very good at any of this, are we?" Callum switched on the kettle and leaned heavily against the counter for support.

"We're terrible," Jon admitted. "But I suppose we'll get better."

"We can only hope." Callum fell silent. "I bet there are plenty of people who'd be shocked if they could see us now. And maybe a few who wouldn't. What did you tell Roy about wanting to use the place?"

"Just that I needed a break. I knew he wasn't intending to come here himself; someone's lent them a villa in the South of France for a month. Besides, it would never occur to him that I might not be here alone – or perhaps with Justine." Jon was busying himself with small domestic tasks, with setting out plates and knives and the butter dish on the table.

"I assume Roy knows you have a history? With men, I mean."

"It was a long time ago," Jon told him. "I don't really want to discuss it."

"All right. But does he know?"

"Yes." The first two slices of toast bounced up out of the toaster. Jon transferred them to the table and pushed more bread into the machine. "Eat it while it's hot; I'll have the next lot."

Callum had succeeded in producing two mugs of tea, and now he sat at one side of the table while Jon slipped into place opposite him. "A picture of domestic harmony," he said, thoughtfully. "So, was Roy himself a part of your history?"

Jon was staring at him, trying to decide between outrage and resignation as a response, but in the end he could hardly summon the energy to be annoyed. Callum could be inept and over–intense at times, but there was not a shred of malice in his soul.

"It was," he repeated clearly, "a long time ago. Neither of us had a clue what we were doing. We were lucky to keep the friendship afterwards."

"You were," agreed Callum. "But I can't imagine anybody ever seriously falling out with you. 'One would as soon assault a Plush Or violate a Star'."

"Mention that to my ex–wife some time, would you?" suggested Jon. "She still thinks I'm the Demon Incarnate."

"Because of Roy?"

"No. She never knew about that, thank goodness. Do you truly imagine she'd have stopped at ridicule if she had?"

Callum grimaced. "I've read a couple of her books," he said. "I picked them up in Darwin and read them on the set. She can be pretty vicious, can't she? According to her, you're one of the most incompetent fools that ever trod a stage."

"It amuses her," said Jon, without rancour. "And it gives her a useful income. Between us, we can just about manage to send our daughter to a decent school. I'm quite willing to put up with a little mockery, if that's the end result."

"Everything for love, eh, Jon?"

"I suppose so, if you want to look at it that way."

They were silent again for a little while, concentrating on eating, and then Callum said, thoughtfully, "So Roy Arbour's the skeleton in your closet, is he? I suppose I should have guessed."

"No, he isn't. You are. You must realise that we stand a very good chance of ruining one another's career completely if ever a word of this gets out."

"Trust me," said Callum, "I can ruin my career all by myself, I don't need any help from you." But he seemed unwilling to elaborate further, and returned his attention to his tea and toast with an air of utter world–weariness that seemed to indicate that he had given away far more than he intended to.

He was scarcely in a more cheerful mood later that same morning, when – after another few hours of sleep and a leisurely exploration of one another's body under the searing water of the shower – Jon found him once again in the kitchen, leaning with both hands on the worktop, looking sightlessly out of the window. It was one of the few in the house which did not have a satisfactory view, giving instead onto a narrow strip of uninspiring garden and a small shed, and Callum seemed quite fixated with this lacklustre prospect.

Jon slid up behind him and wrapped both arms around his waist, but Callum did not turn. Instead he put one hand over Jon's and said, "Listen, there's something we need to talk about. Can we go for a walk or something?"

Jon's lips touched his ear. "It's going to snow," he said, doubtfully, "but we can if you like."

"Please, love. I'm feeling restless."

"I think there's a path down through the woods to the beach," offered Jon.

"Perfect," said Callum. "An empty beach in the middle of winter. Just exactly the kind of thing I'm in the mood for."

Minutes later they were picking their way in single file down a rocky track, through a straggly shaw of oak, ash, beech and rowan. It was steep enough to make them glance around for handholds from time to time, and to make the prospect of hauling themselves back up later less than inviting, but for the time being their only object was the expanse of grey–white strand which had seemed so tempting from the bedroom window. There was no sign of tracks on it anywhere and, having the atavistic desire of all humans to mar perfection if they thought they could get away with it, they were intent on leaving footprints in the sand.

They reached the bottom of the path, climbed over a wall and dropped onto a narrow plinth, from which they were obliged to scramble to a flat rock. From there they picked their way from boulder to boulder for perhaps a dozen metres, until the rocks gave way to pebbles, and then to shingle, and finally to coarse, gritty sand, damp underfoot, and they stepped out of the shelter of the trees and felt the force of the wind.

"Hardly the most peaceful place," Jon commented, mildly. "We couldn't have had this conversation by the fire, over a glass of wine?"

"No."

"All right, then." And they walked for several paces, side by side but not speaking, towards the curling edge of the water. When they reached it they stood staring across its rippling surface, inhaling its salty fragrance, listening to the susurration of the waves. Jon bent and picked up a flat pebble, skimming it a few miserable feet until it plopped embarrassed into the sea. "Pathetic," he acknowledged, shrugging. He had half–expected Callum to take up the challenge, but he remained standing with his hands in his pockets and a miserable expression on his face. "What is it, love?" asked Jon at length, moving to shelter him from the wind and noticing that there were tears in the corners of his eyes. The sharp wind could have done that, of course, but he was certain it had not.

"I don't know where to start," confessed Callum, unevenly. "You have to realise that this … this thing with you … happened when I wasn't expecting it. I wasn't prepared. There were – there are – a lot of loose ends."

"You were seeing somebody else?" Jon ran his hands reassuringly up and down Callum's arms, not quite holding him, not quite chafing warmth into him, but a little of both. Callum seemed determined not to meet his eyes.

"Not exactly. But … you remember Thea? You remember how we didn't think we'd heard the last of her, and then she went quiet again and we thought we'd got away with it after all?"

"Yes?" Cautious, encouraging, although with a sinking heart.

"Well, it turns out … she's pregnant. She wrote to me at my agent's address. Marked it 'Private and Confidential' but of course they opened it, and Lenny rang me in Australia to tell me all about it."

"Oh." Jon digested the words carefully. "When's the baby due?"

"Next month. Don't bother counting back, the dates work out – unfortunately. And I won't say she's blackmailing me, exactly, but I have an idea she could cause me problems if she wanted to. She could say I'd raped her, for example. You know what happened to Craig What's–his–name a year or so back."

"Yes. But surely he was acquitted?"

"He was, but not before it did a lot of damage to his life. There are people who wouldn't touch me with a bargepole if I had that sort of thing hanging over my head, Jon, and you know it. Lenny and his solicitor advised me to deal with it quietly and generously ... and always wear a condom in future." There was no mirth in the laughter that followed these words, but his eyes engaged with Jon's as though seeking his approval. "So we came to a discreet arrangement: a lump sum now and so much a month until the kid's eighteen, all private and on condition that she doesn't make any public statement naming me as the father. Not that it won't leak out, what with the people in Lenny's office, the solicitor and his lot, and anybody Thea or her parents might have told. But having treated her well and given her everything she asked for should count for something, shouldn't it?"

"I would hope so."

"And ... " Callum gripped his arms, fingers fastening like steel bands around the thick sleeves of Jon's sweater, digging through to the spare muscle beneath. "It's a self–defence mechanism," he admitted, apologetically. "Misdirection. How can I possibly be gay if I'm impregnating random females all the time? I'd rather get a reputation as a bit of a cad with women than be outed to the world as some kind of screaming fairy queen."

"You're hardly that," was the judicious response. "It's not as if there had been a great many men in your life."

"Maybe not. But there are some who could tell the tale if they wanted to. They're pretending to be straight at the moment, but that's never a reliable arrangement. Thea could be a great insurance policy if anyone ever decided to open his mouth." He looked up anxiously. "I'm not going to tell you who they are."

"Of course not. Do I know them?"

"I doubt it. They're in the profession, but I don't think you've been in any of the same productions. You could have run into each other socially, I suppose."

"I'm going to assume not," said Jon. "For my own peace of mind. And yours, I imagine."

"Absolutely, love. Thank you."

"I'd rather not know," Jon explained, in case the point hadn't been made sufficiently. "I don't want to find myself being uncharitable to anybody because they knew you before I did; I'm afraid that could very possibly happen."

"Jealous?" Callum managed something like a smile. "You? Never. You'd knock yourself out to be fair to them, probably at your own expense. But I don't want that hanging over us, love. We've got enough problems, with Thea and the baby."

"Hmmm. So, you're going to be a father?" Jon was making a determined effort to sound positive about the prospect, but Callum was not deceived.

"So it seems. Not a hands–on father, though – more of an occasional father, like you." He stopped, shaking his head. "It's crazy," he said. "You get together with someone, you're happy with them, the sex is great … and you end up with a baby. That's the way it's supposed to happen – only I feel as if I've got all the right bits in completely the wrong order. I've messed things up royally, haven't I, Jon?"

Jon folded him closer, dropping a reassuring kiss onto his cold brow. These were not ideal conditions in which to hold a conversation of this sort and he would have been glad of an excuse to haul Callum back to the folly and warm him up, except that this was the time and place Callum had chosen and he had no desire to interfere with that.

"No more than anybody else," he said. "We all do stupid things, and we all look back on them later and wonder what on earth we could have been thinking. Mistakes are what make us human, and learning from them gives us strength. I hope you're not expecting me to be angry with you – or even mildly disappointed?"

"Well, I did think you might feel let down," admitted Callum, glumly.

"But we weren't even together when it happened."

"I know, but it was starting to feel as if we belonged together, wasn't it? I can't make myself think of it as anything but a betrayal."

"Well, not of me. If you've betrayed anybody, Callum, you've betrayed yourself. But it sounds as if you've dealt fairly with Thea – and remember, she must have known what she was doing all along. I'm sure there was a moment when she could have had an abortion, and apparently she chose not to. So, whatever happened between the two of you that night, you've made your choices – and I'm more than willing to stand by you in yours."

"I know you are. It would never occur to you to do anything else, would it?" There were large, fat tears rolling down Callum's cheeks now. He sniffed inelegantly and tried to turn a sob into a laugh. "You're the thousandth man, aren't you, love? The one who stands by you to the gallows–foot and after? You know the poem, don't you?"

"Of course," Jon smiled.

> *"One man in a thousand, Solomon says,*
> *Will stick more close than a brother.*
> *And it's worth while seeking him half your days*
> *If you find him before the other."*

"Yes, that's it. That's who you are, isn't it? My thousandth man?"

"I hope so. And I hope you're mine." And he kissed Callum, there and then, out in public on the beach, just to make sure that he was perfectly understood.

It was some minutes before they came to their senses again, and realised that the threatened snow had begun to fall. They were not the large, languid, feather–like flakes which settled decorously on eyelashes and hair, but the small spiteful variety which seemed so much wetter than their fellows and invariably took the quickest route through outer clothing to chill the skin beneath.

"Time we went indoors," said Callum, soberly.

"That or turn into snowmen." But neither of them made any discernible movement in the direction of the tower.

"If you play your cards right," Callum whispered, tilting his chin with a rather obvious attempt at flirtation, "I might be persuaded to rape you in front of a roaring fire."

Jon considered the remark for a moment. "Appealing as that sounds," he countered, "could I have the rape without the roaring fire? All in all, I think I'd rather be screwed to death than burnt."

"Wouldn't everybody? But yes, if you insist – one rape, hold the roaring fire. Satisfied?"

"Not yet, but I suspect I'm going to be soon." And his hand slid lower, to fasten lasciviously on the front of Callum's jeans as if claiming ownership of their contents.

"Careful, love. There's somebody up there in the woods; I thought I saw someone with a dog."

Jon laughed but released him anyway. "Only an idiot would be out in weather like this," he countered, wryly.

"We're out in weather like this," Callum reminded him.

"Case in point, I think." But they were moving steadily now towards the wall, and to the point where they had scrambled over it, and there was indeed a dog fossicking about among the wintry rock pools – a black Labrador with a hyperactive tail.

"Hello, mate," said Callum cheerfully, "Where did you come from?" The dog snuffled loudly, bounded over and tried to leap into Callum's arms as if he were its dearest friend in all the world and he scratched it vigorously between the ears. "Not out here on your own, surely, are you?"

The dog spared him a pitying look that seemed to express its disappointment that humans were so irredeemably stupid and transferred its attention to Jon, its front paws planting themselves firmly on the sleeve of his sweater.

"Yes," said Jon, "you're absolutely delightful, but I think somebody's calling you." A female voice could be heard somewhere a little above them, and as the distance closed the cry became identifiable as "Muttley? Muttley?"

"Go on, Muttley, back to your mum," Callum told the creature, taking Jon's hand and beginning to lead him towards the shore. They had only gone a few paces, however, when a woman bundled up in waterproofs and a woolly hat emerged some distance to the right of where they stood, and stepped through a gap in the wall that they had not noticed earlier. "Well, bugger me," exclaimed Callum, "there's a proper path!"

"Bugger you? I'm sorry, I thought you just said … ?"

A moment of blank incomprehension, and then Callum was laughing immoderately. "You're quite right, love, I did, didn't I? Well, bugger you, then, if you prefer, there's a proper path – it must come out somewhere above the house."

"I suggest we find out," offered Jon, and they turned their steps towards it.

At the bottom of the shallow ramp they met the dog's owner. She was a small woman, so muffled against the elements that they could hardly make out her features. "Good morning," he said to her, civilly.

"Good morning." She was smiling up at him, but that was all the conversation they exchanged. She was far too intent on catching up with her dog.

"So much for keeping it private," said Callum as they moved off. "I'm pretty sure she saw us."

"I expect so," sighed Jon. "It would be just our luck if she turned out to be a rabid theatre–fan and recognised us both."

"Or Thea's mum," was the glum rejoinder, "and used it to screw more cash out of me."

"Or my agent, and tried to charge you for my services."

"Ouch. I could never afford you. But we'd have smelled the brimstone, wouldn't we, if it was her?"

"True. Well, I suppose we'll find out soon enough if there are going to be unpleasant consequences."

"That's right. 'Sufficient unto the day', and all that crap. Now, come on, love, I've got plans that won't involve you doing a great deal of talking for a little while. Whimpering, yes, possibly; talking, no, definitely not."

"If you insist," agreed Jon, and slipped his fingers docilely back into Callum's grasp.

Callum squeezed them, and began to haul him up the path again with some vigour.

"I do, Jon," he said, with assurance. "I absolutely do."

◆

◆

INTERVAL

◆ ◆ ◆

Act 2

Scene i
(The kitchen at the Old Crown, March 1997. The room has been completely refurbished, with new kitchen units. JON and IZZY are contentedly drinking tea at opposite sides of the table.)

♦

"It looks wonderful," said Izzy, in satisfaction. It was half an hour since she had arrived, and she had needed only moments to dump her bags in the garden room and take her shoes off before sitting down to a cup of tea with Jon; now she was beginning to evaluate the changes since her previous visit. "It must make a difference having the freezer in here, instead of having to go outside."

"It does. Although we were lucky not to lose the whole lot when the main fuse blew."

Izzy laughed. "Karen told me about that on the phone. According to her it wasn't so much luck as forward planning. She said Callum was here when it happened – I suppose that must have been soon after his father died. He doesn't really strike me as the practical type, though; I don't imagine he was a great deal more use than the proverbial chocolate fireguard."

Jon allowed himself a brief moment of reflection. It was nearly three weeks since he had seen Callum, and the only evidence of their past encounters was a _Monòpoli_ 50,000 lire note pinned to the kitchen notice–board. However their self–imposed exile from one another was coming to an end at last: this was Saturday, and rehearsals for _The Duchess of Malfi_ were to start on Monday.

"He did his best," he said. "I wasn't here, so he had to do most of the mopping–up and look after the builders. They missed him when he'd gone; they kept asking when he was coming back."

116

"It's a shame he didn't want to stay again this year," mused Izzy. "He's quite pleasant to have around. Where's he lodging, do you know?"

"White Elm, I believe." The evasion tripped too carelessly off Jon's tongue; he would have to become inured to the language of lies and half–truths before the season was out, if there was to be any keeping his relationship with Callum secret.

"Is that star treatment, do you suppose?"

"That may have something to do with it, but I think it's more likely to be connected with that girl who was following him around last year. You remember, Thea? I wouldn't be surprised if he was going out of his way to avoid her."

"That's a shame," groaned Izzy. "It's a high price to pay for popularity. I take it you've never had anyone following you around like that, Jon?"

He laughed. "Rosemary set a private detective on me once, if that counts. He was trying to find out whether I'd taken up with anybody else after she threw me out, and he came back on and off for about six months. She must have been disappointed; I was living like a monk at the time."

"And you still do. Honestly, if ever a man was less likely to be guilty of double–dealing … I don't think I ever want to meet your ex–wife, though, she sounds like a tough customer."

"She is. I don't know why I imagined the two of us would suit each other."

"Maybe you didn't imagine it," suggested Izzy. "Maybe it was her idea."

"You're probably right," he conceded. "Looking back, marrying her seems an extraordinary thing to have done. I don't recognise myself at all." He fell silent for a moment, then started again with patently false cheerfulness. "So, from one uncomfortable subject to another – how are your parents?"

"Ouch!" grimaced Izzy. "You really know how to twist the knife, don't you, luv? Well, Dad's his usual self, thank you: bumbling, deaf, focussed on his work. He did find time, though, to tell me he'd seen

Judi Dench in the *Duchess* in 1971 – it was all I could do to stop him dragging out the programme. Apparently she was absolutely wonderful and he thinks I'm very strange casting for the part; it seems I lack emotional intensity. You'd think he'd never seen me arguing with my mother."

"Oh." Having been witness to Izzy's Lady Mac the previous season, Jon could hardly imagine anyone faulting her on emotional intensity. To one who had seen Judi Dench in the role, however, perhaps Izzy's Duchess might be a slightly less thrilling experience. Whether Jolyon Thorpe spoke from a position of knowledge or simple unthinking prejudice, though, was another matter entirely. "Will they be coming this time?" It seemed the remark least likely to give offence.

Izzy shook her head. "As far as Dad's concerned, what we do here isn't much of a step up from amateur theatricals. That's because he's never heard of any of us, not even Pete and Roy. There's no such thing as name recognition with my dad unless there's a title in front of it. If you were *Sir* Jonathan Stapleton, now, he would have heard of you."

Jon bit back the obvious remark, that very few people had ever heard of him anyway. "But surely your mother will come?"

"Only if it fits in with her other plans – and you won't wish for it either, luv, if you know what's good for you. She reduces me to the intellectual level of a twelve–year–old; I always end up wanting to stick my tongue out behind her back. I don't suppose I could get up and emote my little socks off if I knew she was somewhere in the darkness planning one of her lectures about motherhood as a woman's most sacred duty and only noble calling. It's positively mediaeval." She stopped, and sat staring out of the window at the miserable grey sky; rain was falling steadily, as it had been for two or three weeks already, and sometimes it felt as if the saturated earth could absorb no more and would crumble under the strain.

"Well," said Jon, "you can forget all that now, and concentrate on rehearsals."

"Yes, I always enjoy this part. Have you let your other rooms yet, by the way? You told me about Catherine and I'm looking forward to seeing her – we did a telly together a couple of years ago – but what about the other two?"

"Ah, of course, you won't have heard," he told her, brightening. "Bill's coming back to play the Cardinal. It was all very last–minute, he didn't know if he'd be free, but he'll be getting here some time tomorrow. He's having Jax's old room."

"Good old Bill, that's great! But we'll be rather an elderly lot this year, then, won't we, with both him and Catherine? Aren't there any younger ones coming in?"

"Not until after the mid–season break. There's a new lutenist joining the pit orchestra then, and he's having the other room until he can find something more permanent. I'll probably take the opportunity to get it redecorated before he moves in; it's about time it was done again."

"You really keep on top of all that sort of thing, don't you?" Izzy asked, impressed. "You're incredibly domesticated."

"I have an eye for detail," agreed Jon, "which is a nice way of saying I'm a pedant. But keeping it out of Roy's hair is the way I pay my rent. I was hoping we might have had time to install a bathroom in the coal store once we'd moved the freezer out – we've been planning that for quite a while now – but the kitchen took so long that we ran out of time. If you're back next year, though, you should have the use of a downstairs bathroom."

"Excellent. That'll make life easier. But I'm trying not to think that far ahead," she finished on a plaintive note.

"I know," agreed Jon, thinking of Callum and of how fleeting and insubstantial their time together had seemed. "I must admit, I don't really want to think about the future too much either."

Bill's arrival the next evening coincided with a deluge of Biblical proportions, and he unloaded himself and his luggage from the taxi regretting loudly that he had left his foul–weather gear behind on the set of his sailing movie.

"When I think of what they spent creating a wild sou'wester on a sound stage," he said, with heavy irony, wiping his dripping face and hair in the kitchen. "They could have waited and moved it here and saved a fortune."

Jon shoved a cup of coffee at him and grinned. "There isn't a huge seafaring tradition in Shapley," he said, "being so far from the coast. And I'm not sure the river's deep enough to take a man–o'–war."

"From what I saw when I arrived," retorted Bill, "it soon will be. 'Deep, deep as the ocean'," he quoted, lugubriously. "It floods here sometimes, doesn't it?"

"Oh yes. Hence the board in the Market Place showing the high–water levels. Hence the cost of insurance. The river has a habit of getting out of bounds every ten or fifteen years or so; sometimes it gets as high as Charlie's Chipper."

"Really?" Bill looked astonished. "But that means … "

"That we'd be in trouble here? Yes, but fortunately it's never got much beyond the corner in all the time I've lived here – although we've had most of the village shut off at times, and the buses have to go round the back and up Worthy Lane. The main road isn't really 'Walter Street' at all, you see," he went on. "For three or four hundred years it was 'Water Street', because half the year it was under water. That's why there are only orchards on the other side, apart from the church. You couldn't build houses there unless they were on stilts."

Bill considered this. "That's why you have to go upstairs to get into the pub, then, is it?" he asked.

"Yes. The beer cellar floods on a regular basis. But don't worry, I've put you in the room at the front this year; if push comes to shove you can throw a plank over the windowsill and make a bridge. You'll be able to cross the road without getting your feet wet."

Bill's face twisted into a grimace of appreciation. "Nice idea," he acknowledged. "But I might just ask them to pipe it directly to my room, so that I don't have to go outside at all. The ultimate labour–saving device, that would be, not even having to walk as far as the pub."

"It sounds the last word in luxury," acknowledged Jon, with a smile, and settled down to enjoy an evening of Bill's undemanding company.

The following day was the first read–through of *The Duchess of Malfi*, and as there was to be no minibus service for the initial couple of weeks it was a question of reversing Jon's increasingly elderly car onto the pub forecourt and inserting three damp and bad–tempered actors into it. Their route to the rehearsal room, conditioned by water on the surrounding roads and traffic signals out of commission, was less straightforward than it might have been, as a result of which the three of them fetched up late and not exactly in the sunniest of moods. They need hardly have worried, however; nothing was happening when they blundered in together clutching their play–scripts, and their mood lifted on regarding the familiar scene. Coffee and biscuits were set out to one side, and Ewen and two or three of the hardier souls were by the fire door in the contemplative stances of smokers. They looked grave enough to be discussing something of earth–shattering importance, or at the very least planning an execution.

"Have no fear," announced Bill, marching into the middle of the throng, "Bill is here!" He began to relate in exhausting detail the trials and tribulations of their journey, accompanied sporadically by Izzy; they sounded mellow and good–humoured together, like a duet for baritone and alto saxophones.

The resulting chaos made a useful cover for Jon's reunion with Callum. He slapped the younger man cheerfully on the shoulder and said, with feigned briskness, "Callum! How's your new accommodation?"

"Fucking freezing, mate," was the dispirited response. "I've just been complaining about it."

"He has, too," came a voice from out of the mêlée. "Ad–bloody–nauseam."

"Really? It's cold?"

"It's right on the water, isn't it? I didn't think of that. And I haven't figured out the heating yet; it comes on at night and in the morning but I have no idea how to make it come on all the time. I nearly froze to death yesterday."

"But at least there's no flooding where you are?"

"None. It's all on the river, rather than the canal; I suppose the lock gates must be keeping it back."

"Good. One less thing to worry about, then. What's the place like otherwise?"

Callum laughed delightedly. "Wonderful. A little floating palace. Everything brand new and just fitted–up. Bloody lonely, though," he added, in a softer tone. "Come and cook for me at the weekend, love? If you can get there, I mean."

"Of course." Jon risked a shy smile, which Callum returned in similar coin. Then he made a determined effort to change the subject. "So, how do you think Ewen's looking?"

Callum grimaced. "Dreadful," he said. "Has he been ill?"

"He says not, but I don't know that I believe him."

"It's those coffin–nails," said Callum. "They'll get him in the end. Once you start that filthy habit, you never stop even if it kills you – and it usually does."

"Never been tempted yourself, then?" asked Jon.

"Not remotely." And Callum lowered his voice to a caressing whisper. "I think I've got enough vices already, don't you?"

By Wednesday of the same week they were blocking their movements on a painted area of floor representing the stage. They were a motley assemblage of human beings, all still to a greater or lesser degree wedded to sheaves of paper with crossings–out, underlinings, and interlineations in different–coloured pens. Bill's script was a psychedelic miracle illuminated with arrows, butterflies and men with big noses, and he stumbled around looking over the rims of his half–moon spectacles like a science teacher faced with a delinquent class. He did, however, lend gravity to the proceedings; whenever Ewen's temper seemed about to fray it took only a word from Bill to bring things back into order – a useful attribute Jon was inclined to envy.

"We'll take the murder of Antonio next," murmured Ewen wearily. It was late afternoon, and with questions and queries and practical problems at every turn they still had not made it to the end of Act V. Most of the cast, having been run through, strangled, poisoned or otherwise disposed of earlier in the play, were sitting, standing or leaning around the walls in attitudes of disinterest; only Jon, Callum, Bill and some walk–ons playing servants were necessary for the present scene.

"It isn't murder," protested Callum, still energetic despite the long day he had put in. His character was heavily involved in the action and had a great many lines to deliver. "It's an accident. I mistake him for the Cardinal."

"Well, yes," replied Ewen, unenthusiastically. "Thank you for proving you've read the play – but since this is the third day of rehearsal I rather hoped you had."

"Sorry." Callum would not be quelled. "Just pointing out that I wouldn't murder Jon under any other circumstances. Bill, on the other hand … "

"You'll need an army, whippersnapper," growled Bill. "And a box to stand on."

Callum grinned at him. "A good little 'un can beat a good big 'un any day," he averred cheekily.

"Yes, well, perhaps we can concentrate? We'll have curtains here; I've got some hospital screens coming tomorrow … "

"Quick nurse, the screens!" put in Bill, reflexively.

"Ah, yes. Absolutely. But for now, Bill, you're stage right; Jon, you're at the back, Callum you enter downstage left, and none of you can see the others. I want you thrashing about in the curtains like Hamlet killing Polonius – 'A rat, a rat!'"

"'Mad as the sea and wind when both contend Which is the mightier'? I can do that. How many times do you want me to stab him, Ewen?"

Ewen shrugged. "Oh, two or three," he said, carelessly. "Let's just make sure he's dead, shall we, even though he's still got half a page of dialogue to deliver?"

"Sure thing. Good job I hate you so much then, eh, Jon?" A smile, freighted with meaning, and then Callum took up his position. He was using a transparent plastic ruler as a sword, and had thrust it into the pocket of his jeans to be drawn in sinister fashion the moment he stepped between the drapes.

"Right," snapped Ewen. "Enter Antonio and servant. Carry on, boys."

"'Here stay, sir, and be confident, I pray';" said the servant. "'I'll fetch you a dark lantern.'"

"'Could I take him at his prayers,'" intoned Jon, "'there were hope of pardon.'"

"'Fall right my sword'!" Callum stepped forward, his pretend weapon raised in sinister fashion, and struck Jon two or three mortal blows to the chest. Jon, more startled than anything, toppled over in a loyal attempt to die in a heap, but had to press his face to the floor – smitten not so much by his death wound as by the giggles. Rumpled, mischievous, armed with a plastic ruler, Callum looked more like a child pursuing a playground vendetta than a vile Jacobean assassin plotting sinister vengeance, and Jon had temporarily lost his grip on professionalism.

"All right." Ewen's words cut his ordeal short. "This is not the shower scene in *Psycho*, and we'll do it without the Jack–the–Ripper eye–roll if you don't mind. Jon, don't defend yourself, you don't see him coming. Again."

Callum reached down to help Jon to his feet. "I need to talk to you." He snatched the moment when Jon's cheek drew level with his own and screened him from the rest of the company. Jon nodded, and did not meet his eyes again for several moments. When he did, they were all business; he was stabbed, he fell, and he gave his dying speech.

I would not now
Wish my wounds balmed, nor healed, for I have no use
To put my life to. In all our quest of greatness,
Like wanton boys whose pastime is their care,
We follow after bubbles, blown in th' air."

"'Break, heart!'" declaimed Callum, emotionally.

"'And let my son fly the courts of princes'." Jon's head tipped back over Callum's arm, and Callum lowered him to the floor and stood up quickly, as if horrified to witness what he himself had done.

"Fuck. I've lost the line."

A sigh issued from Ewen. "Dear boy," he said, "if you weren't the shit–hottest thing since Larry O tried out for the chorus I would even now be planting my boot up your plebeian backside. As it is, I need a ciggie–break – and you can use the time to find your line. If you lose it again after that, you'll be writing it out a thousand times after class. Ten minutes," he added, to the room in general. "Let's all go for a pee and take a deep breath, shall we, and then push on through the rest of the scene. We should be out of here by six, with luck." He strode towards the fire door with his hangers–on in tow, and Izzy cast a sympathetic glance in Callum's direction before joining the throng heading for the ladies' room.

"Well?" asked Jon, as the hall emptied swiftly.

"It's here." Callum did not glance around.

"What's here?"

"It." A moment of mutual incomprehension, then Callum said, "The baby. It's a boy."

"Oh. When?"

"This morning. My agent phoned at lunchtime. She's calling him Connor. Connor Henley."

Jon's eyebrows climbed. "Congratulations," he said, automatically. "I think?"

Callum was looking stunned. "Probably. We'll talk about it at the weekend. You are still coming over?"

"To cook for you? Yes. Do you want me to bring the food?"

"If you like," was the quiet response. "Just don't bother bringing any clothes."

The exclusive Old Coal Wharf development at White Elm, where Callum had his temporary headquarters, was just that – exclusive. Situated on what had once been a colliery's private stretch of canal, it was gated both from the water and from the land and surrounded by trees. The developer had divided the site with some ingenuity, building a house for himself on half of it while the remainder was devoted to moorings for residential narrowboats to be let as holiday accommodation. These were not, however, for navigating up and down the short length of canal available to them; instead they were the equivalent of floating luxury cottages with mains electricity and flush toilets, and they were to arrive one by one on the backs of low–loaders from boat fitters around the country.

Gertrude was the first. Splendidly painted in dark blue with a traditional rose–and–castle design on the side, she sat at the end of a newly made road behind an anonymous security gate; Jon had to pause to key in the code, and then ease the car at walking pace along a track punctuated with speed bumps. It was after midnight; they had given their all in the *Duchess* twice during the day, and then Jon had returned to Shapley with Izzy and Bill and set off from there again in his car. The story to account for his absence was simple enough: now that renovations at Fardels were reaching a critical stage and Roy and Pete were still out of the country he was required to meet regularly with Tony the manager, who was overseeing day–to–day progress on the building work. To this end, Jon had decreed, he would occasionally sleep over at Fardels after a Saturday night performance, have the meeting in the morning and return in time for lunch; otherwise it would cut too deeply into what he laughingly referred to as his leisure time.

Callum was waiting on the wharf, dressed in disreputably slouchy tracksuit pants and a sweatshirt from an American college he had never so much as flown over in a plane, let alone attended.

"I heard the gate," he said.

"I'm not surprised; it's so quiet here." Jon climbed wearily out of the car, bringing a box of groceries with him. In response to Callum's enquiring look, he said, "Well, you did ask me to cook for you."

"I did. But I hope what you've brought will do just as well for breakfast."

"It will."

"All right, then, come to bed."

The boat's interior was crisp and minimal and just as palatial as Callum had promised, if somewhat lacking in personality. Everything shone, from the laminate flooring to the brass hatch casings in the overhead; the cushions on the banquette were deep and square as if they had never been sat on, and the ingenious little kitchen was too perfectly clean to be part of anybody's home.

"I've hardly dared do more than boil a kettle," Callum confessed, as Jon unpacked his groceries into the fridge. "Everything's here, though, and all the instruction books are in the drawer. I just chickened out."

"Hmmm." Jon looked around him. "Should I interpret 'come and cook for me' as 'come and teach me how to cook'?" he asked, thoughtfully.

"Not exactly. I'm not totally helpless. I'm just not interested in food unless somebody else is taking responsibility for it."

Jon nodded. "Well," he said, "show me the rest of the place." Not that there was much to be seen. In a space less than seven feet wide and arranged like a large caravan, virtually every aspect of it was visible from where they stood.

Callum patted the curved bulkhead separating kitchen and bedroom. "Bathroom," he said. "Full–sized shower. Not as good as the one at Portofino, but I expect we'll manage. Proper toilet, loads of hot water. And we've got a full–sized bed, too."

"Good," mused Jon, as he was led by the hand into the handsomely–appointed compartment. "I could sleep on a clothes line."

"What makes you think you're going to be doing any sleeping?"

"Tyrant," Jon complained, without malice.

"Yeah, right," was the dismissive response. "Tell me you don't want to fuck me through the mattress?"

"Of course I do. I always do. Just not sure I'll be able to, that's all."

"Oh, don't worry, love," Callum told him, insouciantly. "By the time I've finished with you, you won't be in any doubt." And, to judge by the things his busy hands were already doing, he was intent on proving his point as rapidly and effectively as possible.

An hour or so later, drowsing side by side under the one muted lamp still alight on the boat, they were becoming reacquainted with one another in luxurious affectionate touches and indulgent kisses. It scarcely seemed to matter what they talked about, as long as they talked; even after a week of rehearsals, watching and interacting with one another in a professional capacity, the desire for the sound of each other's voice had not diminished in the slightest.

"I'm supposed to bulk up for this movie," Callum said, lazily watching Jon's fingers stroke a path over the still–negligible curve of his biceps. "*Planetfall*," he explained. "Rossi's a rufty–tufty engineer, not a cream–faced loon. I've got to catch Bryce by the fingernails when he falls down a mineshaft, and he's nearly three inches taller than me. So they've put me on these protein drinks and signed me up with a personal trainer, and I'm supposed to go running two or three times a week – which I haven't done since I stopped doing P.E. at school. Mind you, I had quite a turn of speed in those days. I was a fly–half," he added. "How about you?"

"Rugby? Perish the thought. I was a flannelled fool, not a muddied oaf. A wily spin–bowler, or so I thought at the time. I took nine wickets in a match once – against the worst school in the league."

"Who were they, St Borstal's?"

"Dotheboys Hall. They were all starving orphans."

"Of course." Callum had taken his hand now, and was stroking the slender fingers individually. "I can just see you, plotting and planning like some evil genius. You'd look good in whites, too, all tall and cool and elegant."

"You'd look good in shorts," was the immediate response. "All hot and sweaty and covered in mud."

"Pinned to the ground by a dozen muscular blokes? You'd like that, wouldn't you?"

"The idea has its attractions," Jon mused. "Although, of course, I've seen you hot and sweaty plenty of times."

"You've made me hot and sweaty plenty of times. But why don't you watch me work out some time? I'm using the fitness centre at the Greyhound in Gostrey."

"I don't think that's a good idea, do you?" Jon quelled the notion with gentle regret. "We're both too well–known locally; word would get out. But I'll watch you run, if you like."

"I go early in the morning."

"That's all right. I'm sure I'll have no trouble … getting up." There was just a suspicion of innuendo behind the tone.

"I don't suppose you will, love. You never do. Tomorrow, then, if it's not raining? And then what?"

"Then I'll take advantage of you, of course," Jon told him. "After all, you'll be exhausted and out of breath; I'll be able to do whatever I want with you."

"You can do whatever you want with me anyway," was the quiet reply. "That's always been the case."

So the following morning, and on many others thereafter during the run of the *Duchess*, Jon got out of bed when Callum did, and sat loyally on the towpath watching Callum pound circuits around the picnic ground and the car park, on grass and clinker paths and newly–laid tarmac, screened from the road by a stately stand of elms and a scrubby hedge of laurel, and the only witnesses were the somnolent ducks, the nesting blackbirds and, later in the season, the butterflies and buzzing insects. He watched him hunched up on cold mornings, and stretched out on warm ones, and for longer and longer spells as the months drew past, and on almost every occasion he crammed his body into the narrow shower cubicle with Callum afterwards and took him slowly up against the wall while warm water slicked down languidly over their perfectly united bodies. It was, declared Callum, the best possible exercise routine, and he was soon beginning to reap the benefits of it in improved muscle tone and stamina, in healthier skin and deeper respirations, and in greater vitality generally.

Ewen's health, conversely, continued to deteriorate as the season progressed, and he began leaning more and more heavily on his senior cast members, Jon and Bill. Indeed, from time to time, he left Bill to take the occasional rehearsal on his behalf, citing a medical appointment somewhere or other. Still, his condition remained the elephant in the room, observed by all but never discussed, and the mid–season break seemed to be coming at exactly the right moment for all of them as strength and willpower began to wane.

"Are you going to see your daughter?" Callum asked, when they were drowsing away the early part of a Sunday morning aboard the *Gertrude*.

"Of course."

"And she lives in London?"

"Yes. Why?"

"I was thinking you could stay with me," Callum offered, bluntly. "My downstairs neighbours have gone home to Hong Kong for a whole month, so we'll have the house to ourselves. We'll have to be careful, but it's better than staying at a B&B the whole time. Cheaper, too." He stopped, then added, "You've never been to my flat."

"I haven't, have I?"

"Well, then, it's time you did. It'll be great – and you won't have to keep on getting up early to 'have meetings about the farmhouse'," he laughed.

"You agreed that we had to keep it all a secret," Jon reminded him.

"I know. But sometimes it seems too high a price to pay. Is there someone who can take over feeding the doves and everything for you?"

"Izzy, probably. I think she's staying in Shapley; she and Catherine are planning to go sightseeing and do a lot of girly things."

"'Girly'? Catherine's what, sixty–odd?"

"Well, to hear them talk you'd think they were both teenagers," was the laughing reply. "But they're planning to do … whatever women do when they have days out together. Shopping? I don't really know."

"They're a closed book to you, aren't they?" Callum asked, softly.

"Not entirely. My daughter's educating me. I'm not a complete primitive."

"Good. So, can you and I spend some time together and do a few girly things of our own? Fix each other's hair, file each other's nails, try on lipstick?" Then, in response to the look of horror on Jon's face: "Well, all right – chill out with a beer and watch sport on the telly, then? I've got meetings to go to about *Planetfall* – costume fittings and so forth – but I can arrange those for when you're seeing Justine, so they don't cut into valuable time we could be using for something else. I'm sure there must be a few condom flavours we haven't tried yet."

"No doubt," was the sober response. "As long as it isn't grape again. They were disgusting."

"They were, weren't they? I've been getting rid of them, discreetly – leaving them in pub toilets and so forth. I'm sure they'll find good homes eventually."

"Anything but grape."

"Absolutely. But I should think, wouldn't you, that we might be able to dispense with them altogether soon. It's been nearly six months, after all, and I haven't so much as considered laying a finger on anybody else."

Jon shuddered. "Nor have I," he said. "Really?"

"Really. Why don't we make that our plan for London? You and me, skin to skin, nothing in between? No more banana, no more cola, no more anything but us."

"You," said Jon distinctly, "are a randy little tart."

"I am, aren't I? I'll assume you like that idea, shall I? Only it seems to be having quite an effect on you already."

"I do. It is."

"Well, let's wait and do it properly in London. Make an occasion of it."

"Agreed."

"Good. Meanwhile, can I pass you anything?" Callum's stubby square fingers were playing in a little bowl beside the bed where colourfully–wrapped condoms were jumbled like boiled sweets. "Any particular flavour?"

"Anything at all," said Jon, helplessly.

"I know, love. Just as long as it isn't grape."

The last performance of *The Duchess of Malfi* before the break was a businesslike, lacklustre affair. Everybody seemed to be on automatic pilot, even Bill, and Izzy's normally carefully–judged portrayal went over the top at an early stage and descended into hysteria of cartoon proportions. The emergence of her mother from the audience after the final curtain would have given even the most casual observer a demonstration of Izzy's capacity for emotional intensity, however, especially when aspects of Prunella Thorpe's voluble critique of the production thundered out through the walls backstage.

"Poor kid," Bill muttered to Jon as they passed along the corridor. "I'd heard her mother was a bit fierce."

"She's terrifying," Jon admitted. Up ahead, Callum was in conversation with Maisie from wardrobe about a split in the knee of Bosola's breeches, which seemed to have emerged spontaneously during the killing of Antonio.

"So why does Izzy put up with it? She's a sensible girl, over twenty-one; surely she doesn't need to subject herself to that?"

"I'm sure she doesn't." Jon was barely concentrating; Callum's hands were moving on himself in places Jon would have preferred his hands to be: thighs, groin. "But it's her mother," he shrugged. "We put up with things in the name of love that we wouldn't otherwise contemplate. The people we love are the people who have the power to hurt us most; that's always been the way."

If Bill was following the direction either of Jon's gaze or of his thoughts, he gave no indication of it. "Well," he said, "I suppose so. I just don't like to see it happening, that's all."

"No," agreed Jon, "I know." And he passed ahead of Bill into the end-of-term hubbub in the communal dressing room.

That night Jon did not make the pilgrimage to White Elm; there was no excuse for it, as he would have time to talk to Tony during the week, and the need was decreasing anyway now that rebuilding was nearly completed and Roy and Pete were due home. They would be returning to the Pink Palace for a while, however; there seemed a shocking number of decorative choices to be made concerning Fardels, and the idea of moving into a house that was not complete to the last teaspoon and bar of soap seemed never to have occurred to them. There was, therefore, the looming horror of another party at the Pink Palace to contemplate before performances began again on the last Monday of the month.

First, however, came the visit to London, and five delicious days and nights in Callum's company. It would not be accurate to suggest that every minute Jon spent with his daughter was devoted to yearning for his lover, and he deliberately kept his thoughts away from the notion that in future they would be making love without protection; he was too adult, too sensible, and too good a parent to allow his mind to wander like that. There were, however, moments when he found himself turning round to make some remark to Callum, only to discover that he was not there. It was as if, although Callum and Justine had never met, no family scene could be complete without the two of them together, and that in itself was becoming something of a concern.

Nevertheless he enjoyed his time with Justine, discovering that she was neither too old for Hamley's toy shop nor too young for *Les Misèrables*, and that she embraced both with an open–heartedness that made him glad of her existence. In the past she had always seemed to be a little girl, and little girls were foreign creatures to him; now, on the cusp of puberty, she had begun to acquire some of the characteristics of a young lady – occasional poise, elusive gravity, and from time to time even a genuine pause for thought. Whatever the differences between himself and his ex–wife, Jon was more than happy to concede that Rosemary's upbringing of Justine looked certain to deliver to the world a valuable and intelligent young adult in a year or two's time.

These were the thoughts crowding in on his mind as he picked his way carefully towards Tufnell Park, not an area of London with which he had any previous acquaintance. His instructions indicated a railway station, a main road, a parade of shops and a cluster of Victorian streets where many houses were divided into flats. In the upper half of one of these, surrounded by someone else's furniture, he found himself in Callum's arms again at last.

"Thank God you're here!" The door was barely closed behind them before Callum was kissing him frantically, an expression of nervous importance in his eyes. "Did you have a good time with your daughter?"

"Actually, yes."

"You sound surprised."

"I am. I've never really been sure whether she sees me out of love or duty, but as she grows older I suppose it's more likely to be love."

"Idiot," Callum told him. "It's you; how could it not be love? Now, let me get you a drink, and then you can sit around looking decorative while I do something clever about dinner."

"Dinner?"

Callum grinned. "Don't worry, I didn't cook anything. I subcontracted – to a professional caterer. All I have to do is ping it in the microwave, and even I can manage that." He led Jon into a large, awkward sitting room, where a massive fake–leather couch dominated the furnishings. Set up next to it was a table with two chairs, tidily arranged for an intimate meal. "Not the most glamorous location in the world but I wanted to do it right. Tonight's important, isn't it?"

"Yes, it is."

"I've been thinking about it a lot," confessed Callum, quietly. "Have you?"

"I didn't dare."

"Probably wise. It made me want to … You know?" A gesture indicated the temptation Callum had been fighting. "I've been so turned–on I could barely concentrate. Bloody meetings were a nightmare," he added. "I've got to have green hair for this film: green, I ask you! And eyelashes. Everything's got to be dyed." He paused. "Chest, too. The things we do for art."

"Why, do you have to get your shirt off?"

"I'll be astonished if I don't have to get my knickers off," was the crisp retort. "When these guys pay for a pound of flesh, a pound is exactly what they want. But I think I'd draw the line at having my pubes dyed green," Callum added, solemnly. "Unless they substantially improve the money, of course."

The food was good; whoever prepared it knew precisely what they were doing, and had succeeded in producing a menu that was almost completely Callum–proof. That did not, however, mean that he was able to relax while they were eating; instead he was continually bouncing up like a jack–in–the–box offering wine or salt or a clean knife from the kitchen, a tiny disaster area seven or eight steps along the passage. Only after the umpteenth reassurance that there was nothing missing and everything was marvellous did he eventually return and sit down heavily, clutching a large napkin between frantic fingers.

"I'm overdoing this, aren't I? Am I spoiling it?"

Jon reached across to take his hand. "You don't need to impress me," he soothed. "I'd be happy to eat fish and chips out of a newspaper. You know I would. We've done that sort of thing before."

"We have. But I wanted to make an effort. I don't want you thinking that all I ever do is take – especially the way things are between us in bed."

"I thought you liked that?"

"Of course I do. But maybe you'd prefer it if … if you didn't have to do most of the work most of the time."

Jon shook his head. "It's not exactly work," he commented, smiling. "And I'm happy. I like what we do – even when we don't do anything. I don't evaluate your performance with a checklist, you know." He was trying to make a joke of it, but the attempt failed miserably. Callum looked away, and again Jon squeezed the hand he held. "Darling. Every minute I spend with you is something I never expected to have."

"Oh, Jon!" The exclamation held a lost and desperate quality. "There are honestly times when none of this seems real to me. All the hiding, the … little stolen bits, the secrets. It makes me wonder … if nobody knows about us but us, do we even really exist at all?"

"If a tree falls in the forest and nobody hears it, does it make a sound?" Jon mused, profoundly. "That's what you mean, isn't it?"

"Yes, that's it exactly. I think … I almost think I want to find a way to make it real, you know. Properly real, so that other people know about it. Half of me wants to be out and flaming and all over the papers and get the whole business over and done with once and for all."

"And the other half?"

"The other half doesn't, because it's scared of where that might lead us. Scared of getting it wrong, I suppose. It's a big decision, isn't it, who you want to spend the rest of your life with?"

Thoughtfully, Jon bit his lip. "Much as I'd like to," he began sadly, "I can't see it working for us on a long–term basis – can you? I mean, it's not as if there's anything I could offer you. You've seen the way I live; I don't even have a home of my own. It would be nice to think that you and I could have some sort of future together, but I honestly don't see how. And anyway, your path in life is going to take you far away from me; you're going to be a movie star; you don't need the likes of me holding you back."

"It's not 'the likes of' you I want – it's you! And you wouldn't be holding me back, you'd be … "

"What? Your boyfriend? Your husband? 'That queer actor who only got famous by sucking Callum Henley's dick'? Do you really think that's the way I want to be known, for the rest of my days? Besides, I'd cramp your style catastrophically and you know it as well as I do. I have a life, Callum; it may not be exciting, but it's mine – and until you came along it was working exactly the way I wanted it to. Peaceful," he added. "Private. Safe."

Callum's eyes lowered, and what might have been a smile touched the edges of his mouth. "I thought you'd say something like that," he acknowledged. "It's the reason I haven't tried asking you before … if you'd be interested in making it permanent, I mean. Moving in together. Joint bank accounts, that sort of thing. I know it would be difficult, but I'd give it a go if you would. Would you want to, if we could?"

Jon withdrew his hand, carefully folded his table napkin and put it to one side. "I've come closer to wanting it with you than with anybody else in the world," he admitted, gravely. "And that includes the woman I married. If things were different, if the law was ever changed, there's no question in my mind – you'd be the one. But things aren't different, Callum, and as it is we wouldn't stand a chance. I have no desire to ruin whatever we've got at the moment by wishing for something that isn't going to happen. Have you?"

"I suppose not."

"Good."

Callum's mouth flattened again into a line, and he regarded the debris on the dinner table with a jaundiced eye. "That wasn't a bad meal, was it?" he asked, tiredly.

"It was very nice."

"Hmmm. So, would you like dessert? Or would you rather have me?"

"That depends." Jon took a deep breath, watching his world slowly right itself as Callum made a determined effort to push away whatever misgivings had assailed him. "Is dessert something that will spoil if we leave it?"

"Profiteroles. They'll be fine in the fridge – unless I decide to eat them off your scrawny chest later on, of course."

"Well, that would save on the washing–up. But to reply to your question ... "

"Profiteroles or me?"

"Yes. There really is no need for me to give you an answer, is there?"

"No." Decisively, Callum threw down his napkin. "Come on, stud, it's time you took me to bed."

Callum's bedroom was narrow and cramped – narrower and more cramped, even, than Jon's quarters at the Old Crown – and it hung out over the downstairs kitchen at the back of the house like a belated afterthought. It had a view of other people's gardens, dustbins, sheds and trellis fencing, all overhung with the sodium haze of the city, and it was cold. A one bar heater mounted on the wall buzzed and crackled as its element warmed up; it looked lethal, in a downmarket sort of way. Callum should have had something better and smarter than this, but it seemed that he did not feel ready to accept it. At least, not yet.

"It's crap, isn't it?" The apologetic note was back in his tone.

"No. It's not how I pictured your room, though, I must admit." In answer to Callum's lopsided look of enquiry, Jon made an effort to continue. "I don't know – silks, four–posters. You seem to deserve a more luxurious setting than this."

"Well, yes. But this is real life, love, not the movies. Some of this is the stuff I grew up with. This chair, the rug, the curtains: they were all in my bedroom when I was a kid. I used to wrap that rug around me and pretend to be a bear. That was my first ever taste of the acting profession."

"A bear. A teddy bear? That's what you remind me of, all golden and furry."

"Don't laugh, I was a grizzly bear; I was absolutely terrifying."

"Of course you were, darling." Jon's arms slid around his waist and pulled him close. "Of course you were." He sighed. "Out there in the world, I fail at almost everything, but when I'm with you I feel as if there's one thing I do occasionally get right."

"I've never had any complaints," Callum told him, his hands sliding under Jon's sweater and possessively across his warm back. There was something delightfully familiar about it all, about the fact that it was the two of them, and there was a bed, and they knew one another so well by now, and yet it was always fresh and new and there were always exciting things to be learned. The mere fact that they could still make one another tremble and gasp and moan was, in itself, as much enticement as they had ever needed to do this again and again ... and again. "Only I wish there was more space."

The bed was pushed right up against the wall; it was going to be nearly as awkward getting in and out of it as the one on the narrowboat, with one of them constantly having to climb over the other. If they had not been quite so used by now to spending their nights as a random tangle of limbs and appendages, it could have been supremely inconvenient for them both.

"I could afford better, I know," Callum went on, humbly. "I should buy myself a place, really – Lenny's financial advisor thinks I should start investing in property as soon as possible, and a flat of my own would be a good first step. But somehow it doesn't really seem important to me."

"Then don't let him push you," was the quiet response. "If you're happy where you are, and you can afford it, there's no earthly need to move. Change for its own sake is not necessarily the same thing as progress."

"And there you have it," Callum laughed. "The Stapleton philosophy in a few well–chosen words. Even so, it's a bit tatty," he admitted, with a shrug.

Jon slid an affectionate arm around his shoulders. "'Better is a dinner of herbs where love is, than a stalled ox and hatred therewith'," he quoted mildly.

"True. And there is love, Jon, isn't there? On both sides?"

"Yes, darling. There is."

"Good. I was afraid I'd really screwed things up for a while back there. I'm not sure I'm ready for any of the stuff that's been happening to me lately – the films and the meetings and the people and the money. I'd much rather be like you and take it all in my stride."

"But I'm not nearly as successful as you're going to be," Jon reminded him, softly. "I'm a featured player, not a star. Just keep your head, don't rush into anything, and remember where you came from; you'll be fine."

"Will I?"

"I guarantee it," Jon told him, kissing him again.

And after that it was like a sweet, slow dance, gently separating one another from their clothing and leaving it piled on the bedroom chair from Callum's childhood home, until the last garment – Callum's white tee–shirt – joined the rest, and Jon took half a step back to cast an appraising eye over the improvements to his physique.

"You're definitely putting on muscle, aren't you?" he asked, quietly.

"Mmmm. I thought you'd approve."

"I do." A hand slid over the gentle swell of a boyish breast. "You're filling out."

"Just a bit." There was a ragged edge to Callum's breathing. "You know what I want?"

"Naturally." Jon turned and lifted the edge of the duvet. "In you get."

In a flash Callum scooted past him and was quickly on his side with his arms held out. Jon, however, made him wait; he sat on the bed and, with a fine air of droit de seigneur, ran proprietorial fingers through the downy hair on Callum's chest.

"Will you really have it dyed?" he whispered, huskily; the strange notion had caught hold of his imagination in ways he had not been expecting.

"Probably," was the distracted response. "You know what the punchline of the story is, don't you? The *Planetfall* thing?"

"No. What?"

"Oh, of course – you haven't read the books. You should, you know. They're not just your average space operas."

"No?" Jon was stroking his stomach almost obsessively.

"No. There's a love story, too. Rossi and the Commander … "

"The Commander?"

"Bryce. I'm going to have to kiss Bryce."

"You're making a gay sci–fi film?" Jon's head lifted. "Oh, I see. You're joking."

"No, I'm not. You need to read the books. It only comes out gradually, but … well, there are just these two guys on this spaceship in the middle of nowhere. You don't really think they spend their nights apart, do you?"

"God. I had no idea."

"I know. It did a slow burn on me, too, but yes … I'm going to be up there on the silver screen with my face fifty feet wide, kissing Bryce Gullory for all I'm worth. Do you think you're going to be madly jealous, darling Jon?"

"I don't know. Maybe. Maybe not. It all depends on how far you're willing to go with him, I suppose. For example, will you both be naked?"

"We might be." Callum was savouring the power of the tease, enjoying its effects on Jon – and Jon himself was totally lost in the word–pictures the two of them were creating, which had the liminal, transgressive quality of a borderline fantasy, of a thing that could so easily have been horrendously wrong and yet was still surprisingly and wickedly attractive.

"Will he do this?" And Jon's mouth closed, where Callum had wanted it to be from the first, on the raised knot of a yearning nipple, sucked it in between harsh teeth, bruised it with a ferocious ardour.

"I expect so." Shattered and breathless, Callum could scarcely form the words. "He knows how much it turns me on."

"Oh, really? Does he? And what about this? Will he do this, too?"

The mouth moved, settled for the first time on unsheathed hot flesh, took it in, soaked it, sucked it, teeth pulling sharply at ridged skin, tongue probing the minuscule slit in the crown.

"Oh, you bastard, you absolute bastard, I'm going to … " But it was already too late, and with a spastic jerk of his hips Callum let loose uncontrollably, flooding Jon's open and accepting throat. "Fuck!"

"Oh yes," said Jon, and bent to kiss him, and to season his lips with his own seductive flavour, "I think I can safely promise you that."

"That was really something," Callum said, quietly, some time later. "I don't think I realised quite how different it would be. How much better I would be able to feel you."

"I know. It's difficult to imagine anything more intimate, isn't it? Having seen how much you enjoyed that, I'm rather looking forward to experiencing it for myself," he confessed, almost shyly.

"Likewise," was the optimistic response. "Always provided, of course, that I can control myself a bit better than I did this time. I still can't believe you actually swallowed it, you know. Who the hell taught you how to do that?"

"A gentleman doesn't tell," Jon told him, smoothing his hair and dropping a kiss onto his brow.

"And you are at all times … Oh, but love, I never imagined even for a moment … "

"Hush. It isn't really all that difficult."

"Good. Because it's definitely something I want you to teach me."

"I'm not sure it can be taught," was the amiable correction, "but feel free to practise on me any time you like."

"Oh, I will. As soon as I get my strength back. You can be quite the caveman, can't you, darling, when you're in the mood?"

"You inspire me," laughed Jon.

"I noticed. It was all that talk about me and Bryce, wasn't it? Maybe you secretly fancy the idea of watching me do it with someone else?"

Jon considered the idea solemnly. "Well, if I do," he said at length, "we're in the right profession, aren't we? I suspect there'll be no lack of candidates for the role from now on."

"Meaning whoever I might find myself playing opposite in the future? Well, yes, if your imagination happens to turn that way, it should have plenty of scope for running riot over the next few years. I'm being offered all sorts of mad projects now, with all sorts of mad people, and *Leichhardt* isn't even out yet. I suppose I'm starting to get known around the industry."

"It's this absurd habit you have of always being good at your job," commented Jon, idly. "That sort of thing can get an actor quite a reputation, you know."

"Well, I'll have to try to break myself of it then. Turn in a few really crap performances, forget my lines, fall over the furniture, that sort of thing."

"I doubt you could do that even if you tried; it would be alien to your nature not to do everything to the absolute limit of your ability. And that includes this activity too, by the way."

"Thank you, darling. One does one's best." Callum turned his head, and his lips brushed across the curve of Jon's ear.

"So, what kind of mad projects are you talking about?"

"All sorts. A couple more films – a Victorian detective thing, which I don't much fancy – and Petruchio in *Taming of the Shrew* at the National for the summer. What are our lot at home planning next year, do you know yet?"

"*Rosencrantz and Guildenstern Are Dead*," supplied Jon, without hesitation.

"Oh, really?" Callum considered for a minute. "Not a lot for me in that, though, is there? I definitely don't want to play Hamlet, and that doesn't leave much. The Player King, I suppose, but I'm a bit too young for that. What will you do – Claudius? Polonius?"

"I don't know. Nothing's been said so far. I may not even be in it."

"Well, if you're not, come to the National with me instead. I'm sure I can shoehorn you in somewhere. Hortensio, maybe?"

"You're going to do it, then?"

Callum was silent for a while. "It's still in the balance," he said. "I'd be more likely to, if you were going to be there with me. But I can't see how I'd fit into *Ros 'n' Guil* – so it looks as if I'm going to be wanting some form of employment next summer, doesn't it? Why don't you come and lodge with me for a change? I'll buy a two–bedroom flat and you can 'stay in the spare room'." He made lazy air–quotes with the fingers of his left hand to illustrate the offer.

"Well, possibly. But then again … "

" … possibly not," concluded Callum. "All right, love. Think about it and let me know as soon as you've decided."

"Yes, I'll do that. But at the moment I'm rather more concerned about Roy and Pete's party, if you really want to know; that seems more pressing than anything else right now. I wish there was some way of getting out of it without offending them."

"Why? Still concerned that you'll be the one getting chucked into the pool?"

"Naturally."

"Don't be daft! I haven't known them long, but even I can see that they have far too much respect for you to treat you like that. No, I suspect it's probably my turn this year. I'll bring a change of clothing, just in case."

"Why? Why on earth would you be expecting that to happen?" Jon sounded utterly scandalised at the idea.

Callum laughed. "Because I've been working with Bill Wildman for some time now and I'm starting to get an idea of the way his mind works, that's why. Trust me, I have good reason to believe I'm right at the top of his hit list."

"Bill?"

"Yes, Bill." Callum stopped. "Do you really mean to tell me you still haven't worked out who it was that chucked Jax in last year? Apart from you and Izzy, who was it that was most infuriated with the silly cow?"

Jon turned to him in astonishment. "Are you suggesting it was Bill?"

"Of course it was Bill! He lived in the room immediately below her, didn't he? Surely you must have heard him muttering about all the noise she made when he was trying to sleep?"

"I may have … "

"You honestly didn't notice, did you? There were times last summer, my friend, when Bill could have seen that girl roasting in hell, believe me. If he hadn't been going off to Hampshire every other weekend filming, I don't suppose he would have got through the season without committing murder. Even so, he might not have done it if I hadn't slipped him fifty quid and a bottle of Scotch. So, you see, I know where all the bodies are buried – and, in true murder–mystery fashion, that means I'm next. Which also means that I'd better be well–prepared for my big wet tee–shirt moment – rising out of the water dripping, just like Colin Firth."

"Only half a head shorter," teased Jon, indulgently.

Callum affected annoyance at the sly suggestion. "Are you implying that I'm vertically challenged, Jonathan?" he asked, in mock outrage. "Or maybe that my respected professional colleague Mr Colin Firth is in some respect deformed?"

"Neither. Only that perceptions of beauty vary such a lot – and I never really understood what everybody saw in him, that's all."

"Ah." Callum considered this remark thoughtfully for a while, and then delivered his final verdict on the subject in no uncertain terms. "Well, Colin's a good–looking bloke and everything, and I've liked a lot of the things he's done, but one thing's for certain – you can bet your bottom dollar nobody's ever tried asking him to have his pubic hair dyed green!"

◆

(Some months later; a modern restaurant
self-consciously pretending to be old;
the fake oak beams jar with the modern
plastic window-frames. JON and CALLUM are
dining together at a very small table;
they are both obviously extremely tired.)

◆

By the middle of August there were only six weeks left of the *Duchess* and even the indefatigable Callum was beginning to manifest all the symptoms of end–of–season malaise.

"Bloody play's going on for ever," he grumbled, staring at Jon across a booth in the Chophouse at the Greyhound Hotel. It was several steps up–market from either the Bistro Upstairs at the New Crown or the ill–fated Blue Rajah, an establishment Callum hadn't been able to bring himself to enter since his encounter with Thea the year before, and taking in a post–show dinner here rather than meeting for a secretive rendezvous at White Elm had been his idea. Jon had allowed himself to be persuaded by the argument that it would look odd if fellow cast–members and former house–mates did not dine together at least occasionally, and sat watching Callum in a mood of amused indulgence.

"We're celebrating," Callum had grinned, when the invitation was issued.

"What exactly are we celebrating?" asked Jon now.

For answer Callum took out his wallet, unfolded it, and produced a slightly mangled photograph of a baby.

"The first picture of Connor. Well, the first one to reach me, anyway. Can you believe he's five months old already?" There was a note of peevish resentment in his tone. "I'm sure she's busy," he said. "Babies are a lot of work, or so I've heard. Do you think he looks like me?"

Solemnly Jon compared the photograph with the face before him. Fair hair, luminous blue eyes and cherubic features were common to both, but what he held in his hand was essentially a picture of an amorphous pink blob wrapped in a white blanket; more than that it was impossible to say.

"Not especially," was the thoughtful response. "But he's a baby. Don't they all look like Winston Churchill?"

"I don't know. Did Justine?"

"No. She looked like her mother. She still does."

"Well, from what I can remember, Connor looks a lot like Thea. Except, of course, that he's got his clothes on." Callum tucked the photo safely back into his wallet. "Anyway, I've been invited to visit him after the play ends, and I wondered if you fancied going with me?"

"To see your baby?" Jon's forehead furrowed in consternation. "Wouldn't that cause complications? How would you explain me, for a start? And anyway … "

Callum tilted his head in enquiry. "Yes?"

"Um, it's possible," Jon began, slowly, "I might have to work. I've got a fairly substantial offer to do a TV thing after the *Duchess*. And I mean immediately after," he continued, with an apologetic grimace. "It starts shooting the Monday after we wrap here. The last Monday in September."

"Oh God. So you won't get a break at all then?"

"Unfortunately not. It's a six weeks' location shoot to start with, then two weeks in the studio in the middle of December."

There was a studied silence from across the table, until Callum said quietly, "I was going to suggest we went away for a few days before I start on *Planetfall*. Italy, Spain, somewhere warm. Florida."

"Oh." It was almost impossible to know how to respond to this, but Jon made an effort not to be dismissive. "That would have been lovely," he said. "Albeit fraught with difficulties. It doesn't matter where you go in the world, there's always a risk of running into someone who recognises you. Alan Marshall was on a bus tour in New Zealand when somebody in the seat in front turned round and said 'Didn't you do the voice of Captain Beaver in that toothpaste commercial?' And look what happened to Jax at the airport."

Callum smiled. "I'm not convinced she didn't march up and down with a loudhailer announcing that she was Jacinta Burroughs and she'd once played a hairdresser in *Coronation Street*," he responded, ruefully, "but you're right. We'd be on some glorious beach in the middle of nowhere smearing each other with suncream and things would just be getting interesting when some yobbo would stumble over and say he'd seen us in the Scottish play and we were absolute rubbish."

"Except that a yobbo wouldn't have seen the Scottish play in the first place," was the amiable reply. "They're all waiting for that blockbuster sci–fi picture of yours."

"Oh, they'll hate that. They'll expect it to be all ray–guns and monsters and what they'll get instead is existentialism and angst." Callum squared his shoulders, determined to master his disappointment manfully. "So, tell me about this wonderful role that you're taking in preference to spending time with me, then. I didn't know you'd gone up for anything recently."

Jon took a deep breath, grateful for the forbearance with which his announcement had been greeted. He'd been half expecting tantrums, but apparently the invitation to become acquainted with his son had put Callum into an even more than usually benevolent frame of mind.

"I didn't go up for it," he admitted. "It came to me out of the blue. You know Edgar has his own production company?"

"Edgar Treece? Yes. Doesn't he run it with his … daughter or something?"

"Stepdaughter. She does the admin, he's the asset. Anyway he's doing a series about Lord Curzon when he was Viceroy of India and he wants me to play Curzon's sidekick – Oliver Russell, Lord Ampthill. Apparently Russell was a rowing man, and Edgar thinks I've got the physique for that – even though I can't row. I'm going to have to learn how to, between now and the end of the run."

"Goodness." Momentarily Callum was taken aback. "Victorian?" he asked. "Dreadful old side–whiskers, is it?"

"A little pointy beard, like King George the Fifth. I'll have to start working on that, too."

"Hmmm. And mine's got to go before the film. Its going to be quite like old times this winter, then, isn't it?"

"Yes. Except ... "

"I know. Except that I'll be on my own in Tufnell Park and you'll be ... where?"

"In a hotel in Manchester, as far as I know. Roy and Pete will have to take charge of their own renovations for once."

"It won't kill them." But Callum's head was bowed now, and he was playing pensively with the rolled edge of a linen napkin. "We're not going to see much of one another for a while, are we?"

"I'm afraid not. And if you do Petruchio in the summer ... "

Callum groaned. "Are you absolutely sure I can't persuade you to come and join me in that? They're offering Katharina to Izzy, you know – a one year deal, the same as mine. It would be so good if we could all be together again."

"It would," acknowledged Jon, "but I can't. I've more or less given my word to Ewen now. It's the Player King," he added, diffidently. "Don't tell me you wouldn't do it if you had the chance."

"I would, and if it's ever offered I will. So, are we going to see anything of one another over the winter at all?"

"Well, there's Christmas. Surely you'll get a break then?"

Callum's face fell. "I've booked to take my mother to Australia for three weeks," he admitted, desolately. "It'll be the first anniversary of my dad's death, and I wanted to distract her a bit. My sister's buggered off," he added, in a tone of complete indifference. "She's moved in with a bloke called Steve who I've never met and hope I never do. Apparently he's got a Union Jack tattoo and he hates blacks, queers and Jews."

"He sounds delightful."

"He sounds like my dad, multiplied a thousand times," came the dispirited response. Then, with a determined effort, Callum rallied. "Well, what does that leave? Any windows in the schedule when you're not actually working and you could come to London for the occasional weekend? Or maybe I could come to Manchester while you're there? I believe they're going to let me have Saturdays and Sundays off from time to time."

"Most of November and the start of December," replied Jon. "I'll ask Caro to keep those weeks free. But if anything comes up after Christmas I'm afraid I'll have to take it."

"Understood." Callum sighed. "It's going to be a long few months, isn't it?"

"It is. But neither of us is in any position to turn work down. And it's not as if … " Jon stopped abruptly.

"Not as if we were married?"

"No." Even in their quiet corner of the restaurant, where they were perfectly certain the sound of their voices would not carry, it still seemed an outrageous thing almost to have said. Jon was uncomfortably aware that an offer very nearly the equivalent of marriage had been made and rejected so recently as to make the recollection painful. He supposed there might come a time when he would regret the instinctive decision he had taken then, but for now he was determined to stand by it. "Of course," he went on, trying to make it sound more casual than he felt, "this is the downside of something like this. We have very different commitments, and we're not in a position to arrange our lives around one another without drawing the kind of attention we'd rather avoid."

"It's the sacrifice you make," agreed Callum, solemnly. "So far, though, I'd have to say I think you're worth it."

"Thank you," was the quiet response. And then, in a somewhat defeated tone, "But it hasn't even started to get difficult yet."

It soon did. The diminishing number of excuses for staying out overnight, combined with the necessity of spending every Sunday morning learning to row, served to disrupt their cosy weekend routine completely. It was still possible for Jon to snatch a few hours at White Elm on the occasional Sunday afternoon and evening, but now that a second narrowboat, *Cordelia*, had arrived on the scene, there were sometimes other people letting themselves in through the security gate, strange children playing with frisbees on the grass, and the sick smell of grilling sausages in the air.

"Not quite as exclusive as it once was, then," he remarked cynically, one purple–and–gold twilight when the television on the other boat was loud enough for them to hear every word of some moronic gameshow.

"Alas," was Callum's weary sigh. "I think we've had the best of it, don't you?"

It did not take Pete and Roy long to re–establish the frantic pace of their social life once they had moved lock, stock and barrel into Fardels. The first thing they did was invite everybody they knew to partake of drinks and nibbles and help them ceremonially mark out where they eventually intended their pool to be – and, since their circle of friends had widened further as a result of their travels, 'everybody' comprised quite a large number by now. It included, for example, a BBC drama producer by the name of Jeremy Bracegirdle who was patently scouting for contacts to exploit and names to drop. The fact that he was young, suave and moderately good–looking had escaped nobody's notice, least of all his own, and he appeared firmly set on squeezing every ounce of value from it. In particular, he was determined to scrape an acquaintance of some kind with Callum who, since the Thea incident, was more than marginally nervous of him.

"God, keep that man away from me," he muttered, taking refuge between Jon and Izzy and trying to vanish into the background. "He's already floated two or three impossible projects nobody in their right mind would touch with a bargepole. Whoever heard of doing *Robin Hood* on radio, for instance?"

"That could work, actually," observed Jon, in his mildest tones. "Depending on which version he intends to use; some of it's quite poetic. He wants you for Robin, I suppose?"

"Yes. With Pete as Little John and Roy as the Sheriff." Callum fell silent for a moment, then returned to the subject rather more thoughtfully. "He's talking about six half–hour episodes a year for the next four or five years. I've never done much radio; what sort of time commitment do you think that would involve?"

"Not much," Jon informed him. "Two or three weeks at most, assuming you can find time to read the scripts and prepare them thoroughly beforehand."

"You should do it," Izzy put in, crisply. "You need as much variety and exposure as possible at this stage; don't just stick to film and stage work because that's what you're comfortable with. Do the occasional telly if it's offered – make sure it's something worth doing, though, like Jon's *Curzon* thing – and as much radio as you can fit in." Then, seeing Callum's puzzled expression, she explained further. "It's free, you see," she said. "Nobody can ever complain that they don't have access to good quality drama as long as they can get it for nothing on the radio. If it's there and they don't go looking for it, that's their problem – but we don't want to be accused of elitism, now, do we?"

"No." It was clearly not a view Callum had heard her express before, and his look registered astonishment. "We don't."

"Besides," added Izzy, "you've got just the face for radio."

"Thank you." And the remark was just silly enough to make all three of them smile immoderately for a moment.

"Are they doing it in Birmingham?" asked Jon, after a while. "If so, you could come back to the Old Crown for a few nights if you wanted."

Callum heaved a sigh and, if there was a momentary flicker of panic in his eyes at having to turn down an invitation which in other circumstances he would have jumped at, it was noticeable only to Jon. "I would," he said, "except that Roy and Pete have invited me to stay here. Anyway, it looks as if they're actually going to be doing the first lot while you're up in Manchester so I'd have the house to myself – and I'm starting to get very tired of my own company."

"As a matter of fact," said Izzy casually, "I was hoping to stay on myself after the season finishes. Catherine's got a guest shot in *The Archers* and we're also working on a project together. I thought I could push it forward a bit during the day while she's out at work, and the two of us could get together and compare notes in the evenings."

"So, you and Catherine … both intend to stay on?" Jon asked, bewildered.

"Yes, luv, if that's all right with you? I mean, I can stay in the house until you get back from Manchester if you like, so that it's never empty at all? I'm taking the winter off this year," she added, luxuriously.

"Daddy's got an exhibition in January, and I've got a standing invitation to spend Christmas in Hawaii, so I'm not taking on any new commitments at the moment. Besides, if I'm going to do a whole year of Katharina I need to charge my batteries a bit first, and I can't do that if I'm scooting madly round the place grubbing after every available penny."

"God," growled Callum in mock–annoyance. "And my preparation for playing your husband is going to be thwacking bad guys and snogging Bryce Gullory. You'll absolutely wipe the floor with me next summer, won't you?"

"Well, yes," said Izzy, sinking back into her seat with a satisfied smile. "But that's the natural order of things anyway – the superior intellect will always tell. As well, of course, as being precisely what the playwright intended me to do."

If opening the *Duchess* had been something of a damp squib, and the houses throughout the season less than stellar, the closing two performances had been sold out months in advance. A certain proportion of the theatre–going public, having a taste for *Schadenfreude*, always booked for the final matinée just to discover what kind of indignities the actors were prepared to inflict on one another in the name of practical joking – and perhaps to winkle out evidence of animosities among the cast – and there was always a 'last–night' crowd fully the equivalent of the first–nighters and often even more enthusiastic as they watched the season's company disband and set off in quest of new adventures almost before their eyes.

This particular occasion was the source of ironic satisfaction for Jon; cheated of his parting from Callum the year before, this time he did at least have the chance of taking a more considered farewell. However the absence of any plan for continuing their association was troubling, and he found it impossible to shake the conviction that no matter what might have been promised it was all about to collapse in a welter of disappointment and disinterest. He didn't know whether he had expected anything else, really; holding onto a comet like Callum Henley had always seemed beyond the capabilities of someone like himself, and he made a determined effort just to be grateful for the happiness they had been privileged to share. He had never expected it to be more, or imagined it would last.

Callum, on the other hand, was all for making plans, however speculative. They would meet when they could, they would spend time together as their schedules permitted and continue to enjoy one another enthusiastically. For the sake of peace and quiet Jon agreed with every word and reassured him that he intended exactly the same, but a rat of doubt was gnawing at his vitals nonetheless. He knew only too well what so often became the fate of good intentions.

This state of affairs still obtained when they took to the stage as Antonio and Bosola that final Saturday afternoon in September, with end–of–term wildness already established among their fellow cast members. Indeed, if the present audience had come less to see the matinée and more to witness the antics of the company they were unlikely to leave unsatisfied: the accumulated frustrations of the *Duchess of Malfi* company provided them with enough unscripted entertainment for even the most demanding of palates. The entrance of the Duchess and her brother the Cardinal, for example, was accomplished with the Duchess's bodice half–open and the Cardinal sporting what appeared to be a pink lace garter on a surprisingly shapely calf. Neither gave any indication of being aware of these aberrations, however, and they played their scene with all the tragical foreboding that could be inserted into it.

Some small part of Jon's mind noticed but did not respond to Izzy's semi clothed condition. He had seen worse, after all: one early production he had been in had required him and several other members of the company to dress in loincloths and stand around looking menacing, and he had shaken off the last remnants of body–modesty then. Nor had a woman's cleavage ever been of interest in itself; he was capable of aesthetic appreciation when presented with as fine a specimen as this, but he had never quite understood the male obsession with the female breast. He considered himself a connoisseur of more recherché treasures; chests, in his opinion, should be smaller, flatter, and far less obvious. Besides, Izzy was his friend; he had ceased to think of her as a sexual being long before she had made her only–half–joking proposal of marriage to him the year before, and her state of undress failed to register as of any greater significance than Bill's extraordinary leg–wear. He was too absorbed, indeed, in preparing his own contribution to the mayhem – a sneak assault on Callum which he had planned in detail. It required split–second timing and no little boldness, but could be carried out without risk of disaster to either of them.

They were in the wings, waiting for their cues in the murder scene, when Jon struck. The actor playing Antonio's servant was ahead of them, giving his attention to the flaming torch he carried, and the stage and its surrounds were in almost total darkness. Alongside was the velvet wall of a quick–change booth, its curtain looped back, and Jon reached out one lazy hand and unhooked it as if he hadn't noticed exactly what he was doing. He had, however, calculated this manoeuvre to a nicety; with his other hand he grabbed Callum and hauled him into a pool of even deeper darkness, pulling the curtain around them, and for thirty seconds that felt like thirty minutes Jon kissed him, deeply, mercilessly and inappropriately, his free hand adventuring among the lacings of Callum's codpiece.

"You won't forget me in a hurry," he whispered, breaking away, leaving Callum panting for breath, and in a sudden whirl of curtain, cape and sword he was gone, stepping onto the boards exactly as he had eight times a week since the beginning of the season, his timing not impaired by so much as a fraction – and if there was greater relish than usual about the way Bosola accomplished the death of Antonio at that particular performance, as indeed there was, nobody but themselves ever became aware of the reason for it.

It seemed for a while, too, as if Jon had escaped any more tangible retribution than the defiant expression in Callum's eyes, but when they lined up to take their bows he was not surprised to find his hand being grasped and once again having something firmly pressed into it – this time a small, scratchy–cornered object whose feel he was perfectly accustomed to even in the dark. A little, square foil packet. A condom, of course.

"Grape," Callum assured him, over the relentless enthusiasm of the audience. "You won't forget me in a hurry, either."

The evening show went more according to the book. At this stage of the proceedings even the most pedestrian production was often accounted a triumph, largely because those concerned were glad to be escaping and moving on to other things, and the *Duchess* had never been an out–and–out disaster – although some of the critics had been less than kind, and the paying public had stayed away in droves. It had never seemed likely to be a commercial success but – as Izzy was keen to remind them all – money was not always the appropriate motivation for mounting a theatrical production; sometimes there were less tangible benefits to be considered. The last–night audience understood this in abundance, and rose to its feet to applaud the intention and the gusto with which it had been carried into effect rather than the play itself; if there was one thing the local theatre–going public appreciated more than anything else, it was a Damned Good Try.

The party afterwards at the White Horse had everything the party the year before had lacked. Callum – who had taken his rightful place as the life and soul of the event – was fully occupied in regaling an eager audience with renditions of some of the scenes he would be undertaking with Bryce Gullory in the near future, Catherine and Izzy were squeezed into a corner discussing the respective merits of the Brontë sisters, and Bill and Jon sat shoulder to shoulder watching the antics of their younger peers with an almost parental fatalism.

"'And thus the whirligig of time brings in his revenges'," Bill sighed, pushing his pint away. "We get a few months off to go and earn some real money, and then we all troop back here in the middle of March and start the whole rigmarole again."

Jon grimaced. Callum was, mercifully, out of sight at the moment, although his voice could occasionally be heard from the other bar. "At least we'll do better financially with *Ros 'n' Guil*," he said. "I think this one's hit Ewen rather hard."

"Why? He's not out of pocket on the deal, is he?"

"No, I don't think so. But he put a lot of effort into it, and it didn't work out quite the way he hoped it would."

"It should have done," Bill mused. "All the ingredients were good."

"True. But Jacobean revenge tragedy has a limited shelf life these days, and it was probably a bit too ambitious. *Ros 'n' Guil* is going to be much more mainstream isn't it? And more lucrative, too."

"Even without His Nibs over there?" Bill asked, tilting his head archly in Callum's direction.

"Even without him. What could he possibly play in it, after all?"

"One of the leads, I suppose," Bill shrugged.

"Oh no, that wouldn't work! They've got to carry equal weight, and he's too big a star already; we've got nobody who could stand up against him, and that would make it terribly one-sided. Besides, he'll be an excellent Petruchio and Izzy will make a wonderful Kate; I think they're both doing the right thing, going to the National instead."

"You weren't tempted to go along with them, then?"

Jon laughed softly. "Not really," he said. "I like my life here. Besides … "

"Hmmm." Bill was not slow to recognise the sorrowing fall to his words. In the past few days they had each had conversations with Ewen which had left them in a less than optimistic frame of mind. "Yes," he added, thoughtfully. "We've got our work cut out for us next summer. Have you ever actually done any directing before?"

"Only a bit. It was disastrous. It was a student play called *God's Pig* and I did just about everything wrong that I could possibly have done. I'm lucky my cast didn't stage a mass walkout. Mind you, there were only five of them."

Bill chuckled, but it was a dry sardonic sound and did not exactly inspire confidence. "I'm not a lot more experienced myself," he admitted, ruefully. "As you say, student stuff, and one thing at the Edinburgh Festival which you don't want to know about. We did it three times a day in a marquee in a permanent howling gale and by the end I wanted to kill everybody involved – including myself."

"I expect we'll muddle through somehow," Jon told him, trying to sound confident. "It's not as if Ewen's going to be totally incapacitated, after all. He'll be there most of the time; we'll just have to be ready to take up the slack when he isn't. How difficult can it be?"

"As long as we agree our plans in advance and try not to undermine one another," Bill said, "we should be all right. Living in the same house is certainly going to help."

"And having Rory and James under the same roof won't hurt either," completed Jon, with satisfaction. The casting for the summer had been more or less agreed upon by now: Bill was going to give one of his 'doddering old eccentrics' in the role of Polonius, and the two young leads were assigned to Rory Cooper and James Rudge, an Australian actor to whom Rory bore a startling resemblance. The play's inherent confusion between Rosencrantz and Guildenstern would be well–served by their physical similarities, and this had been hailed as one of Ewen's finest casting coups to date. Less felicitously, he had opted to bring back Douglas Pirie as Claudius and Jax Burroughs as Ophelia. The latter pair, mercifully, were to be accommodated elsewhere and had no intention whatever of darkening the doors of the Old Crown.

"No girls at all next year, then?" Bill asked, smiling.

"Not one," Jon confirmed. "Matthew's staying on in your old room. I don't think he particularly wants to move out now, he's settled where he is. Well, he's not a great deal of trouble," he added, letting his attention wander again to where Callum was once more the centre of attention.

"Unlike some people we could name?"

"Oh, Callum's not so bad when you get to know him," Jon mused, allowing himself to be distracted from the serious nature of the conversation. "He's a bit young and thoughtless, but time will take care of that. It usually does," he concluded, wistfully – and was happy enough when Bill seemed inclined to change the subject fairly shortly afterwards.

There was no time to recover from the end of the *Duchess* before Jon found himself, late the following morning, in his car heading north. A room had been booked for him at a small, friendly hotel near the studios, and he fell into it with weary gratitude and total absence of expectation. It did not really seem appropriate to start missing Callum at this stage; no doubt he would, as the weeks and months rolled past, but they had parted with every stated intention of meeting again – Callum to remove his belongings from *Gertrude* into the less austere surroundings of Roy and Pete's guest bedroom, Jon to leave Antonio behind and think himself into the skin of a quintessential Victorian.

Being back in Edgar's undemanding company, however, looked likely to make it all a whole lot easier. Edgar's stepdaughter, Jenny – his only living kin since her mother had passed away – seemed fully dedicated to looking after not just Edgar and his business interests but also his friends and associates. Her eye for detail extended even to Jon, and his room when he arrived contained flowers, fruit, and a basket of necessaries intended to turn it into a temporary home. There was also a note in Edgar's handwriting suggesting dinner that evening. Wryly he supposed this must be the sort of treatment Callum was used to, although it was a novelty to him; his previous catalogue of incidental barristers and fathers–of–the–bride had never merited such indulgences before; he usually arrived to find printed instructions from the studio, identification for getting him in through the gates, and a message reminding him that the car – or more likely the minibus – would pick him up at a certain time to take him to make–up, and would he please be sure to have breakfast first because nothing would be provided on set until lunchtime. It was only with enormous difficulty that he managed to quell the urge to telephone somebody – anybody – and tell them all about it in cadences of breathless awe. Izzy, perhaps – or Callum, if it would not have caused such utter consternation at Fardels. Instead he mastered himself enough to sit down at the dressing–table and pull out a sheaf of hotel writing paper, upon which in his meticulous handwriting he began to keep a very precise and comprehensive diary of his experiences for the future entertainment of his daughter.

By the end of the second week he felt as comfortable as he had on any other project in the past – more so, in fact, than he had expected to feel in Callum's absence. They had become so used to one another, both as lovers and as colleagues, that he had anticipated the separation making more of a mark on him than it had. It was not that he did not miss having someone to curl up against, even though his nights with Callum had been snatched and infrequent and – apart from brief periods 'playing house' in the diverse environs of Portofino and Tufnell Park – they had scarcely enjoyed one another's company for longer than a weekend anyway; it was simply that he had learned to make the change from lover to actor so thoroughly and completely by now that it felt like the closing of a door. Callum was tucked away safely behind that door, confined to a different compartment of his life, and it was almost possible to forget about his existence for hours – and even whole days – at a time.

It was refreshing, too, to concentrate on Edgar and his people. They had all been together for many years – Jenny, indeed, was the most recent addition to the crew, having taken over her late mother's duties as far as organisation of Edgar's life was concerned. Also present, although not directly concerned in the *Curzon* project, was a tall and distinguished–looking actor by the name of Nigel Carlyle who specialised in playing aristocrats and politicians and the occasional smooth–tongued charmer. He and Edgar had been friends for decades, and they were now in the final stages of assembling a project they had long been working on together. Whilst Edgar was preoccupied with *Curzon* on the set, therefore, Nigel sat with Jenny in a trailer making endless telephone calls and trying to fit together a massive three–dimensional jigsaw puzzle with the working title of *Hawker and Duffy*.

"There'll be a part in it for you, young Jonathan," he said cheerfully. "If it goes to a series, which we hope it will. You can have your choice of jolly good chaps to play … priests, detectives, murder victims. You can even be a baddie if you like."

Jon stared at him in disbelief. "Can you really see me as an axe–murderer?" he asked, laughing. Nigel's confidence in him, obviously inherited from Edgar, was charming but in his opinion totally misplaced.

"Well, maybe not weltering in gore," conceded Nigel. They were out of doors, and he was puffing away on a lunchtime cigar whilst Edgar and Jenny had their heads down over some detail with the script supervisor. "But there's a chap in one of the books – *Prophet Motive* – who embezzles half a million from his firm and murders one of his colleagues to cover up for it. He's the quintessential mild–mannered man pushed to extremes. Right up your alley, I'd have thought."

"Possible," conceded Jon, intrigued. "What does he do with the money?"

"Double life," chortled Nigel. "Multiple wives and families stashed all over the map. They think he's away on business four nights a week, whereas what he really does is jump in the car and move on to the next one."

"Good grief. I'm not sure I'd be all that convincing as a man with even one wife, let alone more – somebody the other day referred to me as the most famous incompetent husband in the country!"

"That wasn't you, that was Finn," came the crisp response. There was no need to ask whether Nigel had read Rosemary's books: everybody had read them, and everybody looked sideways at Jon on account of them. "It would be quite a fun twist, though, don't you think? Stick two fingers up to the ex–wife?"

"It's tempting," Jon acknowledged.

"About time you fought back, old man," Nigel told him, expansively. "And you can trust your Uncle Nige to help you out."

That evening, when Jon returned to his hotel, there was a message for him at the desk. Mr Daniel Bosola had telephoned; he was in Manchester and would appreciate a call from Jon if he had the time. He went up to his room immediately and dialled the number.

"Jon?"

"Callum … ?" Somehow, though, the next words just would not come. It should be something conventional, some question about why and where and how and what on earth, but the connections refused to form in Jon's brain and he simply sat there on his bed listening to the matching silence at the other end of the line; listening to the sounds of Callum's room; listening to Callum breathe. "Are you all right?" he ventured nervously, after a while.

"I think so, thanks." But it was an entirely conventional assurance;

there was no sense of conviction behind it whatsoever.

"Where are you?"

"The Midland Hotel. It's a great big place in the city centre. Can you come over and stay the night with me? I want to talk to you about something."

Frantically Jon considered. His schedule lay open on the dressing–table and a quick check showed that he wasn't needed until after lunch on the following day. "I suppose … " His brain was whirring. "I could get a taxi," he said. "Be there in an hour or two?"

"Yes. Listen, I'll give you the room number … just walk in through Reception and come up in the lift, nobody will challenge you. That's why I chose it, it's anonymous – I've got a double room and nobody cares who I share it with. We can eat on room service and you'll never need to show your face outside the door."

"All right."

"Good." The massive exhalation of breath at this point indicated exactly how tightly Callum's nerves had been wound beforehand. "I really need to see you."

"I'll be there as soon as I can," Jon reassured him, softly. "Should I bring anything?"

"Only a toothbrush. I've got the rest."

An unworthy suspicion crossed Jon's mind. "This isn't just … ?"

"God, no, love, heaven forbid! This is important, and I have to tell you about it face to face. I don't actually care if we don't … " He trailed off there, awkwardly. Except in some of their more impassioned moments, neither of them had ever quite had the vocabulary to talk about the details of their sex life; in the cold light of day they were bashfully inclined to resort to euphemism and ellipsis. It was a moment which could have been supremely awkward, had not Jon been overwhelmed with affectionate sympathy for Callum's inarticulate blundering.

"I missed you, too," he said, calmly. "I don't think I realised how much until I heard your voice again."

"Then get yourself over here as quickly as you can," was the gravelly response, "because if I have to wait very much longer to see you I'm going to spontaneously combust, and that can be hell on the carpet."

"We can't have that," soothed Jon. "But unless you put the phone down, darling, I can't very well set off to meet you – can I?"

"Oh, bugger!" said Callum, and the line went dead between them, and five minutes later Jon was heading out of the hotel into the grey Manchester evening, wondering what in God's name he was letting himself in for this time.

"I'm not cut out for all this secret agent stuff," he said, an hour and a quarter later.

Callum stood back from the door and admitted him into a large, airy hotel room whose principal ornament was a bed with a sumptuous purple throw which argued viciously against the regal red of the carpet.

"I know, love. I'm sorry." Once the door was closed and firmly locked behind them Callum hugged him and pressed an almost–formal kiss to his cheek. "I like the little pointy beard," he said, stroking Jon's chin approvingly. "Very butch. I take it nobody tried to stop you downstairs?"

"Not at all. Nobody took any notice of me."

"I didn't think they would. I told the management I was hiding from a demented female fan – which, God knows, is not a million miles from the truth. But if you'd gone to the desk they wouldn't have admitted I was even here. I did mention I was expecting a colleague to join me for a meeting, though."

"Which could possibly be the world's most transparent excuse," observed Jon.

"It doesn't sound very good, does it, now that you mention it? But, then again, these people make their living out of being discreet."

"Which is the reason you didn't want to come to where I'm staying?"

"Exactly. I checked up on it; Edgar's got you booked into the kind of cosy nook where everybody knows everybody else and they get worried if you don't come down for breakfast. Here, nobody gives a stuff – especially if we make it worth their while."

Jon sighed. "It all seems rather unnecessary though," he said.

"I'm sorry to say it isn't." Callum guided Jon over to where a couple of armchairs and a coffee–table were grouped together, and they sat facing one another in silence for a moment. Conversations with Ewen had tended to start like this recently, and the next words had often been *I'm in remission* or *It's more chemo, I'm afraid.* Ewen had always made superhuman attempts to spare his hearer's feelings, and Jon had never really understood why.

"You'd better tell me straight away. Is it something dreadful?" he asked, solicitously prepared for anything from unemployment to contagion.

"Dreadful enough," was the low–key response. "Embarrassing, more than anything else. Look, do you mind if we eat now and save the talking until we go to bed? I'm so damned tired!"

It was such an unusual thing for Callum to have said – Callum, who could work everyone around him to a standstill and keep on going like the bunny in the battery advert. Astonished, Jon cast an appraising sidelong glance at him and found that even two weeks' absence had sharpened his perceptions; he was seeing things he had never seen before. There were deepening laugh lines around Callum's eyes, the texture of his skin had altered, and there was perhaps the faintest suspicion of grey beginning to show in his hair. He was rather young for that, admittedly, but Jon's own first grey hair had appeared exactly on his twenty–first birthday; he supposed it all depended on whatever genetic legacy one's parents had passed on.

"That's not like you," he observed, in his calmest tones.

"I know. Why don't you tell me everything that's been happening to you and see if you can't cheer me up a bit? My stuff will keep until later; I'll feel a lot happier talking about it with the lights off, anyway."

"All right," Jon smiled, reassured now that it could not be anything as terrible as he had first imagined. If it had been death or serious illness Callum would still have wanted to shield him from it, but he would at least have broken it straightforwardly. This, whatever it was, was obviously a complicated mess and he was half–ashamed of needing Jon's help to cope with it.

"But first we'll order dinner," went on Callum, with a flash of boyish practicality. "I'm not going to drag you halfway across an alien city and burden you with my problems and roger you through the bloody mattress without even feeding you, although I have to confess that rogering isn't exactly high on my list of priorities at the moment."

"That's a shame." Jon pulled the room service menu towards him and opened it at random. "Perhaps I should order the giant Cumberland sausage, in that case?"

It had fallen dark before their meal arrived. Callum stood at the door and took the tray from the waiter; Jon did not exactly try to hide from him, but neither did he make his presence blatantly obvious. Whatever they ate afterwards was serviceable without being exciting, purposeful rather than enjoyable. The slight tension in the atmosphere was very different from all the relaxed times they had shared in the kitchen at the Old Crown or on opposite sides of *Gertrude*'s little table, and Jon found himself paying more attention to Callum than to his meal.

"So tell me about this thing Edgar and Nigel are doing," Callum said, as though desperately casting around for a topic that might fill the unaccustomed silence between them.

"The *Hawker and Duffy* books by Elinor Chase," Jon said, between mouthfuls of ... something or other. "*Sinner City, Axe of Omission, Prophet Motive ...* "

"I know, I know. A cop and a Catholic priest investigate murders together."

"That's right. Edgar's playing Chief Inspector Hawker, Nigel's going to be Father Duffy. It's their pet project, they've been trying to get the money together for years – and then it all had to go on hold because Edgar's wife was ill. And then of course she died. They're only just getting it back on the road now, but Edgar's determined to do it before he gets too old. He's almost at the mandatory police retirement age already."

"Well, Jack Warner was still doing *Dixon of Dock Green* at the age of eighty."

"So I understand – but that's not Edgar's ambition, believe me."

"Anything for you in it?" asked Callum, hopefully.

"Some chap with multiple mistresses," Jon told him with a wry grimace.

"Ah. Nice. I like the irony. So – if a married man has a girlfriend she's called his mistress. Does that mean that if he had a boyfriend he'd be his master?"

It was lame enough, but Jon considered it with his usual gravity. "I don't know. Are you saying you'd like to be my master?"

"God, no, love, nothing like that. That's not really my sort of thing, is it? No, what I meant was – there isn't a proper name for what we are, is there? I think that's rather sad."

"Friends with benefits?" suggested Jon, recovering slightly.

"No," replied Callum. "It's more than that, but I don't know exactly what it is."

They finished their meal, put the tray outside, and prepared to go to bed, moving around one another economically in the small space, talking about nothing. There was a determined ordinariness about the whole proceeding, both aware that sex – if it occurred at all – would be an afterthought and not the reason for their being together. On the whole, though, Jon did not know that he minded very much; it was as good to be needed as desired, and it was something of a relief to be made aware that Callum cared for him on more than just one level.

Jon was the last to finish in the bathroom. He stepped out of it and switched the light off, undressing in the darkness and sliding easily between crisp sheets into a tangle of warm arms. Callum clung to him just a little more fervently than he usually did, his body taut, his breathing harsher than it should have been.

"Tell me," Jon said, as they wound themselves together in that dear, familiar way and lay listening to the hiss of the cistern refilling, the click of the cooling lightbulb, the murmur of sheets against skin. "What's worrying you?"

"Oh Jon. I don't know what I'd do if I didn't have you to talk to," Callum told him, shakily. "Dump it all on Izzy, I suppose. Well, she knows the worst – she was there when it happened. Thank goodness I didn't have to fill in too many of the blanks for her, she'd got most of the story already. Not this bit, though." A broad hand slid slowly over Jon's shoulder. "She has no idea that you and I ... "

"All right, I understand. But tell me what it is that's happened."

Callum groaned. "Thea, of course. Thea's happened. Again. You could have put money on it, couldn't you? Except that you always like to give people a chance to behave decently first. You know she'd invited me to go over and see Connor? Well, I had a day off from *Robin Hood* yesterday, and like an idiot I decided to go."

"Why 'like an idiot'? What on earth could be wrong with visiting your son?"

"Nothing, you would think. There shouldn't have been, at least. But you're being far too rational, Jon; you've forgotten what we're dealing with here. The woman's completely and utterly bonkers."

"Oh?"

"Yes. Remember how I asked you to go with me, and you said you didn't think you could?"

"I remember." Instinctively Jon was stroking Callum's neck and back as if soothing a frightened cat. There was obviously a saga to be unfolded here, and to judge by Callum's tone it wasn't going to be a pleasant one. "So?"

"So ... sound decision on your part, as it turned out. But anyway I didn't want to go alone – I never know what to say to people about babies, apart from anything else – so I thought maybe Izzy wouldn't mind going with me."

"Really?" This was surprising, but when he considered it further Jon realised it was a logical choice: Izzy never seemed at a loss in any situation, and he could imagine Callum looking to her if he felt at some kind of disadvantage. "You know," he mused, "that was a good idea. I'm glad you came up with it."

Some of the tension seemed to melt from Callum's body. "So was I," he admitted, "at the time, but I was afraid you wouldn't approve. You might have thought it was ungentlemanly to involve her, or something."

"She was involved already," Jon pointed out. "And she didn't seem to mind too much before. No, I think you did the right thing. Go on."

"Well," sighed Callum, "when they told me they didn't need me for the day I had a sudden flash of inspiration and called Izzy to find out if she was free, and luckily she was. So off we went together to see Thea at her mum and dad's place in Croydon – and, let me tell you, even for someone from the arse–end of Swindon, Croydon still feels pretty much like the badlands."

"I'll have to take your word for that." Jon deepened his embrace, easing Callum more firmly into his arms. "I wouldn't know."

"We found the house all right," Callum went on, regardless. "A nice place, they're obviously not short of a few bob – and there were Thea and Connor living in the granny flat and everything was perfectly friendly, and I got to play with my son while Thea and Izzy talked like normal people. It was great having her there, Jon; she took all the heat off me and gave me a chance to get to know Connor a bit. He's quite a cute little kid – not a lot to say for himself and he smells a bit funny, but we got on all right. Izzy took a couple of pictures of us together; if they turn out well, I'll send you one."

"Thank you, darling. I'd like that."

"I know, love – you're just a sentimental old softie at heart, aren't you?"

"I am," confessed Jon, unrepentantly. "So what happened next?"

Callum sighed. "We stayed about an hour, Thea's mum brought us a cup of tea, it was all really civilised – exactly what I'd been hoping for, innocent trusting fool that I am."

"Well, there's nothing wrong with that, is there?" prompted Jon, encouragingly.

"I wish," came the dispirited response. "Unfortunately, the second we stepped outside again we ran headlong into some tit with a camera who insisted on taking pictures of me and Izzy leaving the house – and Connor and Thea waving to us from the doorstep."

"Pictures," Jon echoed, mystified. "Why? What on earth would anybody want with those?"

Against his shoulder, Callum groaned. "It's the bloody film," he uttered, wearily. "We haven't even started shooting yet, but the publicity is absolutely horrendous already. Every geek or freak who ever read the books wants to talk to me about how I'm going to approach playing Rossi – as if it was more challenging than the Scottish King or Bosola or anything I've ever done – and I've been invited to one of those big science fiction conference things they have in the States … you know, where the fans dress up as the characters, like they do for *Star Trek*?"

"My God, really?"

"My God, really. There isn't a single foot of film in the can, all I've done so far are make–up and costume tests, but all of a sudden I'm public property and every move I make is news – at least for the sci–fi crowd. I must admit, I wasn't really expecting that."

Jon kissed him quietly on the cheek. "I'm sorry, love. It must be awful."

"It is. And now this strange sci–fi magazine has all these pictures of me with Connor and Thea and Izzy and God knows what bollocks they're going to make up to go with them; it all depends on what kind of crap Thea's been chucking out, I suppose."

"Thea?"

"Oh, come on, who else could possibly have set it up? She didn't turn a hair when the bloke popped up from the shrubbery and started snapping away at us; she was expecting him, that was obvious – she smiled and waved just like the Queen Mother. Thea sold me out, Jon, and Izzy right along with me. She only went along to keep me company, and now this whole damned thing's going to be hanging over the pair of us for the next year or so, whether we like it or not. I can't exactly see Thea letting it drop without a fight, can you?"

Jon considered the scenario briefly. "All right," he acknowledged, "I see what you mean. You're worried about exposing Izzy to that kind of scrutiny."

"Of course. What has she ever done to deserve it, after all?"

"Nothing, I know. But I'm sure you've talked to her about it already, and I'm also sure she said the same thing I'm about to say – that it won't do any harm when it comes to publicity for the *Shrew*. It may not be exactly what you wanted, but some people will come to the play on the strength of it – just to get a look at you."

"She did say that," Callum admitted, nuzzling his neck sleepily. "She didn't think it would be a bad thing either. She said she was happy to be my escort for the whole year if it would help – provided she didn't run into Mr Right in the meantime."

"Bless her heart, I always knew you could rely on her."

"Absolutely, she's a good egg. I've never really had a female friend before – not one who'd put herself out for me the way she has, I mean – but she's a lot like you. Somebody I can lean on if I need to."

"Yes," acknowledged Jon, trying to push away a tiny invasive pang of jealousy. "That's a good description. I've always considered her utterly dependable myself."

"She is. But meanwhile we've got Thea selling stories to magazines – and my agent's getting calls asking for comments and interviews about my private life rather than my work. He's putting up a stone wall, but you know what happens if you do that."

"They start trying to tunnel underneath," Jon completed, cynically. "They talk to everyone you've ever worked with, people you were at school with, relatives you've forgotten you had … "

"Exactly. And what follows on from that is everything I want to keep hidden has to be buried so far underground even I don't know where to find it again. And that, in turn, means … "

"Me," Jon finished for him, as though it were inevitable.

The silence that followed this remark was awful, hollow and echoing. In the end it was only with difficulty that Callum finally steeled himself to speak again.

"Yes, love. I'm afraid it does mean you."

"Naturally."

It was surprising how easy it was just to agree, to accept that there was no alternative, that it absolutely had to be this way.

"It isn't the end of anything." Callum sounded almost desperate. "It doesn't have to be. Only – we're going to have to give one another a wide berth for a while and not meet up unless there are plenty of other people around – at least until I finish working on *Planetfall*." He reconsidered. "*Deadfall*, too, I suppose, and maybe even *Firefall*. This wouldn't be the greatest time to be outed, would it, for either of us, what with me doing *Planetfall* and you doing *Curzon*?"

"No." Jon was aware that he was being virtually monosyllabic, but there really did not seem very much to be said – and Callum was the one doing all the talking anyway, which seemed appropriate. Nobody would care whether a man who played a minor part in a minor historical drama about Lord Curzon was gay or straight or got his thrills from buggering camels; Callum was the only one who counted here; Callum should be making these decisions. "Tell me what it is you want us to do," he breathed. "Go our separate ways and forget any of this ever happened?"

"God, no. This has been ... so good for me, Jon. So great." But Callum's face was mashed miserably into Jon's shoulder. "I can't think," he went on. "I want you to make it all go away, disappear and never bother us again – babies, photographers, sci–fi fans, the whole stinking lot of them – and magic us back to one of those mornings on *Gertrude* or the day we walked on the beach at Portofino and met that woman and her dog. I know you would if you could, love, but the really shitty part is that you can't. Nobody can. That doesn't make me stop wishing for it to happen, though. This is a bastard of a mess we're in, and I can't see any way out of it at the moment."

"I know. Neither can I. But that doesn't mean there isn't something we can do; we just haven't thought of it yet. This ... relationship, affair, whatever it is ... will only be over when we want it to be over, and not a moment before. You tell me when you want to end it and we'll both walk away without regrets. Until then ... I'm sure we can find a way to keep it going somehow."

"That's my Jon," came a drowsy murmur from somewhere close against his neck. "Always the sensible one. Don't ever change, love, will you, for the sake of whatever shreds of my poor sanity are left? I need you always to stay exactly the way you are right now."

"Naked and underneath you?" teased Jon, placing a kiss next to Callum's eyebrow. "Is that what you had in mind?"

"Hmmm," was the distant answer he received. "'S really the only way ... "

◆

Jon awoke in the morning to warmth and comfort and the well–loved sensations of sharing a bed with Callum; he had lost none of his Labrador puppyness and was sprawling with angular elbows and knees seeming to occupy more than their fair share of the space, one muscular forearm resting alongside Jon's cheek. Jon opened his eyes to see Callum watching him cautiously from beneath his heavy lashes.

"Morning, love."

"Good morning. Did you sleep well?"

"Better for having you here." Callum rolled over onto one side and swam a little nearer. His hand disappeared beneath the bed–covers and settled warmly on Jon's hip. "I wish I could take you everywhere with me."

Jon smiled and let himself be pulled into a comfortable embrace. "I sometimes think you need a keeper," he conceded.

"If only you'd been there the other day, instead of Izzy … "

"It would still have happened," Jon reminded him. "And she's a lot easier to explain than I would have been. People will just assume you're seeing her."

"Doesn't that bother you at all?" asked Callum.

"No. Professionally it could be very good for both of you."

"And most importantly … it's Izzy."

"As you say."

And whatever else might have been said upon the subject was swallowed up in a sequence of frowsy morning kisses, in slow fingertips on lazy flesh, in the tranquil pleasures of undemanding early morning sex; nothing energetic, just the exchange of gentle, quiet hands and at last a soft, lingering conclusion.

"I'm going to miss this," Callum whispered, his arms wrapped tightly around Jon's neck.

"We've been apart before," Jon reminded him, petting his hair and trying to impart reassurance where he felt none himself.

"Yes, but then we knew there'd be an end to it. This time … "

"You feel as if it's going to last forever?"

"Yes."

Jon thought about it. "Perhaps we can get a cottage somewhere," he said. "Maybe we can borrow Portofino again before the summer."

"Or we could go abroad," Callum suggested, on a slightly more optimistic note. "I've always wanted to see Venice."

"Very romantic: all singing gondoliers and water–lights on the ceiling."

"The ceiling would probably be the only thing you'd see for the entire week," was the cheerfully earthy response.

"Oh. Then as far as I'm concerned it might just as well be Scunthorpe!"

"Or Wigan. Or Heckmondwyke. They would probably be cheaper."

Jon shuddered. "You really know how to sweep a man off his feet, Callum, don't you?"

"Not 'a man'," answered Callum, sombrely. "Just you. Never seemed worth doing with anybody else, but you … But we're going to have to put it back in its box for a while, aren't we, until this stupid Thea business has blown over again?"

"I'm afraid we are. But we'll stay in touch, of course?"

"Of course we will. I'll phone you. Probably a lot, actually, while I'm doing *Planetfall* – I have a horrible feeling working with Bryce is going to drive me to the edge of dementia. And I'll have to let the flat in Tufnell Park go soon, the Press have found that already, so I might move into Izzy's mum and dad's basement until I can get something more permanent sorted out. They've got a flat down there where they used to keep the au pair."

"It sounds perfect for you," smiled Jon. "An oubliette. They can lock you in and throw away the key."

"I wouldn't mind – as long as you promise to visit me sometimes, in my lonely isolation?"

"Perhaps."

"And perhaps not, is that what you're trying to say?"

"Who knows?" Jon gave a long, deep sigh, and let his fingers tangle idly in Callum's chest hair. "I stopped trying to work any of this out a long time ago and I haven't got a clue how it's going to end up. The only thing I know is that I'm grateful for every moment we've had so far, and if it all grinds to a screeching halt tomorrow it's been absolutely

172

wonderful and I won't forget a second of it."

"Me too. But it isn't going to end tomorrow, is it?"

"No, darling, of course not," said Jon, making his most steadfast effort so far to believe in the literal truth of what he was saying.

◆

(The kitchen at the Old Crown; it is daytime, spring 1998, and there is a hopeful light in the room. JON and BILL are relaxing over cups of coffee at the large central table)

♦

"Seen anything of Callum lately?" Bill asked, idly reaching for a chocolate biscuit. He had only been back in the house an hour or so, but it felt as if he had never been away.

"Callum? No. Why?" Jon looked up distractedly. He had been pondering a letter from his London tenants, giving warning that they would be vacating the flat at the end of May. They were, it appeared, pregnant – at least, that was the way they expressed it – and wanted a less urban environment for their child. They were heading for Wiltshire to open a pottery.

Bill shrugged. "I can't help thinking I'm staying in his room," he said. "Even though Izzy had it last year. There's just a sort of Callumness about it somehow."

"Cheek." Jon stuffed his letter back into its envelope. "It's been completely redecorated since he lived here."

"I noticed. Did that after you finished *Curzon*, did you?"

"Not personally. All I did was open the door to let the workmen in. Same with the new bathroom downstairs."

"Yes. That looks good, too." Bill glanced around in satisfaction. "It's nice to be back," he said. "I've always liked the atmosphere here. It's peaceful."

"Perhaps that's the doves."

"Perhaps." Bill fell silent for a while, contemplating the infinite, then sniffed disapprovingly. "Had a rough time in the papers, hasn't he, Callum? All that 'Callous Henley' business. Clever, but hardly accurate – it doesn't look as if he treated the girl too badly. Is she trying to con him into marriage, do you think?"

Jon looked up in alarm. "I hadn't thought of that. It's not as if they'd ever had much of a relationship."

"Well," said Bill, "I don't know anything about it, but from the outside … What was it, then, a one–night stand?"

"Something of the sort, I think. I know she was a lot keener on him than he ever was on her." It would hardly be giving much away to acknowledge Callum's lack of enthusiasm for any long–term involvement with Thea. His statement, through his agent, had made it plain enough. Jon could have recited it from memory, and only with difficulty restrained himself from doing so.

> Although Thea and I are no longer involved
> with one another
> we are both committed to the welfare and
> happiness of our son,
> Connor Henley Dawson,
> and will be sharing responsibility
> for his upbringing.

Spare and functional, the dead hand of Lenny's prose was evident in its composition. Callum had wanted to put in something about joys and sorrows; Lenny had overruled him.

"You know, nobody would care about him if he wasn't doing this sci–fi thing," Bill ruminated, absently. "Without that he's a jobbing actor like you and me, but as soon as you make a movie – especially if you get your kit off the way he's doing – people think they own you. They had pictures of him in the papers virtually naked."

"I saw those. There's some kind of circulation war going on; half the tabloids are calling him a love–rat, the other half can't get enough of him. One lot even gave away free tickets to see *Leichhardt*."

"Hmmm. Not surprised, I hear it's a bit of a turkey."

"Not really. It's a good film, just not a popular subject. It would have helped if they'd made their minds up whether Leichhardt was a genius or an idiot: playing both at once didn't give Callum much to work with."

"Well, I haven't seen it – and I'm surprised you managed to find the time."

Jon grimaced. "I've had a light winter since *Curzon*," he admitted. "And plenty of time after Catherine and Izzy moved out. I did have some voice–overs, but generally work's been thin on the ground. I had to amuse myself somehow."

Ruefully Bill acknowledged the sentiment. "Still," he said, "bloody *Leichhardt*." His body language said it all.

"I thought I might learn something," Jon smiled. And, indeed, he had: slipping quietly into the back of a half–empty London cinema with an almost unrecognisable Callum and sitting for two hours in darkness while the bones of his hand were crushed to powder, he had learned a great deal – not about Leichhardt or Australia, but about Callum's insecurity and self–doubt and inability to sit still. They had ducked out before the end and were in a taxi back to Bayswater before Callum let out the breath he seemed to have been holding throughout the film.

"Did you hate it?" he had asked, then.

"No," was the simple answer, and the conversation ended there.

It had been a strange interlude, the snatched few days in London; Jon had never imagined that the Thorpes' basement flat would be a rat–infested dungeon, but neither had he expected stark lines and white shiny surfaces, nor self–consciously rustic cushions and kelims. It was an odd setting for Callum, and although he had been living there some months already he rattled around in it like a boy wearing his elder brother's cast–offs. He was obviously uncomfortable with his life; endless call–backs for *Planetfall* meant he had still not finished with it, and the start date for the *Shrew* was looming. The one for *Ros 'n' Guil* was even more imminent; there had been only a small window of opportunity, not even a week, for them to get together, and they had grabbed at it with all four hands. But Callum was unsettled, hyper-alert to sounds and movements, stepping out of his way to avoid shadows and protecting Jon from observation almost as if he were in purdah. Even when they were alone in the flat with the curtains drawn and the lights off, he was still unable to relax.

"You just don't know when they'll pop up next," he said, more than once, and Jon was hard put to it to know whether this counted as reaction to a trying experience or incipient paranoia. He had never been in a similar situation himself; it was difficult to empathise with anything so far beyond the limits of his experience.

"Does Thea know where you're living?" he asked.

"I hope not. But they could always follow Izzy, couldn't they?"

"Possibly." He was holding Callum in his arms, and they were naked, but for some reason neither sleep nor sex seemed possible at the moment. Instead they lay together chasing demons in the dark, all Callum's fears and insecurities spilling out to be muffled against Jon's accommodating shoulder.

"I should buy a place," said Callum. "Something with good security, something out of the way. I should turn myself into a company. I should hire somebody to look after me."

"A bodyguard?" asked Jon.

"A minder. A driver or a PA. Bryce seems to need six or seven people around him all the time and I'm never sure what any of them do. He says once your fans get hold of you they never let you go."

"Bryce?"

Callum sighed. "He's a bit of a nutter, I know, but he's quite a good bloke – and he knows the business inside out. The movie business, that is. I don't think he knows a thing about acting – he just gets on and does it."

"How did your love scene go?" It felt wrong to be asking, somehow, when they were as intimate as this; however the kiss with Bryce had been hanging over them both for several weeks now and the need to know about it had begun to burn a corrosive hole through Jon's confidence.

"Awkwardly. It's not as if we hadn't rehearsed it, but I kept feeling everybody could see right through me. I've never felt so exposed doing any scene before. It's not a great romantic encounter or anything, just a character moment, so it has to look as if we do it all the time without even noticing – but it felt like a big deal to me when it shouldn't have. I couldn't relax, so I started flinching every time he touched me – and he kept getting angrier and angrier all the time. In the end I thought the top of his head was going to fly off and his brains would boil out all over the floor."

"God, that sounds awful."

"It was. No matter what I did, I couldn't shake it off; I've never hated kissing anybody so much in my life. And the strange part is – I don't actually hate Bryce. What I did hate – and I didn't think I would – was anybody seeing me kiss a man. It just felt too personal somehow. It was more of myself than I wanted to reveal."

Jon folded him close. "But you got the shot?" he asked, concerned.

"In the end. It took most of the day, and I think the crew had me down as a raging homophobe by the end of it – which is ironic in the circumstances." Callum paused, and a bitter chuckle escaped him. "Gives a whole new dimension to suffering for one's art," he offered wryly.

By the time Jon's mid–season break came around that year the potters had departed the Hackney flat and moved their bump and their expectations to new quarters in Amesbury. He had an opportunity, therefore, to inspect the apartment and prepare for putting it on the market; considering what similar properties were currently fetching in the neighbourhood, this seemed as good a time as any to cash in on his investment. It was not as if he had ever felt any great attachment to the place, either, which he thought was just as well as he glanced around. It had not been trashed – indeed, the potters had looked after it carefully – but their artistic natures had expressed themselves in decorative choices which sat oddly with his conservative nature. The blood–red walls in the sitting room worked well enough with the durable natural fibre flooring and black sofa he had left in place, but he wondered how anyone ever survived waking up to a bedroom the colour of a workman's high–visibility jacket which he was sure he'd be aware of even with his eyes shut. It would have to be the first room to get a coat of paint, but not until after he and Callum had slept there. He would have to hope the boy's nerve held, otherwise he might find himself dealing with the aftermath of a psychotic episode on the strength of it.

Callum arrived late that night in a minicab, paying it off at the corner and walking the rest of the way with a rucksack on one shoulder and a baseball cap pulled low to hide his eyes. He fell into the flat gracelessly, in a seemingly disagreeable frame of mind.

"Batista's an idiot and Bianca's a tart," he complained, dropping his bag and backing Jon roughly against the wall. "I mean it, the silly old bugger's senile – and she's slept with every male in the company already, excluding me. And him, presumably," he added, although he did not sound especially certain.

"Do you want something to eat?"

But it was difficult to remain civilised when Callum was all hands and tongue, determined to dispense with the amenities, apparently in the mood for something quick and dirty. Jon had never known him so freakishly out of sorts before, so totally at odds with the rest of the world.

"You," said Callum gruffly. "I want you." His hands were already tugging urgently at Jon's clothes.

"Not here." Jon captured the hands and pushed them away. There was a draught under the front door, and the smell of cats had wafted in from outside. Nobody in their right mind would have sex there when there was a perfectly good bed. "The bedroom's behind you. Are you sure you're not hungry? It's steak and kidney pie," he added, as though it might have a bearing on the decision.

"Sex or steak and kidney?" Callum made an elaborate pantomime of debating the matter and ended up shrugging helplessly. "Where's the bathroom?"

Jon indicated a door. "Give me a moment to turn the oven down."

"Don't be long."

There was something peremptory about the tone which made Jon hurry; he switched the oven to its lowest setting, pushed the pans of vegetables off the rings and cast a regretful glance in the direction of the set table and the wine breathing on the window–sill. Callum was obviously full of pent–up aggression, and if his thumbnail sketch of the *Shrew* cast was anything to go by Jon could well understand that there were frustrations which needed to be exorcised through the medium of something vigorous and unrefined. Nor did he object to the notion in any way; reduced to its most basic components, this was what his relationship with Callum was about – supply and demand, the atavistic requirement for functional sex. He wondered if it had ever been any more than that.

He did not have long to debate the matter, however; Callum was on him the moment he got in through the bedroom door. Mercifully the lights were switched off and the true awfulness of the décor remained hidden in the shadows; shadows which also yielded Callum, naked, hot and hairy, his body smelling of sweat and exertion and the oily odour of greasepaint.

"Come on," he grumbled, impatiently. "You're wearing far too much."

"Sorry." Jon moved quickly, his carefully–chosen outfit of pale jeans and dark sweatshirt flying item by item into the darkness, and he was scarcely out of his briefs before he was pushed to his knees on the cheap textured carpet.

"You know what I want."

"Of course." He leaned closer, took a familiar grip, prepared to do this as he had so often before. Usually in the past it had been Callum taking the receptive sexual role and indeed relishing it, giving himself up entirely, adopting a submissive attitude that at times was flirty and almost girlish. Not always, however – and now it was obviously not what he had in mind, as he held Jon's chin in one strong hand and steadily fed him pulsing flesh. This was an unprecedented demonstration of puissance; Callum tonight was entirely different, muscular, dominant, eager to demonstrate mastery over the situation and over Jon. This was Callum in control, Callum testing his limits, and it was at once a thrilling and a terrifying proposition.

Jon relaxed his jaw, letting his mouth be taken, letting himself be used without regard.

"You'd let me do this, wouldn't you?" Callum said raggedly. "You'd really let me fuck your face. Would you like me to fuck your face for you, Jonathan? You know I'd do it right."

Only an inarticulate grunt was possible in response to this, and since it could have been taken either for acceptance or refusal it seemed supremely irrelevant in the circumstances.

"You would, wouldn't you?" Callum whispered, bending as low as he could manage, his hands stroking the back of Jon's head and his neck. "You'd let me do any fucking thing to you I wanted, no matter how much you hated it."

Another grunt, but the digging–in of Jon's fingernails and the iron grip pulling Callum closer gave a less ambiguous answer. Years of vocal exercises, of opening his throat to access the deeper chest and stomach voice, of projecting all the way to the back of unsophisticated provincial theatres, finally justified themselves; he could take this unmannerly pounding without complaint, he could relax and make himself a passive vessel to receive every morsel of accumulated anger.

"Why do you have to be so fucking gentle all the time?" taunted Callum, frighteningly certain of himself. "Why do you have to be so bloody sweet? Isn't there ever anything more you want from me? Couldn't you just fucking do me really hard for once and make every bastard problem go away?"

Jon wanted to tell him that it wasn't like that, it could never be like that, he wasn't that person. He wanted to drive away the rage, to cure whatever had caused it, rather than to have to reciprocate it. If it was roughness and violence Callum wanted, he was going to have to look elsewhere; Jon just wasn't built that way. He was perfectly prepared to give until he had nothing left, but there were limits to how much he was willing to take. Then again, there was no basis for any of it; these were dangerous words, but they were words alone – there was nothing behind them except pain, exhaustion, embarrassment and the desire to expel weeks of frustration, sexual and creative, in one massive outburst of foulness. This was Callum lancing his soul, freeing himself of every poisonous thing that had built up inside him since the last time they were together. It was not surprising it was urgent, and distorted, and in its way completely vile; it was also absolutely necessary, and nothing at all to do with love.

"Bastard," growled Callum, once more, and let go into him. There was a brief sickening sensation as tension throbbed and flailed against his gullet, and then Jon gentled his grip on Callum's flesh and resumed his reassuring caresses. He wanted to say that it was all right, that he understood perfectly, that he would always be there and would be whatever Callum wanted him to be, but he did not know if he would ever be able to speak again; it had all been too apocalyptic for words to be of any significance now.

"Sweetheart?" Callum had withdrawn immediately and was already sinking to his knees, his skin cold and damp in the awfulness of the bedroom. "Are you … ?"

"Yes." It seemed his voice was working after all. "I'm fine."

"I shouldn't have … "

"You should. Of course you should."

"No."

Of all the ridiculous things that could have happened, it looked as if they were about to get involved in a playground spat about blame – if blame there was to be. Jon was at particular pains to circumvent it.

"Callum." He wondered how many times he'd actually used the boy's name in the bedroom, rather than the 'darling' which always felt more natural. "I promise you, it's all right."

"But you didn't … "

A hand slipped into Jon's groin. He had scarcely even begun to get hard, but this had never been about mutual satisfaction in the first place – merely about servicing a need.

"It's all right," he repeated.

"It isn't." Callum was shaky against him, beginning to comprehend the implications of what he'd done. What he'd said. "I can't believe I did that. I think … I think I just needed to hurt somebody, and it didn't matter who."

"Yes." Jon stroked his hair, soothed him, pulled Callum into his arms, tried to impart some measure of comfort. "We all have that inside us. Isn't it better for you to turn it on me than somebody who might be damaged by it? I'm not afraid of you." Which was a lie, of course, but what Callum needed to hear at the moment.

"Are you telling me I didn't hurt you?"

"Not really. Or at least it's nothing I won't recover from."

"You shouldn't have to. I shouldn't have done it in the first place."

Jon shook his head slowly. "Many people do worse than that in the name of love. If you'd asked me, I wouldn't have refused you – so where's the harm?"

"It isn't like me," said Callum. "I'm not an abuser."

"I know." But it was cold and uncomfortable sitting there on the floor, and the bed was close at hand. "Come on, let's get into bed and you can tell me what it is that's upsetting you. Bianca's a tart and Batista's senile, I think you said? Sounds like every theatrical company I've ever been involved with."

And he knew, with depressing clarity, that he would be scraping dried–up steak and kidney pie into the bin the following morning, and that all his meticulous preparations would be for nothing because the only thing Callum had ever really needed was to talk.

And talk he did, and Jon listened, almost until dawn. It was like a dam bursting, and all the internal politics and shenanigans of the company at the National came flooding out. Callum and Izzy had walked unwittingly into a group already at war within itself, with a director famous for changing his mind and trying things that didn't work, for pushing his actors around as if they were pieces on a chessboard and for thinking he had the right to control every aspect of their private lives as well as their conduct on stage. The story of Thea and the baby had pursued Callum to his new employment, and he had found himself dividing opinion among his fellow cast members almost equally. Some of them had sympathised, some had asked questions about Connor or demanded to see his picture, and some more down–to–earth ones had slapped him on the shoulder and called him a lucky bastard. All this had seemed like a terrible intrusion at a time when he only wanted to be left alone to get on with his work, and the situation was hardly improved when pictures of him being kissed by Bryce Gullory made their way into the papers. It was all an unholy muddle, a situation only exacerbated by the reaction of his mother to the latest burst of publicity.

"She's never off the damned phone," he said, the tension back in his voice as he spoke about her. "Twice a day at least. I've tried to persuade her to keep to regular times, but she seems to think it's her God–given right to break in on what I'm doing whenever it suits her and spend half an hour complaining about how Katy hasn't been to see her. When she phones the theatre they tell her I'll ring back as soon as I can, but she calls six or seven times in a row and shouts at them for trying to stop her talking to her son."

"That's ... " Jon was searching for a word that would not be hurtful.

"Dementia? I know it is. I'm trying to get the ball rolling to get her diagnosed, but it all seems to be happening very slowly. If it wasn't for Izzy ... " He stopped. "It's like having a big sister to look after me," he said, gratefully.

"Good."

"And then I get people who think they have the right to ask me whether I'm gay or straight," Callum went on rawly. "I played the Scottish King; that doesn't mean I go around murdering people in my spare time. Kissing a man for a movie doesn't make me gay, any more than kissing a woman makes me straight. You'd think people in the profession – of all people in the world – would get that, wouldn't you? And then my mother ... my mother ... " There was an awful hitch in his voice, a warm piteous dampness against Jon's neck, and then Callum seemed to draw himself together with tremendous effort. "My mother called me a dirty little queer," he murmured, painfully. "She said she never wanted anything more to do with me, but the simple fact is that if I don't support her she'll have nothing and nobody left to lean on. God knows where Katy and Steve are, they went up north somewhere and left her to cope on her own, and the house is an absolute tip. Auntie Ada's doing her best but she's older than my mum and she's just as baffled by it all as I am. We're going to have to find a private care home or something, and persuade my mum to go and live there – and on top of all this, eight times a week I have to march out on stage and be fuckin' brilliant or I get letters of abuse from punters who think I've ripped them off somehow, and nobody seems to care what I want at all. I'm not a selfish man, Jon, am I? I hope I'm not, anyway. But sometimes all I want to do is jump up and down and scream at the top of my voice 'Me, me, can't you see me? Where am I in all of this?' Is that what being an actor is about, do you think? Does it mean the real you has to disappear completely and nobody ever sees you for who you are any more?"

"No," said Jon, softly. "I can see you, darling boy. I still know exactly who you are."

"I know you do, love, bless your soul. And I meant what I said – you'd do just about anything for me if I asked you, wouldn't you?"

"Of course I would," acknowledged Jon. "Including walking away from you, if I thought that's what you needed."

"I don't want to need that," said Callum, stubbornly.

"No. But nobody wants to need glasses or a hip replacement either, only sometimes you just have to accept the inevitable and give in to it. Sometimes it's the only sensible thing to do."

"Not for us, though, love. We're not ready to give up yet, are we?"

"No," acknowledged Jon. "Not yet. But I'm afraid that isn't quite the same as 'never', darling, is it?"

It was like this for weeks throughout the summer – the occasional snatched few hours of closeness when all that seemed to matter was holding Callum together somehow, interspersed with late–night telephone calls freighted with stress and misery in which Jon gave as much of himself as he could and always willingly. As the year drew on, however, there was less and less to give; Ewen's illness had begun to be more apparent, and Jon and Bill were constantly fending off questions and trying to keep control of a fractious company in his increasing absence. It was a situation which could not be expected to continue for long, and Jon was constantly waiting for some official axe or other to fall on them. Management, however, seemed content to ignore everything not brought directly to their attention, as long as some kind of *modus vivendi* could be maintained. This left the responsibility squarely on Bill and Jon's shoulders, but mercifully so far it had not proved an impossible burden to carry.

When the telephone rang one Sunday afternoon close to the end of the season, however, Jon reached to answer it with a sinking heart. It could only be bad news, because it was always bad news these days. Whether it was another relapse for Ewen, the latest misadventure of Callum's mother, or the distant echo of pennies finally dropping at headquarters and shit belatedly hitting fans, he could not remotely begin to guess, but he knew he wasn't going to like it one little bit.

In this, however, he was wrong for once. Edgar Treece's voice on the other end of the line was warm and reassuring, and Jon felt as if he could have sunk down into it and soaked himself luxuriously for hours.

"Jon? How are you, old man?"

"A bit ragged," he answered, honestly. "It's been a bastard of a week." The feeling that they were approaching the endgame with Ewen had grown throughout the summer, so that even Bill was beginning to look haunted by it, and Jon was aware that he himself had lost condition too. Already painfully thin, he had managed to shed enough weight during the season to make his costume hang loosely on him and earn a few pointed stares from Maisie – although she, in common with everyone else in the company, was now aware of the significance of Ewen's illness and the strain it had loaded onto Jon and Bill. She had dedicated herself to silent support and trying not to complain about anything, but had been unable to resist a little dig on the subject of his waistline.

"Don't work yourself too hard," she counselled, and all of a sudden he'd wanted to tell her all about Callum and how afraid he was for him these days. The words had been on his lips, but he had turned away without speaking them aloud.

Edgar, however, would know nothing of any of this; this was a localised disaster affecting only their own small theatrical neighbourhood, nothing that would have held any significance in the wider world.

"I'm sorry to hear that," he said, urbanely. "Bad time to talk?"

"No," said Jon. "I'd be glad of something to take my mind off it."

"Ah. Well, then." And there was an almost audible gathering of forces at the other end of the line. "Thing is, Jon, I wondered how you were fixed for next year. Early part. Any plans in place yet?"

This was the way the question was usually phrased when it was the preliminary to an offer of some kind – gentle probing of availability and interest in the guise of friendly chit–chat. With happy memories of his time in the *Curzon* company still fresh in his mind, Jon was more than ready to consider any offer Edgar might intend to make.

"Nothing so far, no. My agent's always on the lookout for radio or telly stuff at that time of year, and I can usually pick up something or other. It tends to be a bit sporadic, though. Why do you ask? Have you got something specific in mind?"

But Edgar countered with another question. "Are you doing a summer season locally again next year?"

"Ummm … that's actually rather complicated. Things are quite fluid at the moment. I can't explain in any detail, I'm afraid."

Edgar digested this response thoughtfully. "Well," he said, "I may be about to make it all a lot more complicated for you. You see, my old chum Nigel hasn't been very well lately."

"Oh." But with death and decay seeming ever–present at the moment, this did not exactly come as a shock. "I'm sorry to hear that. Is it anything … I mean, I don't want to pry, but … "

"Kidneys," said Edgar, bluntly. "He's got to have regular dialysis, and he's going on the list for a transplant, but at his age … well, younger people tend to take priority, and that's the way it ought to be."

Recollection of Nigel's larger–than–life personality and his apparently endless goodwill surged through Jon's mind. What little he knew of chronic kidney failure seemed to indicate that it was a long drawn–out, painful and tedious business which would sap the resolve of even the most boisterous individual. Nigel must have been a lot like Callum when he was younger – frantically energetic, a finger in every pie – and the thought of him reduced to a shell by some merciless affliction was deeply depressing.

"Poor old Nigel," he said. It was impossible to know what to say, really; they were empty words which comforted neither speaker nor hearer but had to be uttered nonetheless.

"Well, yes. But he's been remarkably cheerful about it. Grateful to have kept going as long as he has, he says."

"Yes," admitted Jon, "that sounds like him."

"Absolutely. Have to bash him with a brick to kill him, I suspect. Anyway, Jon, long story short ... Nige and I have been talking about this TV project of ours, *Hawker and Duffy*. Network liked the pilot and they want to pick it up for a series, but it seems Nige isn't going to be well enough to carry on after all. He absolutely wants it to go ahead without him, though, and I wondered ... that is, we wondered ... " A deep breath, a very conscious pulling–together of his thoughts. "Jon, how would you feel about taking over from Nigel and coming in to play Father Duffy? We both think you'd be perfect for the part. In fact, you would be – you are – our first and only choice."

"Oh." He had been standing, casually, not paying much attention to his surroundings, but all of a sudden Jon was aware of having dropped forcibly into a chair and was now staring uncomprehendingly at a wall he had seen a million times before. "Are you ... s–serious?" From nowhere he had suddenly developed a stammer.

"Yes." Edgar's tone was grave. "Hard work, I'm afraid, and we film in Leeds, so you'd need to think about moving north, but I know you're a single chap so I'm hoping that might not be too much of a problem for you?"

"Um, I suppose it wouldn't." It was a startling prospect, nonetheless.

"Well, I'll talk to your agent about the fee, but I can tell you it'll be more than the pittance we paid you for *Curzon* – and I thought perhaps a couple of thousand on top might help, by way of a relocation allowance?"

"You don't need to ... "

But Edgar wasn't listening. He had a speech all prepared and he was damned well going to get every part of it out if it killed him.

"Twenty weeks a year for the next three years, renewable annually after that," he went on. "Leaves you plenty of time to take theatre parts and so forth, the rest of the year – although we'll be asking you not to do anything too similar for the duration. No more Roman Catholic priests, that is."

"I don't think I've ever ... " Jon racked his brains. He had played one or two Church of England vicars in his time, mostly in creaky old

Whitehall farces, but they tended to be comic stooges rather than serious characters. He'd never had to impersonate a clergyman in earnest before. "I'd have to learn the religious stuff," he said, weakly. "I'm not Catholic. Someone would have to show me what to do."

"Absolutely. We've got a lovely chap called Father Terence who helps us out with all that sort of thing. Did you do Latin at school?"

"Yes."

"Well, that's a start. Can I take it you might be interested, then?"

"Oh! Yes, I think so." Jon stopped. "It's all a bit sudden," he said. "I had no idea … I mean, I'm thrilled, but I need to think about it. Give me a couple of days?"

Edgar's laugh was a deep mahogany sound, rich and dark and expensive. "My dear chap, nobody's going to rush you into it – just testing the water. Let me make a formal approach through your agent, not committing you to anything, just getting things moving. See if you can get hold of a couple of the books and I'll send you a tape of the pilot and the first two or three scripts. If you like, you can chat to Nige about it as well … here, I'll give you his number." Jon scribbled the digits automatically. "Take your time. I think you're right for this, and so do Nige and Jenny. We're not going to start thinking about alternatives unless you turn us down. But not a word about Nigel's illness yet; we're not letting on until we absolutely have to – preferably not until we've cast a replacement."

"Of course."

"Are you sure you're all right?"

"Yes. I will be as soon as I've recovered, anyway. I'm really grateful for the offer," he added, almost as an afterthought. "Thank you, Eddie."

"Welcome, old thing. Call me if you've got any questions. Or Jenny – she's got all the bits and pieces at her fingertips as usual. It's going to be a wonderful team to work with, Jon; I'm sure you'd be happy if you joined us."

"I know I would," admitted Jon. "But it's a lot to take in all at once. I need to work out the implications." There was no denying that he would have relished an opportunity to talk it over with Callum, to get his advice and input, to decide with him whether or not it was a good idea – but that would have put too much pressure on Callum at a time when he was already struggling to cope. The last thing he wanted was to burden him with additional worries. "Do you mind if I mention this to Bill Wildman?" he asked. Callum might not be available, but when it came to commonsense professional advice Bill was pretty much unequalled. It would feel good to lay it all before him and hear what he had to say on the subject.

"Of course. I know you won't discuss Nigel's little problem in any detail – just say he can't commit to the project after all. Sure I can rely on you to do the right thing, old man."

"Thank you. It does sound fun," Jon added, wistfully.

"It does rather, doesn't it? And if I can't have poor old Nige along, Jon, I'd just as soon have you. Have a think about it, will you, and let me know?"

"I will, Eddie," he promised. "Thank you again."

Jon remained sitting in the chair long after the call ended, staring at the phone, wishing he had Bill to talk to, wishing Callum was somewhere he could reach him, and wishing he had a generous enough spirit not to be grateful that Nigel's infirmity had brought him such an attractive offer. If he took the job – and it would require something cataclysmic for him not to – he would have to think about making a generous donation to some kidney research charity to propitiate the Fates. Nigel's ill–luck seemed to have turned into his own good fortune; on such reverses, and on such cosmic ironies, were the foundations of classical theatre laid.

"'As flies to wanton boys are we to th' gods,'" he said, aloud. "'They kill us for their sport.'"

Bill, predictably, was enthusiastic. He went off to his room abruptly and returned brandishing a copy of *Frankincense and Murder*, the fourth *Hawker and Duffy* mystery.

"Got the first three somewhere," he said, vaguely. "Probably at home, or I might have lent them to somebody, but this one's as good a place to start as any. This is the one where Duffy finds a dead man in his confessional one morning."

Jon's eyebrows climbed, and he took the volume cautiously. "Do you know the books well?"

Bill chuckled, aware of what he was really asking. "Well enough to know you're ideal casting," he admitted. "If Nigel's name hadn't been attached to the part from the beginning I'd've been trying to talk you into going for it. Nigel's probably a bit too old, actually – Duffy does have some fairly active stuff to do. He cycles everywhere, for a start, and if I remember rightly he's got to shove a door in with his shoulder in one of the books – it might even be this one. And he's supposed to have done a bit of boxing in his youth."

"Does he have a first name?" asked Jon.

"Fergus," came the crushing response. "But I don't suppose you'll have to do it with an Irish accent. I can't imagine Nigel used one in the pilot, did he?"

"I haven't seen it yet. Eddie's sending it over."

"Good. Well, don't make your mind up 'til you've watched it, but I can't think of a single reason why you'd want to turn this down."

"I'd have to move to Leeds," Jon reminded him, smiling. "And, as you say, I'd have to play a man called 'Fergus'."

"Bummer," smiled Bill. "Well, in that case, mate, you should avoid it like the plague, of course."

Given the circumstances, the light–hearted mood could hardly have been expected to last. Although they were close enough to the end of the run now to have a reasonable hope of surviving without major disasters, it was plain to the entire company that this would be their last season with Ewen – knowledge solidified when he announced his intention of submitting his resignation. The fact that he had already begun to make plans for the next summer's production, and took substantial pains to convey every nuance of them to Bill and Jon as if he saw them as his natural successors, seemed like either fatalism or the most lunatic optimism – especially as Jon had already reached the private determination that he would not be returning to the company at that time.

He watched the *Hawker and Duffy* pilot several times in succession in his upstairs sitting room, once in company with Bill and half a dozen bottles of beer, most often alone. He particularly enjoyed the way Edgar's tweedy geniality gave way suddenly to steely analytical comment, and was delighted to note that Nigel had not made Duffy the kind of wide–eyed adoring sidekick it would be impossible to play. There was a certain amount of character development there already; Duffy was unworldly, naïf perhaps, and always tried to see the best in people, but he had the capacity for leaps of intuition which Hawker came to value. Most encouragingly of all, Nigel had managed to get out of the way in the pilot an awkward sequence which had the two men graduating to the use of their first names; it was a relief not to have to utter the words "Call me Fergus" and try to keep a straight face while doing so.

"Are you going to be around next year?" he asked Bill, idly, as the closing credits rolled.

"Probably. If whoever takes over decides to keep to Ewen's plan, I could end up playing Prospero; must admit I've always fancied having a crack at that."

"Yes, me too, one day."

"Slippery slope, though. You do Prospero, then you do Lear, and the next thing you know you're being wheeled on in a bathchair to play Priam in *Troilus*, with a beard right down to your knees. There's no going back after that."

"All the same," mused Jon, "working's got to be better than not working. I take it you won't be applying for Ewen's job, then, Bill?"

Bill snorted. "God no. One season of helping out with it was enough for me, thank you! Christ knows how you kept your temper with some of those little bastards, Jon; I should think you'd be in line for a sainthood one of these days."

Jon laughed. "Plenty of practice," he said. "Working with Callum."

"Ah, yes. If you can keep a lid on him, I should think you can keep a lid on anybody. Isn't he supposed to be doing the second season of *Robin Hood* fairly shortly, by the way? The first one turned out rather well, I thought."

"It did, actually," Jon conceded. "Yes, they start in a couple of weeks' time, but he'll have to fit it in at weekends because he'll still be playing Petruchio in London during the week. Roy was telling me the other day they're doing most of the recording on Sundays and Mondays this time, just to accommodate Callum."

"Ouch. That sounds like bloody hard work, but I suppose it won't be for long."

"No. And they must be making it worth his while or he wouldn't do it."

Bill's nod indicated agreement. "No doubt about that. Didn't fancy getting involved in it yourself, then?"

"Wasn't offered," answered Jon. "Not sure what I could play, really. Sundry peasants with Mummerset accents, I suppose. Just as well; it doesn't leave me with any contracts I need to get out of if I take on the Duffy thing."

"Which you will, of course, be doing?" Bill's eyes had narrowed and his inflection was melodramatically heavy.

"Yes. My agent wants all the t's crossed and all the i's dotted, but once we've got the paperwork sorted out I'll be happy to sign it. In fact," he admitted, ruefully, "it would've had to be a much worse part for me to think about turning it down; I need the money. A couple of good years in something that pays at a decent scale and I can be financially secure for the first time in my life. I can buy a house, and I might even be able to fund a pension. Plus my daughter's getting to the age now where I ought to start thinking about university for her. She's twelve," he added, in response to an enquiring look. "She wants to be an archaeologist."

"Good God. My two louts are fourteen and sixteen and neither of them's manifested any sign of possessing a brain cell yet. The only thing Sam ever wants to do is play rugby, and Brendan thinks they'll take him in the RAF with nothing more than a certificate for woodwork and a charming smile. They probably will, too. But their mother and I are planning to call it a day," he added, matter–of–factly. "We just can't stand the sight of one another any more. She likes it far too much when I'm away on tour; I've thought for a while that she might have a fancy man, but the truth is I don't actually care a great deal whether she does or not." He stopped. "Maybe I should just move in here permanently, Jon. What do you think?"

Jon was staring at him in open–mouthed astonishment. "You know what, Bill? I think you probably should."

It seemed to Jon, whenever he thought about it later, that work had really been the only thing still attaching Ewen to life; with that solitary anchor removed, he no longer had any reason to stay. Jon went to see him once or twice in hospital, sat beside the bed and made notes as Ewen drifted in and out of consciousness under the influence of massive doses of painkillers, knowing that he would never again see the world outside his stuffy room. The notes he made were mostly nonsense, inspired by drug–induced ramblings, but sometimes there were threads of insight in them. Jon noted them all, content to allow Ewen the illusion that even in his last days he was contributing something to the company and the profession which had dominated his career. At the end, when Ewen's sister phoned to say that he had gone, Jon bundled up the notes and handed them over to Bill.

"You might find a use for them," he said, bleakly, and went off to call Pete and Roy.

"Oh, shut the fuck up," said Roy when he answered. "Not you, Jon, the bloody dog. Peter, darling, will you please take the wretched thing outside?" It always boded trouble when Pete was addressed as 'Peter' – which, after all, was not his name. It indicated that all was – at least temporarily – not well within one of the longest–established relationships Jon was aware of. "They're both getting on my nerves," Roy vouchsafed, confirming the theory. "Is it Ewen?" he asked, when the mayhem in the background had subsided to a tolerable level.

"Yes. He died last night. The funeral's on Monday morning."

"Ah, good," said Roy. "I mean, 'good because that means we'll be able to go'. We could bring Callum with us, if you like?"

"Callum?" Stupidly he repeated the name. He had been thinking of Callum as safely elsewhere, as not connected with Ewen's death in any way, but of course he would want to be informed about it. He would also want to attend the funeral if he possibly could, and therefore they would be seeing one another soon. They might even sit side by side in the church. At some stage he would have to tell Callum about Edgar's offer, too, and what he intended to do about it, and in the back of his mind was the notion that Callum would probably not approve. It was not real drama, it was series television, and he felt like a mercenary doing it solely for the money.

"Callum. You can't have forgotten about him, Jon, surely?"

"No, but ... I've been a bit preoccupied lately."

"Of course you have." Roy, too, seemed somewhat distracted. Perhaps he was looking out of the big gable–end window of the Fardels sitting room, watching Pete and the unknown dog capering about in the yard. One of them would be throwing a ball and the other one would be catching it, although he did not like to speculate which was which; Pete and a dog would no doubt enjoy one another's company immensely. "Was it awful?" asked Roy, his tone sympathetic.

"Not really. Not for me. It was for Ewen, of course. But it was mercifully quick in the end. He just ... stopped."

A respectful silence followed. "Was it the fags, do you think?" asked Roy, bluntly.

"Probably. They certainly wouldn't have helped."

"No, they wouldn't. So, Monday morning? I'll ring Jeremy and get him to organise a day off from *Robin Hood*. He might come with us, actually; I think he's interested in applying for Ewen's job."

"The poor man isn't even in his grave yet," protested Jon, mildly outraged.

"I know, dear boy. But it's a dog–eat–dog world out there, isn't it? The bigger a bitch you are, the closer you get to the top."

"Meaning?"

"Meaning ... on that basis alone, young Bracegirdle's heading for the heights of his profession. God help you, Jon, if you ever get on the wrong side of him; he doesn't believe in taking prisoners."

"I'll bear that in mind," said Jon, more grateful than ever for Edgar's intervention in his life.

◆

Monday morning started out surprisingly sunny for the time of year, but there was a cold breeze blowing. Sitting squashed in a church pew with Maisie and her husband, Jon was at least able to concentrate on making a proper farewell to Ewen. Bill had not been able to attend as he had long–standing business in Cardiff connected with his divorce; Izzy had remained in London with Catherine, taking meetings about their Brontë project, and Jeremy Bracegirdle had mercifully not put in an appearance. Otherwise all the usual suspects were in attendance – Rory and Jax sitting apart, Douggie Pirie skulking at the back as if expecting the spire to collapse on top of him at any moment, James Rudge and Matthew Linton the lutenist serious and self–contained together in a way that made Jon wonder whether there was anything he had missed concerning them. Not that he cared, in particular; other people's lives were other people's business. If he spared any attention for anyone other than Ewen and his immediate family, it was only for Callum. He was in the row behind, with Pete and Roy, providing the filling in the sandwich – or perhaps a buffer zone between two warring states, because all certainly did not seem to be well in that establishment. Sometimes, during the hymns, when Jon was trying to think about the words and what they meant, there would be just a hint of Callum's lighter tones audible against the baritone bellowing of his companions. Callum could sing all right, but not to the standard of those two heavyweights; with a couple of West End musicals behind them, Roy and Pete were inclined to assume the starring role whenever vocal talent was required – and even, and most especially, when it was not. There was something quite poignant about it all, as if Callum were a child drowned out by overbearing parents. Jon could well imagine that when he stayed with them he didn't have very much say in ... well, anything at all, actually.

Afterwards they gathered in the churchyard, with Roy obviously in impatient mood.

"We won't be going to the crematorium," he said, with one of his lordly gestures. "We don't want to leave the dog on his own any longer than we have to. Not only will he howl the bloody place down without us, but he's quite likely to eat the furniture too – and some of it was actually rather expensive."

Jon looked at him blankly. He remembered thinking that he ought to have asked them to explain the dog, but the past week had been so awful that none of his memories of it really fitted together any more – and very little of it made any sense to him even when they did.

"Well, I'd like to go," said Callum. "Can I hitch a ride with you, Jon?"

"Of course. I can drop you back at Fardels later."

"Thanks." But Pete was already swinging his car keys around on his index finger and trying to drag Roy away by force of personality, and a moment later the pair of them were striding across the church car park, barely nodding to sundry theatrical acquaintances as they passed.

"Dog?" asked Jon, numbly watching them go.

"Stupid black thing," Callum supplied absently. "Some relative of Roy's is in hospital and they're looking after it for her. It takes Pete for a lot of long walks; Roy says they go out worrying sheep together."

Jon chuckled, feeling rather out–of–place considering the occasion, but as usual with a funeral once the formal business was over there were all sorts of conversations breaking out among the mourners and very few of them had anything to do with the deceased. Most people were even now sorting themselves out for the journey to the crematorium; the hearse had left already, so had the vicar in his modest hatchback, and various black–clad women were marshalling the rest of the congregation into cars.

"Come for a walk," said Callum, tugging at Jon's arm and indicating the churchyard. "I want to talk to you. It isn't the best time, I know, but it may be ages before we get another opportunity."

Jon glanced at the crowd in the car park. He should really go to the crematorium, and then back to Ewen's house to drink dry sherry and eat ham sandwiches and say something fitting to the family. He could surely find some means of not saying that Ewen had destroyed himself slowly with smoking and stress, because they knew that well enough already. But the alternative was Callum ...

"All right," he agreed, and let himself be led away.

◆

They sauntered idly at first, as if they were inspecting tombstones. *Clarence Walsh, 1873; Hester McMahon, 1904;* overgrown, decorated with green cullet, windmills and dead chrysanthemums. Nobody glanced in their direction, and eventually they ducked around the corner of the church and were hidden from sight by the fold of a buttress.

"They'll never realise we're not there," Callum said, optimistically. "Come on, let's sit on the bench."

The one really grand tomb at this side of the Poets' Church was provided with its own little yew arbour, and in the arbour was a bench. The grass around it was wet; they slogged through it scattering fallen raindrops in every direction.

"Oh God," groaned Callum as they dropped into the seat. "That place will never be the same without Ewen, will it?" He nodded towards the grey roof of the theatre, starkly visible beyond the trees.

"He's been there a very long time," Jon murmured, conventionally.

"It must have been tough for you and Bill. You were the only ones who really knew how ill he was, weren't you, almost to the end?"

"Of the company, yes. I don't know what he told his family."

"No, of course not." Callum sighed. "Roy and Pete didn't have a clue until he put in his resignation, but you know how wrapped up they always are in their own business. They seem to think JB's going after Ewen's job – you know, Jeremy Bracegirdle, the guy who's producing us in *Robin Hood*? I gather he's blotted his copybook at the BBC. Had an affair with the wrong person or something."

"Really?"

"Swings both ways, apparently – and, before you ask, no, I have no idea whether the other half in this case was male or female. Either way, it wasn't the best possible manoeuvre, career–wise."

"No." Jon reached across and took his hand, scarcely surprised when it remained limp beneath his fingers. "You don't really want to talk about them though, do you, any of them? Not even Ewen."

"No," admitted Callum. "Actually, I don't."

"You want to talk about us."

"Yes." A troubled inhalation, and then without looking at him

Callum said, "It's possible we might have reached the end of the road, darling, at least for now."

Jon looked away. "I can't say I'm surprised." Somehow he managed to remain absolutely calm, as if the face of stoicism he had gradually assumed throughout the season was protecting him from all emotion. "It's been horrible lately, hasn't it?"

"It has. I've felt like a criminal, meeting you in all those awful places and never having any proper time together – and I'm sure it isn't doing either of us any good. This movie star business has got completely out of hand – I never wanted any of it to happen, although I must admit I was quite interested in the money."

"I know. But I keep seeing you interviewed in newspapers and magazines and I think you're coping beautifully."

"Thank you, darling. I hope I am. But it feels wrong to drag you through it all, to make you hide away and come running after me to strange and remote locations in the hope that we might get a few days of peace and quiet to ourselves. In any case I can't seem to relax any more, and I'm beginning to wonder if maybe we're in danger of forgetting why we started all this in the first place – the pleasure of each other's company. It's almost becoming … too much like hard work," he completed, with a regretful groan.

"Oh dear." Jon considered the words for a while, clinging steadily to Callum's unresponsive hand. "Yes," he said at last, "I see how that could be a problem. What do you think we ought to do about it?"

"Let each other go," sighed Callum, sounding firm but unutterably miserable. "I can't see any alternative. If we end this now, while we still have happy memories, we can both look back on it afterwards as something positive we shared – not something that looked as if it was going to destroy the pair of us completely."

"I never imagined that it would," corrected Jon. "But I've told you before – you only have to ask. The last thing I ever want to do is hold you back."

It was a long time before Callum found an answer to this, and when he did he seized Jon's hand and squeezed it almost brutally. "You're too good for me, you know? You always have been."

"I suspected as much," was the determinedly upbeat response. "So, what exactly are your plans?"

"Nothing much. Stay where I am for the time being, finish the awful bloody *Shrew*, do *Deadfall* in the summer, see what's available after that. I'm not short of offers, but there's nothing really exciting happening at the moment. Lenny thinks I ought to try Hollywood, and I could certainly get plenty of work over there. It's just a question of finding the right project, as usual."

"Good. Then I promise I'll go to all your movies on the day they open."

"You'll hate them. They're all going to be as crap as *Leichhardt* was."

"*Leichhardt* wasn't crap. It was just too intellectual for some people's tastes."

"Yes, well, by the time *Planetfall* opens I'll probably be grateful to be offered a stereotyped British villain in some cheesy daytime soap. Honestly, I have a feeling I'm going to be box–office poison the moment people see that kiss with Bryce – but there's a part of my mind thinking it would be no bad thing after all."

"Well, you can always come back here and play bit–parts," consoled Jon, feeling a weight lifting from his shoulders as he spoke. "I'm sure JB would give you the occasional walk–on if you asked him nicely."

"He would, too," was the morose response. "And that's probably about all he'd give me, too, unless I'm willing to get my knickers off for him." But the forbidding expression on Callum's face discouraged any further enquiries on the subject. "What about you, now that Ewen's gone? Are you staying on? And what's Bill planning, do you know?"

"He's coming back, actually. Towards the end Ewen was talking about him doing Prospero next year – and unless the new director cancels that … "

"Unlikely, don't you think? *The Tempest* always goes down well."

"It does. Anyway, Bill's going to be moving into my quarters at the Old Crown. I haven't had time to tell you about it yet, but I've been offered the chance to take over Nigel Carlyle's part in *Hawker and Duffy*."

"Good grief, really? I didn't know Nigel was leaving! But that's wonderful, Jon – what a fantastic break for you! You are going to take it, aren't you?"

"Yes, I am. I've already signed the contract."

"Good man! That sort of thing is the Holy Grail in our job, the one thing everybody in the business is always after – one halfway–decent TV series and you could be set up for life."

"Assuming it lasts," Jon reminded him cautiously. "These things are always a bit of a gamble."

"Not with you and Edgar in it; there isn't the remotest chance of the bloody thing not lasting!"

Jon did not choose to remind him of all the ways in which a speculative project like this might go wrong. "It's based in Leeds," he said instead. "I'll have to move there, but I should have just about enough money to buy a house now that the flat's been sold."

"Your own place," Callum enthused. "How great would that be? No more living in other people's rooms, no more second–hand furniture!"

"Oh, I wouldn't go quite that far," smiled Jon. "I'll have to start from scratch, after all. But in due course I might treat myself to some new stuff, if everything works out well. And if I've got a place of my own," he added wistfully, "I can have Justine to stay with me sometimes."

"Of course you can, love. That's got to be something to look forward to, hasn't it?"

"It has. Although I must admit … the price I'm paying does seem to be rather high." His fingers stroked slowly, tenderly, across Callum's palm, and they looked into one another's eyes for a moment and unsurprisingly discovered that they were both fighting back tears.

"Blood's thicker than water," Callum choked. "Put her first. Promise you won't think about me at all."

"You say that as if you thought it would be easy," complained Jon.

"I don't," admitted Callum. "But I bet you'll learn to do it, all the same."

Later, when he looked back on that time, Jon could never be quite sure which had been the exact moment of their breaking–up. It might have been that conversation in the churchyard when Callum dropped his bombshell, or the actual physical parting a short time afterwards when Callum stumped off to get a cup of coffee and waste a couple of hours in town before taking a taxi out to Fardels, or the moment two weeks later when an exchange of parcels had been completed and Jon realised with no very great surprise that he seemed to have lost his favourite nubbly green sweater and acquired instead a hideous heliotrope tee–shirt.

The day after that, the same florist's van once again pulled up in the car park of the New Crown. The same delivery man crossed the road with an armful of multi–coloured roses.

Jon received them, smiling cordially, and went to put them in water. He searched them thoroughly for a card and found that, as he had expected, there was none.

Later that morning he took the roses next door and gave them to Karen. He kissed her affectionately on the cheek in parting, grabbed up his overnight bag, and set off for Leeds to start looking for a house.

◆

(The basement kitchen of a house in Yorkshire. The windows are high and small under a vaulted brick ceiling, but darkness and rain can be seen outside; it is Easter, 1999. JON and JUSTINE are sitting at the table eating a meal.)

♦

"So what's it like playing a Catholic priest, then?" asked Justine, around a mouthful of treacle sponge. "Do you feel all holy and stuff, and do you have to be really good all the time?"

Jon had collected his daughter from the station only a few hours previously and was still marvelling at her safe arrival unaccompanied, although once her mother had put her on the train and virtually strapped her into a first–class seat there were not a great many places she could have gone. He was also trying to work out whether she was his daughter after all or possibly some sort of change–ling, but determinedly set that puzzle aside to give her question mature consideration.

"It is a bit odd," he admitted, thoughtfully. "I suppose it's like any part, really – you spend a lot of time working out what you can do and what you can't. I mean, most people probably think religion's quite serious – even a bit dull – but that doesn't mean the people who practise it can't have any fun."

"No," shrugged Justine. "I get that. Not 'no fun', just 'no sex'."

"Well, yes. I mean, no." Jon laughed awkwardly. He tried to imagine himself at the age of thirteen having a conversation with an adult which included the word 'sex' and found that it just wouldn't work. In fact at her age he wasn't sure he'd been aware of what his parents' generation had described as 'the facts of life' at all. His own discoveries along those lines had been furtive, almost accidental, whereas he supposed Justine had probably received a full technical briefing with PowerPoint slides and very possibly practical demonstrations as well, and he didn't know whether to envy her or be slightly horrified.

"So what does he do for fun, then, your man?" she was asking, oblivious to his confusion.

"Well, I'm sure it's nothing anybody your age would enjoy." His tone was almost apologetic. "He doesn't go to discos or anything." He hoped kids still did that; trying to work out what the interests of a teenager might be these days had left him feeling positively antediluvian. Justine was patently no longer a chubby–faced little girl with little girl interests; she seemed to have changed almost overnight into something as leggy and wayward as a foal, with straight copper–coloured hair to her shoulders and large clear blue–grey eyes which saw a little more than he would have liked them to. If he had expected to be able to deal with her on the same superficial level he had previously employed during a hundred hot and expensive days out – pacifying her with ice cream, cheeseburgers and cuddly toys – he was obviously doomed to disappointment: this version of his daughter was more challenging than he had expected. Fortunately, however, Rosemary had given him a lot of information about Justine's likes, dislikes and other personal foibles – enough ammunition for him to be moderately confident he could keep her entertained over the Easter break at least. "He might organise them, though," he conceded. "He does work with a city centre boys' club."

"Hmmm. Well, does he do any kind of sport?"

"He plays cricket. He coaches boxing. He jogs."

"Oh, tragic!" Her face contorted into a disapproving smile. "He really is a bit of a saddo, then, isn't he, Dad?"

"I suppose he probably is," he conceded. "Although in a lot of ways I think he's admirable. You know I don't share his religious faith, but I do envy him the certainty of something to give his life a purpose."

Justine had stopped eating and put down her spoon. "That makes sense, I suppose. I mean, it would be nice to think we all had a purpose, but I'm never sure how much religion helps. Isn't it better if we just think things out for ourselves?"

He was somewhat taken aback. The last time they were together she had been talking non–stop about a band called Steps and had somehow bullied him into taking her to see them; that was what had made him question whether she was really his child at all or had just arrived from some planet newly in contact with Earth. To have gone from pre–teen idiocy to abstract philosophical musings in only a few months struck him as remarkable, but he imagined there was no real reason why growing–up should happen gradually; there might very well be sudden and unexpected leaps along the way.

"You could be right," he admitted, letting her see how impressed he was. "Although there are some people who would call that anarchy."

She grimaced. "I know. But Jake says if we have minds we ought to use them properly or they'll stop working altogether."

"Jake? Do I know Jake?"

Justine grimaced. "He's really Mr Jacobs, our new English teacher. We do Rupert Brooke and stuff with him." The casual, off hand way she spoke indicated that this was of supreme importance to her.

"Oh, good. I didn't realise you liked poetry. Does he make it interesting?"

"Yes, he does. He reads it like he understands it, like it actually means something. Before him, we had Cruella de Vil – Miss Russell; her real name's 'Celia' but we called her Cruella. She made everything sound like a shopping list. You know …

Half a league – and –
Half a league – and –
Half a league – and …
Onward!

Like it was the ingredients for a pudding or something. Mum says she Left Under A Cloud, and that's when we got Jake – which is great because you can really get what he's talking about. And he didn't laugh about me wanting to be an archaeologist, either." The implication was clear: the unsympathetic Miss Russell had been dismissive of Justine's dearly–held ambition.

"I'm glad about that," he said, sincerely. "It must help to have an inspirational teacher." Although his own school days were a long way behind him now, he could not quite keep an edge of envy out of his tone.

"Why?" she asked. "Didn't you?"

"I'm afraid not. I went to a school that distrusted art and poetry, and they only managed to bring themselves to teach Shakespeare by crushing all the life out of him. We stuck to the histories, and only the boring bits of those. I think if I'd ever hinted that I wanted to be an actor I might have been thrown out on my ear."

"Goodness! How on earth did you end up going on the stage, then?"

He smiled wistfully. "I was very shy," he said. "My mother sent me to verse–speaking classes to 'bring me out of myself', and it just sort of grew from there. My father never liked it, though. He thought it would make me grow up to be some sort of softie."

Justine's narrow face twisted again. "Poor you. Mum says you're really only a bit pathetic these days. She says you used to be a whole lot worse, which is why she put you in her books in the first place."

"Pathetic?" It was not as if this was a new accusation, but hearing it from Justine came as something of a shock.

"I don't know, thick or wet or something. She said she never really knew who you were or what you wanted out of life, and she didn't think you did either. She said you liked to drift and let things happen to you; you never went out and tried to make things happen for yourself."

"Oh." He digested the words carefully. "She's probably right. I'm not the sort of person who makes things happen; I must admit, I do like a quiet life. But coming here has shaken me up a bit," he admitted. "I'm out of my rut and I've got a lot of new challenges to deal with. Maybe it'll do me some good."

"I think it has already," his daughter opined confidently. "You've got a better hair cut, for a start – and that awful beard's gone, too. Is that how vicars are supposed to look?"

"He's a priest, not a vicar," corrected Jon amiably. "And I don't think there's a regulation style – although they should be neat and tidy, of course."

"And behave themselves," she reminded him, grinning.

"I know. I'll have to curb my riotous lifestyle, won't I? Cut down on the parties, the drinking and the women?"

"It'll be a strain, Dad, I know, but it'll do you good in the long run."

He laughed. "Your mum warned me you were a cheeky monkey," he told her, affectionately. In fact Rosemary's six pages of notes had pointedly included the word 'outspoken', which he had found amusing at the time and was enjoying even more now that he came to experience it for himself. It was as if he and his daughter had never really relaxed together before, and were starting to learn about one another for the first time. She was a revelation, and he was quietly delighted and not a little proud of her.

"I take after her," was the waspish response. "I'm a chip off the old block, everybody says so."

"You're not going to write books about me too, are you?" he asked, pretending to suspect her intentions.

"I don't know yet," came the judicious answer. "It all depends on whether you do anything to deserve it."

They were watching television when the next bombshell hit. They had both expected the classic comedy film to be as good as all the critics said it was, but unfortunately each had been disappointed in a different way. Justine managed to conceal her restlessness nobly, however, almost until the denouement. Then she betrayed her wandering thoughts with the remark, apparently apropos of absolutely nothing, "You know you're going to be a TV series, don't you? Finn, I mean. They're making him for ITV, with Rory Cooper playing you. Mum says he looks nearly as gormless as you did when she first knew you. She said I ought to warn you so it wouldn't come as too much of a shock."

"No, I didn't know about that." After all, he had never had any involvement in the books except inspiring them, and the incidents in them were not drawn so closely from life as to be actionable. Privately he had always thought of them as exquisitely attenuated revenge for whatever it was he had done to disappoint Rosemary – which must have been pretty much everything. "I expect your mum's pleased? She should get a tidy sum out of the television rights."

"She will. She says we can have a big holiday somewhere when the money comes through. Maybe Florida or the Caribbean or somewhere really hot. I'm not all that bothered about sitting around on beaches any more, though. I think I've probably outgrown that sort of thing."

"Well, you ought to go somewhere that's got archaeology as well," he suggested idly. "Greece or Italy perhaps?" It had begun to occur to him that his daughter's chosen subject was something he knew little about, despite having once been in a production of *Death on the Nile*. He was going to have to do some reading if he wanted to be able to communicate with her.

"Or Turkey or Egypt," she chipped in. "I know. Anywhere but bloody Florida. Tell me the best place you've ever been to on holiday?"

Jon thought about that for a long time. "I went to Portofino," he said at last. "I loved it there, even though it was in the middle of winter. It's still the best holiday I've ever had."

"Italy," nodded Justine approvingly, and he did not take the trouble to correct her. "Yes, that would work. I'll have to see if I can talk Mum into taking me there instead." But mercifully the film was re–engaging her attention and she let the topic lapse, and for a while after that Jon sat staring at the screen and thinking about something else, and wondering if he had taken leave of his senses altogether.

It was five months since he and Callum had seen one another or even spoken. There had been an exchange of Christmas cards, of course … lavish and eccentric from Callum, tasteful and almost formal from himself … and then Jon's change–of–address card had obviously caught up with Callum wherever he was, and roses had followed on the day after he moved in. Not that he had ended up needing to transport much stuff from Shapley, although Bill had kindly obliged by borrowing Rory's clapped–out old van and helping with the shifting. It had been mostly boxes of books. The outgoing residents of the new house were emigrating and had been happy enough to sell off much of their furniture as part of the deal.

Just as well, really; Jon had been plunged headlong into a shooting schedule on *Hawker and Duffy* which left little time for shopping, and the prices in some of the city centre shops had made his eyes water.

That sort of thing would have to be postponed until at least the end of June, when the first season should be nicely in the can and he would have a chance to get to know his new surroundings properly. For now, though, he – and Justine, and the occasional visitor – would manage with what they had.

But apart from the Christmas card and the roses there had been no contact whatsoever with Callum. *Planetfall* had opened over the festive season to the usual razzmatazz; a glorious over–the–top gala première in New York had made it into most of the newspapers and even some TV news broadcasts, so that for an uncomfortable forty–eight hours or so Jon had barely been able to turn around without coming face to face with Callum's cheesy grin or the raised waving hand which showed off little green house–shaped cufflinks holding together a shirtsleeve that was undoubtedly silk. Less comfortable still, he had been accompanied by a vacuous–looking Izzy in a floor–sweeping burgundy gown, every inch the celebrity fashion–plate such an event required a female companion to be. For a serious Shakespearean actress to allow herself to be viewed as arm–candy was a development Jon had hardly been expecting; his response to seeing her draped languidly over Callum and fluttering her eyelashes ditzily for the paparazzi had been the closest he ever came to uncouth – but whether he had been outraged for her professional dignity or quietly seething with jealousy at her proximity to Callum was a question he studiously did not examine.

He had meant what he said about standing aside and letting Callum continue to the top without him. He had meant it sincerely, and he knew in his heart it was the right thing to do, but there had been times since – especially on the first night alone in his cold new millstone grit cottage a hundred miles from everything he knew – when he had seriously questioned his own sanity. That night he would have had Callum back at any price – ambitions, neuroses, inconsistencies, betrayals, heartbreak and all. He had never felt so lonely in his life before; there were no doves in the garden, no neighbours at home, no friends within reach, and the heating was not working. He had hunched in the darkness beneath an inadequate duvet cuddling a hot–water bottle, contemplating cold cereal for breakfast and the prospect of having to shovel snow off the path in the morning, and had wondered whether he was making the worst mistake of his life. Then he had thought back over all the other mistakes he had ever made and come to the conclusion that he was still only lurching from one disaster to another, and that nothing had really changed for him at all.

And, the following day, there had been two dozen multi–coloured roses from Callum. He had sat and cried over them for a solid fifteen minutes before making himself a comforting cup of tea and going outside again to finish gritting the path.

Justine was starting to think about going to bed an hour or so later when the telephone rang.

"Oh, I bet that's Mum," she said, heavily. "Checking up on me. Like you wouldn't have called her ages ago if there had been a problem." She rolled her eyes comically, making it clear that in her book legitimate adult concern was just another name for fussing.

Privately Jon agreed with her and did not approve of being monitored quite so closely, which was the thought uppermost in his mind as he answered.

"Oh good, you are there!" Jon's heart sank into his boots as Callum's bright voice came clearly from the other end of the line. It would have been an ominous coincidence, except that Jon had been spending a good deal of time thinking about him lately and the odds were not exactly spectacular. Callum was speaking loudly enough to combat something noisy in the background, an amplified, distorted voice and the sound of passing footsteps on a hard floor. "Listen, I'm in Sheffield, I can be at your house in an hour and a half if that's okay? Don't say 'no', Jon, please … I need to see you. It's important."

"Well, yes, but … "

"Good man! I must rush, the train's in already. I'll see you later!"

"Wait a minute … "

But the phone had crashed down, and Jon was left listening to the disconnection tone and staring distractedly at Justine across the kitchen table.

"Anything wrong?" she asked, sounding uncannily like her mother always had in moments of crisis.

"No, I don't think so." He was trying to control emotions he could not even name. "That was a friend of mine; he's coming over later on to talk to me. I suppose he might want to stop the night, so you'll probably see him in the morning."

"Oh. Where is he going he sleep?"

"In the library. I'll make up a bed for him on the sofa."

"Library!" Justine laughed. "It's not a library, it hasn't got any books in it; you just think that sounds posh!"

He smiled. "The books are in there all right. I haven't unpacked them yet, that's all."

"Well until you do you can't call it a library, can you? It's a storeroom. Your friend will have to sleep in the storeroom."

"All right," replied Jon, dutifully. "I'll tell him that. I'm sure he'll be thrilled."

If he had expected it to be difficult to persuade Justine to go to bed after this revelation, he had underestimated his daughter. She was no longer six years old and her curiosity had been tempered with something which began to look like patience. She could wait, and he would either tell her all about it in the morning or he would not. At any rate she took herself off to bed in good order – and although he suspected that she was listening to music long after lights–out it was not something that particularly concerned him as long as she was happy. It wasn't as if either of them had to get up early in the morning, for a change.

He tidied the kitchen and cleared the boxes from the couch in what would eventually be his library. That was about as far as he was prepared to go until Callum made his requirements known; making up a bed for him in advance would be, as Justine's voice was telling him all too clearly in his head, 'just sad', and he did not want to be gulled into any false assumptions about Callum's plans in case disappointment followed. However there was no denying that he was longing to see his darling boy again, absence having worked its usual insidious magic.

When he was ready, he went and sat in the lounge with the lights off. If Callum was coming by train he would get a taxi up from the station and it would be easy enough to watch for it and open the door without him having to ring the bell – and thereby minimise the chances of waking Justine. It was not that he was anxious to conceal Callum's presence from her, but the less complicated explaining he had to do the better he would feel.

Of course he would hardly have known where to start, even explaining it all to himself. He had just about reconciled himself to a life which didn't include Callum Henley; he had thought he was beginning to settle in to his new circumstances, although he missed what had previously passed for his social life. Edgar, Nigel and Jenny were concerned to fill in some of the gaps for him, however, and the fact that actually being a home–owner had moved him up far enough in Rosemary's estimation to allow for a proper visit from Justine was a blessing. He could put down roots here, he felt, depending on how long the series lasted and what other work might come along in the interim. There was really no need to keep on looking backwards, or to concern himself at all with whatever Callum might be getting up to in his absence.

Which only went to show, he told himself ruefully as he watched the taxi turning into the lower end of the street, precisely how naïf he had always been. The only thing he should ever have expected from Callum was the unexpected.

The car pulled up outside a little before 11.30, and Jon took a deep breath and threw open the door. It was raining again, as it had been earlier. Callum was swathed in a large coat and hat and fell through the doorway carrying a travelling–bag exactly as he always had when they were living together at the Old Crown.

"Hello, darling, I'm so glad to see you!"

Jon shushed him and disentangled the damp arm which had draped itself insistently around his neck. "My daughter's upstairs," he said, abruptly. "Asleep, I fervently hope."

"Oh? Oh!" Callum paused. "You should have warned me on the phone."

"You didn't give me a great deal of time to say anything, did you?"

"No. I was too afraid you might say 'no'. You would have done, wouldn't you, if I'd let you have a chance?" Callum ran a hand across his face. "Stupid, as usual. I'm always getting it wrong these days."

Jon felt a momentary twinge of sympathy for him. Much was expected from Callum in professional terms, but on a personal level he still sometimes showed himself as an insecure boy only superficially coping with the adult world.

"Well, you're here now," he said, warmly. "And I'm not about to chuck you out on a night like this. And I haven't thanked you for the roses yet, by the way."

"What? Oh – when you moved in here, do you mean?"

"Yes … and the ones before that, too."

Callum shifted from foot to foot nervously. "Least I could do," he said. "In the circumstances. Look, do you mind if I take my coat off? I'm dripping all over your nice clean carpet."

There was a moment of indecision, and then Jon steeled himself for the challenge. "Come down to the kitchen; I'll make us a coffee and we can talk without disturbing Justine."

"Thank you, love. Appreciate it. Downstairs, eh?"

"In the basement," supplied Jon, leading the way.

"Unusual," smiled Callum, following obediently.

In the brighter light of the kitchen it was possible to see properly what Jon had only briefly glimpsed before, that not only had Callum's hair been cropped so close to the scalp as to be little more than a short blond stubble, but the skin around his eyes was pale and puffy, and the eyes themselves seemed to have sunk into a crazily distorted version of his face.

"What on earth happened to you?" he asked, taking Callum's coat and hat and hanging them by the wood–burner to dry. Callum pushed off his shoes, too, and paddled across the floor in damp grey socks.

"Allergic reaction," was the downbeat response. "I was doing make–up tests for *Deadfall* last week, and it turns out there's some new ingredient in the eyelash dye which doesn't agree with me. We've managed to get hold of a batch of the old stuff now, enough to get through the shoot, but I had a couple of days where my eyes were so swollen that I couldn't open them at all. Gave me a whole new appreciation for radio, I can tell you. But I can't work for a while, and of course I'm not allowed to drive because I can't see properly, so I'm going everywhere by public transport – trains and taxis – for the time being."

Jon made two cups of coffee, and sat opposite him in their old familiar poses. "Poor old you. But whatever were you doing in Sheffield?"

Callum snorted. "Looking for Katy and Steve, of course. Last thing I heard, that was where they were living. But when I went to the address Katy gave me there was nobody there and hadn't been for months. Which could explain why my letters weren't being answered, I suppose; they're probably all still in there on the doormat."

"Very likely. Was there some particular reason … ?"

"For wanting to find her? You bet. I've had to put my mother into a care home, and I'm starting the rigmarole of selling off her house. I wanted to know if there was anything Katy wanted out of it before I do. I mean I could put it all into storage, I suppose, but that isn't cheap, and most of Mum's stuff isn't really worth holding onto. But if I can't find her, I can't ask her, can I? The neighbours seem to think she's gone to Newcastle, but I don't think I can actually bring myself to go up there and start looking around without more information. I seriously think I'm going to have to admit defeat and hire a private detective to track her down – which won't be a popular move when she finds out about it."

"Oh." Jon's face creased. "I'm sorry to hear about your mum." He thought for a moment. "It sounds unbelievably stressful." Instinctively he reached over and patted Callum's hand.

"Thank you, love – it was. But at any rate when I got to the station in Sheffield I was planning to catch the next train back to London – only they announced one for Leeds first and I thought to myself, literally on the spur of the moment, 'What I really need is a bit of TLC from Jon.' You've always been able to calm me down and make me feel better about things, and that was what I felt I needed more than anything else. I suppose I haven't got the right any more … I mean, you might have somebody else for all I know … but I knew I had to see you. I didn't actually think about whether it would be convenient until later."

"I understand." It was easy to say, and surprisingly easy to mean. Jon had never experienced any animosity towards Callum; annoyance, yes, at some of the choices he had made, but there was no bad feeling between them. Their twenty–two–months' experiment had left them with happy memories of one another, and if they had moved on and left each other behind it was because that was the way the world was made and there was nothing they could do about it; they had never stopped caring for one another, as far as Jon was aware. "And no, there's nobody else at the moment."

"I suppose you have to be quite careful, actually." It was the same question Justine had asked, albeit phrased more knowingly. "Given the part you're playing?"

"Yes. No scandal. Edgar's very keen on 'an air of respectability', as he calls it. 'Whatever it is, dear boy, just keep it out of the papers', that's what he says."

"Good old Eddie. I've heard nice things about him. You must be enjoying working on the show?"

"Tremendously, thank you." But his own answer struck Jon as stilted, and he wondered why he was unwilling to give anything away to a man with whom he had enjoyed such an uninhibited sexual relationship. For nearly two years there had been no secrets between himself and Callum; now it seemed perhaps there were, and he was not comfortable with the knowledge. It was as if they were starting all over again, as if their time together had been erased or simply did not count at all. "I'm glad it's not some creaky old bodies–in–the–library thing; we do get to deal with contemporary issues – guns and drugs and so forth." He was struggling to find something to say that would not be too gushing, yet his relish in the project showed through clearly. "We've filmed in some wonderful places: Temple Newsam House, and the Cow and Calf Rocks at Ilkley for example. They had me hanging on to that by my fingertips at one point – and it was the coldest day of the year, too."

Callum laughed. "They're turning you into a bit of an adventure hero, then, are they, love?"

"I suppose so. I haven't had to punch anybody yet, thank goodness, but I have had to bash a burglar over the head with a candlestick."

"Slippery slope," Callum warned him, cheekily. "Next thing you know it'll be four inch plastic action figures and collectable sticker-books. We've got those for *Planetfall*. It's not even a children's film, but it doesn't seem to be children who buy those things anyway."

"I know, I've seen them on sale." Jon would never admit exactly how close he had got to buying a miniature plastic version of Callum, with Rossi's green hair, red boiler suit and startling silver eyes, before an attack of sanity had hit him and he had backed away from the toy display very quickly. Nevertheless he could not suppress a shudder.

"Everything all right, love?" Callum asked. "Feeling awkward, are you?"

"Yes. This is strange."

"It is," Callum agreed, sitting back. "This is a lovely house, Jon. How many bedrooms have you got?"

His attempt to change the subject was appreciated, and Jon could not help smiling at its clumsiness. "Two. Ish. There's a room on the ground floor which could be either a bedroom or a study. I'm going to turn it into a library, but at the moment it's full of boxes."

"Books, of course?"

"Naturally. I hadn't realised I'd accumulated so many."

"Your greatest vice," Callum laughed. "I know. Apart from me, of course."

"Apart from you, yes." Another silence lapsed, then Jon said brightly, "I saw you on TV at the première of *Planetfall*. I see you took Izzy with you."

"Yes. Didn't she look fabulous? We have a quid pro quo: I let her drag me to daddy's exhibitions, she lets me flaunt her in front of the cameras. It's just another part to play, really – and I must admit it's convenient: it stops her parents asking when she's going to find a

216

husband. You'd have thought an unconventional artist like Jolyon Thorpe would be a bit more broad–minded, but it turns out he's all about posterity these days. Plus it doesn't do me any harm to have an adoring girl hanging off my arm while people are watching me snog some big six–foot bloke up on the screen." The defensiveness in referring to the kiss with Bryce had not diminished; in fact, it seemed to have increased. Jon could not help wondering whether Callum had been subjected to even more prurient interrogations by journalists. If that was the case, however, he had apparently managed to get by without saying anything too controversial. "It also sends a message to Thea that I'm not in the market for any kind of formal commitment to her and Connor."

"Oh! How is he? Have you seen any more of him lately?"

"Saw him a couple of weeks ago," Callum laughed indulgently. "He's just turned two. I've got some new pictures somewhere, I'll dig them out. He's walking and talking and he seems pretty bright – not that I know much about children, you understand. I took Auntie Ada to meet him on his birthday; she says he looks just like I did at that age, all blond and chubby. Mind you, that's me at any age."

"Not now," said Jon. "You're not chubby now."

"Well, no, I had to lose a bit for the film again this time. It'll all go back on when we finish shooting, though." Callum had reached into the side pocket of his travelling bag and brought out an envelope. "Here we are, happy snaps … me, Connor and Ada. She's really the only member of my family I'm in contact with at the moment. The only one with all her marbles, at any rate. There's no way I can talk to my mum about Connor, she wouldn't have a clue what I was telling her."

Jon took the pictures and examined them. "I see what you mean about Connor," he smiled. "There is quite a resemblance. Were these taken at Thea's parents' house?"

"No fear, I won't be going down there again after what happened the first time! No, she brings him to my agent's office now. She likes it there, her eyes are always out on stalks for big–name stars to rub shoulders with. Lenny's a bit too crafty for her, though; he's careful not to arrange for anyone else to come in while she's there."

"Sneaky," commended Jon.

"Sneaky," Callum conceded grimly, "is a great quality in an agent, and it's what Lenny does best. But anyway he's a lovely little chap – Connor, not Lenny – and he always seems pleased to see me."

"Connor, not Lenny," Jon finished, with a laugh.

"Yes." A deep breath, and Callum seemed to relax further. "So, do you keep in touch with Bill? Have you heard the latest from the Old Crown?"

"Some of it. I gather JB's living in your old room this year."

"He is. Supposedly only until he finds a house, but Pete apparently told him he could live there rent–free – so I don't suppose he's in any hurry to move out, do you? James was going to have the garden room originally, but Bill's given him and Matthew the whole of the first floor to make up for it and told them they can rearrange the furniture to suit themselves, so they've made it into a little flat with a bedroom and a sitting room rather than two bedsits. They seem to be quite settled together."

Jon smiled. "I wasn't sure," he said. "At Ewen's funeral, I thought perhaps … but then something happened and I stopped thinking about them." He watched the twist of Callum's face almost with satisfaction, feeling that at least the boy should recognise what he had done.

"There's a lot of it about," muttered Callum. "Domesticity, I mean. They're apparently planning some sort of commitment ceremony. Roy wants them to have it in the garden at the Old Crown – he's offered to have it tidied up specially, and he's even told them to hire in caterers and charge it all to him – but of course they're dithering. Honestly, Roy can be a bit of a managing old queen, can't he, when he puts his mind to it?"

The observation drew a laugh from Jon. "Oh yes. Most of the time it's well–intentioned, but I must admit I wouldn't want him interfering in my wedding – if I was going to have one, that is. Rosemary's mother was bad enough."

"Pushed you around a bit, did she?" Callum's look was sympathetic.

"She didn't like me at all. She thought I was a slippery customer.

A 'finagler', that's what she called me. She as good as accused me of being after Rosemary's money, which was news to me – at that point I didn't even know she had any."

"Oh! That's where the name comes from, is it? 'Finn Nagle'? In the books?"

"That's where the name comes from in the books, yes. Apparently there's a new one out at the moment."

"You haven't read it?"

Jon shrugged. "I gave up on them a long time ago, I'm afraid. Some of the things Finn gets up to stretch credulity too far; he used to be funny, but he's turned into a bit of an ape. I expect that's because I'm not providing her with any new material these days and she's having to make it all up."

"I heard her reading one of her own short stories on Radio 4 about a week ago," Callum said. "She was good. Why did she ever give up acting in the first place?"

"I don't think she has. Not completely. But she put on a lot of weight after Justine was born, and she was finding it difficult to get cast. She taught for a while, and then she just gave up and concentrated on writing. Very successfully, too, as it turned out."

"That's putting it mildly. She must have made a small fortune taking the piss out of you."

"Well, that's all right, isn't it? I'm sure I must have been rather comical at the time, although I don't suppose I am any more."

"You sound disappointed."

"Not really. I got a certain amount of name recognition out of it, which was very useful from time to time – only I don't suppose it fits in very well with the Roman Catholic priest thing, does it?"

"Probably not. And that's much more like you, isn't it, all serious and thoughtful and concerned for other people? I saw Nigel in the pilot; he was good, but I thought he looked terribly tired. I should imagine you'll bring a lot more energy to it."

"I hope so. I'm certainly putting a great deal in."

The conversation lapsed again, and a strained silence fell. Then Callum said, slowly and without meeting his eyes, "I've missed this, you know. I've missed you. I'm making bad decisions lately, and I've got to wonder if splitting up with you was one of them. It made sense at the time … but then so have a lot of other things which afterwards I wasn't sure about. I've been second–guessing myself like mad for months now, trying to think through all the implications of everything I do. Kissing Bryce, for example … " An awkward pause. "Maybe I shouldn't have done that. Maybe I should have refused. I've got people on the West Coast telling me it's the worst mistake I could ever possibly have made. The smallest suspicion of anything queer and they drop you like a hot brick – and I can't afford to be dropped like a hot brick, what with my mother's fees to be paid. Have you any idea how much care homes cost these days?"

"No. Mercifully it's something I've never needed to get involved with."

Callum was still looking away. "Well, you've been lucky. I tell you, Jon, we're in the wrong business; we should be running a care home if we want to make any money. But I ran into a lot of anti–gay sentiment in the States. There are people over there who think God has a special hell created just for us."

"There are people everywhere who think that," Jon told him. "As well as quite a few who don't."

"I know. But isn't it strange how the ones who hate us always seem to shout the loudest?"

"That's because it's still more socially acceptable to be anti–gay than gay," was the quiet reply. "Nobody's ever afraid people will find out that they're straight. Nobody ever gets criticised for kissing someone of the opposite gender in a movie."

"Tell me about it. I've really had a struggle to keep my temper with some of that homophobic newspaper lot. But anyway, it feels more and more to me as if I'm dancing on a tightrope … come out once and for all and commit myself to a gay identity and put up with the consequences, or keep on trying to look as if I'm straight until I've got enough money in the bank for it not to matter any more."

"And how much is enough?" asked Jon. They had been down this road before.

"That's the problem, I don't know. How do I know my career won't tank and leave me sweeping the floor in Tesco's for the next thirty years? I didn't get much of a fee for *Leichhardt* and I'm on a percentage with Rossi so it's going to be a while before I see any real income from any of my pictures. Meanwhile I've got living expenses, and I've got to support my mum. It's not as if she had savings either, just the house." He ran a despairing hand across the soft velvet pile clinging to his skull. Jon was manfully suppressing the urge to run his fingers over it, to stroke them down the warm sweet–scented skin at the back of Callum's neck and leave extravagant kisses in their wake. "Even so," Callum went on, breathily, "I thought it was worth asking … could there ever be any circumstances in which you might be willing to take me back?"

The question was unexpected. That Callum had been feeling sorry for himself and regretting a series of wrong decisions was one thing, but that he would try to turn the clock back and re–establish their relationship was something Jon hadn't considered likely.

It was tempting, of course it was; he had such happy recollections of warm limbs tangling round his own, and of that remarkable sensation of specialness – of chosenness – which had always sparked towards him out of Callum's eyes. He would not have been human if he hadn't wanted that again, if he hadn't been wrestling with the desire to throw caution to the winds and drag the boy to bed and make love to him right now, Justine or no Justine, and bear with the consequences in the morning. Unfortunately, however, there was Callum's mercurial nature to be taken into account as well: he was prone to thought–processes Jon was unable to follow, and things that made sense to Callum rarely made sense to anyone else. If he committed himself to all that again he would be facing exactly the same obstacles as before, plus new ones thrown in for good measure: his own tentatively established career, as well as Callum's increasing public profile. There would be no more hiding out in quiet corners of restaurants, no more indiscreet adventures in quick–change booths, no more flirting with public exposure; they would have to be so discreet as to make the Cold War KGB look like garrulous gossips, and he could think of nothing better suited to drain all the life out of something which had previously been sweet and uncomplicated. No, the idea would have to be nipped in the bud, as firmly as possible, if either of them was ever to be able to maintain a hold on his precarious sanity.

"Callum, darling," he said, "surely you realise everything's different now? It worked before because we were living quite close to one another, except when you were away filming. Now – the distances involved would make it virtually impossible. And we'd both have to be more careful than ever that it didn't get out. Honestly, one whiff of anything scandalous and *Hawker and Duffy* would be looking for another priest. I don't want to do that to Edgar, and I don't want to do it to myself either – not now that I've got financial security for the first time in my life. Besides," he added, more rationally, "I'm not convinced it's really what you want. I think you're just feeling depressed and unappreciated and you want somebody to hug you and tell you everything's going to be all right – and I can do that without having to get back into a relationship with you. Plenty of other people could do it, too, if only you'd let them. Izzy, for example."

"Izzy?"

"Well, admittedly you might not want to confide in her about your sexuality, but I'm sure you'd be able to lean on her when it comes to the problem with your mother."

"I already do," confessed Callum sheepishly. "I have, in fact, rather a lot. She helped me find the care home, and she's been holding my hand through all the legal bits and pieces. But in the middle of the night, when you're not there … "

It seemed so heartfelt and was so similar to what he had been feeling himself that Jon almost wavered. Then his sensible brain cut in and he made a determined effort to listen to his head rather than his heart … or any more treacherous part of his anatomy.

"You can always ring me," he offered. "Any time of the day or night, I'll talk to you. But I honestly don't think I can turn round and go back now. Everything would happen in exactly the same way all over again, and once was more than enough for me. It doesn't mean I don't still care about you – of course I do! It's a matter of self–preservation, that's all; I need to put myself first for once. I'm sure you understand."

"Yes, love, I do." The maturity of the response was something of a surprise. "The plain truth is, I bollocksed it up. Couldn't get off the bloody fence, could I? Still can't. I just want the world to be different, I suppose. I want it not to be wrong for you and me to be together." He paused, made a sour face. "And after that," he added, with a laugh, "I want some candy and a real gun that shoots."

"I'm sorry," Jon told him, as gently as a man could who had an infinite capacity for compassion.

"No, love. I'm the one who should be sorry, coming here uninvited and raking it up again." He seemed to reach some kind of decision. "I think I'd probably better be on my way now, don't you? Would you mind calling me a taxi, and I'll see if I can find a hotel room for the night? Or maybe there's a late–night train – I could probably be home by breakfast–time."

"Don't be ridiculous!" This was one of the most absurd suggestions ever to have passed Callum's lips, and Jon had no hesitation in making his feelings clear. "I'm not letting you out again at this time of night in this weather – you'd drown before you got to the end of the path! You're sleeping here tonight; I'll make up a bed in the library, it won't take more than five minutes – and I've got the heating on already, so it should be warm enough for you."

Callum was staring at him across the table, speechless.

"I know it's nothing like you're used to," Jon went on, apologetically. "I suppose it's all five star hotels and room service for you now, is it?"

"No." Callum shook his head, but it was obviously a lie. "Well, you know, people like to show off. But that's not what I was brought up to, and sometimes it doesn't feel as if it can all be for me."

"It won't do you any harm to keep your feet on the ground," observed Jon, a fraction more tartly than he had intended.

"I know. I have to keep reminding myself of that." Callum smiled, a little unsteadily. "You're right, love, as usual, and it's kind of you to offer. Well, if I'm staying, perhaps you'd point me in the direction of your bathroom?"

"Top floor, second on the right. If you could avoid waking Justine

I'd appreciate it."

"Of course. Anything I can do to help with sorting out the room?"

"No, that's all right. By the time you get back down here it will all be done."

It was simple enough to make good on that promise. The airing–cupboard in the kitchen yielded bedding and a pillow, and by the time Callum crept downstairs the library was starting to look like a comfortable place in which to spend the night. Jon had even rearranged the desk lamp so that it could be switched off from the couch, and the chill was definitely off the air.

"I can get you a hot–water bottle, if you think you'll need one," Jon offered as Callum stepped in from the hallway.

"I'll be fine, love. Stop fussing."

"All right." But there was a distinct reluctance to separate from one another, and in searching around for a topic of conversation that would keep him in the room a few moments longer Jon heard himself say inanely, "So, what's your next project after *Deadfall*?"

"Oh god," groaned Callum, "more legit theatre I'm afraid – with Izzy again, thank goodness, or it wouldn't be even slightly bearable. She's talked me into doing Leontes in the *Tale* while she does Hermione. I seem to remember that you've played the part yourself?"

"Leontes?" A dismal tour of depressed industrial Wales loomed ominously in Jon's memory. It had been the closest thing to purgatory he could have imagined, and yet all that unremitting misery night after night had helped him flush the humiliation of divorce through his system. "I did," he admitted. "I hope you have a better time of it than I did."

"I don't consider it a particularly cheerful play," admitted Callum, "for all its frolicking shepherds – but it's part of the repertoire so I suppose I ought to have a go at it. How about you, what will you be doing when you've wrapped on *Duffy*?"

"Duke Theseus, regional tour of the *Dream* – Exeter, Monmouth, Lancaster, Bedford, Gloucester. Bryan Aven's doing Oberon and Grete Sanger's Titania."

"Goodness! I haven't seen Grete for years. I found her a bit of a cold bitch, to be perfectly honest, but I bet she'll make a great Titania. You've worked with Bryan before, though, haven't you?"

"I was his understudy, a million years ago. We haven't done anything together since."

"Well then, it'll be a chance for you to catch up with him," Callum promised. "I hope everything turns out all right."

"Yes – and so do I, for you and Izzy." But Jon was staring down dubiously at the couch. "You know, you can have my bed and I'll sleep in here."

"No, thank you, love. If I'm going to be sleeping in your bed, I'd prefer you to be in it with me. You wouldn't want to reconsider that, I suppose?"

Jon shook his head. "I can't," he said. "Not only because … But not with my daughter in the house. She's too young, and even if she understood I'm not sure her mother would. I'm only just getting to know Justine for the first time; I don't want to risk it all going wrong now."

"Meaning … maybe you would if she wasn't here?"

"Meaning … she is here, so it's irrelevant. But the offer of the bed still stands."

Callum shook his head. "No, that's all right, love, you wouldn't be comfortable on a couch – your spine's longer than mine. There have to be some advantages to being vertically challenged, after all."

"You're not." Jon was quick to refute the self–deprecating comment.

"Compared to you, I am," laughed Callum, to ease the awkward moment. "Izzy says I'm a short–arsed runt. I think she said 'runt', anyway."

"I expect so." Jon was quite surprised to find himself actually smiling. It was a long time since he and Callum had been able to relax together, since there had been this easy humour between them. Somewhere along the way they had stopped being themselves and started playing roles in which neither had ever been entirely comfortable; it was as if artifice had entered into their relationship, and there had been no place for honesty any more. "You'll be all right here, then?"

"I'll be all right," Callum assured him, and gently took hold of Jon's shoulder and placed a kiss of gratitude on his cheek. "Get some sleep, sweetheart. You look worn out."

"Actually," admitted Jon, "I am. Sleep well, I'll see you in the morning."

"Good night, love," said Callum, as the door closed between them, and Jon headed off upstairs to the safety of his own room and a maelstrom of disordered thoughts.

He made his way downstairs again a little after seven the following morning, moving as quietly as he could so as not to wake either of his guests. The door of the library was closed as he tiptoed past, and he smiled towards it like a miser gloating over a hidden hoard. There was another hour or two with Callum over breakfast to look forward to, introducing him to Justine, getting him fed and prepared for his journey home and seeing him off to the station, and although it might be awkward and might threaten his resolve not to get entangled with the boy again it was still a prospect to be relished.

With that in mind, he began to think about providing food for the masses. There was plenty of bacon and eggs and several cartons of fruit juice lurking in the fridge, and he'd bought in some miniature packets of breakfast cereal to make sure he had something that would appeal to Justine. This would give him an excuse to lay the table properly and demonstrate that despite several months of living on his own and eating meals in front of the television he had not lost the rudiments of civilised behaviour.

Not that he would be required to exercise his domestic talents for an hour or so yet; nobody but himself ever got up early if they didn't have to, and Justine was seldom aware of the necessity. Callum, however, he might expect to see sooner: the couch in the library was an accommodating old thing but even for the vertically–challenged it would not be comfortable for an entire night. He would surely be driven to put in an early appearance, filling the basement kitchen with an indefinable Callumness that Jon would store away and cherish for the future. It sometimes seemed as if he shed gold dust wherever he went, and Jon was absurdly careful to treasure every speck and grain.

He looked up from the mug of tea which was slowly rebuilding his soul and his consciousness after a moderately agonising night. He hadn't slept well, nor had he slept badly; instead he had teetered between the two without rhyme or reason, waking partly rested but with his mind still weary from the night before. And why not, indeed? The unexpected irruption of Callum into his tranquil and ordered existence had reminded him of things he had compartmentalised and tried to forget. Or, if not to forget, at least to deal with rationally and consign to the past.

It had been working, too: long hours of filming, plus an extensive period shadowing Father Terence and learning how to behave like a priest, had left him in a state of pleasant exhaustion most of the time since his move. On top of that he had managed to find time to redecorate the bathroom, which had been a charming shade of what Bill referred to as Channel–passenger–green, and put up pictures here and there around the house. It had started to seem to him as if he didn't mind the absence of Callum from his life at all, or as if this was just another extended parting while one or other of them worked elsewhere. But theirs had never been intended as a permanent arrangement; they had simply been in the right place for one another at the right time, and it would be foolish to try to make any more of it than that. Or so he had always thought before.

It seemed, however, that Callum was not content to leave it at that – and maybe Jon wasn't, either; after all, over on the notice board by the fridge he still kept the 50,000 lire *Monòpoli* note from the first time he and Callum had kissed. Elsewhere in the house, in a folder which would never be found by anyone – except executors, perhaps, or methodical burglars – there were newspaper and magazine cuttings: Callum as Rossi, Callum as Leichhardt, Callum as Bosola and Petruchio; there was even a picture from the *Radio Times* featuring Callum as Robin Hood, at a photo session where he seemed to have been giggling the entire time. There was probably something ... well,

227

Justine would have called it 'sad', Rosemary would have said 'pathetic' … about keeping a cuttings file on the boy as if Jon were some demented fan, but when it came right down to it there wasn't much else to keep. Blurred photos of them in shared situations – the occasional party, sunning themselves in the back garden of the Old Crown – his watch, and the heliotrope tee–shirt which lurked under a plastic cover in Jon's wardrobe were his only tangible souvenirs. All the rest was memory, and some of that was less than sweet.

Well, the recollection of that first kiss was one he particularly treasured. It had all been so new and promising then, and although he had been aware of the travails that lay ahead he had managed to ignore them and delight in Callum, in the tantalising forbiddenness of their secret, in the snatched shared moments which had made the workaday world bearable for them both. He had saved the *Monòpoli* money because it summoned up the mental image of that evening so perfectly: candlelight playing off the blue in Callum's eyes, and the unexpected sensation of triumph as he rolled the boy across the floor and revelled in his kisses. It had been one of the headiest moments of his life so far, and he never wanted to forget it.

The *Monòpoli* note was pinned to the board with a businesslike red map–tack. Behind that was an envelope which looked like the ones Jon kept in the desk in the library. He didn't recollect having pinned anything in an envelope to the board, so he got up and leaned over to examine it. The superscription on the outside was 'Gruoch', and the writing would have been identifiable in just about any circumstances.

"Callum?" he said, aloud, and his heart dropped through him like a stone.

The envelope was sealed. He had to tear it to get it open, and his hands were shaking. Inside there was a sheet of the awful lined paper he used for lists, but given the chaos his desk was in since the move Callum had done well to find even that. A drawing in blobby pen at the top was obviously supposed to represent a bunch of roses; Callum had coloured some of them in lighter and darker shades of blue.

Darling, the note began, *it's 5 a.m. and I'm going to wander off and see if I can find a taxi or a bus to take me to the station. I'm sorry to run out on you like this, but I feel it's for the best — don't you? It was wrong to try to talk you into something you obviously don't want, and you were very sweet not to lose your temper with me last night. I'll probably be scooting off to live in the States shortly anyway, so I'll be out of your hair for a while — and maybe by the time we meet again it won't be anything like so awkward between us any more. But I'm glad I came, if only for the chance to see how comfortable you are in your new house. Sorry I didn't get to meet Justine, though — maybe another time? If you ever need me for anything, Roy or Izzy will know where to find me — and I'll be back every so often to do more Robin Hoods and see my mum and Connor. I wish things could have been different, but maybe the world isn't ready for you and me just yet. We won't forget each other in a hurry though, will we? It was all a lot of fun.*

At the bottom there was no signature, as he had come to expect; merely a large, looping, flamboyant capital 'C', typically Callum in that it gave away everything and nothing all at the same time.

Jon read through the note once more, then folded it and put it into his pocket. How, for God's sake, had he managed not to notice that Callum's coat, hat and shoes had been removed from their places beside the stove? Or perhaps he just had not wanted to trust the evidence of his disbelieving eyes? But there was no denying it now, the boy had gone, damn him. He had walked out of the house and out of Jon's life without so much as a goodbye, and this was all he had left behind.

Well, that was that, he supposed. It was over. He could go upstairs and put his head around the library door, but he knew what he would find: the bedding folded neatly, everything exactly as it should be except that Callum was not there. And, for some reason, Callum not being there hurt a great deal more this time around than it ever had before.

He was still sitting with a cup of cold tea and thoughts he could not put a name to when Justine came yawning down the stairs some considerable time later.

"Morning," she said, slumping into the room with tousled hair, wearing something pink and stripey which was far too bright for such a sombre occasion — or indeed for any occasion at all. Jon roused himself only with an effort.

"Good morning, darling. Would you like tea, coffee, or fruit juice?"

"Tea, please." She sat down heavily. The effort of descending from the bedroom had clearly been too much for her. "Where's your friend? Is he still here?"

A moment of panic, and then he said smoothly, "I'm afraid he couldn't stay; he had to catch an early train. He would have liked to meet you, though; he said he was sorry to have missed you." He was proud of having got these few words out without any suspicion of a tremor – at least until right at the very end.

"Pity," she said. "He's got to work, then, has he?"

"Yes. He's making a film at Pinewood. It's called *Deadfall*."

"Oh, neat. That's one of the Dylan Judd ones, isn't it? Callum Henley's in those. I saw him in the first film and I thought he was cute. Does your friend work with him at all?"

"I believe he does," smiled her father. "I'll ask him, next time I see him. Now, there's bacon and eggs and cereal and toast – what do you think you might like for breakfast, sweetheart?"

"Toast," said Justine firmly, and pulled the world slowly back around onto its proper course as she did so. "And butter. And marmalade."

"Toast and butter and marmalade it is," he told her, turning away to get it organised. As he worked he listened to her chattering away about nothing at all, and reminded himself adamantly that he was better off without the complication that was Callum in his life – and that he would not miss him, not even the slightest, the most inconsequential, the most unimaginably infinitesimal little bit.

◆

◆

INTERVAL

◆ ◆ ◆

Act 3

Scene i
(A small old-fashioned pub in West
Yorkshire, smoky and faded; JON and BILL
are hunched over a table in the corner.
It is the late evening of a summer day in
the year 2000.)

◆

The following April, surprisingly without fuss or palaver, Douglas Pirie
married Jacinta Burroughs. The announcement – smugly after the
event – caused a minor earthquake in the theatrical community,
especially that segment of it which had for a long time been centred on
the Old Crown at Shapley. Jon heard the news in a telephone call from
Bill Wildman, who had spent the previous summer playing Prospero to
Douggie's Caliban and Jax's Miranda but had noticed nothing in the
way of closeness between them then. He had, however, to his
astonishment, been summarily recruited to bear witness to a ceremony
in a South London Register Office where the bored staff had failed to
recognise any of them. Even that seemed not to have dampened Jax's
spirits, though: Douggie had been offered an enticing new role playing
a mystery–solving English butler in an American TV series, and the
California lifestyle was a stronger lure than Jax could ever have dreamed
of resisting – even if it came with Douggie as the price.

By the time Jon collected Bill from Leeds City station at the
beginning of his mid–season break, however – it coincided with the last
couple of weeks of filming on _Hawker and Duffy_, enabling Bill to make
a guest appearance in the final episode of the second series – the
runaway romance of Jax and Douggie had paled into insignificance
beside a still more fascinating topic which had supervened: in the
ensuing weeks, and also unknown to anybody in advance, Callum
Henley had married Isabella Thorpe.

The subject of this unlikely liaison was not raised until some time after Bill's luggage had been dropped off at Jon's house and they were high on a hillside in an out–of–the–way pub with flagstone floors, nicotine–stained Lincrusta on the walls, and thin, flat cushions on the benches. The fact that it also happened to serve the best bar meals in the vicinity was the attraction; dining alone had begun to wear on Jon's nerves, and he was becoming an expert on the local eateries.

"The steak and kidney pie's good here." He pushed a laminated menu over to Bill. "So are the chips."

"You don't look like a man who eats a lot of chips," groaned Bill. "You look as if a good wind would blow you over. You never put on any weight; I don't know how you do it."

"Metabolism," Jon suggested, with an apologetic smile. They both ordered pie, then settled into a corner and leaned together conspiratorially across a small round table. Bill was hugging a pint of strong beer, Jon sipping delicately at a glass of fruit juice: West Yorkshire Police were having one of their periodic purges on drinking and driving, and he had no desire to run afoul of them. It would do his reputation, and that of the show, no good for Father Duffy to be breathalysed.

"So," said Bill, after a while, "what happened with Callum? I knew he was spending time with Izzy, but I didn't realise they were that close."

"Neither did I," admitted Jon. "It came completely out of the blue." He did not explain with what empty emotion he had seen the photographs – Catherine Senior throwing confetti over lounge–suited Callum and Izzy in floral pink and matching hat – which had appeared in a couple of magazines. Nor did he mention that the specks of green at Callum's wrists were cufflinks in the shape of Monopoly houses. "But they had been virtually living together at her parents' place."

"I thought that was just a practical arrangement," said Bill, in his down–to–earth manner. "After all, he lived with you for quite a while and he didn't marry you."

"True," Jon shrugged. "Actually, I don't know what happened. I've had no contact with Callum since ... " He deliberately failed to come up with the exact date although he could have named the day, the hour, and even the minute. "Well, for more than a year. Ewen's funeral must have been the last time." That late–night encounter the previous Easter did not enter into his calculations at all.

Bill sniffed. "Not surprised," he said. "He's been busy filming, hasn't he? And they did the *Tale* at the National together of course. Did you see that?"

"No. Did you?"

"I looked in. It was a bit slick for my taste, and the guy playing Autolycus couldn't sing. Some new kid, Oliver something, straight out of drama school and pretty wooden. Callum and Izzy had to carry a lot of dead weight on that one. Maybe by the end of it they felt they only had one another to lean on?"

Jon's eyebrows climbed. "It could be that. I believe something similar happened with the *Shrew*." Callum's scathing assessment of Baptista and Bianca was vivid in his memory "I'm amazed they went back for a second season after that."

"So am I." Bill's eyes narrowed. "Economic cowardice, I suppose. We'll sell ourselves like tarts on a street corner if the money's good. Except you, of course," he added, emolliently. "You've got a great little earner going with this Duffy thing, haven't you? Regular income, decent residuals – and the scripts aren't bad either."

"No, not at all. Most of them are excellent. In fact it's all turning out rather nicely." If it was a relief to steer the conversation away from Callum's marriage, Jon gave no indication of it. "You'll enjoy working with the team, it's a friendly set–up. Although," he added, "Eddie's a bit miffed that there's no cricket to take you to: the West Indies aren't here until July, by which time you'll be back at work."

"Story of my life," grumbled Bill. "You'll go, though, won't you?"

"I expect so, although we do tend to attract attention these days. I'm going to concentrate on radio and voice–over work during the winters in future; I don't like being too visible."

Bill chuckled. "No, it can be a bit of a disadvantage. But if you think you've got it bad, that's nothing compared to Callum. He's got fans who dress up as Rossi and follow him everywhere; it's no wonder he'd want to get himself hitched to somebody sensible like Izzy. In fact," he reflected as their meals arrived, "it shows better taste than I gave him credit for. I mean, he's a nice kid but I never suspected he had a brain. Maybe he'll prove us wrong about that, eh, Jon?"

"You never know." Jon turned his attention to his steak and kidney pie.

"'I say, we will have no more marriages'," quoted Bill, ruefully. "'Those that are married already – all but one – shall live; the rest shall keep as they are.' Bloody Hamlet had it right, didn't he? All this marrying gets in the way of the important stuff in life – Shakespeare and drinking."

Jon was watching him with ironic amusement. "Is your divorce through yet?" he asked, feeling he knew the source of Bill's disaffection with marriage.

"*Nisi*. Not *absolute*. Another three weeks to go."

"Hmmm. How do you feel about that?"

"Feel?" Bill examined the word as though it were an alien concept.

"Happy?" Jon prompted. "Sad?"

Bill shrugged. "Neither," he admitted, flatly. "Sense of inevitability, really. In a couple of years' time I'll be fifty; my career's going nowhere, I'm living in somebody else's house, and all I've got to show for twenty years of marriage are two great oafs of sons with no real sense of direction." He sniffed. "At least I wasn't stupid enough to take up with some little gold–digger half my age, though, like Douggie. No fool like an old fool, eh?"

"She's not half his age," Jon pointed out. "Fifteen years younger, I believe."

"That's bad enough." Bill was obviously not in the mood to let it pass. "It's too much, isn't it? You're an adult while they're still a child. What do you even talk about with somebody like that – and how the hell are you supposed to keep up with them in bed?"

"That's never been a problem for me," Jon told him, unguardedly. He was thinking of Callum, and how in their more intimate moments there had been no evidence of the age gap between them.

"No, you lucky bastard!" Bill had obviously heard the words, but had put his own interpretation on them. "You'd never be stupid enough to let yourself get tangled up with some brainless little bimbo, would you? In fact, given the way your marriage to Rosemary turned out, I'd be astonished if you ever felt like getting involved with anybody ever again."

"Well, I won't pretend it hasn't crossed my mind from time to time." It seemed safe enough, now that it was over, to admit that perhaps there had been, just briefly, someone of significance in his life; Jon knew that Bill would honour his confidence and wouldn't probe for further information. "There was someone I was very attached to, for a little while. But we decided it wasn't going to work in the long–term, and I think we probably did the right thing."

"Not Izzy, was it?" Bill's eyebrow quirked suspiciously.

"It wasn't, no. Why do you ask?"

"I know you're fond of each other, that's all, and it would have made sense in a way. You'd have been a better choice for her than Callum, in my opinion."

"Thank you. But I have no intention of ever getting married again."

"Sensible man."

"I hope so. What about you?"

"Probably not. Can't imagine who'd have me, for a start. But I'm not really thinking that far ahead at the moment; too busy feeling a great weight's been lifted from my shoulders, if you must know. And so does Angela, apparently – she's going back to her maiden name, as if she can't wait to wipe me out of her life. I was supposed to be the one getting rid of her, not the other way round." Bill's peevishness was almost comical; he was doing everything but pouting.

"Works both ways," Jon soothed. "And, if it's any consolation, some wives never take their husband's name at all. Rosemary always kept her maiden name, and that's how she registered Justine; that's why I'm Stapleton, but my daughter's surname is Pacifico."

Bill groaned. "I always thought Angela was grateful to ditch her family name," he said. "Higginbottom. But being Mrs Wildman can't have been any picnic, either. James and Matthew were talking about hyphenating their names when they moved in together, but they decided against it in the end. They didn't think either Rudge–Linton or Linton–Rudge sounded right. Did I tell you they'd bought a house?"

"I think you did. Nowhere near JB, I hope?"

"No fear, he picked up a place somewhere close to the old Pink Palace. Got it for a bargain price, too, the bastard. I've had one or two tenants since the boys moved out, but nobody for any length of time. It's just me and the doves there these days. In fact my eldest, Brendan, is coming to stay for the summer. I've fixed him up with a job in the kitchen at the New Crown to get him out of his mother's hair for a few weeks."

"Good idea. Is Roy still trying to persuade James and Matthew into some kind of elaborate coming–out ceremony, do you know?"

"I think he's got other problems at the moment," grunted Bill. "They've gone very quiet on the idea; Matthew was always a lot keener on it than James, anyway. But I keep getting either Roy or Pete on my doorstep late at night complaining about the other one. Mostly it's Roy complaining about Pete, but not always. There's something going on there that frankly I don't want to know about – and neither do you, I suspect. You should be grateful to be out of it."

"I think I am."

"Absolutely." Bill dug into his mound of chips again, and then said, "So, will Izzy take Callum's name, do you think – or will he be modern enough to take hers?"

"I'm betting neither," opined Jon. "I'm betting there'll be no change – in that respect, at least." In other respects, though, he could not imagine Callum making the adjustment to married life at all. Nor, aside from Izzy's many virtues, could he think of a single reason why he might have wanted to.

For the rest of that year Jon could barely open a paper or switch on a television without being confronted by Callum and Izzy, although it was months before he heard from either of them directly. Then it was an apologetic note from Izzy, begging forgiveness for not having forewarned him and their other friends of their intentions and pleading a sudden attack of romantic madness as the cause. It had been done impulsively, she said, and they hadn't had time to let anybody know. Even her parents hadn't been there, only Catherine and Lenny, Callum's agent. She went on to issue an invitation for a reconciliation bash, a sort of late wedding reception combined with an early Christmas party, for which they had taken over the ballroom of a London hotel and at which they were preparing to entertain just about everybody they had ever met in their lives. They hoped he would come and help them celebrate the start of what she called their new creative partnership. There was nothing of Callum at all in the note; he had not even signed it.

Jon read it several times. He pinned it to the notice–board in the kitchen with the *Monòpoli* money and the card with the blue wrens on the front. For several days he considered what his reaction ought to be, then declined on the basis of a prior arrangement to spend the week with his daughter – a prior arrangement which he then went to a great deal of trouble to make. Afterwards he was glad he had done it. The event was covered in one of the gossip magazines which, seeing itself as a cut–price *Tatler*, had decided that anyone not present was so far off its radar as to be irrelevant. Being ignored by such a publication was among his life's ambitions, and so Jon was quietly satisfied with the decision he had made – especially as it brought him an extra few days of Justine's increasingly welcome company. It gave them a chance to get a little more practice at being father and daughter, roles into which they were gradually beginning to grow.

The Christmas card Jon received that year was signed 'Callum and Izzy', in her handwriting. There was no large, elaborate, single 'C'. There were no roses. Nor was there any further invitation.

In January, he started work on the third series of *Hawker and Duffy*, and in March his lover's wife came to Yorkshire to take a guest–starring role in an episode.

The moment he set eyes on Izzy, Jon decided that he had no option but to forgive her. After all, there was no way she could have had any idea of the turmoil her marriage had caused him, and what had been done was as much Callum's fault as her own. So he kissed her on the cheek and asked after Callum, and found himself apologising for his absence at their celebration.

"I think you had the right idea, luv," she said cheerfully, as they sat side by side in make–up. Truth to tell he did not require a great deal of attention – the usual foundation to combat shine and a little something to emphasise the curl of his eyelashes – but it was a quiet morning and the chance to sit and shoot the breeze with an old friend must not be allowed to pass. They had always been on good terms, and he hadn't realised how much he would miss her. "Actually, it was awful. It was stinking hot and it felt as if there were thousands of people eating our food and drinking our booze, and at one point Cal and I just looked at one another and wondered who the hell most of them were. I mean, every moocher we've ever met turned up to eat us out of house and home – even the dreaded Thea. Well, there'd be no keeping her away, would there, as long as it was free? She came all the way from Croydon in a taxi which she somehow persuaded Callum to pay for. Basic black and sequins and made up to the eyeballs like a raccoon. Spent a lot of time trying to ingratiate herself with James Rudge until he put her right on that one, and then she tried to wind herself round Bryce – same result, although I've got an idea he ended up paying for a room for her and persuading the hotel staff to put her to bed. We couldn't have sent her home in that condition, that's for sure. Callum was very worried about her."

The notion that Thea could not hold her drink – or at least was out of practice at it – did not exactly come as a surprise. "I'm sorry it was a disappointment," he said, as sincerely as he could.

"I'm not. It was one of those duty things, where you wipe out as many obligations as you can simultaneously. We did have a few people there that we were glad to see, but as for the rest … it was mostly a case of 'done it once, don't need to do it again'. Have you ever met Callum's Auntie Ada?"

"No. Was she there?"

"She was. Sat drinking gin with Catherine and talking about Tyrone Power; they had a whale of a time together. They're not that far apart in age, when you come to think about it. I mean, Catherine's the same age as my mum – and much more fun to be around."

This brought another thought to mind, and Jon heard himself asking: "Did Callum ever catch up with his sister, do you know? I remember he was trying to find her."

"God, that was ages ago! Yes, he did. She'd moved to Scotland with that boyfriend of hers and promptly had a baby, although I don't think he's made any attempt to marry her. She doesn't want anything to do with us, though. Apparently Callum kidnapped her mother and put her into a care home when obviously what he should have done was look after her himself. Oh, and he shouldn't have sold the house and he's probably pocketed the money. As if he needs the odd two hundred thou these days. I mean, have you any idea of the business *Deadfall* did? And *Firefall* will be out in the summer; it should break all previous records. Callum will be a millionaire by the end of the year."

"A ... million?" In Jon's vocabulary, that was an unimaginably large sum.

"I know. It doesn't really seem possible, does it? He's still the scruffy boy in the pink tee–shirt, somehow. Thank goodness he got rid of that awful thing, though, I hated it. I think I've managed to move him upmarket a bit, I'm delighted to say; I keep telling him, he's like something out of *My Fair Laddie*!"

"Sow's ear to silk purse?" Jon had rather liked Callum as he was before, all rough around the edges; smoothed down and tricked out, he would no longer be the Callum Jon had known. But he would, undoubtedly, go further in his profession like that; it was all a question of playing to one's audience, he supposed.

"That's right, luv," grinned Izzy. "Between us, you and I might make something of him yet."

"Oh no," said Jon, "you don't need me. You seem to be doing a pretty effective job on your own."

"That's me," she laughed ruefully. "Izzy Thorpe, puppeteer. Watch me pull the strings and see my puppets dance!"

During the filming of that episode, sections of which took place on open moorland miles from the city centre, it became apparent to Jon exactly how tired Edgar had started to look. On the sets in the studio he hadn't really noticed that Chief Inspector Hawker, usually so dynamic and dominant, had spent more time than usual lately sitting behind his desk and allowing the story to come to him. Once they were out in the bright fresh air, however, he began to realise how often Edgar was to be discovered propped up against a gatepost, a drystone wall or a solitary moorland cross, seeming to smile and take his ease but actually recruiting his energies for the next assault. Now that Jon looked, too, he could see that the lines around Edgar's eyes had deepened, that there was a pallor to his skin that make–up couldn't hide. There was also a slow deliberation to his speech as if his words were being produced with more care and labour than usual, and he wondered why on earth it had taken him so long to recognise the symptoms of an underlying malaise.

It would be fair to say that they were all tired, however, and counting the weeks to the end of shooting. Picking up scenes from the cave rescue episode had distorted the production schedule and it was sometimes difficult to remember which story they were working on at any given time. Increased stress was almost palpable throughout the company, and even the unfailingly courteous First AD – a chubby, blue–eyed young man by the name of Jack – had started to look frazzled around the edges. During a break in filming while they waited for a large dark cloud to pass across the sun, he confided to Jon and Izzy over coffee that Edgar's health might, in its own way, have become as unreliable as Nigel's.

"I'm not sure. They're closing ranks. Jenny's looking worried."

"I did think he was looking a bit blue around the mouth," said Izzy, soberly. "That's often an indication of heart trouble; my grandfather was the same. Mind you, he lived to be ninety–three."

"Edgar's barely sixty," Jon observed. He wondered whether he himself had guessed there was a problem and tried to put it out of his mind, or whether he had simply been unobservant. He hadn't known Edgar long, but having worked together over the last two or three years they had become friends as much as colleagues. Had he been too self–absorbed to notice that Edgar was struggling, or had the change been so gradual it hadn't seemed like change at all? They were all getting older and losing their former vitality; perhaps he had just assumed it was all part of the ageing process.

"There'd be no show without him," observed Jack, trenchantly. "Duffy on his own couldn't carry a series – no offence intended, Jon."

"None taken, and you're absolutely right. If Edgar's ill, we're all going to be looking for a job."

"It might not be a bad idea to start checking out alternatives," Jack went on, dully. "Nobody wants to, but it's hand to mouth in this business. If Edgar can't keep going … I don't suppose you'll be wanting anybody for your *Wildfell Hall* project, Miss Thorpe?"

Izzy, who had been staring at a distant horizon, turned to look at him in some surprise. "It's 'Izzy'," she said, "and I might. Give me your card and I'll pass it to the producer. No promises, but I'd rather work with somebody I know. Are you based in Leeds?"

"Manchester." It was clear in his accent for the first time.

"Of course. Well, I'll give you a strong recommendation. Only maybe it won't be necessary?" she added, wistfully.

"I hope not," Jack agreed – and the three of them entered into a conspiracy of silence on the subject of Edgar's health, and did not touch on it again for quite some time.

By the end of the season's filming, Edgar's difficulties were no longer such a secret. He was being cosseted and indulged to an extraordinary degree, guided and supported through every scene, and although he made valiant efforts to project his familiar bonhomie it had begun to seem like self–parody long before the final shots were in the can and everybody assembled on the police station set for the wrap party. Even then Edgar was acting a part, sitting at one end of the buffet table talking to people, attended by Nigel who thanks to his dialysis schedule actually appeared to be in marginally better health at the moment. Still, however, nobody was prepared to discuss future plans until Jon found himself elbow to elbow with Jenny and staring across at two men who seemed to have become unaccountably elderly in a short space of time.

"Is he really as ill as he looks, Jen?" he asked, keeping his voice low.

"Eddie?" she shrugged. "I don't know. He refused to see a doctor until we'd finished the series. I've made an appointment for him next week. If it's bad news … Well, it depends on Nige, I suppose. They're partners in the company; if one of them can't carry on, the other one takes over automatically. And I stay with the company," she added, briskly. "I don't do nursing, I'm useless at it and I hate it, anyway. If that's what he needs, we'll pay a professional. My job is to keep the business running and keep the money coming in."

Jon looked at her in admiration. She was younger than himself and several inches shorter, but she had the strong chin and determined expression of a battler.

"That's reassuring. I know I'd be glad to have you looking after my business interests."

"Well, I am, in a way," was the reply. "You're as much a part of this now as Eddie and Nige and we couldn't do it without you, either. And your agent is one of the toughest I've ever dealt with: She's like a lioness protecting her cubs."

"I'm afraid she is a bit fierce," he apologised. "In a good way, I hope."

"In a very good way. You should stick with her. But tell her it's not likely we'll be filming series four at the usual time next year: Nigel and I have a plan in place to delay by six months and shoot in the autumn, providing Eddie's well enough. So you may be looking at filling up a whole year before we can get back here, Jon. Usual caveats, don't take on anything that would reflect badly on your character. Is there anything for you in *Wildfell Hall*?"

"I'm afraid not." He had explored the possibility with Izzy, but had reluctantly come to the conclusion that there was no obvious role to suit him. Besides, Geraldine Bland had been putting out feelers in his direction about a radio *Bleak House*, in which she wanted him to play John Jarndyce. It was not so well–paid, of course, but would be better fitted to his temperament and would give him a chance to take a rest before it started. "I do have other options," he assured her.

"I don't doubt it," smiled Jenny. "Stay in touch and I'll let you know what's happening. And you could drop in and cheer Eddie up from time to time, if you're in the neighbourhood."

"Of course," he said. "I would have done that anyway."

"I know. Apart from Nigel, you're the best friend he's got in the world."

At the start of the summer holidays that year Justine came to stay again, this time bringing along her Aunt Diana, Jon's sister, on one of her rare visits from New York. Her professional commitments and Jon's were so often in conflict that they had seen little of one another for years, although when things were quiet they made an attempt to keep in touch by phone. She had been so enchanted by Jon's descriptions of his Yorkshire idyll, however, that eventually she had found a window in her schedule to make a visit, so timed as to enable her to travel up from London with Justine. In the evening, when she had finished being charmed by the house and its surroundings and Justine had abandoned them in favour of something absolutely unmissable on TV, Jon pushed a glass of wine into his sister's hands and sat with her to unwind.

"So." Diana unpinned her long hair; she had never been ash–blonde before, but unquestionably it suited her. "Is there anybody new in your life, Jon?"

He shrugged. There had been conversations like this before, all stemming from an excruciating one when they were teenagers when they had each shyly admitted doubts about their own sexual preferences, and although he had learned how to deal with them over the years they had never been much more comfortable than the first.

"I don't really meet anybody," he said. "I've made a lot of friends, but there are no romantic interests among them."

"Damn. I was hoping you'd tell me something to cheer me up. Something to restore my faith in human nature. No boyfriends, then. I'm assuming no girlfriends either?"

"Nobody of either gender."

"Hmmm. I used to think you had the right idea, you know. Being bi should have doubled your chances of finding a partner. Instead it just seems to have confused the issue."

"I'm not sure I ever really was bi," he vouchsafed. "Trying to believe

I was made it all feel easier at the time, that's all. I wanted so desperately to be normal – or as near normal as I could get."

"You are normal," Diana told him. "But I know what you mean. Mum and Dad would've been horrified if they'd seen how we turned out, wouldn't they? She asked me once if I thought you were a pansy. 'A pansy', for God's sake. I said you were just sensitive, and she told me that was nearly as bad. She had a bee in her bonnet about what would happen if you ever had to go off and fight in a war. She said you'd be no good at all, and that was when she told me I should have been a boy. In other words, it would have been perfectly okay for me to go and get killed in a war, but not you. How twisted is that?"

Jon grimaced. "'They fuck you up, your mum and dad. They may not mean to, but they do.' Philip Larkin obviously knew what he was talking about."

"I don't think Mum ever understood the irony," confided Diana. "Until the day she died she was still telling me to find a good man and settle down. If you remember, I was with Tamsin at the time – and I was 'out' to everybody in my life except my mother."

"And I'd split up from Rosemary and didn't have the guts to tell her why," he returned. "I should have had the courage of my convictions, shouldn't I?"

"I don't know. What good would it have done, after all? You'd have confronted her with a truth she didn't want to face, and then she'd have died disappointed in both of us. Better to leave her with her illusions, I suppose. Whatever you do is bound to be wrong; you just have to choose the way that hurts the smallest number of people. What do they call that, 'damage limitation'?"

"I suppose so."

Diana laughed. "How's Roy these days, anyway?" she asked. "Do you see anything of him, now that you're not living in his house?"

"Not much. He still does a lot of overseas tours – and believe it or not he's gone into farming."

"Farming! That doesn't sound like Roy at all! From what I can remember he was always elegant and polished. I can't really imagine him getting his hands dirty – can you?"

"Well, there's a manager who looks after everything on a day–to–day basis, but Roy takes quite an interest in the business."

"Or perhaps in the manager?" suggested Diana mischievously.

"Perhaps," he smiled. "I wouldn't know."

"Of course not. I take it he's still living with Pete?"

"As far as I know. They've had their ups and downs, but I don't see Pete wanting to branch out on his own if he doesn't have to. For one thing, he wouldn't have a fraction of the earning power if he wasn't being towed along behind Roy. Well, only in Canada, and he didn't want to spend the rest of his life there – that's why he left it in the first place."

"Big–fish–small–pond syndrome," was the sympathetic response. "How well I recognise it! I'm sorry to hear they're on the outs, though; it must be something in the air. Settled couples breaking up, I mean."

"Maybe." He leaned back and regarded her from a long way off. "Are you going to tell me what happened between you and Alice, then? Only I thought the pair of you were fixed for life?"

"So did I." Diana mirrored his comfortable pose. "And I'm not sure I know what happened, to be honest; it was all so slow and gradual that I didn't notice it at the time. It's not as if she went off and had some great big passionate affair with a Third Flautist or anything – at least, if she did I haven't heard about it. And I certainly didn't do anything of the sort."

"No. It isn't really your style, is it?"

"Definitely not. But anyway, it just sort of – decayed, somehow. Alice started saying maybe we wanted different things out of life, and that was true in some respects: I wanted to stay in New York and she wanted to travel … We could probably have worked that out, but we kept noticing other things we didn't agree on, and most of them were stupid and petty and we said things that people who love each other should never say. I did some work for a movie company and she called me a mercenary bitch. She went all counter–culture and alternate–lifestyle on me and started harping on about how we were ruining the planet. Not 'us' as a species, you understand. Apparently I was doing most of it myself by leaving lights on, taking cabs, buying man–made fibres. Hate–crimes against the universe, she called them."

"Fanatics can be very hard to live with," Jon observed. "Whatever their fanaticism."

"You've got that right. Honestly though, Jon, when she started talking about taking a year out to find herself and walking to India I'm afraid I flipped. I asked her who was going to pay the mortgage, and do you know what the answer was?"

"I can guess. Possession is theft. We don't really need all this stuff. Burn it on the sidewalk and don't look back."

"Pretty much. You know the type?"

"Midlife crisis hippies? I've met one or two in my time. There's a stage carpenter in Bradford who used to be a commodities trader in the City until he decided it was immoral and he should be doing something with his hands instead. He's a friend of Edgar's. Everybody's a friend of Edgar's."

"You're fond of him, aren't you?" smiled Diana. "Although I take it he's not the one who left the pink tee–shirt in your wardrobe? I saw it when I was hanging my clothes up, and it didn't exactly seem your sort of thing. That's why I wondered if there might be somebody new."

"Ah." Jon hadn't expected her not to notice, of course, and he could have packed it away when he was vacating his bedroom and moving temporarily into the library, but he'd chosen not to do so. He had wondered if she would ask. "That's a very old shirt."

"Meaning, whoever he is, he's not around any more?"

"Meaning – he's married."

"Oh dear. At least that's one thing I can be sure Alice won't be doing. Not until they make it legal for people like us anyway. I take it you're still in love with him?"

Jon shrugged. "I've been asking myself that question." Just for once it would be good to talk about Callum to someone who stood a chance of understanding – even though he had no intention of revealing his name. "I won't know unless I see him again, and that doesn't seem very likely at the moment."

"If you have to ask the question," she observed, "the answer is you probably are."

"Maybe." That was as far as he was prepared to commit himself. "It won't do me any good. Somebody else has got him now, and I can't bring myself to hate her for it. From what I hear, it's doing him the world of good. I wouldn't begrudge him the chance of being happy with a woman – if that's what he actually wants."

"I know you wouldn't," yawned Diana, her long day winning out over her determination to stay awake. "That's you all over, generous even if it breaks your heart. But it's the same thing, isn't it – me and Alice, you and Mr Pink Tee–shirt? 'If you love something, let it go; if it doesn't come back to you, it was never yours in the first place.'"

"'But if it does come back, it's yours forever'?" he continued, wistfully. "Thank you, Di. That's a nice idea, but I'm not going to be holding my breath waiting."

The telephone call which came one Friday evening in early August would have been an awful shock if Jon had not been prepared for it. His agent had rung during the week to say that Callous Films were checking his availability to play Banquo in a big–budget movie and was he interested, and she had hardly needed to explain to him that Callous Films was composed of little more than Callum Henley himself, determined on launching himself into a secondary career as a director. The sickening thud of inevitability which fell through his entire body at the mention of the Scottish play had answered all his questions in advance.

"They start next month," Caro said briskly. "You'll have finished *Bleak House* by then. The only question is whether you think you can bear working with that little tit Henley again."

Caro's antipathy to Callum was nothing new. She distrusted his rise to movie prominence intensely, thought him devoid of talent, hated everything from the sound of his voice to the colour of his hair and jumped at every opportunity to make a caustic observation about him. Nor was he the only one she despised in similar fashion; indeed, her refusal to be awed by influential members of the acting profession was one of the things he liked about her. Caro Llewellyn was not an easy woman to impress.

248

"I have my doubts," Jon admitted frankly. "But I'll listen to what he says." If nothing else it might give some indication of the state of his own feelings for Callum, although he could not help reminding himself of Diana's apposite words. Even admitting to doubt was conceding the possibility … the certainty … that he was not yet over him, and probably never would be.

In the circumstances, he managed to remain remarkably calm when the phone rang at a little after eight on the appointed evening.

"Hallo, Jon." Warm and confident – although how much of that might have been counterfeited for his benefit Jon could not have said – Callum sounded older somehow. Perhaps he was just tired. "Long time no see."

"Callum. How are you?"

"Mustn't grumble," said Callum, as though it didn't matter how he was. "What's the news on Edgar? Is he picking up a bit?"

The word was out now about Edgar's health, although the word was somewhat garbled. There had been mention of a 'heart murmur' and the need to rest, with the possibility of an operation later in the year – a valve replacement, perhaps. Jon had spent time with him as promised, but they had stayed away from that particular topic altogether; instead they had sat in the sunshine and watched Ricky Ponting score a century, and the world had been a fine and trouble–free place for both of them for a while.

"A bit, thank you," he conceded. "It might be a very long haul for him, I'm afraid."

"Only to be expected. Well, I'm glad he's got friends around to help him through it. But I didn't ring you up to talk about Eddie, of course."

"No." Jon heard his own voice as if it belonged to somebody else, distant and reserved, product of a determination not to encourage Callum in any way. Whatever the boy wanted he could damned well ask for it this time; Jon was not going to be meeting him in the middle any more.

Callum, however, was ploughing on regardless. "This Scottish film," he said. "I need somebody brilliant to play Banquo. Somebody who can make a lot out of a little, which is what you always do. I know you'll tell me there are other people out there who can do it better but trust me, Jon, there aren't. And we felt – that is, Izzy and I felt … Well, the point is – do you think you could possibly stand the thought of working with me again?"

There it was, the infamous sixty–four thousand dollar question, and just at the moment Jon did not have a sixty–four thousand dollar answer. He let a long silence elapse while he thought before replying, so that Callum felt obliged to prompt him anxiously from the other end of the line.

"Jon?"

"I … don't know," he said, at last. "I've often wondered whether I would or not. It's been such a long time since we … "

"Since Ewen's funeral?" Callum put in sharply, as though to forestall any more emotional reminiscence. It seemed that his late–night pleadings the following Easter and his subsequent disappearance were not to be discussed. "Nearly three years, I know. But Izzy said … I mean, she got the impression you might be interested in doing it."

Looking back, Jon had to admit that he had certainly given Izzy more than an indication that he would be willing to work with her; he would scarcely have contemplated her *Wildfell Hall* scenario otherwise. That was a far cry, however, from agreeing to become embroiled again in the beguiling world of Callum Henley.

"That was kind," he said vaguely. "I suppose I might."

"Your agent seemed to think you'd be able to work to our timetable," encouraged Callum, and though the words were slick there was something uncertain in the tone.

"Then I probably could." Jon did not like the way it sounded but was unable to help himself. "I don't know. Work is work, of course, and I've never been one to turn my back on a reasonable offer. Caro mentioned the fee … I must admit it's very generous."

"No more than you deserve." Jon had the distinct impression that Callum had only with difficulty held back from attaching the word 'love' to the end of the sentence. "Listen, why don't I send you a shooting script, and when you've had a chance to think about it perhaps you could come and discuss it? We're still in Bayswater," he added, humbly. "I'm running the company from the house. Do you get to London at all these days?"

"I do. I'm living in Leeds, you know, not Lhasa; London and back in a day is perfectly feasible from here."

"I'm sorry. I think what I meant was … if I was you, I don't know that I'd ever want to leave. How about lunch here, a week today? I can get the script to you by courier tomorrow, although it's pretty standard stuff. Izzy's Gruoch, of course, but we can't get either Rory or Jax this time – he's got some TV series and she's disgustingly pregnant, according to Iz. Just as well, really, I don't think they'd work together anyway. I think the pair of them ended up hating one another, and Jax marrying Douggie probably hasn't helped much."

"True." The parallels with Jon's own situation had not escaped him, although Callum seemed unaware of them.

"Well, there are a lot of other people on board that I'm sure you know – I'll put a cast list in with the script. Shame we couldn't have had Edgar for Duncan; Izzy was rather taken with him when they met."

"He's a nice man," Jon agreed, solemnly. "Lovely to work with. Sober and sensible and gets on with the job."

"Just like you, Jon; no wonder you make such a good team." A silence, then: "I've watched some of them, you know. The episodes. They're very good. You're very good in them."

"Thank you. I've seen … your films." He had, too, making a solo pilgrimage to each one the moment it opened in the city. He had watched Rossi in the throes of both triumph and disaster, seen him die in the second film and be resurrected in the third, and finally seen him mourning the loss of his love, his life and everything he had ever known at the cataclysmic end of *Firefall*. Rossi's desolation had been almost palpable then; or perhaps it was just that it corresponded so well to the emptiness Jon had felt inside.

"I've just finished a new one. In Tunisia. A war film."

"I know."

"You keep up with my career?"

Jon bit his lip. He hadn't meant to reveal quite as much, but he supposed it wasn't really all that damning. After all, they were still friends – weren't they?

"I ... "

"Of course you do," Callum returned, crisply "I don't know why I was surprised. I just thought ... maybe you'd seen enough of me to last a lifetime?" But the words conjured up an image – or was it a memory? – of Callum spread naked across the white–on–white bed at Portofino when they'd gone there for what he'd always thought of as their Christmas honeymoon, all creamy–golden and intense and abandoned as though trying to cram his entire life into a few hours of pleasure; as if charging some emotional battery which had long since been drained to uselessness.

"I wouldn't ... exactly say that," Jon conceded, with reluctance. "I don't hate you, Callum. Did you think I did?"

"Not really. But perhaps I thought you should."

And that, acknowledged Jon as they finally managed to end the call, was one of the most perceptive things he had ever known Callum to say – and all the more uncomfortable for being true.

Mercifully Jon had managed to pull himself together by the time he arrived at the Thorpe house in Bayswater for lunch the following week. The place did not seem to have changed since he and Callum had enjoyed a few days there three and a half years earlier – if 'enjoyed' was quite the right word, considering that Callum had been convinced there were tabloid reporters following him everywhere and was oppressed by the fear of being outed against his will. Which brought to mind a whole new series of questions in relation to Callum and Izzy's wedding, photographs of which had appeared in the press. If it had been as secret and unpremeditated as they had tried to maintain, Jon wondered who had taken those pictures and why?

Callum greeted him at the door of the house, not the basement flat this time, and ushered him into a hallway decorated in the finest taste.

"This is all Izzy's doing," he explained diffidently. "Pru and Jo are living most of the time in Paris now. If they come back at all, they use the flat downstairs. That is, they would if it wasn't always full of my work stuff."

Jon had a vision of filing cabinets and desks piled high with papers, but dismissed it quickly. For what Callum was intending a telephone and a contacts book would be all he needed. Perhaps he simply liked to entertain himself with the illusion of having a busy office.

"You want to eat first or talk?" asked Callum.

It was on the tip of Jon's tongue to defer to his host on that one, but then he changed his mind. "Let's eat," he said. "It's been a long morning."

"Of course." And with surprising meekness Callum escorted him into the dining room.

The meal was pleasant enough – simple, heaven knew, because Callum's cooking still left a lot to be desired. There was a cleaning lady or personal assistant who took care of that kind of thing when Izzy was out of town – as she was, currently up north filming *Wildfell Hall*. Whoever it was had prepared the pasta dish in advance, and there hadn't been much skill involved in heating it up, distributing it onto plates and adding salad. Indeed, more effort had been required to extract the cork from the wine and fill two goblets without wasting any. Callum's hands were not as steady as they had once been.

"Well," he asked, when they had eaten and retired to the sitting room, "did you look through what I sent you?" A copy of the script was prominent on a side–table between them.

Jon ran a slender finger across the top sheet and looked up. "I've read it."

"So – what do you think?"

"There's nothing revolutionary about it, is there? The same part, the same lines. I could do it in my sleep."

"Of course you could. Doesn't mean you're not perfect for it though."

"I don't know. I've got a lot of television commitments these days."

Callum seemed disappointed at his lack of enthusiasm. "A month," he said. "That's all I'm asking. We'll fit it around your other stuff, if you want to do it."

"Well, I suppose it might be possible …

"Good man!" Callum sprawled back in the opposite armchair. A cream polo necked sweater framed his face and his hair was a wild golden tangle, collar–length and out of control. His blue eyes were picking up the play of sunlight through stained glass panels in the Victorian sash windows. "But I'm sensing a problem. What's on your mind?"

Jon leaned back, in retreat from a personality stronger than his own. "I've never been keen on covering the same ground twice. I'm not sure how much more I can do with this part; I thought I'd left it all on stage the last time we did the play. Besides, surely you'd prefer to have somebody younger in it this time."

"Not necessarily. You and I have the kind of chemistry that you just can't fake. We've had some mad adventures, Jon, haven't we? Do you remember those awful swords in that first production, which used to bend if you hit them too hard? And that flea–bitten old fur robe I had for the banquet scene? I'm sure it was made out of somebody's cat."

Reluctantly, Jon acknowledged the tug of memory. They had been good times – epic times – and there was a lot he recalled with fondness. "The cardboard crowns," he said, despite himself. "The night you put your hand through the scenery."

"That's right," returned Callum. "The start of the run where I had to wear Douggie's boots. It felt as if his feet were still in them!"

Jon found himself smiling as his mind danced back along pleasant byways of recollection: Jax drunk off her skull at a party in the White Horse and coming to grief tangled in a roller towel – he wondered whether Douggie had been told about that, or if he had found out about her proclivities for himself – Ewen's laugh which turned too easily into coughing, Maisie threatening to iron Callum's costume with Callum still inside it. That summer had been much too surreal for words.

"It was fun, wasn't it?" He wondered exactly who was controlling his mouth.

"It was, but this is going to be different. It isn't going to be a straightforward adaptation of the play; there's more we can do with it, if you're interested."

"Such as?"

Callum took a deep breath. "Such as – supposing Mac and Banquo had been lovers? Wouldn't that give the story an extra dimension, for a start?"

"My God. You really want to give the world a gay *Macbeth*?"

"Hush! Don't say the name! Go outside and spit and throw salt over your shoulder – or at least quote something from the *Dream* to neutralise it!"

"Later. I'll do all that later. Are you out of your tiny mind, Callum?"

"Probably. But think about it for a moment, will you? Suppose I'm not just betraying my country but somebody who's given me his heart and his trust for years – somebody I've actually been sleeping with on a more or less regular basis. Doesn't that make the whole thing much more tragic?"

"Or 'not sleeping'," put in Jon, "as the case may be."

"Or 'not sleeping', exactly."

"Well, it's different. And you married Gruoch, what – for dynastic reasons?"

Callum's lips pursed. "Precisely. And you got married, too, don't forget – you've got a son, after all, Fleance."

"Well, yes. Although it's possible I didn't know you at the time."

"All right, so you're nothing like as mercenary as I am – but we both knew that already, didn't we?"

Jon's eyebrows lifted. This was one of the baldest and most self–aware statements he had ever heard from Callum, and although he had expected a certain increase in maturity in the time they'd been apart it still came as something of a shock.

"All right," he said. "I'm listening. Tell me more."

Callum grinned. "I knew you'd be intrigued! Well, I'm making the wife the bad guy in this version: she's the one who wants me to be king, and she's the one who wants you out of the way. She couldn't do it if I wasn't dangerously unstable, of course, but it doesn't take much to wind me up and set me loose. In fact, I'm thinking of having Izzy double as First Witch to underline the point. What would your reaction be to that?"

Jon considered for a moment, scanning the play in his memory. "You'll be cutting out Hecate completely?"

"I think so – don't you?"

"And making Gruoch prime mover in the plot against Duncan?"

"Absolutely."

A thoughtful silence supervened. "What exactly would you be asking me to do?"

Callum's eyes shone with a mixture of mischief and apprehension. "That's where we get to the tricky part," he admitted, grimacing. "I'd want you to be madly in love with me, and then I'd want you to be betrayed. Do you think you could manage that for me, Jon?"

"I'm not sure." The response was as dry and uninformative as Jon could possibly make it. "It's not as if I had relevant experience to call upon, after all."

His words fell with a dull thud and for a moment he wondered if he had gone too far, but Callum rallied swiftly.

"Come on, don't be like that! I thought we'd put all that behind us long ago – and if we haven't we should have done by now, shouldn't we?"

"If you say so." Jon was making an effort to keep the rawness out of his tone. "So, what will you be doing while I'm breaking my heart over you?"

"Murdering Duncan and stealing his kingdom, of course! I was already off the rails, you see – in fact, you were probably the only person holding me together. By the time Gruoch came along, I didn't take much pushing to tip me over the edge; she's turned me mad long before she goes mad herself. You see, we're saying here that witchcraft is real and she's got all sorts of supernatural powers, and once you accept that it opens up hundreds of possibilities. I mean, she can disguise herself so that even I don't recognise her, and she can fly back from the blasted heath on her broomstick before my message ever gets there – I'm even thinking of sending her off to murder Lady Macduff! But the point is, Jon, Gruoch can influence me into doing anything she bloody well likes – and what she wants most of all is to get rid of you. Anyway, Izzy and I have the whole play to demonstrate the nature of our relationship but you and I only get a few scenes so we're going to have to make them all count. That's why I need you; there's nobody in the world who can put as much emotion into a part as you can." He stopped. "No, I take that back. You don't put emotion in, you draw it out. That's a very different skill."

It was a sharply analytical comment, and showed that Callum had given the matter considerable thought. "Thank you," Jon told him, softly.

"Welcome, love." The endearment just seemed to slip out, and to be unnoticed by both of them; it made little difference to the tone of the conversation whether they acknowledged their previous connection or not. "So, what do you think?"

"Ah. Well. For a start, I think I'm too old and hardly the type, but I suppose you'll tell me that's irrelevant."

"Definitely."

"Then you'd better explain what, exactly, our characters' relationship may have been in the past?"

"That's easy. I think you looked after me when I was just starting out. I think you took me under your wing and protected me from the world, but I don't know if it was ever more than that. I know I did the most important part of my growing–up when I was with you."

Jon did not dare to meet his eyes. He was no longer sure whether they were talking about their fictional counterparts or themselves, and he was determined to make his responses neutral enough to serve for either.

"And sexually?" he asked. "What was that all about, would you say?"

Callum's response was calm and rational. "We needed each other," he said. "It worked between us, that's all."

"And you imagine, do you, that people will believe in that?"

"Why not? After all, it happens to be true. Age is irrelevant, Jon; personality is more important – we are what we are, and we can't change that. I need you to help me show how complex this man is: he's a killer and a traitor on the outside but underneath he's just a needy child. You know as well as I do that if society hadn't forced him to marry Gruoch he could have settled down with Banquo and there would never have been a tragedy. If he could have come out of the closet early enough, subsequent events would all have been very different."

"That could be said about a great many of us," Jon informed him waspishly.

"It could indeed, love. It could indeed. Well, are you going to do it or not?"

Jon passed a hand across his eyes. "I don't know," he said, thoughtfully. "It would be quite a challenge, wouldn't it?"

"It would. And if you listen, you can just about hear Ewen spinning in his grave."

"I doubt that," Jon responded. "I should think he'd have given his eye teeth for the chance to do something as unusual as this. But are you sure your backers will let you get away with it?"

"Yes." Callum was concentrating on the contents of his wine glass, and did not look up. "I've run it past them and they're all for it. They like a bit of controversy. If they wanted a conventional interpretation they'd hardly have asked me to direct it, would they?"

"Fair enough. But if I do it … That is, if I can fit it in with everything else … "

"Of course."

"Well, if I do it … I take it you're not talking about anything overt? No passionate kissing or groping, for example?"

"No. We'd need to be extremely subtle about it, in fact. I want it to be there for anybody who knows how to read it, and for the rest of the world it'll go right over their heads." The gesture that went with this was like the swatting of a fly. "We can be as open or as closed as you like, Jon, I won't force you to do anything you're not comfortable with. Only, I want you to put it all up there on the screen and let the audience see what's in your heart. You can do that, can't you?"

"I can," acknowledged Jon. "Although I'm not sure I want to."

"Because … ?"

It was the question Jon had been dreading. He set his glass aside, squared his shoulders and let the pain of the last few years show in his face. "Has it never occurred to you that I might find it difficult to play your lover after everything that's happened between us in real life?"

"Oh," Callum was momentarily nonplussed. "I thought … "

"I know what you thought. Did you ever wonder what I might think? I certainly don't recall you asking me."

"But you're … we're … It never actually meant that much to you, did it, Jon? You gave it up when I asked you to, and as far as I can tell you've never looked back since. And you did make it clear … you know, that night … that you weren't interested in starting it up again."

"I gave you up because that was what you wanted me to do. My opinion was never sought, as far as I could tell."

"Are you trying to say I didn't give you any choice?"

Jon drew a steadying breath. "Well," he said, "be honest, Callum, did you?"

Callum was staring at him now, his eyes large and round, his composure gone, the wine and the script forgotten at his side. Slowly, and with heavy inevitability, he was beginning to fit pieces together in his mind and assembling a picture that was different from the one he had originally believed he saw. The working of his thoughts was so apparent, so obviously a source of pain to him, that Jon had no option but to sit and wait for the outcome which, when it came, was just what he had silently predicted it would be.

"No, Jon, no," said Callum, in an appalled and devastated tone. "I don't suppose I ever did, did I?"

◆

(A stuffy, crowded screening room in which a film is being shown. JON and IZZY are sitting together. CALLUM paces nervously at the back of the room, intermittently biting his thumbnail.)

◆

Work on what inevitably came to be known as the Scottish film began later that year. Jon, steeling himself to a professional attitude, turned up on time, remembered his lines, and did not bump into the furniture. It was not the most pleasant experience he had ever had on a movie set, but he did everything the director asked of him and tried to forget that he and Callum had ever been more to one another than colleagues. Indeed, it was not difficult, with Callum so extremely unlike himself – dark–haired, high–cheekboned, intense and nervy, he was fully convincing as the kind of overwrought young man whose susceptibilities could be worked on by a woman of talent and ambition, and produced a performance which showed his character as an automaton guided to destruction by a wife whose motivations could only be guessed at. In deliberate contrast Jon made Banquo sensitive, a good father, the kind of friend Callum's character should have been grateful to have; unfortunately Izzy, as a shoulder–padded Thatcherite harpy, convinced her husband that friendship was weakness and that Banquo and Fleance lay between him and his legitimate ambitions. Later, even after her supposed death, Izzy's manipulative Gruoch remained a baleful presence in the film, and the question hanging over the closing reel was whether her character's suicide was merely an illusion and her cursed spirit would haunt succeeding generations for centuries to come.

Watching a rough cut of the assembled footage in a London screening room soon after principal photography had been completed, Jon could scarcely form an objective response. He had never enjoyed seeing himself on screen and only did so when he could not avoid it, but Izzy had begged for his support. Uncertain about her own performance – over–the–top megalomaniac villainesses were not her usual métier – she had even offered to have a cab at the door with its engine running in case either of them felt the need to make a hurried exit. However, they had survived with morale more or less intact. In fact it was generally agreed that, once the rough edges had been smoothed over in the editing suite and a full orchestral score laid down, the result would be a startling new interpretation of a Shakespeare standard.

"They'll either love us or they'll hate us," said Callum, smiling with his mouth whilst the expression in his eyes was one of dread. "Either way, it's been an adventure, hasn't it?"

"'It was the best of times, it was the worst of times'," Jon quoted as they parted at the end of the evening.

"'It was the age of wisdom, it was the age of foolishness'," responded Callum without hesitation. "Suppose I need you to come and be foolish for me again, Jon? Do you think you might be available?"

"I don't know," was the rejoinder. "But you'll always be welcome to ask."

And that was how matters stood for many months afterwards. Callum was busy in post–production; Izzy and Catherine were negotiating the rights to some Enid Blyton stories; Pete, Rory and James Rudge were preparing to tackle *Love's Labour's Lost* under the direction of the ubiquitous JB. Roy, on the other hand, was off somewhere exotic, turning in one of his trademark mild–mannered assassins for a spy movie featuring Bryce Gullory and Matt Damon. Every so often he phoned Jon to impart details, not of this project but of the commitment ceremony he had finally dragooned James and Matthew into accepting, and for which he had cast himself in the combined role of sugar daddy and fairy godmother. In volunteering to foot the bills for the occasion he had established himself as producer and director of a theatrical entertainment, and there was no detail he did not take an active interest in, even from a distance, and relay to Jon at inhospitable hours of the night.

Jon, at a loose end for once, went home and dug out the notes for a biography of Henry Irving he had first contemplated writing in his student days. There was a surprising amount of it in existence already and, given leisure and peace to complete the research and turn the text into something more scholarly, there might possibly be a market for it. His increased public profile from appearing as Duffy would not hurt, and even his agent expressed cautious optimism – at the same time making sure he did not lack for an occasional guest role in some television show or other. Thus, in quick succession, he played a murderous head–waiter, an absent–minded academic, a dispossessed aristocrat and the bespectacled solicitor reading the will to the family. None of these took more than a day or two, and he was happy to retreat to his cottage and his piles of reference books at the end of each assignment.

In March, indications were received that a kidney might soon be available for Nigel. A man who had been in a persistent vegetative state since being hit over the head at a football match the previous year turned out to be an ideal match. Now, following a legal battle, his life support was to be switched off; every harvestable organ had been promised to somebody, and Nigel was to be one of the recipients. He was warned not to stray too far from a telephone and to be sure of getting to the hospital within an hour or two when the time came.

"Have to cancel white water rafting down the Orinoco, then," he said. "I was looking forward to that."

"Maybe after the operation?" Jon suggested, smiling.

"Believe it when I see it, dear boy," was the half–hearted response.

Edgar, at the same time, had begun to rally considerably. Rest, medication and a stringent diet had knocked ten years off his age, and it was possible to see him making substantial progress in shaking off the effects of his illness – although there were occasions when he and Nigel sat side by side comparing symptoms like men twenty years older. At such times Jon could only observe them with amused fascination. If nothing else, it would enable him to refine his occasional depictions of elderly frailty: no experience was ever wasted in an actor's life.

◆

Nigel went into hospital in April. Jon spent hours sitting with Edgar and Jenny at their house, waiting out the surgery, willing the telephone to ring. When it did, and they were given a cautiously optimistic report on Nigel's progress, Edgar seemed to fold in on himself and give way to prodigious weariness.

"They've always been fond of one another," Jenny said, after Eddie had shambled off to bed. "They're like brothers. You never know what one of them is feeling until you've seen the effect it has on the other. They should have bitten the bullet and moved in together years ago."

It was not the first time she had expressed this sentiment, but it was the clearest demonstration Jon had ever had of what she meant.

"Emotionally they're a couple, aren't they? They get on better than some married people I know."

"They're on one another's wavelength," she concurred. "But I'm starting to worry that at some point there'll only be one of them left – and whichever one it is, he'll need support from you and me to carry on running the company. That's why they've asked me to sound you out about becoming a partner, Jon; they want you to have ten per cent of the shares now, rising to forty when one of them dies. They want to remake their wills with that in mind, as long as you have no objection."

"I can't … " He was about to demur, the default response of a modest man, then thought about it again. "I should probably accept, shouldn't I?"

"I think you should, unless you absolutely hate the idea. They want the company to continue after they're gone, and I think they'd like you to pass it on to somebody else in turn. Obviously you'll have to make your own decisions about that when the time comes."

Jon considered for a moment. "I don't know much about TV production," he admitted, apologetically, "and I was really very bad as a director."

"Maybe – but you know what makes decent drama and what doesn't, and how to tell if anybody's good at their job. Most of the rest is just common sense and instinct anyway. Nobody ever taught Eddie how to run a production company – he picked it up by making his own mistakes. But you're sensible and you're not likely to ruin everything with insane schemes, so you're the sort of person they can trust. This company is their baby; they want you to look after it when they can't."

"All right." He was surprised how easy it was to say and how comfortable he felt with the idea.

"All right?"

His mind was churning. Of all the possible futures he had envisaged, all the likely outcomes of the second half of his career, a sidestep into production had figured nowhere on the list.

"As long as you're there to help," he added, humbly.

"Absolutely. This company is as much my life now as theirs. Besides, I own ten per cent, so it's in my interest to make it work. I imagine you and I can be business associates, can't we, Jon?"

"I see no reason why not." But her words provoked a tension in him, and he found himself casting uneasy glances in her direction. After all, they were pretty much of an age; he hoped she didn't have any other sort of association in mind.

"Don't panic," she told him, quietly. "Business is all I'm interested in. Besides, I've been around theatricals most of my life and I'm getting quite good at sorting the sheep from the goats. Friends and business partners, nothing else."

Notwithstanding the sensation of relief her words produced, it occurred to him that his indecision could be read as unflattering by a woman who was neither young nor attractive. Jenny was as down–to–earth as could be imagined, but it would be wrong not to recognise that she had her sensitive emotional side.

"I'm sorry." He wasn't sure that didn't make it worse, somehow.

"You needn't be. I like our friendship the way it is, and I wouldn't want to change it. Except that one day in the distant future you're going to be my boss."

"A terrifying prospect." He attempted to smooth things over with a joke.

"You're not alone in that, I promise you," was her quiet response. "Let's hope the pair of us have time to get used to the idea before we put it into practice!"

◆

Jenny's doomsday scenario retreated into the distance as the year progressed, however. Nigel began a steady recuperation in and out of specialist convalescent facilities and, buoyed by his progress, Edgar began to throw himself enthusiastically into preparations for the new series of *Hawker and Duffy* in the autumn.

As he was beginning to settle to the notion of returning to the show, however, Jon was startled to receive an invitation to attend the commitment ceremony for James Rudge and Matthew Linton, to take place at the Greyhound in Gostrey over August Bank Holiday. He did not know either James or Matthew well, having met them only in company with Roy, and supposed this invitation had been made at the request of his friend who no doubt stood in need of moral support. Without giving the matter much thought, therefore, he accepted – and was then plunged into an agony of indecision as to whether or not he ought to buy them a present. Roy provided the solution by offering to add Jon's name to the gift he and Pete would be giving, which only left Jon with travel arrangements to make – and, as he would be working until Friday evening, this meant driving down on the morning of the ceremony. Everything was in place well in advance, therefore, and he was able to give his full attention to work that week.

Which, as matters turned out, was nothing like enough to protect him against the disaster which struck him out of a clear blue sky.

Waking up was more difficult than it should have been. Jon's eyelids worked like rusty roller–shutters, opening in instalments: first a little, then a little more, tentatively admitting light before slamming closed again. He was warm and safe, but his body was a miscellany of discomforts and his mouth tasted as if no fresh water had visited it for months. He doubted he would be able to speak, but didn't see the necessity either. In fact there was no necessity for anything; going back to sleep would be a better idea than making any attempt to interact with the world.

"Dad, are you awake?" It had been a good idea in theory, demolished by the sound of Justine's voice beyond his line of sight. "I was wondering when you were going to put in an appearance."

Jon tried to turn his head, but the pain in his shoulder wouldn't let him twist far enough to make her visible.

"J's ... " His mouth was too furred–up to shape her name. "Wha' ... you ... ?"

"Hang on a minute."

He heard the sound of liquid being poured, and a moment later a plastic cup appeared under his nose. He sipped a lukewarm antiseptic flavour, the best water he had ever tasted.

"More?" asked Justine. He could see her properly now.

"Please." A whole word this time – vowels, consonants and all! He was quite impressed by the way it sounded in the circumstances. "Thank you."

"No problem." She moved her chair and sat down, grinning. "You look bloody awful!"

"Do I?" He would have laughed at her astonishment if he'd had the energy.

"How did it happen?"

He tried to shrug, then thought better of it. "Fell downstairs. Broke my collarbone."

"And three teeth, and concussed yourself!" She obviously knew more about it than he did and her question had therefore been a rhetorical one.

"Yes." Truth to tell, he was massively embarrassed about the whole business. He was rarely required to perform anything resembling a stunt, and on this occasion it had gone spectacularly wrong. He had shoulder–charged a prop door which was intended to resist at first and then give way, after which he was to turn to the girl he was rescuing, deliver his line and usher her down the fire escape. Unfortunately at the cry of "Action!" he had shoulder–charged the door as required, found it resisting more than he expected and, instead of stepping away and asking the carpenter to have a look at it, he had slammed into it again and gone through far too quickly and no longer on his feet. After that there had been some sort of impact with the railings on the fire escape, several collisions of various kinds, and a lot of confusion involving an ambulance, an A&E Department, a barrage of questions and a doctor who shone a torch into his eyes – and all while he had been trying to apologise to Eddie for ruining the take.

By the time he'd reached this room in what appeared to be a brand–new hospital, all he'd wanted to do was sleep – and he'd done a lot more sleeping since. But Eddie had been there for some of the time, clasping his hand in the ambulance – he might be sixty and in failing health but he had a grip like steel – and drawing a laconic comment from the paramedic in attendance.

"Bugger me, *Hawker and Duffy* holding hands in my cab!"

And Eddie had stuck like glue throughout triage and X–ray and treatment, and had still been there when Jon was tucked into bed, bandaged to the eyeballs, his left side a mass of pain, his consciousness peeling away under the influence of whatever drug he'd been given. He thought Eddie had been there when he fell asleep, and maybe when he surfaced hours later to be informed that his family were on their way. He remembered wondering whether Diana was in England, and if so how the hospital could possibly have known. Then it became apparent that his brain wasn't working because he should have remembered whether he had family or not, and when he considered the matter in detail he decided the only solution was to go to sleep and hope he might understand better when he woke up again.

"How long have I been here?" Really, 'what happened?' and 'where am I?' were lines that should have been outlawed decades ago; they'd been done to death in a hundred thousand clichéd movies already – some of which he'd been in himself.

"Since Thursday," Justine said. "It's Saturday now."

Saturday? He'd lost a day somewhere. He remembered having lunch on Thursday in the studio canteen, so the accident must have taken place in the afternoon. Had Eddie stayed all night, then, and if so where was he now?

"I couldn't come yesterday," Justine was saying. "I had a piano exam in the afternoon. When they rang up they said you wouldn't be conscious anyway, so Mum and I decided I'd come up on the early train today; I got here three hours ago. Mum would have come with me, but she didn't know if you'd want to see her – and she reckons I'm big enough and ugly enough to travel on my own anyway. She says she pities any poor rapist stupid enough to try it on with me."

That sounded like the sort of robust thing Rosemary would have said – not complimentary, but reassuring after a fashion. At least it demonstrated faith in Justine's ability to look after herself.

"Obviously it worked," he smiled awkwardly. "Where are you staying?"

Justine shrugged. "I'll be all right at your house, won't I? I've got a key, and all my stuff's there. Jenny says I can come and go by taxi and charge it to the company, and phone her if I'm worried. But I'll stay with her and Eddie if you want me to."

Jon looked at her. Somehow, while he was asleep, she seemed to have grown up; she was sixteen now, obviously ready for a measure of independence: his misfortune could be the making of her.

"No," he said, "that's all right. There's food in the freezer; you can look after yourself for a day or two, can't you?"

Justine wrinkled her nose. "Of course I can. I'll stay on after you come home, too, just to make sure you're managing all right. Mum'll be ringing every five minutes to check up anyway, if I know her – and I can watch videos in the evenings, if that's okay with you?"

"If you want to."

"They're sending you home on Monday. Eddie and Jenny are going to pick you up in the car."

There was no denying her enthusiasm; she seemed to have constituted herself his guardian and protector while he was unable to take care of himself, and he would be a fool to reject such amply demonstrated goodwill.

"Thank you," he said. "Could you ring Roy Arbour for me? I was supposed to be going to a wedding today; he'll have to make my apologies. His number's in my blue book, wherever that is."

"It's here," said Justine. "I've got all your stuff in a plastic bag. Your watch is buggered, I'm afraid. You must have landed on it when you fell."

"Oh." One of the last mementoes of his time with Callum. "Have you thrown it away?"

"Not yet. Do you want me to?"

"No. It was a present; I wouldn't want to lose it, even if it's broken."

"I'll take it back to the house, then, shall I?"

"Yes, please, if you would."

Justine smiled. "All part of the service – I'm going over this afternoon. Eddie and Jenny are coming to see you later, and I'll be back this evening." She sounded terrifyingly efficient all of a sudden, as if she were the adult and he the child. "Eddie's really upset about the accident. He says it was all his fault."

"It wasn't. It was mine."

"He said you'd say that. He says you said it over and over again in the ambulance. But it doesn't matter what you think because there'll have to be an investigation anyway, and Eddie says he'll probably have to pay a fine. He wanted to stay, you know, but Jenny made him go home with her. She said she'd resign if he didn't. She reckons that's the only thing that frightens him these days!"

"He relies on her." Jon leaned against his pillows. The room had started to swim, and he felt as if someone had been pouring acid into his eyes. "He'd never manage on his own. But it really wasn't his fault at all."

"Well, you can argue about that when you see him," Justine told him. "Given the condition you're in, I wouldn't suggest you try fighting until you're feeling better. Not if you want to live to finish filming, anyway."

And Jon was going to make some trenchant response to that, really, as soon as he could remember what it was, but just at the moment it didn't seem quite as important as a detailed inspection of the insides of his eyelids, a slow slide into the haze of pre–sleep, and surrender to the safety and comfort of the healing dark.

As promised, Jon was driven home by Edgar and Jenny during the course of the following Monday, after which he retired to bed and took no further part in the proceedings. The next afternoon, by arrangement with Justine, Roy arrived in a taxi, bringing – in addition to his overnight bag – a bottle of champagne and a sheaf of gladioli worthy of

Dame Edna Everage at her finest. He was all charm and bonhomous cheer, but to one who knew him as well as Jon there was something a little too determined about the twinkly good humour, something so forced as to be almost painful. It took an actor, he supposed, to know when another actor was putting on a show.

"The champagne," said Roy, settling in, "is from the wedding. Everybody was sorry you couldn't make it. Especially me – I could have done with the immoral support. But I see you've got plenty of flowers already."

Bouquets had been arriving at regular intervals during the morning – from the crew, from Eddie and Jenny, even from Nigel whose own recovery was progressing satisfactorily. There was also, tucked away on the windowsill and half–hidden behind the curtain, a bunch of multi–coloured roses which had arrived without a card or other means of identifying the sender. Justine had been all for ringing the florist to make enquiries; Jon had calmed her with something vague about a friend with a penchant for practical joking. He had managed to insinuate that the culprit might be Bill, and was now hoping Bill wouldn't take it into his head to send flowers for real; he didn't think it likely, but doubted his powers of invention would be up to devising a second explanation if he did.

"People have been very generous," he said, as Justine bustled from the room in search of a container tall enough to take the gladioli.

Roy reached across urgently and took his wrist. "How much can I say in front of her? Do you need me to keep my big fat trap shut about the wedding?"

"Not really – she must have seen the invitation, it's still on the board in the kitchen. Just try to avoid outing anybody who wouldn't want to be outed, will you?" The look that accompanied this remark was direct and meaningful, leaving Roy in no doubt whom he was alluding to.

"All right. But having a commitment ceremony isn't exactly keeping it off the radar, is it? I've brought pictures, if you're interested; I printed them off last night. How about you, Justine? Would you like to see photos of a wedding with no bride?"

She blinked, re–entering the room and setting down a plastic waste–

bin full of water which was the only receptacle that would hold long–stemmed flowers of any description.

"I knew it was supposed to be a gay wedding. James and … somebody?"

"James and Matthew," supplied her father. "They're friends of Roy's."

Roy was scattering pictures on the coffee table. "Well, a wedding is a wedding is a wedding, I suppose – and this one had everything: confetti, cake, cheesy smiles, family mayhem. I expect you'll recognise some of the people in the background, at least."

Preoccupied with the flowers, Justine glanced over briefly. "It's a sweet idea – but it isn't legal, is it?" There was no criticism inherent in the words; this was merely an observation.

"It's not illegal, either," responded Jon. "Just not officially recognised. But if they wanted to make their relationship public, this was probably as good a way as any to go about it."

"Not that it was ever really a secret," Roy put in. "They should have been hyphenated years ago, like Gilbert–and–George or Marshall–and–Snelgrove or something. Nobody talks about James or Matthew separately any more; they might as well have been married. Unfortunately the law doesn't allow that yet – although I know there's been a fair bit of lobbying lately."

Justine was giving her concentration to the flowers, declining to look at the pictures while her hands were wet.

"Well," she said, "I don't understand why anyone would go to all the trouble of having a wedding if it doesn't mean anything. Couldn't they just hang on and wait until the law's been sorted out?"

Roy and Jon exchanged glances.

"My love," said Roy gently, "generations of queer men and women have died waiting for the straight world to wake up and take notice of them. Not to get too political about it or anything, but there comes a time when you have to put your foot down and insist on being who you are. Besides, nobody has any idea what might be around the next corner; it's really a case of grabbing your happiness while you can. And, let's face it, we're all a bunch of theatrical old queens … there's nothing we like half so much as dressing–up and showing–off!"

"Very true," laughed Justine. "So what did you wear, then, Uncle Roy?"

"Blue suit, darling, and a fabulous waistcoat – there's a picture of it somewhere – explosion in a paint factory, like the one Simon Callow had in *Four Weddings and a Funeral*. I worked with him once," he mused. "He played my boss. We didn't get on, which is odd because we have so much in common, but that doesn't mean I wouldn't steal from him – or anybody else – should the occasion arise."

"No shame in stealing from the best," agreed Jon, with a conspiratorial grin.

"Not that you'd know, of course, never having stolen anything from anybody."

"As long as you believe that," Jon smiled, "it means you haven't noticed yet."

"Is that Pete?" Justine pointed to a bulky figure at the edge of one of the group shots. She had dried her hands and was examining the pictures for faces she knew – of which there were precious few. James and Matthew under a rose arch; James and Matthew with their families grinning and trying to pretend they were comfortable at a wedding between two men; James and Matthew cutting a heart–shaped cake ... Here and there a well known face appeared in the background, but for the most part they were snapshots of people's cousins and grandmothers and best friends from drama or music school. "Why's he looking so miserable?"

Roy sighed. "He was in a bitch of a mood all day. Someone stepped on his toe in the morning, and after that he wanted to kill everybody he met." Jon looked up sharply across Justine's bent head, but Roy's expression warned him to silence. "It's a long story and not particularly edifying; let's just say that he wasn't at his best, shall we? I could have done with your dad along to referee, Justine; he always adds a note of sanity to the proceedings. Trust you to find a way of weaselling out of it, Jonathan!"

Thus Roy steered the conversation away from what appeared to be a somewhat delicate subject, and back to the absorbing topic of Jon's accident.

Towards the end of the evening Justine left them on their own, having earlier assembled a more than passable dinner with Roy's enthusiastic assistance. He had once played a chef in a film and now treated them to a reprise of the performance he had given then – screamingly funny, but not a great deal of practical help.

Justine excused herself after the meal and headed off to soak in the bath before bed. Roy made himself comfortable in the sitting room with Jon, the pair of them equipped with coffee and the box of designer chocolates which had accompanied Nigel's flowers.

"You've got half a florist's shop in here," Roy said, as Jon pressed back into the cushions on the sofa. "Who sent the roses?"

Jon shrugged. He still found himself doing that, even though it was not particularly comfortable since his injury. "Someone I've worked with, I suppose. Izzy Thorpe, perhaps?"

"Izzy Henley," Roy corrected. "As you very well know, she's 'Sadie, Sadie, married lady, Still in bed at noon'. It all seems to be working out reasonably well so far." The words were blithe enough, but there was an undercurrent of bitterness in the tone. Even though he was far from at his best, Jon was not about to let such a blatantly–dropped hint escape him.

"Indeed it does," he said. "There was never very much to stand in their way, was there? But what about you, Roy? I get the impression there's something bothering you."

Roy sat back in his chair and groaned. "You never said a truer word, dear boy – but where do I start? With the fact that I've kicked Pete out of the house, I suppose. He spent most of yesterday moving his stuff into one of the spare rooms at the Old Crown, and I should imagine Bill Wildman hates me for it already."

"You kicked him out?" Incredulous, Jon repeated the words. "Can you actually do that? I thought you owned the place jointly?"

Roy laughed, but there was no humour in it. "Whatever gave you that idea?" he asked. "All the property's in my name – well, Arbour

Estates', anyway, which in effect is me. I paid for every stick and stone myself – Pete doesn't own a thing except a few suits, and much good may they do him. I can't wait to see how far he'll get on his own."

"On his own?"

"Completely. The shit hit the fan during the weekend." Roy enunciated the words as carefully as if they were Shakespeare. "Somebody was indiscreet, and I finally put the pieces together and realised what had been going on. For the past couple of years, Pete's been screwing JB behind my back."

Jon's coffee mug nearly fell from his hand. He mastered it only with difficulty and set it down again. "I'm sorry? You did say JB?"

"I did. Jeremy Bracegirdle, infamous cocksman. Oh, there's more, much more … JB's been working his way through the company, of course, which is what he got edged out of the BBC for doing – and we all know he doesn't discriminate; he's an all–purpose fuck. Some of the girls didn't mind, and one or two of the boys, but when he put the moves on the wrong straight boy he ended up with a complaint to the management. I don't know all the details," Roy added, glumly. "I was out of the country, *making mit der fake Cherman accent* and trying to kill Matt Damon – who, let me assure you, is quite a charmer but totally out of my league. Anyway I gather *Love's Labour's Lost* was a hotbed of … well, hot beds. Pete only seems to have done the dirty with JB – albeit over a period of something like three years – but JB's been putting it about with reckless, and not exclusively gay, abandon. Anything that moves, and quite a lot that doesn't, sooner or later Bloody Bracegirdle will attempt to roger it."

"But … Pete?" Jon was stuck on that basic concept. He had always thought of Pete and Roy as a couple, and although they'd had their ups and downs they had seemed suited to one another from the beginning. If they were to separate now, it would remove one of the pillars of his universe; he wouldn't know his place in the world if they were not together. The earth was shifting under his feet; he was beginning to feel vulnerable.

"Pete. I know for a fact that they've been doing the horizontal tango since *The Tempest* and I'm pretty sure Pete used to visit JB when he was

274

living at the Old Crown – although I haven't got proof of that, of course. What I do know is there were times when he should have been at home and he wasn't. I suppose, if I thought about it at all, I imagined he was picking up random boys and having random sex with them. It never occurred to me that it might be the same person over and over again – or that it could be him."

Silence fell, painful and confused. At last Jon, struggling to assimilate what he had been told, said kindly, "I'm sorry, I didn't know about any of this. I never suspected it for a moment." Indeed, he had cheerfully ignored such hints as had begun to come his way; he had felt there was enough turmoil in his life without adding more, a determination which now seemed unforgivably selfish.

"Why should you? 'Unto the pure all things are pure'. You wouldn't treat a lover that way, and you don't expect anybody else to either. I wish I was you sometimes, Jon; everything always seems so simple for you."

"It isn't," Jon said, apologetically. "It's rarely simple."

"I know. But leave me my illusions, will you?" Roy's voice quivered for the first time since he had begun his recitation. "I like to think there are things I can count on when the world goes to hell, and one of them is that you'll always be the same old reliable Jon. This has made me realise that I really wasn't very nice to you when we were together. In fact I've wondered whether what's happened since wasn't divine retribution for the way I treated you back then. I'm very sorry about it all, you know."

"I know. You said so at the time. But it's past, Roy; we're different people now. We were never meant to be together, were we? Not like that, at least."

"No, we weren't." Roy's tone sounded a modicum more hopeful. "My tastes are far too unrefined, I'm sorry to say. With the best will in the world, Jon, nobody could ever accuse you of being rough trade. But it was fun while it lasted, eh?"

"Definitely," Jon assured him. "I wouldn't have changed it for the world."

◆

For a while after that they confined themselves to discussing Pete's inadequacies, centring on the proposition that he was boorish, lacking in talent and in some mercifully unspecified way selfish in bed. Roy talked until every complaint against his lover had been rehearsed in detail, then pushed his mug away and sighed.

"I'd have the bastard back if he seemed even remotely sorry for what he's done, but he just doesn't seem to get it. It's not him going over the side that bothers me so much as the fact that he did it with that piece of excrement Bracegirdle. I've never understood why any sensible man would get involved with him at all – which begs the question whether Pete had any sense to start with. I used to think he was just one of the big dumb good-looking ones, but I'm beginning to wonder if he's actually incredibly stupid."

Jon felt this was harsh, especially in view of the fact that Pete had been bright enough to hook himself up to someone who had provided him with a comfortable home and a luxurious lifestyle for years, but refrained from saying so. "We all make mistakes," he murmured instead.

"We do indeed. Only some of us admit to them and try to put them right, while some stomp up and down like Miles Gloriosus insisting we have the right to behave like arseholes. Pete seems to think he doesn't actually owe me anything – like respect, for example, or even loyalty. Irony being, of course, that I was working my way round to asking him if he wanted to make it permanent. He's always been fairly sniffy about that sort of thing in the past, but I thought if he saw it working for James and Matthew ... "

"Oh, Roy, surely not!"

"I know. It was a mad idea, I see that now. I suppose I imagined Pete would be so overwhelmed by the sight of the boys exchanging rings that he'd drop a sentimental tear and go down on one knee there and then. Pete, I ask you, of all people – what was I thinking? The oaf doesn't have a romantic bone in his body – obviously I'd been living in a fool's paradise. Not that I begrudge James and Matthew their day out in the frock or anything. But as for Pete, he can sink or swim all by himself from now on; he doesn't get another penny from me unless he crawls here on his hands and knees and says he's sorry – and actually seems to mean it this time."

"And how likely do you think that is to happen?"

Roy looked down, inspecting the toecaps of his perfectly polished shoes before he lifted his gaze again. When he did, there was a fullness in his eyes which looked remarkably like tears – except that Roy Arbour had never been known to cry in his life without being paid to do so.

"Well," he said, "let's just say there'll be herds of formation–flying pigs doing loop–the–loops over Shapley before that comes to pass."

"Squadrons," said Jon helpfully.

"What?"

"They wouldn't be herds of pigs, if they were flying. They'd be squadrons."

"Ah. Of course," acknowledged Roy, with what might almost have been a smile. "Squadrons of flying pigs. I stand corrected."

And, after that, they were silent again for a very long time.

Jon did not sleep well that night, whether as a result of his conversation with Roy or because he was at all times vaguely conscious that his guest would be passing an uncomfortable night on the couch in his study.

In the morning, when he went down to the sitting room and opened the curtains, he brought the multi–coloured roses in from their exile on the windowsill and placed them in a more advantageous position on the coffee table. Then he sat and looked at them properly for the first time, wondering whether Callum had in fact gone out and bought them himself or whether he had instructed some employee to do it, and in either case what he had meant to convey by sending them. It was over between them and had been for years, but in another sense it had never really been over at all. Diana had been right about that, at least: his feelings towards Callum had scarcely been diminished by the years and the miles between them – and not even by Callum's marriage to Izzy. It all made perfect sense to him, although whether it would to anyone else remained open to question.

He was still staring at the roses when Roy appeared in the doorway, shoeless, jacketless, his hair a rumpled tangle and stubble on his chin.

"God," he said grimly, "look at you, all clean and tidy and neat and fresh – and I feel like something the cat dragged in. That spare bed of yours leaves a lot to be desired, Jonathan."

"I'm sorry. Shall I make you some coffee?"

"In a minute," Roy smiled, sitting down. "And then I'll cook us both breakfast, if you like ... I suspect Justine's intending to have a lie–in this morning."

"Possibly," Jon answered, absent–mindedly. "She often does."

"Good for her. She must be a massive consolation, all things considered."

"Yes." Jon had not quite thought of his daughter in such terms before, but he could hardly deny it. "I'm very proud of her."

"Naturally." Roy ran a hand across his bristled chin. "So," he said at last, "are you going to tell me who it really was that sent the roses? Was it Izzy? Or could it have been another member of her family?"

"Another ... ?" Jon looked up, and found Roy watching him. Although he had spent much of his film and television career being menacing, he had the capacity to radiate an aura of benevolence on occasion which his friends found comforting.

"Ah. I see I was right." Roy stopped, then continued. "Let me tell you a story, dear boy, about something that happened a long time ago in another country, to somebody who might or might not have been a cousin of mine. Let's call her Cousin Sophie, for the sake of argument, and pretend that she's getting on a bit. She might – or might not, whichever takes your fancy – live all alone with her dog, in a cottage by the sea."

Jon was aware of colour leaching from his face. He knew that he was wide–eyed and open–mouthed, not quite comprehending what Roy was saying yet experiencing a sudden apprehension at what might follow.

"Always supposing," Roy went on gently, "that I had a property nearby, I might conceivably have asked Sophie to wander over occasionally to make sure my guests were behaving themselves. We'll imagine, shall we, that Sophie doesn't know much about theatre and wouldn't be able to put names to the faces of anyone she saw? She described you rather charmingly, however: a tall, thin man with beautiful manners. And of course I knew who I'd lent the cottage to, so I had no doubt who she meant. But when she told me that she'd seen you on the beach with someone … Well, her description was so vague it could have been pretty well anybody."

Tension drained from Jon's body, leaving him weak. He made an attempt to say something – anything – but none of the words made sense either separately or together. He was remembering the beach, the snowy day, the blissful warmth of Callum in his arms. It had all been far too long ago.

"Which is where the matter would have ended," continued Roy, "if Sophie hadn't had to go in for a hip replacement round about the time that Ewen died. We ended up having the dog at Fardels for a few weeks, as you probably remember, and Callum dropped in to stay while he was there. Humans will sometimes keep secrets for you if you ask them nicely, but animals are nothing like as obliging; they don't know what they're not supposed to tell. The way Muttley and Callum fell on one another's neck when they met, it was pretty obvious that they'd run into each other somewhere before and that they'd absolutely adored one another on sight. If I hadn't already worked out who it was you'd taken down to Portofino with you that time, I'm sure that would have been enough to convince me." He paused, then went on in an altered tone. "I don't know how secret you thought you were being, Jon, but Pete and I have known for a while. Or guessed, I suppose I should say. For myself, I haven't said a word to a soul … but I have no idea what Pete might have seen fit to discuss with JB while they were up to no good together. Personally I think that if Bloody Bracegirdle had ever believed you and Callum were an item he might have tried to use it against you – or at least made some attempt to smuggle himself into Callum's knickers – but in all the time we've been working on *Robin Hood* together he's never given any indication of suspecting Callum wasn't straight. Not that it would have been enough to stop him in any case, one suspects; with the Bracegirdle it was always a question of 'so many men, so little time'."

"God." Jon buried his face in his hands. It was not comfortable and he wished he hadn't attempted it, but there was relief to be obtained by hiding from Roy's too–knowing gaze.

"Look," his friend continued, "don't get upset. I don't suppose Pete said anything, and I know I didn't. Sophie hasn't a clue who Callum is – although she knows you, of course, from *Hawker and Duffy* – and the dog's not telling. So I'm going to assume, unless you insist otherwise, that you and the blond boy had some kind of desperately romantic affair during which, if there's any justice, you shagged the living daylights out of one another at Portofino – and that you were ecstatically happy right up until the moment he kicked you in the teeth and married Izzy Thorpe instead? Since when, if I'm not mistaken, he's probably wishing he hadn't been quite so bloody stupid as to let you out of his sight in the first place?"

"I … can't answer that," Jon told him. "The last part, I mean."

"Ah. But the rest is true?"

"More or less."

"Good! I always suspected you had a crush on him, but I never thought he had enough intelligence to drag you into bed and have his wicked way with you. I'm glad I was wrong about that. If it's not too much of an intrusion, dear boy, may I ask how long the whole wonderful business lasted?"

If Jon was disconcerted by the question, he took care not to show it. "On and off, just under two years."

Roy shook his head. "And you never breathed a word about it – either of you – until after it was over. Well done, old thing. Bloody well done."

"We had a gentleman's agreement," said Jon. "We promised we'd never tell."

"Of course you did." Roy gripped his uninjured arm for a moment. "That's just the sort of thing you would do. Well, it's safe with me; if I haven't said anything by now, you can be sure I have no intention of doing so. But the question remains, of course: does he still love you? And do you still love him?"

"That's two questions," Jon protested, mildly. "One of which I don't know the answer to."

"And one of which you do," countered Roy, with a sympathetic smile.

Roy's visit was short. He was gone soon after lunchtime, leaving Jon and Justine alone. He was in sober and reflective mood as a result of his conversation with Roy; she, in the first flush of a passion for housework, had announced a plan to spring clean the cottage from top to bottom before she left. The fact that it was nearly September was no bar to her determination, it appeared.

That afternoon Jon retreated to his study and got out the notes for the Irving book. He looked at the pages and they looked back at him, and not a single original thought appeared in his mind. It was impossible to concentrate on anything except Roy's parting words.

"You know you're right together," he had said then.

"I know. It wasn't my decision."

"Rubbish. He trampled all over you, and you let him."

"Do you seriously think I could have stopped him?"

"I don't know," Roy had said as he climbed into the taxi. "I only know you didn't try."

And although he was not a man given to regrets and recriminations, Jon could not help admitting the sense of what Roy had said. Possibly he could have held on to Callum, if he'd tried hard enough, but he was not entirely sure he had wanted to at the time – and even less certain what he would have done had the same choice been presented now. But he missed the nights, he missed the warmth, and he missed the closeness – even if it had only been illusory.

In truth, as time drew on, he was beginning to miss Callum more than he had ever imagined possible.

In that respect, Justine's presence did not exactly help. That very evening, searching along her father's meticulously alphabetised video shelves, she fell with delight on the garish red and orange box containing *Planetfall*.

"Oh, wow, I love this!" she exclaimed, brandishing it enthusiastically. "I saw it about twenty times when it first came out.

I've even got one of those little Rossi action figures somewhere!"

Despite himself, Jon could not help laughing. "I remember you telling me you thought Callum Henley was 'really really cute'," he teased, expecting her to disavow the sentiment now that she was older.

"Well, he is!" was the response, against his expectations. "He's a babe … and he's getting baber and baber all the time."

Jon's eyebrows lifted. "I'm not sure 'baber' is a word," he commented. "But I take it you're still a fan."

"You bet. Did you ever find out whether that friend of yours had met him? You said you were going to ask next time you saw him." When Jon looked at her blankly, she went on. "You know, a couple of years ago, somebody came here in the night and left before I got up in the morning? You said he'd gone back to work on a film with Callum. *Deadfall*, I think it was."

"Oh. Yes, I remember now."

"You were going to ask him if he knew Callum," she continued. "Did you ever get round to it?"

"No, I didn't." He bit his lip. "I'm sorry, I should have told you at the time. That actually was Callum, I'm afraid."

Justine's eyes grew round. "Callum Henley? Really? He was here, in this house? I didn't know you knew him that well!"

It was on the tip of his tongue to tell her exactly how well he and Callum had known one another, but then he checked himself. It was not entirely his story to tell, and having once confessed to Roy – who had guessed it anyway – did not give him the right to reveal it all to Justine as well. Besides, he would scarcely dare to have such an important conversation with his daughter unless he had cleared it with her mother first. Rosemary had some very pronounced views on the subject of homosexuality, and would still be capable of taking Justine away from him if she had a mind to.

"We've worked together several times," he said. "He was up this way on family business, and he needed somewhere to sleep." He was hoping she would not ask why a man with successful movie and stage appearances to his credit had not simply booked into a hotel for the night. "I felt I ought to keep quiet about it," he added apologetically.

There were a number of questions Justine could have asked at this point, many of which would have been awkward for him to answer, but the one which did emerge took her father by surprise.

"Was that why he wanted Auntie Di to work with him, then, because he knew you? I supposed you fixed that up, did you?"

"Auntie Di?"

"You know, when she did the music on *Firefall*?"

"She did?"

"Oh, Dad! Of course you knew about that, don't be daft! She played the bit at the end, where Rossi's crying over the Commander! And then when he fires up all the engines and aims the ship at the planet and all you see after that is flames … that's Auntie Di, playing over the closing credits."

Of course. Jon had been too stunned by the storyline to think about the music, but the plangent harp–notes had sounded hauntingly familiar even when distorted by the speakers in the cinema. He should have recognised his sister's distinctive attack, but the thought had never crossed his mind until now.

"Actually," he said, "I didn't know. Callum and Auntie Di are both professional people; they don't consult me about their contractual arrangements." And he reflected that he hadn't sounded quite so pompous since he'd played the crusty family lawyer earlier in the year, and that he needed to start mixing with younger company or he'd end up completely fossilised before he was fifty.

"Well, she enjoyed working with him," Justine told him, chirpily. "She said he was fun and friendly. Is he like that with you?"

"Sometimes." Jon was irresistibly reminded of his own epitaph to the Scottish experience. "Good and bad, like most other people in the world."

Justine was watching his face intently – and, although he didn't think he had left any particular emotions on display, she seemed to reach some sort of decision on the strength of it.

"Well, I'm not sure I'm in the mood for *Planetfall* tonight," she conceded. "Maybe we want some–thing lighter. How about Uncle Roy in *Demon Chef*?"

"Perfect. He's really funny in that."

"He is. Although not quite as funny as he was last night."

"True. The best performances never seem to get caught on camera," he told her. But he managed to laugh in all the right places nonetheless.

It was a day or two more before he and Justine got round to watching *Planetfall* together, side by side on the couch in the dimly–lit sitting room, both of them caught up spellbound in the action. All the classic moments of the film played out before them in sequence: the rescue of the Commander from the fiery pit, the casual kiss which had first clued–in a generation of movie viewers to the nature of the relationship, the decontamination shower for which most – but not all – of Callum's body–hair had been dyed green. It was nearly five years since that particular scene had been filmed – the year Connor had been born, the year Roy and Pete had moved into Fardels, the year Callum and Jon had been together. How much had changed during those five years was the subject of inevitable melancholy reflection as the movie played.

After it ended neither Jon nor Justine made any attempt to get out of their seats to put the light on, although she used the remote control to switch off the TV.

"That's such a good film," she said. "One of the best things Callum's ever done."

"True. He hates it now, of course."

"Does he? Yes, of course he does. Nothing would ever really be good enough for him, would it?"

"Probably not."

There was another silence, then Justine said, "It's not the kissing and stuff, is it? I mean, he's not embarrassed about having to play a gay character?"

"Hardly. It's grist to the mill in our profession. One week you're a sensitive gay astronaut, next week you're a demented serial killer. You have to be convincing whatever you do."

"And anyway," Justine went on, "he's married, so nobody's going to get the wrong idea about him, right?"

"Also true," acknowledged Jon. "I've worked with Izzy several times, too, as a matter of fact, and we were all in the Scottish film together."

"Yes, I knew about that. I didn't realise you went back such a long way, that's all."

"Oh yes. Izzy's one of my best friends. She asked me to marry her once." And he had no idea why he'd said that, except that perhaps it would serve to establish his heterosexual credentials at a moment when he was feeling vulnerable in that regard. Watching Callum in any of his movies always left him emotionally poleaxed, and in the immediate aftermath of an encounter with silver–eyed Rossi he could scarcely be held responsible for his actions.

"You're kidding!"

"No. But I think she was."

"Good. Not that she wouldn't suit you, Dad, but she looks pretty good with Callum, too – although I've never really worked out why they haven't had a baby yet. It's not as if he can't, obviously, because he's supposed to have had one already with that Thea woman. Maybe she can't. Izzy, I mean. Or maybe she's just too busy with her career."

"That could be it," Jon conceded, uncomfortably. "She's very serious about her work."

"Fair enough. It would be a shame if they didn't, though. She'd make a good mum."

"Yes," acknowledged Jon. "I'm sure she would."

After Justine went home that weekend, Jon returned to work on *Hawker and Duffy*. Many details of the production had been altered to accommodate him: for the time being he was only to be filmed from the side or in close–up, for example, or partially shielded by other people or doors. It was laborious, and so was having temporary repairs to his three broken teeth and covering his bruises with make–up, but at least it got the show back on the road and enabled the company to stick to its schedule. Given the financial penalty that would undoubtedly ensue as a result of the accident, Jon was anxious not to make the situation more complicated than necessary.

That it was gruelling would have been ridiculous to deny. Edgar and

Jenny made sure he ate with them after work and drove him home, which took care of food and transportation, but he had underestimated the long–term stress of carrying around an injury. Everything took longer and was more difficult than it needed to be, and the overall effect was steadily more and more depressing.

In such a mood, a phone call from Roy one Saturday evening came as a welcome diversion.

"Interesting news," he began, archly. "You won't be surprised to hear that JB's got the sack – again."

"Really?" Jon made no attempt to pretend he was sorry. "What for, this time?"

"Not keeping it in his pants, of course. Nothing to do with Pete, either. Apparently he turned up one day in the week with a black eye, and the next day he was packing his bags. Going to sell up here and try his luck in the Southern Hemisphere, according to Bill."

"Oh! And is ... " It was not an easy question to ask. "Is Pete going with him?"

Roy laughed hollowly. "Hardly, dear boy; he's been dumped, from a very great height – for being too old or too hairy or something – and may I be the first to say, 'It serves him right'. I wonder how long it'll be before he comes crawling round begging me to take him back?"

"Not long, I don't suppose." In one respect at least, Jon felt that Roy's character analysis of Pete had been perfectly accurate: he would be absolutely useless on his own. "And will you, when he does?"

"Almost certainly," came the disillusioned response. "His feet smell, he farts in bed, he's got all the personal charm of a warthog with halitosis – but the two of us were a done deal a long time ago, I'm afraid. So, like an idiot, I'll probably let him talk me into it eventually. Although I might just make him suffer first."

"And so you should."

"And so I will," Roy laughed. "Oh, and you may also be interested to hear that everything is apparently not quite so blissful in the Henley household these days, either. Reputedly something to do with an over–endowed actress he met while he was making his desert movie, which you and I both know is a farrago of nonsense. My spies tell me it's more likely to be good old–fashioned 'creative differences', and that if they do separate they'll still be on the best of terms. Nothing hysterical and dramatic about this one, I'm pleased to say."

If the thought of Roy having spies was chilling, the idea that they had detected a flaw in Callum's marriage to Izzy was even more so. Jon had genuinely thought that it was working, and despite his own equivocal feelings on the subject he had always liked both parties well enough to hope that they might have been happy together. Nevertheless there was somewhere in his psychological make–up a little demon of retributive justice that wanted to stand up and cheer at the news.

"'It is the little rift within the lute, That by and by will make the music mute,'" Roy quoted smugly. "Maybe she'll throw him out and you'll be able to have him back. Would you want him, if she did?"

"Yes," he said, and surprised himself by how simple that decision had been.

"Good. Then I hope you'll get the chance. And for goodness' sake, dear boy, do try to hang on to him this time!"

◆

(The basement kitchen of JON's house in
Leeds in late 2002. Outside the window is
a winter night, but inside it is cosy and
warm. JON is alone, busying himself with
the last domestic tasks of the day.)

◆

Series four of *Hawker and Duffy* was in the can and the year was
drawing to a close when Jon's telephone rang late one evening. As he
reached out to answer it, he reflected that he did not need to be psychic
to work out who was on the other end: Callum had absolutely the
worst timing in the world.

"I'm in Arizona," he said unexpectedly. "Filming a Western. At
least, we don't actually start until the New Year. Izzy's coming over to
spend Christmas with me. You know she's going to be back at the Old
Crown for the summer? She's playing Goneril."

"I'd heard. Eddie's delighted – and convinced she'll act him off the
stage."

"Not him!" laughed Callum. "Nobody upstages Edgar Treece and
lives to tell the tale – as you've probably found out to your cost! I must
say I was surprised to hear he was ready to take on anything as
demanding as Lear, given the problems he's had – but I suppose he had
to have a medical and everything?"

"Clean bill of health," concurred Jon. "Nigel, too, or he wouldn't be
directing. But they've got Bill for back–up – he's the ideal right–hand–
man for that sort of situation. For any situation, really. I'm going to try
to get over during the run – Eddie and Nigel have taken JB's house in
Gostrey for the year."

"Ah. He hasn't sold it yet, then?"

"No. He wanted to wait until he had a better idea what his plans
would be, so he's letting it out. I think Edgar made him an offer he
couldn't refuse."

"More likely Jenny did," was Callum's response. "It strikes me she's
the brains of that outfit."

"True," conceded Jon. "Anyway, Callum, it's late … "

"You're right – I should get to the point, shouldn't I? Put simply, Jon – it's shit and fan time again, I'm afraid. There's going to be a story breaking about me over the next few days – timed to coincide with *Ice Cold* opening in London, of course. That's one of the reasons Izzy and I are having Christmas in the desert – hopefully nobody'll be able to find us here."

"Oh? Something uncomfortable, then?"

"I'm afraid so. There's a girl … Lauren Valenti … threatening to say she and I had an affair while we were working on the film. It's rubbish, but you know as well as I do that people are going to believe it. Only I didn't want … " He stopped, pulling himself together with an effort. "I didn't want you to believe it, Jon."

"Then I won't," Jon told him simply. "If you say it didn't happen, it didn't happen. It doesn't matter what I think, anyway."

"Yes it does. I mean, it's not as if I hadn't actually had the odd affair from time to time. Just … not this one, all right? God, if only you could see her – fake tan, push–up bra, nylon hair. Give me credit for having better taste, at least!"

"I do."

"Well, of all people, you should! On the worst day of my life I wouldn't touch her with a bargepole. I had to kiss her for the film, and she wasn't all that special then. I don't know what her angle is, except that she's got big tits and no talent and wants to be famous – and acting isn't going to do that for her."

"She's invented the whole story, then?"

"Yes. Not a word is true. It's all just a great big tacky publicity stunt."

"I see." Jon considered for a moment. "How does Izzy feel about it?"

"She's spitting rivets, as you can imagine. Wants to challenge the silly bitch to prove her allegations – which of course she can't. She's got a whole 'stand by your man' scenario planned, but I'm trying to convince her it'll only make matters worse."

"It would definitely add fuel to the fire," agreed Jon. "I'm sure you're wise to dissuade her if you can."

"I'll tell her you said that, if you don't mind. She likes you."

"I like her." It was one of the crowning ironies of his life, Jon realised. He liked Izzy but had never managed to be in love with her, while for years he had been at least half in love with Callum but frequently hadn't liked him at all.

"I know." Callum had stopped talking, and thousands of miles of silence hung between them. "There's stuff I want to tell you," he said at last. "Stuff I need to get out of my system, but not now. Can I call you in the New Year? I mean, I don't want to make you uncomfortable, but I would appreciate … if you're not too busy … Oh God!" A gasp of exasperation. "I just like hearing your voice, Jon. Can I call you next time I need cheering up?"

"Of course you can."

"You really don't mind?"

"No."

"I don't suppose you want to come to Arizona, do you, and spend Christmas with Izzy and me?" The tone was hopeful but hardly expectant.

"I'd love to," replied Jon. "Unfortunately, I can't. I'm doing six episodes of *With Great Pleasure* starting in January, and I'd like to spend some time with Justine first. Not as exciting as a Western, I'm afraid – worthy, but dull."

"Ah. It sounds wonderful to me – so much like home. This place is full of cougars and coyotes and snakes and lizards and spiders the size of your hand. You don't get those in BBC regional studios, do you?"

"Not since JB was booted out, at least."

"Good one! But you're right – I hope the bastard rots in Hull for what he did. Maybe we should introduce him to the Valenti creature; it sounds as if they'd be ideal for one another." Callum paused, then discarded the notion with an audible shudder. "Ugh, what an awful thought. Anyway, I'll have to go – Bryce is here and we have reservations for dinner. You're sure I can call again?"

"Whenever you like."

"All right, I will. Have to rush now, though, love – catch you later. 'Bye!"

"Goodbye." But the connection had been broken before the word was even uttered, and left him holding an unresponsive phone.

Jon stood in his kitchen for some time afterwards, eyes closed, thinking of Callum with the strong Arizona sun upon him, backed by brilliant sky and the endless mottled grey of the desert. He did not like to admit how tempted he would have been had it not been for Radio 4, but he knew that it would have been one of the more dreadful mistakes of his life – because Izzy would be there, and Izzy was married to Callum and standing beside him in adversity. However welcoming the tone in Callum's voice might have seemed, it was obviously not meant as a come–on, because there was nothing left between them any more.

Except that of course there was: Callum still could not walk away from him, no matter how much better it might have been for both of them if he had.

He would look forward to those telephone calls, though – should they ever materialise. If they did, they would tell him more than he knew now about what might be going on inside Callum's head. If they did not – well, he would have his answer just as clearly, and be able to plan accordingly.

As well as Edgar Treece's *Lear*, that summer was to witness the début of an ambitious new National Theatre production of *David Copperfield*. Jon's agent had been assiduous in putting him forward for any role in it that was even halfway suitable, and he had emerged cast appetisingly against type as the cruel stepfather Mr Murdstone and with the occasional cameo later in the tale. Since everyone except Copperfield himself was required to take more than one role, it looked as if it would make for a lively time backstage. Not since the RSC's epic *Nicholas Nickleby* had an adaptation on this scale been attempted, and if the creative confusion which had held sway then was to be repeated it would require considerable strength of will to survive the season unaffected – or indeed at all!

Fortunately there was time before rehearsals started for Jon to return to his old haunts for the opening of *Lear*. Fardels was shut up and the farm left in charge of its manager, Tony; Pete had lost no time in negotiating a return to his Canadian hospital soap, whilst Roy reciprocated by taking his smooth–tongued villain persona to California where he was living in Mr and Mrs Douglas Pirie's guest apartment. Jon, therefore, begged a few nights' lodging with James and Matthew at their home in Gostrey. James, having done an episode of *Hawker and Duffy* at the end of series four and returned to record a *With Great Pleasure* opposite Jon and on both occasions stayed with him, was happy to reciprocate the hospitality. For Jon, it was a pleasure to spend even a short time in the home of a gay couple who did not devote as much of their day to bickering and jostling for position as Roy and Pete always had. But perhaps James and Matthew's relationship was on a firmer footing; they certainly seemed settled and domesticated in a way he almost found himself envying.

"Like old times, isn't it?" Maisie asked, sitting beside him in the White Horse after the show. Most of the cast were there, and with a few notable exceptions it might have been *The Duchess of Malfi* again, or the Scottish play from the year before that. Bill seemed to have constituted himself master of ceremonies and was keeping Izzy and Grete Sanger entertained with a flood of anecdotes; Edgar and Nigel had their heads together in a corner over fruit juice and plans for the future; the younger cast were exhibiting satisfactory awe, and it was delightful to see how impressed they were with the entire experience.

"I half expect Callum to come marching in at any minute," she continued. "The place doesn't seem the same without him, does it?"

"He's in America," replied Jon, absently.

"What on earth's he doing there?"

"Playing Wild Bill Hickok, I believe." Callum had expressed reservations about the role, but his agent had convinced him that the fee and the exposure made too powerful a combination to turn down. Yet he was haunted by the response to Mick Jagger's Ned Kelly years earlier. "They'll call me a Limey pantywaist," he'd moaned in one late night call packed with doubts and misgivings, "and they'll be right."

"Is he?" Maisie sniffed disapproval. "Too much to hope that he might support his wife's career, I suppose, although I've no doubt she's expected to support his. But perhaps they're not seeing much of one another at the moment; the rumour I hear is that they could be splitting up."

Roy's words of months before returned to Jon's mind, although there had been no firmer suggestion since then that the marriage was coming to an end. In fact, from the little Callum had said on the subject, it had sounded stronger than ever.

"I hadn't heard," he admitted. "Is it something to do with that girl who came out of the woodwork recently?"

"'Woodwork' is right," Maisie told him. "I've seen more animated trees! She only got that part because she slept with somebody or other, believe me. If it was Callum … well, you'd think he'd have learned his lesson after the other one, wouldn't you? About unsuitable women, I mean."

It was on the tip of Jon's tongue to agree with her; then he thought better of it. "Without knowing the circumstances … "

"Yes, you're right, shouldn't listen to gossip. Always plenty of rumours in our business, and the only true ones are probably the ones we never hear!"

"That's a good way of putting it." Jon forced a smile. "But I doubt whether Callum will be marching in, as you say. He's living all by himself in a house on the edge of the Arizona desert. I can't decide if that sounds peaceful or terribly lonely."

Maisie considered the question. "It doesn't sound like Callum, that's for sure. I think you'd enjoy it, mind you; you seem to be quite comfortable on your own. But Callum's different. I wouldn't be surprised if he was hating every minute."

And Jon, remembering the Leichhardt movie, the summer of the *Gertrude*, and the disastrous year when Callum had lived in Izzy's parents' basement, could not help agreeing with her. Callum Henley was not designed for solitude, and he probably wasn't enjoying his own company any more now than he ever had before.

Over Easter, the Scottish film was released to reviews that were decidedly less than enthusiastic. While the more thoughtful papers and magazines took time to decide how they felt about it before committing themselves, the ones specialising in snap judgements were able to get in first – and none of them seemed to have the slightest idea what they had been watching. In fact, few of the reviewers showed signs of any previous acquaintance with Shakespeare beyond the belief that he had written West Side Story some time in the 1950s.

'QUEER GOINGS–ON AT THE CASTLE', one downmarket rag headlined its review, although as the writer had walked out while Duncan was still alive it was difficult to know what value to place on his assessment. Other writers got more personal:

TV's Father Duffy, Jonathan Stapleton, loses all dignity here. Tarted up in a strange blond wig, he is unconvincing as the one–time lover of Callum Henley who, with his rugby player's physique and his wandering eye, is the last person one would ever suspect of being gay – squirm–inducing kisses with Bryce Gullory notwithstanding. If Henley wants to convince us he is anything but 100% straight he is going to have to work harder than this – preferably without involving an actor like Stapleton who is so obviously uncomfortable with the material. What Mrs Henley, the delightful Isabella Thorpe, makes of it all, we can only speculate.

"I'm sorry," Callum said, when he called later that evening. "Maybe I got it wrong. Did I get it wrong, Jon, and everyone was too scared to tell me?"

"No. It's different, that's all. And these aren't the quality papers; they're more used to guns and monsters and films where people drop their trousers."

Callum laughed. "Thank you for that – you've just described my entire cinematic output! Well, the only films I've done that anybody ever remembers, anyway. Did you see where they said *Planetfall* was 'squirm–inducing'?"

"I did. And I was 'unconvincing' as your lover."

"You were. I couldn't quite imagine that myself."

"And you're '100% straight'," returned Jon, chuckling. "None of it matters, it's all total rubbish. You believed in the film when we were making it, didn't you?"

"Yes."

"And do you still believe in it now?"

"Of course. It's just myself I don't believe in."

Jon let out a long, slow breath. "You trust Izzy, don't you, and you trust me? Couldn't you take yourself at our valuation sometimes, rather than your own?"

"No, love," was the soft response. "That's always been the problem. The pair of you value me much too highly; one of these days I'm going to let you both down flat."

"I don't think either of us believes that," Jon told him. "I wish you didn't."

"I know. It's just the way my brain's wired up, I'm afraid. Whenever I think I've done a brilliant job on anything, some idiot takes particular delight in tearing it to shreds."

"Well, 'some idiot' is right. But it makes you try harder next time, doesn't it?"

"Up to a point. Sooner or later I'm going to get the message that it's just not worth fighting any longer, and God knows what I'll do then. Go back to Swindon and get a job in my dad's old factory, I suppose."

The urge was almost overwhelming to reach down through the telephone wire and slap some sense into him – or to wrap both arms around him and hold him until the horrors went away. Callum sounded lost and defeated and isolated in his misery, and whatever small hurts Jon might have suffered at his hands seemed to melt into insignificance beside his need to make the boy feel better now.

"Don't be daft." He put every ounce of loyal affection he could manage into his tone – a formidable store. "Give it a few more days, until the people who know what they're talking about have had their say. Ring me this time next week and tell me if you still feel the same. And remember, 'this too shall pass'."

"You promise?" Callum sounded unnervingly close to tears.

"Of course I do," responded Jon, firmly. "Have I ever let you down?"

"No, love," admitted Callum. "I don't suppose you ever will."

When Callum called a week later, Jon was prepared to meet him head–on.

"Mark Kermode liked the Scottish film," he exclaimed, hardly waiting for him to speak. "He said so, on the BBC website:

It's strange, which is why people don't understand it, but the nice thing is that it exists at all. You've got to give Callum Henley ten out of ten for trying something unusual rather than taking the easy way out and going for populist crap. The man's got talent even if he doesn't always know how to use it. Mark my words, this is the kind of cult movie people will still be talking about in ten, twenty, thirty years' time. It's got something; I don't know what, exactly, but it's got it in handfuls."

"Yes," said Callum. "I did see that. And a few more along similar lines."

"So, are you feeling better now?"

"A bit, thank you."

"Good," said Jon. It was one of their shorter conversations.

He did not hear from Callum again for a couple of weeks, but just before he was due to go into rehearsals for *Copperfield* the telephone rang at its customary unsocial hour.

"I wanted you to be the first to know," Callum told him. "Izzy and I will be going our separate ways in the near future. The marriage thing never worked the way it was supposed to work, but we always said we'd give it three years. Only, the three years were up at the beginning of the month – and Izzy says she's not getting any younger and she wants to be free to try again."

Jon sat down sharply. "Poor Iz!" was his instinctive reaction, realising only too late that it was not the most tactful thing he could have said. "Poor you, too," he added, belatedly apologetic.

"No, no, you were right the first time," admitted Callum. "It's definitely tough on her. But it's going to be as civilised as we can make it, Jon. We're not tearing one another's throat out; we knew this was going to happen and we've had time to prepare for it – almost from the start."

"The start? You mean you knew it wasn't going to last when you went into it?"

"We did, although we weren't ready to admit it then. I don't think either of us approached the business with the right sort of motives, to be honest; we were using one another to hide from things we didn't want to face. Really, as far as Izzy was concerned, more or less any man would have done; all she wanted was a shield between herself and her mother – and I was clean, solvent, available and had all my own teeth so she grabbed me while she could. And it made sense for me, too, as a way of keeping the media out of my private life, so when she asked me ... "

"She asked you?"

"I'm not proud of it, Jon. It didn't seem a bad idea at first, but when the dust settled and we realised what we'd done it was obvious it was going to be an unmitigated disaster. So we gritted our teeth and got on with stage–managing the thing, which is what we've been doing ever since – waiting until we had a way out that wasn't going to hurt too many people."

"Oh, Callum!"

"I know, love. I should have told you before, but ... it just didn't seem right to inflict it on anybody else, you know? Besides, we got along well enough. We make very good house–mates, in fact. We're just not ... "

"Just not husband and wife?"

"No. Well, only on paper, anyway. It's what they used to call a 'lavender marriage' – you know, where one of the parties is a woman and the other one's a raging poof? And don't try to tell me I'm not, love, because we both know different – and one of these days I'm going to have to grow up and admit it to myself as well as everybody else. But I'm making a start. I'm out of the closet to precisely four people already – you and Izzy and two others. It can only get better from now on, can't it?"

Jon could have amended that to 'seven people and a dog', had he been so inclined, by including Roy and Pete and Cousin Sophie and the extraordinarily perceptive Muttley. Instead he bit his tongue. "Are you really thinking of coming out?" he asked, concerned.

Callum gave a disgusted snort. "I don't know. Eventually, I suppose, I'll have to. I thought the Valenti thing was going to force me into it. In fact, I'm not convinced that whole scenario wasn't designed to make me tip my hand, which seems to imply that at least one person's worked it out for themselves. Only Izzy stood by me and made it all go away, so I didn't have to make a decision about that or anything else. But don't you think it's remarkable how some people seem to know my weaknesses and go right to them, time after time? You could almost imagine somebody was setting me up. I know that sounds paranoid, and maybe I'm just seeing conspiracies everywhere – but Izzy agrees with me. Sort of."

Jon sidestepped the whole issue. He did not want to get caught up in persecution fantasies, and anyway his more immediate concern was the effect such apprehensions might have had on Callum himself.

"You sound tired," he commented softly. "Are you getting enough sleep?"

"Not really. But we're just about finished here, and then Bryce is going to lend me his apartment in Miami so that I can work on my new project. Going to try my hand at directing *Richard II*. Do you want to be in it?"

"Stage or film?" But it was a redundant question, and he knew it.

"Film, of course. There's a studio complex in Romania that specialises in mediaeval stuff; they've got castles and hovels and gallows and armour and stunt guys who joust and all sorts of things like that over there. Plus, if we film it there we get EU funding and it only costs a fraction of what it would anywhere else. You up for that? I bet you've never been to Romania, have you?"

"I haven't," Jon told him, not troubling to keep the smile out of his voice. "Ask me nearer the time, and if I'm free I'll definitely consider it."

"Be free," Callum told him, a slight edge of desperation colouring his tone. "I want to work with you again. We're a team, aren't we? The Batman and Robin of the movie business. I'll be Robin," he added. "I've got the legs for the tights."

"You have," admitted Jon, wondering how long it had been since he and Callum had been able to laugh together the way they were doing now – and concluded that it had been, or at least had felt like, ages. "I can't argue. You certainly do have the legs."

Copperfield opened in May. As Jon had knowledgeably predicted, the cast were crushed cheek by jowl into communal dressing rooms with anything up to seven costume changes each, and by end of the first dress rehearsal their semi–underground lair had begun to develop an atmosphere – and a smell – reminiscent of a cattle market. Jon had secured an out–of–the–way corner, squashed behind a door where an actor of larger bulk would have struggled to be comfortable, and had settled in with his Murdstone frock coat hanging up behind him, his Dundreary whiskers set out ready for application, and the young actor cast as Traddles providing a genial bulwark between him and the world. It was a backwater away from the fiercest eddies of confusion and would have served him well enough if he had been able to maintain a certain anonymity in it, as was always his intention in large groups.

He did, however, have a friend in the company – Catherine Senior, Izzy's collaborator on projects such as *Wildfell Hall* and *Blyton*, was cast as Aunt Betsey Trotwood, and inevitably they gravitated together in moments of relaxation during an otherwise punishing schedule. But Catherine, though delightful, had such an overwhelming interest in everyone and everything around her that when the inevitable three dozen – three dozen! Jon reeled at the ostentation! – multi–coloured roses made their anonymous appearance on opening night she was immediately curious about the sender.

"Oh, how wonderful! It's years since anybody sent me flowers like that – and then he was trying to get me into bed! Is someone trying to get you into bed, Jon?"

"I doubt it," he smiled, wondering why on earth he hadn't asked Callum to please, please stop sending the damned things because of the embarrassment they so often caused. Except, of course, that he liked receiving them – they stirred up memories of other times, when they had carried silent apologies or promises or reassurances. He had always thought that was why they were multi–coloured: because they were trying to say so many different things at once.

"You're blushing! Dear man, whoever it is, he or she is obviously determined to have their way with you! I've got a book of flower meanings at home that used to be my mother's – I'll bring it in tomorrow and we'll find out what your message says." And when he looked at Catherine blankly she tut–tutted and shook her head. "Surely you realise that every single flower means something or other? It's a proper code: daisies for purity, lilies for passion, pansies for thoughts … and all the different coloured roses mean different things, although I don't know what they mean when they're all together like this."

"Really," he said, "I shouldn't think the person who sent them has any idea … " But then he stopped. He would have, of course. Callum would know precisely what he was doing and saying and implying. Callum never made empty gestures. Callum did nothing that was unintentional.

Except, of course, the things that were.

By now Catherine had produced a camera and was taking pictures, and Jon found himself trying to turn a perplexed look into a confident smile whilst his brain was churning over the puzzle of meanings and inferences. He left the theatre that day in a ferment of indecision, more desperate to have an interpretation of the gesture of the roses than Catherine could ever have imagined.

When she came in the next morning she announced to anyone who would listen that, according to her mother's book, the accepted meaning of multi–coloured roses was: "'Aspiration; despair; I can never deserve you.'"

This was too much. Jon burned crimson and looked away, waiting for the floor to open and swallow him – which, unaccountably, it failed to do. When at last he had succeeded in calming his thudding pulse and driving the colour out of his cheeks, he turned back and found everyone busy about some task or other – except Catherine, who patted him on the shoulder and made a diplomatic pretence of not noticing that his eyes were wet.

"Ah," she said sympathetically. "Touched a nerve there, I'm afraid. Unhappy love affair, perhaps?"

"Doomed from the start." His voice was a husk of its normal self.

"Indeed. Other party not free, then, one assumes?"

"Married," he confirmed with an awkward shrug.

Catherine's washed–out blue eyes were as fond on him as any mother's. Fonder than his own mother's, as far as his hazy recollections went. "Been there myself," she told him, modifying her jolly–hockey–sticks delivery to something considerably less abrasive. "Hurts like hell, as I know to my cost."

"Yes, it does – sometimes."

"All the time." It was not a question, and carried the certainty of experience.

Jon took a breath before answering. "Yes," he finally admitted. "It hurts all the time."

And Catherine hugged him silently, and said no more about it – but his nickname in the *Copperfield* dressing room was 'Flower' from that moment on.

Early in the season, Justine turned eighteen. Although he was not able to be with his daughter on the day itself, Jon succeeded in securing a break from the play a couple of weeks later, and he and Justine spent the time together at home, quietly discussing her plans for the future. To his astonishment she announced that she intended to study archaeology in Bradford, and that she would therefore be moving in to live with him for the duration. After this she sealed her future occupancy by touring the house making detailed observations about changes that would bring the accommodation up to a standard to receive her, these she outlined to her father over breakfast on the Sunday.

"Plus," she finished, "you'll have to do something about your wardrobe, Dad – it's tragic! Some of the crap I found in there must be centuries old!"

"My wardrobe?" he asked, absent–mindedly. There was a story in the newspaper about Callum and Izzy's divorce, headlined EXCLUSIVE, and – with Callum's incipient paranoia beginning to affect him, too – he wondered where they had got it from, particularly as they had printed a picture of Thea and Connor, and another of Lauren Valenti carrying her bust before her like the jettied upper storey of a house; there was nothing natural about such anatomy.

"You need updating," Justine informed him, patiently. "How long is it since you wore that awful pink tee–shirt, for example?"

"The pink … ?" He looked up at her. "What have you done with it?"

"Nothing." Justine recoiled in amazement. "I'm sorry, is it important?"

"No." He tried to calm his nerves. "I wouldn't want to lose it, all the same."

"Well, don't panic, it's still exactly where it was. I can't imagine you ever wearing that, though, it's such a peculiar colour."

"How do you mean?" He was not fully concentrating on what he was saying; memory had flashed back a sudden vision of the tee shirt hanging on the line at the Old Crown, up against the crimson roses. He remembered Callum's tussles with the washing machine. He remembered playing *Monòpoli* in front of the Rayburn; the faded 50,000 lire note was still pinned to the notice–board in his kitchen, along with the card with the blue wrens on the front and the snap of him as Murdstone with a bouquet of multi–coloured roses. 'Somebody loves you!' the handwritten caption read.

"Well, it's not manly, is it, pink? Not that colour, at any rate. Promise me you never wear it out in public."

"I never wear it at all," he protested – and only realised too late that he had let himself in for supplementary questions. "It isn't mine," he finished, weakly.

"Oh?" Justine seemed about to shrug off the remark, then did something resembling a classic double take and said again, "Oh!", investing it this time with a more attentive tone.

"It belongs to … a friend," he told her, neutrally.

"Of course." And now it looked as if Justine was content and would not be pursuing the matter, so Jon breathed out a sigh of relief. Then she spoke again. "I read a book once … by that woman who wrote *The Shipping News*. There was this guy in it who kept his friend's shirt in his wardrobe for years because … " She faltered, but Jon found that he could not look at her. All of a sudden he knew where she was going with this, and that he would have to go along or lose her trust completely; the one thing he had always hated to do was lie to his daughter. "Because that was all he had, and because they were such a big secret, and because one of them was married." But there her nerve failed and she ground to a halt. "I'm sorry, I'm an idiot. I wanted to pretend you'd had some Great Big Tragic Romance in your life that nobody ever knew about. Forget I said anything."

Jon had been clutching the paper. He set it on the table and smoothed its rumpled pages with long, careful fingers. The familiar picture of Callum and Izzy on their wedding day stared back at him, Callum with those dark specks at his wrists which he knew were the green cufflinks and a grin which seemed to reach out and challenge him. Callum, setting out with so much apparent enthusiasm on a marriage that was never going to last.

"I suppose … " he began, gathering every ounce of courage he had ever drawn upon in thirty years on stage and screen " … you're old enough to know."

"Dad!" Her startled protest stopped him and he looked away, flushing.

"You're right. We shouldn't discuss it."

Somehow he was levering himself to his feet, folding the newspaper to hide Callum's teasing smile. How often that look had been directed at him alone, and in circumstances so secretive hardly anyone had even begun to suspect that there was anything between them. But if it all spilled out now, if it became known somehow – because, God knew, there had been witnesses after all – shouldn't Justine be forewarned? He had never dared raise the subject before but, now that his daughter was of age, maybe he ought to mention it for her own protection. Only the words were not there, and her shocked cry had shattered his resolve. Maybe it would be best kept secret after all. Maybe she wouldn't really want to know.

In this, as it turned out, he could not have been more wrong.

"Dad, are you gay?" Justine asked, after a lengthy pause. She made it sound absolutely normal, like 'are you cold?' or 'would you like a cup of tea?' It ran through his mind even now to bluster and evade, to point to her existence as proof that he could be no such thing, to patronise and make her feel foolish for suggesting it – but he did not have the heart for the attempt. Besides, he had left it too late; she was round the table and hugging him fiercely while he was still trying to work out what on earth to say to her. "You are, aren't you? You're gay. God, I'm so bloody stupid, I should have seen it years ago!"

"You should?" The assertion shocked a response out of him despite himself.

"I think Auntie Di was trying to hint … And things Mum's said … And then there's Uncle Roy. Is he your boyfriend?" But she dismissed that idea as rapidly as it had occurred. "Of course not, he wouldn't fit into that tee–shirt in a million years – and anyway he had Pete. And yours starts with a 'C' because he's the one who gave you the watch … " Her half–sentences went off like airburst missiles around him, detonating more and more sequential charges, starting thoughts which could not be captured and scattered themselves randomly at their feet. "God, you have no idea how terrified I was in the hospital when they gave me that watch and I saw what was on the back! I knew you must have had a relationship with somebody whose name began with 'C', but the only person I could think of was Caro – and I really can't stand her! It gave me the shivers to think about, honestly it did; anybody at all would be better than her! So what's he called, then, Dad? Colin? Clive? Charlie, maybe?"

"Justine, please … "

But it was too late. Her eyes had grown wider still, and they were no longer the size of saucers but the size of dinner–plates, and she had reached out to touch the folded newspaper in a kind of awed fascination before he grabbed her hand and stopped its motion and squeezed the fingers tight.

"Callum," she whispered. "He's called Callum, isn't he? He's called

Callum Henley. That was why you didn't tell me he'd been to the house – because it was supposed to be a secret. Because Callum Henley is your boyfriend!"

His open mouth and stunned expression had already given her the answer, but he knew he owed her more than that; he owed her the truth, and after all his years of obfuscation and concealment, all the ducking and diving and running and hiding, the words were out of his mouth before he could do anything to stop them.

"Yes," he confessed quietly. "Callum Henley is … or rather was … my boyfriend."

He wasn't sure how they got over to the couch after that but he was glad to have it underneath him because at least it meant he couldn't fall any further, and for some reason his legs no longer seemed willing to support him. Nor could he quite understand why Justine was crying, but she had brought the newspaper with her and ripped out the page featuring Callum and Izzy and folded it so that Callum's face was in the centre and thrust it into her father's hands – and now he could not look away from it.

"When … ?" she was asking, shakily.

"What? Oh … six or seven years ago, I suppose, when I was living in Shapley." He traced Callum's printed smile with an unsteady fingertip. "It just happened, I'm afraid. We weren't expecting it. We were both taken by surprise, I think."

"Just happened? You have a secret love affair with a movie star and that's all you can say about it? It 'just happened'? But it isn't over, is it, Dad? It's still 'just happening'?" When he didn't answer, she went on relentlessly. "You don't keep souvenirs of people if you've stopped loving them; you're still seeing him, aren't you? Has he actually been two–timing Izzy Thorpe with you?"

"No, no, absolutely not! He married her … after we split up. We don't … We only see each other professionally these days – and not very often, either."

"But you love him," she insisted. "He loves you. Doesn't he? He must do!"

"I ... " They had been at pains to avoid the use of that word, except as the most casual coinage. He had never really said that he loved Callum, and Callum had never exactly professed to love him. Maybe that was where they had gone wrong. Maybe they should have been more honest with one another about what they felt at the time. "You know, I'm not really sure."

"Yes you are," his daughter told him, sounding so absolutely certain that in that moment he knew it properly for the first time. He looked up at her, all warmth and understanding, and wondered how he had ever managed to father such an extraordinary creature in the first place – and not for the first time the suspicion crossed his mind that he had done no such thing.

"You're not uncomfortable with any of this, are you?" he asked.

Sheepishly, she grinned. "Dad, honestly! What is there to be uncomfortable about? Before long men will be able to get married properly and not muck about with phoney little ceremonies like those friends of yours had last year! It'll all be perfectly normal and nobody will give a stuff any more. Which should have happened years ago, in my opinion."

"It should?"

"Of course. Why should people have to hide what they are and pretend to be something they're not? Wouldn't you like to be able to tell everybody all about you and Callum, really? He's a babe, Dad, I keep telling you – your boyfriend is a bona fide babe; why wouldn't you want a chance to show him off if you could?"

"He's not my boyfriend." He felt this needed stressing before she got completely the wrong idea. "He was, for a while – and then it finished."

"All right. I get that. But he's divorced from Izzy now, so he might want you back mightn't he?" And then another thought seemed to come to her, and she grabbed his arm almost cruelly. "He's the one who keeps sending you the roses! He does want you back! He's still in love with you, Dad, you know he is!"

"I'm not sure I'd go quite that far. We are still fond of one another, though."

"Don't be an idiot. If he walked in through that door now, what would you do? What would you say to him?"

Stupidly, Jon looked across at his kitchen door and tried to imagine the scene. The only time Callum had been in this house he had been disfigured by an allergic reaction to eyelash dye, with his eyes so puffy and swollen he had looked like a goldfish, and still Jon had wanted to kiss him into a stupor and take him to bed and screw him through the mattress, but had been prevented from doing so by the kind of rigid code of honour no self–respecting Victorian could have done without. All those stuffy Dickens and Austen characters he had impersonated over the years must have seeped into his system somehow, he thought. He had put on their codes of ethics with their waistcoats and watch chains; he had straitjacketed himself in their morals and locked his heart away where he hadn't known how to find it again.

"All right," he conceded numbly. "Point taken."

"Good. Because I always reckoned he could do better than that Valenti object who was after him a few months back; I just never guessed how much better! You do realise," she added cheekily, "Mum'll be delighted?"

"Your mother?" He couldn't for the life of him work out why Rosemary would express an opinion of any kind, let alone a favourable one.

"Because now it definitely wasn't her fault, when the two of you split up! She always said she thought there was more to it than you told her then. She'll be glad to know she was right all along."

"It wasn't her fault," he countered. "We established that at the time."

"She thought you were being noble. She thought it was all an excuse for you not being mature enough to settle down."

That was one of the most charitable things Rosemary had been known to say about Jon, and he couldn't help smiling in response.

"I wasn't," he acknowledged. "That's true, as far as it goes. I'm not sure I've ever been mature enough to settle down with anybody, male or female."

"Even Callum?"

"Even Callum."

"Ah," said Justine. "So that's why he went off and ... ?"

" ... married someone else?" he completed. "I imagine it probably is."

It was the first time he had admitted, even to himself, that perhaps he could have kept Callum with him years ago if only he'd been prepared to risk a little more. Perhaps if he had gone to Rosemary cap in hand and explained everything properly, she might have understood his situation and not taken his daughter away from him after all. But then, what had there ever been to explain? And Callum had been afraid to venture out of the closet; he had been concerned with his professional image, with building a façade of heterosexuality, and as a result they had never really discussed their relationship. They hadn't even taken it seriously enough to begin looking for ways around the most immediate obstacles; they had both just seemed to accept that it could never possibly work out for them.

"Justine?"

"Yes, Dad?"

He gritted his teeth. "I got it wrong," he said. "With Callum, and a long time ago with your mum, too. I'm a disaster at relationships, from start to finish; I miss all the signals, and that only confuses the person I'm with."

"No," she said. "That can't be the whole story. You're too modest, that's all; you can't imagine that affection can possibly be meant for you. You need to remind yourself that the people who care for you can't all be wrong."

"And take myself at other people's valuation rather than my own?" he asked, remembering his advice to Callum only weeks before.

"That's it!" his daughter grinned. "Life doesn't always have to be shit, Dad, does it? Sometimes it's ... sometimes it's roses instead!"

"'Sometimes it's roses'," he repeated to himself, as if it was a startlingly novel concept – as indeed it was. "Yes, I suppose for some people ... maybe ... sometimes it is."

In reality, the only practical consequence of coming out to his daughter was that afterwards Jon was able to talk about Callum rather more freely than he had before, to watch the Rossi movies with her in a different way, and to share with her one or two reminiscences of their time together – at the same time enjoining her to secrecy because he had no idea how he was ever going to broach the subject to Callum. Mercifully, however, this was not a dilemma he would have to face in the immediate future: with Jon living in lodgings whilst he worked on *Copperfield* and Callum having moved on from Miami to establish his base of operations in Romania, they had not spoken on the telephone for months.

Jon's contract lasted until September. He left *Copperfield* with only minor regrets as they were due to embark on a strenuous European tour, and series five of *Hawker and Duffy* was to begin filming after Christmas. He was able to spend time with Edgar, Nigel and Jenny when *Lear* finished a month later, and then they set off for the Caribbean to relax and prepare for the following summer – Nigel had agreed to direct *The Merry Wives of Windsor*, in which Edgar intended to play Falstaff. There was no stopping either of them now; they had both recovered their health dramatically and were displaying the vigour and enthusiasm of men ten years younger. Jenny, in frequent emails, complained that she could hardly keep up with either of them any more.

Jon, meanwhile, shuttled back and forth throughout the winter between Shapley and Leeds. Bill had decided to buy JB's house once Eddie's tenancy expired – amid rumours that he had got it for a bargain price, JB being temporarily strapped for cash – which meant that he would be moving out of Jon's flat on the upper storey of the Old Crown. With no obvious responsible tenant forthcoming, however, and not minded to inflict the management of a house full of short–term residents on his sister, Roy's decision from the other side of the world was that the house should be renovated one last time and put into reasonable condition to be sold. He had even hinted that he might consider doing the same with Fardels in the foreseeable future: neither place seemed anything like as attractive to him, now that he was no longer sharing them with Pete. And Jon – whose assignments for the winter comprised little more than recording the voice of Dracula for a video game – allowed himself to be talked into supervising the remedial work, arranging subcontractors and generally managing the project. Shapley was once again the ideal place to be: Eddie, Nigel and Jenny planned to spend Christmas at Gostrey before returning north, and naturally they included Jon – and also James and Matthew – in their plans.

The festive season was memorably riotous that year; the weather was damp and miserable, but inside the rented house – notwithstanding JB's megalomaniac decorative scheme of black, black and more black – the five men and one woman celebrated in traditional style, with roast beef and Yorkshire pudding and Brussels sprouts, with Christmas crackers and the Queen's Speech and carols on the radio, with steam in the kitchen and cake on the carpet. There were gifts, there was drinking, there were happy faces and photographs and endless silly games and stories – and then on the evening of Christmas Day Jon drove James and Matthew home and returned to the Old Crown alone. He was half–expecting to receive a call from Callum, although these had grown less and less frequent as work on *Richard II* progressed. Additionally the telephone service from Romania had proved somewhat unpredictable, and perhaps on this of all days in the year it would not be especially easy to make contact. So he did not wait, exactly, but nonetheless he hoped – but unhappily no call was forthcoming.

His telephone did not ring the next morning, either, although in the afternoon Justine called him from Diana's apartment in New York and thanked him for her gifts, but for the life of him he could not remember what he had sent her – or even what she had sent him.

On the third day after Christmas he was seriously contemplating trying to telephone Callum. He had never done this before – the dynamics of their relationship always seemed to require Callum to be the one making the advances – but he had been given the number of a hotel, where supposedly the staff spoke good English, and told that if he asked to be put through to Mr Daniel Bosola he would be connected to Callum's room – or suite – eventually. But courage failed him. He did not know what he might find himself saying, for a start. 'I miss you' would be too sudden, albeit painfully true, 'I'm lonely' even worse. In the end he convinced himself that he was suffering nothing more than a temporary fit of the miseries, made himself a cup of coffee and settled down to watch *Planetfall* again – for the umpteenth time; wallowing, when one was in this mood, was no bad thing, and at least it sent him off to bed in a better frame of mind.

When the phone rang early the next morning, he leaped to it with enthusiasm and relief. He was going to say everything now that he had wanted to say the night before, and it was no longer going to be resentful and peevish but open and bright, and Callum could make of it what he would. If there was ever going to be concealment between them again, it would not be on Jon's side.

But it was not Callum, it was Jenny – and Jon sat there at his kitchen table and watched clouds filling up the pewter–coloured sky, while Jenny told him in an unemotional and severely practical tone that Edgar Treece had failed to wake up that morning, that it was certain he would never do so now, and that as a result there would be no series five – or six, or any other series – of *Hawker and Duffy* now, and that the world had changed irrevocably once again.

It took an hour to route the call through to Romania.

"Eddie's dead," he said, cutting across Callum's jovially distracted greeting.

There was a pause at the other end of the line, and then he heard Callum shouting, "Get them to shut the fuck up, will you, this is important!" and the background noise diminished somewhat, from pandemonium to a deafening roar. "Hold on!" A door opened and closed, and the quality of the sound altered. "I'm in the toilet," Callum explained, inconsequentially. "It's the only place you get any peace and quiet round here. Did you say *Eddie* … ? What happened?"

"Heart, I should imagine. There might have to be a post–mortem, we don't know yet. He didn't come down for breakfast, and Jenny went to see if he was all right – but he wasn't. She thinks he must have died in his sleep some time during the night. He looked very peaceful, she said; I haven't seen him yet."

"God bless the man." There was a catch in Callum's voice. "The world will be a poorer place without him. Do you want me to come over for the funeral?"

"No. It's not that I don't want to see you, but they'd like to keep it as quiet as possible. More or less family only."

"And you're family? Of course. I'd only be in the way, wouldn't I?"

"I'm afraid you would. I'm sorry."

"No, you're right – I attract attention wherever I go, these days; it just wouldn't be appropriate. Will you let me send flowers, though, at least?"

"Of course. I'll tell you where and when, as soon as I know myself."

"Thank you."

Jon did not know what to say after that. In the end, all he could manage was, "Callum?"

"It's all right, love, I understand," came the quiet response. "Things could've been very different for you and me, couldn't they?"

"Yes," said Jon. "They could. I wish they had."

"I know," responded Callum. "So do I."

A couple of days later, he was able to furnish more details.

"The funeral's going to be here," he said. "At the Poets' Church. Apparently he'd always wanted to be buried between the theatre and the river. Well, it's cremation rather than burial, but they'll inter his ashes there. Down at the back of the church near the yew arbour, I believe."

"Ouch. That's ... horribly appropriate, somehow."

"I know. It turns out Eddie and Nigel made some kind of deal, a long time ago. They're supposed to be buried side by side when the time comes, and that's where they want to be. Nigel's a mess," he added, softly.

"I'm sure he is. I know I would be." It was quiet where Callum was for once. Perhaps he was calling from his hotel bedroom. "Are you sure you don't want me to come over, love?"

"I do," admitted Jon, "I really do, but I still don't think it's a very good idea. You've got *Richard* to finish, and I've got work to do – I inherit Eddie's share of the company, so I'll have to get to grips with that, as well as finding work for the summer. Maybe we can meet up after you get home?"

"If you like." Callum sounded unenthusiastic; he had obviously hoped for more.

"It's not perfect," Jon conceded. "It's the best I can do for now."

"Then I'll take it and be grateful," was the uncharacteristically docile reply, and Jon could not suppress a sigh of relief.

Edgar's funeral took place on the second Friday in January and, as Jenny and Nigel had both profoundly hoped, it was a low–key affair with few luminaries of their profession involved – although many sent flowers. Jon stood next to Nigel during the service, offering a supportive arm or word of reassurance throughout, but when it was finally over and people were milling about outside with cars and umbrellas and the false cheerfulness which is so often a characteristic of funerals he was glad to hand over his charge to Jenny and slide away silently to the end of the churchyard, umbrella low over his shoulders to discourage anyone from approaching.

It was time he made his peace with this place, he felt; here he had sat with Callum what seemed like a lifetime ago, side by side in the yew arbour, screened by the buttress, and here Callum had asked for his freedom – and Jon, being the open–hearted fool he was, had granted it. It had been done gently, with tact and affection on both sides, but there was no denying it had been an ending – and a painful one at that. Yet it was what Callum wanted and thus it was what Jon had given him, because he intended never to accuse himself of holding Callum back for his own selfish motives.

"Jon, is that you?" And if there was one voice above all others that he hadn't expected to hear in these particular circumstances, it was this one.

"Izzy." He lifted his chin and tried to be welcoming, but it was an effort. "I didn't realise you were here. Were you in the church?"

"Yes. At the back, I was a bit late. I've been in Birmingham all week doing something for *Woman's Hour*, and I hired a car … I thought I ought to come, since so many people couldn't – Callum, Grete, Bill and so forth."

"That was kind." But of course she had begun to care for Edgar, after her guest starring role in the series and playing Goneril to his Lear for a season.

"Proper daughterly affection." She looked tired, and he could well imagine why: her schedule had always been intense. Izzy worked harder than almost anyone else he knew, as if she always had more to prove than other people. "This means the end of the show, doesn't it? Do you have any idea what you'll do?"

"I haven't thought about it yet. I think this would have been the last season anyway; we were starting to run out of steam a bit. But we couldn't carry on without Eddie, of course; Duffy on his own wouldn't be enough to hold down a series."

Miserably he looked across the river. Even the swans seemed subdued by the rain, clustering together against the bank in drifts, sleek white heads drooping as if they were wishing themselves somewhere warmer.

"Strange it should have been here." Izzy's tone was wistful. "It's such a beautiful place … when the weather's decent, anyway. I can't imagine anyone ever being unhappy in a place like this." Despite himself Jon laughed – a hollow, mocking sound. "I get the impression you don't agree?"

"No," he said, "you're right, it is beautiful. But it's ironic: when you came up just now I was thinking about a time when I was particularly unhappy here." He was hardly aware of what he was saying, or whom he was saying it to. "I was in a relationship once that ended on this very bench – and I've been avoiding it like the plague ever since; it's full of dreadful memories for me. This is actually the first time I've been back."

Izzy's fingers were surprisingly warm, but then she had dragged them out of a deep pocket to rest them on his chilled hand.

"I had no idea," she said, gently. "How long ago was that?"

"Six years."

"I'm sorry." Her response was automatic, unthinking, and he was listening to the satisfying sound of raindrops slapping onto gravel when she spoke again. "My God … it was you. Of course it was you." It was not a shocked exclamation, just the quiet certainty of pieces falling into place at last.

He turned. "What was me?" he asked.

"Callum." The name seemed to stick in her mouth like thick porridge. "He told me he'd split up with somebody that year, while we were in the *Shrew*, and afterwards wished he hadn't – but it had been too late then to take it back. He wouldn't say who it was." Her eyes were challenging him; he couldn't help remembering how attractive he and Callum had always found her boldness. "But you'll understand why I didn't think it was a woman. It was you, Jon, wasn't it? I know it was!"

He shrugged.

"Oh, God, how perfectly awful for you!" She was gripping his hand tighter now. "How long were the pair of you together?"

He lowered his head and could not meet her eyes. "About two years." His words were almost inaudible against the beating of rain upon the umbrella. "Until Ewen's funeral. He was never unfaithful to you," he told her, trying to be as honest as he possibly could. "Not with me, at least. We were over, long before he married you – and we've only ever worked together since, nothing more than that."

"I know. You wouldn't allow yourself to get involved in anything underhand, would you? You're just not the type."

"It was never suggested." He was striving to be fair to Callum. "Nobody knew there was anything between us. At least, I found out later that Roy and Pete had guessed – and my daughter asked me point–blank, back in the summer, so I suppose it wasn't quite as secret as we thought."

A silence fell then, during which they sat side by side watching the rain fall.

"You're still in love with him, aren't you?"

He took his time about answering, as if trying to spare her the full horror of the knowledge. In the end, however, it would not be suppressed.

"Yes. Are you?"

"No, thank goodness!" She was almost laughing now. "Never was, really. He just seemed like someone I'd enjoy being married to – and, you have to admit, better than the alternative."

"The alternative?"

"Being alone."

"Callum Henley, better than being alone?" he repeated, whimsically. "Yes, you're right. Although sometimes it's a close–run thing."

"Amen to that! I knew all along there had been someone else before he and I got together; he told me there was someone he'd never really managed to get over, and I used to wonder who it could have been – but I'm ashamed to say I never thought of you. You've always seemed so … "

"I hope you're not going to say 'straight'?"

"No, luv, not that! But self–contained, at least – above it all, somehow. Too sensible to get mixed up in the whole sorry business. Immune to loving and losing and misery, I suppose. Safe. I used to like to think that you were safe."

"Yes," he said. "I did, too – before I met Callum. Then I fell like a ton of bricks, and I felt a total idiot. He's so much younger than me and ridiculously talented; I always knew he could do better if only he put his mind to it – which is why I was glad when he married you. It seemed like the grown–up thing to do."

"Bless you, what a sweet thing to say – but it was one of those ideas that sounds great in theory and doesn't really work in practice, you know? Although we gave it a bloody good try."

"I know you did. Callum told me – afterwards. I almost wish it had worked, though; it would have taken the decision away from me."

"Sorry!" Izzy stuffed her arm through his and leaned conspiratorially against his shoulder. "You'll have to deal with that one all by yourself, I'm afraid. It's up to you and Callum to work out what you want now – as well as how to get it."

"Thank you." But the prospect did not seem any less bleak now than it had a few moments ago. "I think."

"You're welcome." It sounded almost casual. "You're really pretty fed up, Jon, aren't you, what with Eddie going like that, and Callum, and the shitty weather and everything?"

"Odd that you should mention it. Yes, I think perhaps I am."

"Right. Well, I don't know if you're aware of this, but depression is largely the result of a dietary deficiency – and fortunately, science has recently come up with a cure."

"Indeed?" For a moment he had awful visions of herbal tablets, granules to sprinkle on his cornflakes – any one of a thousand crackpot fads he'd heard discussed in dressing rooms over the years, from plain old Vitamin C to elixirs made from monkey piss.

"Indeed. I have it on the best authority that depression is caused by a serious shortage of cake, so unless you have any major objections I'm going to drag you off to The Copper Kettle in the High Street and make you eat a whole slice of coffee cream gateau. And, just so that I don't get depressed either, I'm going to take the sensible precaution of eating one myself."

Jon smiled. How like Izzy, to make everything seem so simple! "It's noble of you to want to stand by me in my hour of need," he told her, gratefully.

"What else are friends for?" asked Izzy, as she grabbed his arm and hauled him to his feet. Then she tucked herself in close to his side as they hurried up the church path together, and the heavy rain continued to hammer on their shared umbrella as they went.

◆

(The Old Crown, a few weeks later;
disaster has struck. There is no light
and all is chaos; JON is struggling to
reorganise his possessions and safeguard
the house against a rising tide of dirty
water.)

◆

It continued to rain heavily for the rest of January. During the first
week in February the vicar put sandbags at the doors of the church and
men from the electricity company cast anxious eyes over the sub–
station. Karen and Tim debated putting off a family trip to Disneyland,
but their house was rapidly starting to feel like a prison and their two
boys were steadily driving them mad. In the end they gave in, handed
Jon their keys and instructions for looking after their rabbits and their
pregnant cat, and set off anyway. The gutters of Walter Street were full
and the drains were overflowing as they went.

By Wednesday it was no longer possible for traffic to get through on
the main road and buses were being diverted around the outside of the
village. For forty–eight hours or so the traffic lights went through their
sequence of changes in splendid isolation, and the Belisha beacons
blinked on and off purposelessly in the gloom of early twilight. People
commented on how pleasant it was to be able to cross the road
wherever they wanted to, and peered over the church wall to watch
crows hopping about in the sodden graveyard. A rat was seen in the
yard behind the Templar Building Society, but it scurried off into the
back premises of the charity shop and disappeared from view. The staff
were too busy moving their computers upstairs to take any further
notice; the manager, in wellies and a chunky cable sweater, was
sandbagging the doorway. It was full dark by the time they closed at
five o'clock, with the safe emptied and the hatches battened down, and
still the water rose.

On Thursday, Jon transferred Andrew and Toby's rabbits into cat
baskets and shoved them and their hutch into the back of his car.

318

Forty–five minutes later he set them up with food and water inside one of the barns at Fardels and left Tony to look after them; then he returned and carefully removed Cobweb and all her necessities into his attic bedroom at the Old Crown. By the time he had finished installing sandbags outside both his own and Tim's front doors, and again at the back of both houses, the pub had closed for the day and there was water in the car park. He drove his car to higher ground and parked it on the road behind the supermarket; several other people seemed to have had the same idea, but mercifully there were still some spaces left. Then he strode back down the hill and let himself into the house again, and piled sandbags inside the front door too. He emptied the lower cupboards in the kitchen, stacking everything on the counter tops. The drain in the downstairs shower room was backing up and leaking under the door. He rolled a rug against it and walked away. While there was still electricity and clean water he boiled kettles and filled flasks, and made and ate a substantial meal. His upstairs TV showed him helicopter pictures of the river valley as a sheet of steel–coloured water, bridges and other outlets clogged with debris, cattle clustering on raised areas, cars overturned on flooded roads. The lock gates at White Elm were open; five narrowboats were riding unnaturally high at their moorings.

When the electricity cut out and he lost the television pictures, Jon took his battery radio and went to bed. It was gone nine already, with the rain still hammering against the window. Cobweb had settled in the bottom of his wardrobe, where he had folded up a thick towel for her. In the morning there were five tiny kittens nestled into her fur, and a foot of water in the downstairs rooms. He put out dove food on the windowsill, but only pigeons came.

Tim called him that morning on his mobile. "How bad is it?" he asked.

"It's up as high as Charlie's Chipper."

"Fuck. What about the rabbits, and the cat?"

"They're fine. Your garden's under water, though."

"Bugger the garden." Jon was too tired to make a humorous response. "I'm taking the first flight I can get. Be there some time tomorrow, I hope."

"All right. I'll see you then."

"Cheers, mate."

Jon stuffed the phone back into his pocket and went to clean up after the kittens – yet again.

By lunchtime on Saturday there was a rudimentary meals service being offered at the Bistro Upstairs for anybody who could get through the knee–deep water and leave their boots in the lobby. They had standby Calor Gas cylinders installed for such an emergency, and a freezer full of food that needed to be eaten quickly. The darkened bar served bottled beer and soft drinks, and there were candles on the tables at midday. The black humour of the Blitz prevailed.

Jon had spent his morning transferring as much stuff upstairs as he could manage, locking everything into the lettable rooms: sooner or later he was going to be required to leave the Old Crown – the police had already made that clear – and he wanted it all to be as secure as possible when he did. He wondered whether it would be safe to move the kittens yet. At lunchtime he scrambled out of the front window to avoid disturbing the sandbags – for all the good they were doing – and went to eat in the pub, a jacket potato which must have been in the oven since dawn. He spent half an hour over a bottle of warm lager listening to Derek the plumber explaining why there wasn't any water coming out of the taps – there were pumps which relied on electricity, it seemed, and anyway who knew what contamination might have crept into the system – then wearily stuffed his feet back into his boots and returned to the fray. He put the radio on for company, and the football commentator informed him it was raining in Rochdale.

When the hammering came on the door an hour or so later he was so relieved at the thought of having somebody of his own species to talk to that he scurried downstairs and flung the window open enthusiastically – only to take a couple of steps back in astonishment and watch as Callum awkwardly levered himself over the low windowsill and stepped down wetly into the room.

"I thought you might be glad of another pair of hands." He was making an obvious effort to sound jaunty and upbeat. "Don't send me away, for God's sake – I don't mind getting my hands dirty and I'm quite happy to help with the cleaning up, even if you don't want to keep me around afterwards."

Jon was holding himself together only with difficulty. "Send you away? Why on earth would I want to send you away?"

"Only that … " Callum swallowed nervously. "You don't look all that pleased to see me, love. Have I come at a bad time?"

"Dreadful," Jon admitted. "I've never been so glad to see anybody in my life."

"Oh good." A trademark Callum cheeky grin suddenly broke out across his features, a sly glance up from under the unruly blond mop shot with the first suspicions of grey. This was how he had made his fortune, with the occasional brief outburst of boyishness like sunshine peering between dark clouds; he had parleyed an engaging personal characteristic into a dozen successful screen portrayals. "I can stay then, can I?"

"If I said 'no', would you actually leave?"

"Probably not."

"You think you can charm me into just about anything, don't you?"

"Yes," said Callum. "Because I can."

"I'm afraid," came the weary reply, "you're very probably right."

And then it was all tight arms, crushed chests, and Callum's cheek against his own – and one of them was crying, or it might have been them both.

"Like Alice in the Pool of Tears," said Callum, after a while. His lips were against Jon's throat, and they were both still standing barely a pace inside the open window up to their knees in scummy water. "Did you really cry this much?"

"More," Jon sniffed. "You have no idea."

"Me too. I've been an idiot, love; for God's sake give me another chance."

"I don't know." Gently Jon detached him and they looked at one another for some time. "I can't think sensibly at the moment. I was waiting for Tim to arrive so we could move the kittens to the farmhouse; it's not safe for them here, there could be all sorts of pathogens in the water. According to Derek, it's ninety–nine per cent cattle pee."

"Kittens?"

Jon reached out and pulled the window closed between them and the flooded street. More or less.

"They were born last night ... the night before, I mean. After the power went out. Cobweb, Tim and Karen's cat," he elucidated, in response to a raised eyebrow.

"Ah." Callum looked around warily, as if he expected to find day–old kittens swimming about in the sludge. "And they're ... ?"

"Upstairs. In my wardrobe."

"Of course. Where else would they be? Well, I'll help you move them if you like, since Tim doesn't seem to be here and it'll be dark in a couple of hours. We can leave a note to tell him where we've gone, in case he turns up after we've left. Assuming there isn't something more urgent we need to do first?"

"Not that I can think of. The house is as safe as I can make it – and the police are installing an incident post in the pub, so unless somebody gets in at the back it should be all right. Come on up, I'm more or less ready to leave."

They discarded their boots on the first–floor landing and continued in their socks.

"How did you get here, anyway? You're supposed to be in Bucharest."

"I tried to ring," said Callum. "I couldn't get through. I didn't know if that was you or the Romanian telephone service. There are so many different operators over there, they're always getting their knickers in a knot. After a while I just gave up and booked a flight – Lufthansa have a service from Bucharest to Birmingham. I hired a car and went to Fardels, and Tony told me they weren't letting non–resident cars anywhere near the village so he lent me a pushbike; it's chained to a lamp–post at the edge of the water. Actually I expected to find you hiding out at the farmhouse, but he said something about you rescuing some rabbits and I thought, knowing you, you wouldn't leave the doves unless you absolutely had to."

"I'm afraid they may have left me," confided Jon as they reached the upper landing. "I haven't seen them for a couple of days now; I've been putting food out, but there's been no sign of life since the water came up. I haven't dared to look."

"Would you like me to do it?"

Jon considered the offer for a moment. "No. I'm sure they've just flown off looking for dry land, like the one in Noah's Ark. If it's anything else, I'd rather not know about it yet. I can't do anything, anyway."

"Maybe they're roosting in the trees down by the church. Do doves do that?"

"I doubt it. But you could be right. Stranger things have happened."

"True." Callum was aggravatingly buoyant. "God, this place is exactly the way I remember it from years ago. Didn't Bill do any redecorating?"

"Not up here. Downstairs has all been done quite recently."

"Bummer." Callum was staring around in appreciation. "Reminds me of that first time, you know? The weather was awful then, too. It was more or less the same time of year, wasn't it?"

"More or less. Actually, this was the week we were down at Portofino."

"Just before Valentine's Day."

"Yes."

"Valentine's Day and other wasted opportunities," mused Callum. "Be a good title for a book, wouldn't it?"

"Not one I particularly want to read, thank you," was the response. "Or write, for that matter; it sounds much too sombre for my taste. Anyway, come and meet the kittens."

There was a bundle of mewling fluff in the bottom of the wardrobe, tiny wriggling things with tightly-shut eyes. Callum pulled his heavy jacket off and leaned in.

"Can I pick one up?"

"Carefully."

"Of course." Square fingers isolated the smallest scrap of ginger fur and lifted it up to eye level. "God, the size of it!" The kitten squeaked sightlessly in his hand; Callum traced the narrow stripes on the top of its head. "'Thrice the brinded cat hath mewed'," he whispered to the kitten, as though reciting a nursery rhyme. "'Thrice. And once the hedge–pig whined.' So, how do we get these creatures out of here? What have we got to transport them in?"

Rain battered against the window. The sky had darkened considerably and the bedroom was unlit; it was not easy to see what they were doing.

"I've got a holdall." Jon reached it down from the top of the wardrobe and lined it with a towel. "It'll be warmer for them than a basket. We'll put them in here and carry them carefully as far as Caraways; that's where my car's parked. There's hot water and clean beds at Fardels and we can pick up Tony's bike on the way."

"Good. I could do with a bath. I was up most of the night cutting the bloody film. Didn't seem worth trying to sleep," Callum added, awkwardly. "I knew I wouldn't. I saw the pictures on the news; they were showing White Elm. It looked so awful there, I knew it must be even worse here."

"You saw that? In Romania?"

"They have BBC in the hotel. I've got to the stage now where I'll watch any old crap as long as it's in the right language – believe me, you haven't suffered until you've seen Romanian television." For a moment they worked together to stow Cobweb and her squiggling kittens into the holdall. "Mummy cat and five babies, right? Have you given them names yet?"

"No. I haven't even thought about it. You can, if you like."

Callum laughed. "They're theatre cats, aren't they? Must be, given the dynasty they belong to. I think they should be *John, Paul, George, Ringo and Bert*. The little ginger one is obviously Bert." He had shrugged back into his jacket. "Anything else you want to bring along?"

"Just this." Jon swung up his overnight bag. "Didn't have much with me," he said. "I hadn't expected to be staying."

"Okay. So how do you want to do this?"

"Take turns carrying them, I suppose."

"All right. I'll take the first shift." There was a commotion of squeaking from inside the bag as Callum lifted it up. "Sorry, kittens. It's for your own good, you know. You'll thank me for it later."

Jon merely raised an eyebrow at him, and they started down the stairs together.

As they were putting their wet footwear back on Callum said, "What's the insurance situation, and where the fuck is Roy?"

"It isn't easy for him to get away at the moment; they've written him into *Silver Pantry* as Douggie's brother. Anyway, this is the reason he keeps me around: I shovel shit so he won't have to. The insurance company say they'll send somebody to have a look as soon as the water goes down; I've taken some pictures for them. The worst damage is to the wainscotting in the hall; I think it's going to have to go."

"What, all of it? But isn't it … "

"Listed? Two hundred years old? It is, but I just don't think it's retrievable, I'm afraid. I don't actually know what the walls are made of there but I doubt it'll stand up to much of this sort of treatment. Maybe if I'd been able to hire a pump in time … " He shrugged.

"You can't do everything," Callum consoled him gently.

"True. But it leaves me having to find a source for antique wainscotting of the right period – in a seller's market, of course – or a replacement that's good enough for the Conservation Officer to approve. And all of that assumes that there's even going to be a wall to put it on."

"Ah. I'm beginning to see your point." By now they were passing the bag of kittens from hand to hand through the open window. Then Jon scrambled out, brought the window down as firmly as he could, and turned away from the drowning house. "Isn't Roy planning to sell the place anyway?"

"Supposedly, but he'll have to get the work done first, won't he? Nobody would buy it with all those repairs hanging over it – soaked, leaning, and with no reliable electricity or plumbing. Which means I'll probably have to stay around for at least another year to sort it out."

"You're right," conceded Callum, as they began to push their way out through filthy brown water and gradually ascend the hill. "Nobody in their right senses would pay good money for a dump in that condition, would they?"

Despite continued protests from the kittens and a tedious detour to retrieve Tony's bicycle, they arrived in the kitchen at Fardels less than an hour later. It was barely teatime, but the sky had already darkened and was once again deluging the sodden hills and valleys with rain. All the lights in the farmhouse were on, so was the heating, and there was a note from Tony on the kitchen table.

Milk and bread in fridge, shout if you need anything.

"He knew you'd be tired," Callum said approvingly.

Jon was settling the kittens on a blanket next to the boiler, where three of them immediately flopped over and went to sleep. Cobweb was sniffing the air about her suspiciously.

"He knew you were here," he replied in a flat tone. "No doubt he's drawn his own conclusions." He turned to see Callum staring at him. "I believe Tony and Roy had a fling at one time; some kind of revenge for the JB incident, I presume."

"Ah. I miss everything. I'm completely unobservant."

It was on the tip of Jon's tongue to tell him all about the Muttley business and how he had been outed by a dog, but he did not feel equal to that particular conversation at the moment.

"Why don't you have the first bath?" he said instead. "I'll see what I can find in the freezer for tea."

"Good idea. And then what? Early night?"

Jon looked at him squarely for the first time, noticing how abysmally unflattering the harsh kitchen light was to Callum's slightly fading looks. He was a little too round in the face for perfect beauty, and when he was tired – as he was now – and the sparkle had gone out of his eyes, he became rather a pitiable object. It was all Jon could do not to cross the floor, gather him into a reassuring embrace and offer what comfort he could. He had to remind himself that, in the past couple of days, his own tribulations had been somewhat harsher – and that Callum was supposed to be the one supporting him.

"I expect so," he smiled, feeling his age acutely. "Let's just play it by ear, shall we?"

As Jon burrowed into the freezer for the makings of a meal – a couple of lumps of steak, some chips and peas and a lemon sponge pudding – he heard Callum moving about upstairs, and the water running in the en suite guest bathroom. When he went to investigate, the reason for his choice became apparent; Roy had obviously at some point ceased to use the bedroom he had shared with Pete and the huge double bed was unmade and piled with suits in plastic covers; there were several more hanging in the bathroom. The guest suite, by contrast, was light and friendly; there were sheets on the bed and towels arrayed along the edge of the bath.

"You're sleeping in here tonight, then, are you?" he asked from the bathroom doorway. He did not want to look too closely at Callum just yet. It was only with difficulty that he was managing to focus on what he was doing as it was.

"Yes. Are you?"

"I don't know." Jon sloped away to consider the one remaining guest room, a narrow single, which seemed cold and bleak and just too pathetic to be borne. There wasn't really any decision to be made: he would spend the night with Callum, and deal with the consequences in the morning.

"This takes me back," Callum said, entering the kitchen some time later. "You cooking, me eating. Déjà vu all over again."

Jon turned round, quirked a weary eyebrow at him, and held out a glass of red wine. "With one or two minor alterations, I see."

"Oh, what, the tee–shirt?" Callum managed a bashful expression which knocked thirty years off his age; all of a sudden he was like a naughty child trying to explain a broken window. "Well, believe it or not, my ex–wife gave me this."

"Before or after she became your ex–wife?"

"After. We're still on very good terms, you know." Callum sipped the wine and leaned closer. "God, those mushrooms smell wonderful."

"They're tinned, I'm afraid."

"I don't care. I could eat them tin and all."

Jon was regarding him fondly. "I'm sure you could," he smiled. "But I'm not sure I want to watch you try." He too had changed his clothes, as well as making some attempt at a wash, but was longing for a soak in the bath later on. The fake Victorian roll–top monstrosity Roy and Pete had installed in their guest bathroom was not so much a tub as a junior swimming–pool; one moment of inattention and it would be very easy to drown in it. On the other hand, it would nicely accommodate two men of ample proportions, and this was no doubt the reason it had been chosen. It also had curtains, looped back on fleur–de–lys hooks, which gave it a curious mediaeval air; it could fairly be described as a four–poster bath.

"Anything I can help with?" asked Callum.

"Only the sitting and eating part," was the calm response. "But you can keep me entertained, if you like. Tell me, for example – apart from the obvious reason, I suppose – why my very sensible friend Isabella decided to give you a black tee–shirt with 'Drama Queen' on the front in lavender?"

Callum leaned casually against him, chuckling softly. "Apart from the obvious reason," he replied, "because she's got a friend on the lighting crew at the Donmar Warehouse theatre. They started wearing them a year or so ago and suddenly everybody in London wanted the things. And it's not just lavender, I'll have you know, it's fluorescent lavender. I have it on the best authority that I glow in the dark."

"Something that would absolutely not surprise me," Jon said, "considering that you're an alien." He was beginning to distribute food onto warmed plates, and a moment later the two of them were sitting at the table and preparing to eat. "What shall we drink to?"

"Second chances?" suggested Callum. "Early nights? Drama Queens?"

"Kittens?"

"Kittens. John, Paul, George, Ringo and Bert."

Jon laughed. "You know, Tim probably isn't going to keep those names – especially if some of them turn out to be girls. He rang while you were in the bath, by the way. Apparently there's been some horrendous accident on the motorway and he was stuck behind it for a couple of hours. When they finally got a chance to move on, he was so tired that he headed for the nearest Travelodge and booked in for the night. He'll be here some time tomorrow morning, so he says."

"Oh joy oh bliss," smiled Callum, hacking into his steak. "Hope he has a lie–in – then we'll be able to have one, too."

"Rather sure of yourself, aren't you?"

"Absolutely. Got you back, love; not going to let you go again."

"I'm not sure you have got me back yet. Not completely, at least." Jon was making determined inroads into his chips, but found time to be amused by the echo of Roy's words to him more than a year earlier. "There are still a lot of questions to be answered, and a lot of things I just don't understand."

"For example?"

"For example, if you slept with Thea – which presumably you did, or you'd hardly have had Connor – why on earth wouldn't you sleep with Izzy? She's worth a hundred Theas any day, and it's obvious she loved you; Thea never did."

"Ah. Well, setting aside the fact that Izzy and I loved each other like brother and sister and it never really turned incestuous … the keyword in that sentence is 'presumably'." Half the glass of wine disappeared into an eager throat, and Callum's colour heightened by a shade or two. "The simple truth is, Jon – whatever you may have read in the papers – I've never had sex with a woman in my life. Never really wanted to, either."

Jon's jaw dropped. He forgot what he was doing for a moment, and merely sat there staring at Callum across the table. "I beg your pardon? Did you say … ?"

"No, honestly, it's true. I never slept with Izzy, nor with Lauren Valenti, and especially not with Thea. Her least of all, in fact. Connor actually isn't my son at all, you see, although I'm sure you can imagine how convenient it might have been to let people think he was. Can't you?"

"Of course." A helpless gesture with the fork indicated the two of them. "It provided a smokescreen for ... "

"Absolutely. And with her serving it up on a plate like that, I thought I might as well give it a try if I could. Not that the prospect ever really appealed – but I was young and horny and living in the same house with you and I suppose I was trying to sublimate things because I never thought you'd be interested in me. Only, of course, it didn't work. Embarrassingly enough, I couldn't get into her; I've never known humiliation like it. Anyway, that's why she came back the second night; she wanted to give it another go. For some reason she was absolutely determined – and believe me she tried everything she could think of, but it only conspired to put me off the whole idea. She was totally terrifying in bed, Jon – grabby, loud, demanding, a real toppy bitch. I'd get hard thinking about you, and then I'd shrivel up again every time she looked at me. I ended up with the worst case of blue balls you can possibly imagine – had to stop the car on the way to my mum's to get it out of my system."

Jon's eyes widened. The notion of Callum being so sexually frustrated that he'd been obliged to jerk off in some lay–by or car park whilst driving to his mother's was a hideously attractive one, and one he did not dare to think about in detail.

"So ... ?"

Callum shrugged. "Looking back on it later," he said, "the only conclusion I can come to is that she already suspected she was pregnant, but it was early enough in the process to try to foist the kid off on me. If I'd come inside her – which I never did, not even in the same room! – she could probably have persuaded me I was the father quite easily. I doubt I'd even have asked her for a test; I'd have been too interested in paying her off and shutting her up."

"Which you did anyway," Jon reminded him.

"Quite. She wasn't to know it, but by picking on me she'd got herself into a win–win situation. I could have proved that Connor wasn't mine, but it wasn't in my interests to do so. Lenny and I talked about it, and we decided that if I was going to stay in the closet it would be useful to have Thea guarding the door. So I accepted Connor as my son, let her give him my name, and undertook to pay the bills for him until he turns eighteen. To all intents and purposes, but for a little biological accident, he is my son. And he does, fortunately, look rather like me. It's a dirty rotten shame my dad dropped off the twig when he did. I was looking forward to shoving Connor under his nose and presenting him with the ultimate proof that his poofter son was A Real Man After All."

"So Connor was a boy who needed a father and you were a gay man who wanted to prove he was straight?" Jon mused softly. "In effect, you adopted him."

"That's it. I agreed to more or less everything Thea wanted, as long as she never revealed his actual origins. I suppose you could say she's blackmailing me, but we're both getting what we want out of it."

"And the real father?" Jon asked. "Doesn't he have a say in this? What happens if he wants a relationship with his son?"

"He's had plenty of chances," commented Callum sourly. "He hasn't come forward yet, has he? I don't suppose he ever will now."

"Do you know who he is, then?"

Callum's mouth flattened to a line. "Not 'know'," he said carefully. "'Suspect', however, yes. Before she picked me up in the Blue Rajah that night, Thea had been seeing Rory Cooper – and they started up again when he and Jax got back from Italy. I think I was supposed to be his holiday replacement or something."

"Oh! Then he was two–timing Jax with Thea?"

"Or Thea with Jax, if that's the way you want to look at it. At any rate, he was apparently screwing both of them during the same summer season. Don't you find that blissfully ironic? That my son's father is very possibly the same man who gets paid for taking the piss out of you every week on your ex–wife's TV show?"

Jon's eyebrows climbed. "A job is a job," he said, mildly. "Rory's good in that part, and I stopped thinking of it as having anything to do with me ages ago." He paused. "So – would Thea be the reason he split up with Jax, do you suppose?"

Callum shook his head. "I have no idea – but I don't imagine the two of them were either the first of his conquests or the last, do you? Rory's probably got kids all over England, if that's the way he carries on – and Scotland and Wales into the bargain. I rescued one of them from his neglect, that's all. Like all the rabbits and doves and kittens you take in. Waifs and strays, Jon, waifs and strays."

"We do what we can," Jon acknowledged, thoughtfully. "How much did Izzy know about all this?"

"Not much, when we got married. I told her not long afterwards. The only thing I didn't tell her was that I was desperately in love with you."

"No," said Jon. "I told her that. At Edgar's funeral. Was it you who sent her, by the way?"

"Not exactly. I did ask if she might find time to go, since I couldn't get there myself. I never told her why."

"No, but I did. She didn't seem at all surprised."

"Probably not," laughed Callum. "She's had plenty of opportunity to get used to the idea that the thing you're looking for has very often been under your nose the whole time. Nobody's said anything to me officially yet, but I'm expecting her to marry Bill Wildman sooner or later – and I wouldn't be entirely shocked if it turns out they're in the family way already. She's definitely being unbearably smug about something lately, and it can't all be about you and me!"

Jon lingered so long over washing up, tidying the kitchen and settling the menagerie for the night – a hot–water bottle under the blanket, a safe place in a corner away from draughts, a litter tray and a tasty meal for Cobweb – that he could very nearly have accused himself of procrastinating. In the end, however, he followed Callum up to the bedroom with no thought in his mind more urgent than that of relaxing in a hot bath and a tumbling rapidly into blissful sleep thereafter. Whether Callum had any plans for him in the intervening period was a question he didn't care to dwell upon; he had adopted an attitude of resignation towards the entire business.

Callum was perched on the end of the bed when he arrived, still fully clothed except for bare feet, shuffling idly through the pages of a movie magazine. He barely glanced up as Jon entered.

"Have you seen the rug?" he asked, inconsequentially, indicating the alcove where the dressing table stood. There was a low armchair with pastel pink upholstery, of the type generally and imprecisely described as a boudoir chair, and a fluffy white rug of the screamingly artificial variety. No animal had ever grown fur of that length or colour even in its wildest dreams.

"Ah," smiled Jon. "Ideal for dressing up in?"

"As the world's campest polar bear," was the laughing reply, with the accompanying gesture of a limp–wristed paw–swipe. "Grrrr."

Jon shook his head tolerantly. "I'm going to have a bath."

"All right, love. Want me to come and scrub your back?"

"No, thank you. Not this time." And he passed into the bathroom in a thoughtful mood. This all just felt so easy, so right, that he was half–inclined to distrust it; Callum could not be back in his life again quite as simply as this, could he? And if he was, would he stay? Yet the pieces had begun to fall into place as if they had never been apart, and they were already so relaxed together that he was beginning to forget that there had once been pain. But then, his definition of love had always meant allowing someone close enough to give them the potential to hurt him; he had accorded this privilege to Callum years before, and Callum had taken full advantage of it – but obviously regretted the damage he had done. So on balance he thought he was ready to take the risk again, to let Callum back into his heart – and, indeed, his body, if that was what he wanted. It would be absolutely the last throw of the dice for them as a couple, he felt, but he would always regret it if he did not give the entire scenario just one more wholehearted try.

Jon emerged from the bathroom half an hour later with a towel wrapped around his waist, to find the bedroom in semi–darkness. Only one small light, theatrically–placed above the dressing table mirror, illuminated the space. Callum, looking utterly relaxed and more than half asleep already, was draped in catlike repose across the armchair. He had a bathrobe loosely pulled around himself but not tied, and one toe was toying with the extravagant pile of the polar bear rug.

"This place," he purred, "is positively sybaritic."

His head was tilted back and his eyes closed, and the bathrobe could scarcely conceal his obvious arousal. His face and neck were flushed, his breathing uneven, his expression something between serenity and anticipation.

"'It is the prettiest villain'," Jon said softly. "'It fetches its breath as short as a new–ta'en sparrow.'"

Tactfully Callum ignored the deliberate misquotation. "'My heart beats thicker than a feverous pulse; And all my powers do their bestowing lose,'" he responded, not opening his eyes. "You always know exactly the right thing to say, darling, don't you?"

Jon leaned down. Slender fingers drew the edges of the bathrobe back and spidered over Callum's chest from collarbone to upraised nipple. He stroked delicately, outlining its circumference with a questing touch.

"I've missed the way you do that," Callum sighed and sank further into the chair, his body limp and pliable as water. "Anything you want, love, anything at all." His folded hand opened and so did his eyes as, with the air of a conjurer producing a rabbit from a hat, he flourished a hateful little foil package, scuffed and battered by the depredations of time. "It's the last one. For old time's sake."

Jon took it and examined it. He had hoped never to see another grape–flavoured condom in his life – let alone wear one, let alone taste one. With a cavalier flick of his fingers he threw it away, hearing it land somewhere in the corner by the wardrobe. It skittered down the wall with a sound reminiscent of cat claws on a blackboard.

"No?" asked Callum, grinning.

"No. Not grape, not strawberry, not cheese and pickle, not curry, not caviare. I'd prefer to take my chances without it, thank you very much."

"I'm clean," Callum informed him, soberly.

"I know you are."

"Doesn't mean I haven't … "

Jon interrupted him. "Are we really going to talk about that now?"

"No, love, of course not. But you know you have nothing to fear from me."

"If I was afraid of you, or anything about you, I wouldn't be here – and neither would you. Now, are you ever going to shut up?"

"I doubt it. Unless you're prepared to make me, of course."

"Very unwise to issue such a challenge; I might just take you up on it." Jon straightened, and loosed the towel from around his waist. "Well?"

Callum sat up, hands reaching for Jon's narrow hips, and pulled him close. "Very well indeed," he said, muzzily, burying his face in Jon's groin. "I owe you, don't I? You'd be surprised how much better at this I am these days."

"Just don't tell me who it is you've been practising on. I don't want to know."

"All right. But promise me you'll fuck me properly afterwards?"

Jon gave an exaggeratedly tolerant sigh. "I suppose if I absolutely must … "

"You absolutely must. As hard as you possibly can. It's been such a long time, love, and I need you so much."

"That's scarcely my fault," Jon told him, anchoring his hands in Callum's wayward bright hair, bringing the sweet rosebud mouth down purposefully onto himself and letting the swirling wet sensations encompass him entirely. He barely recognised the long moan of mingled yearning and relief which rose from him to fill the room, the indescribable anguished cry as his soul melted. He had struggled so long and so valiantly against wanting what he could not have, against allowing himself to think that this would ever be possible again, and now here he was, with Callum contrite and compliant and as desirable as he had always been, and absolutely nothing was certain any more. He was terrified of the likely consequences but he was going to do it anyway; he was going to burn his boats.

And oh God, the boy had certainly been practising! He was more accomplished than he had ever been; there had always been more than one talent residing in that glorious mouth, between those pale, sometimes almost invisible, lips.

"Easy," Jon managed, out of breath, his weight on Callum's shoulders. "Easy."

Callum's mouth left him and he turned large docile eyes up to Jon, licking his lips in obvious appreciation. "Too much too soon?" he surmised anxiously.

"Much too much, much too soon. Not that you wouldn't totally deserve it, of course, after everything you've done."

"I know. I'm a complete bastard, aren't I?"

"You are. And I wish I could hate you for it, I really do."

"I am sorry, you know. Desperately sorry. Not that it makes any difference."

"Yes it does." Jon shook his head, assembling his scattered thoughts with difficulty. "Want me to have you on the bed or on the chair?" he asked, trying to maintain a thread of coherence. Callum's mouth was still entirely too close and too pink for comfort, and if he did not concentrate he would find himself plunging into it again, roughly and without conscience, fucking the boy's face the way his own had been fucked, glorying in his helplessness, using him for some form of atavistic revenge. But he did not want to be that man. No matter what might have been done to him in the past, he wanted to treat Callum with respect – which was why he had given him a choice.

"Here," said Callum. "Now. I'm ready. I did myself with lube while you were in the bathroom." He squirmed around, employing the sort of uncoordinated movements which indicated that his bones had turned to jelly and his brain could not be far behind, and knelt with his upper body pressed into the seat of the chair, his knees spread, his pale backside turned invitingly towards Jon. There was a trail of viscous matter glistening on his skin; Jon wiped it away with a fingertip.

"No wonder you were in such a state when I came in," he whispered, awed.

"Waiting for you," Callum gasped, almost inarticulately, and Jon slid into him without further preparation like a hand into an old familiar glove, like a sword returning to its sheath. "I know I'm a tart – but that's where you're supposed to be, love, isn't it? Right where I need you. Right where I always wanted you to be."

"Always?" There was little intelligence left over for speech, when every nerve–ending in Jon's body was concentrating on a slow, profound in and out, on a gentle rocking motion which grew steadily deeper, firmer and more demanding.

"Always. I don't want anybody else, I never did. I only ever wanted you."

"You've got a funny way of showing it," said Jon, and fucked him firmly until he howled and came.

With a certain amount of arthritic creaking and groaning they succeeded in levering themselves into bed several minutes later, where Callum's head came to rest on Jon's shoulder as familiarly as it always had.

"You're still bony," he said, without obvious malice.

"Always have been," Jon told him with a sad inflection. "Always will be, I imagine. And you're still chubby, aren't you?"

"Well–upholstered."

"Chubby."

Callum sighed. "Always have been, always will be," he admitted. "Unless someone wants to pay me to strip off for a film again – then I might make a bit of an effort."

"I'd rather you didn't."

"What, lose weight? Or take my clothes off for anybody else?"

"Either," vouchsafed Jon. "Both."

"Meaning what? You and I are going to be exclusive from now on, are we?"

"We always should've been, shouldn't we, right from the start?"

"You never said a truer word." Callum snuggled confidingly against him, his hairy body warm and sheltering. It was like being wrapped in a blanket, like being protected even from himself. "But in that case I probably ought to tell you who it was I practised on."

"Hmmm." The sound was non–committal. "If you really think I need to know."

"I do, love. I don't want it poisoning things between us in the future."

"All right then."

"Well," said Callum softly, "it was Bryce. He and I saw one another on and off for ages – mostly when it suited him. But it wasn't like it is with you; we never really connected. He wouldn't fuck me, for example, or let me fuck him. He liked me to use my mouth, and when he'd finished ... well, sometimes he did me with his hand, sometimes not even that. Those times, I just had to play with myself while he watched. You know, masturbate. Wank until I came."

"Oh." Jon's mouth twisted in distaste. "That doesn't sound very satisfying for you," he commented, mildly.

"It wasn't, but I felt it was all I deserved at the time. Bryce hates what he is; he'll never be strong enough to crawl out of the closet. He was using me, I know he was, and I knew it then, too – but I was using him just as much. We ended up not liking one another one little bit, but getting together every few months and having sex because neither of us had anybody else. It wasn't pleasant, on the whole, but it made me feel better about buggering up so many people's lives. Yours. Mine. Izzy's most of all. I felt as if I was doing penance for it, in a bizarre sort of way."

Jon did not even need to think about that one.

"Izzy forgave you a long time ago," he said, quietly. "So did I. What you need now is to learn to forgive yourself."

"That's going to take a while, though. If it ever happens at all."

"I know. But you've made a start."

There was a long silence, and then Callum said nervously, "You've really forgiven me for everything?"

"Everything."

"Even the blond wig?"

Jon laughed. "Even the blond wig," he conceded.

"I'm glad. I thought you looked really sexy in it."

"Thank you. You realise you're in a minority, though?"

"I know."

"A minority of one," Jon emphasised, affectionately ruffling his hair.

"I know that, too, which only means that the rest of the world has absolutely no taste. But what was I supposed to do? I love you, and it's a permanent condition I'm afraid. Everything else changes, but that always seems to stay the same. I've tried to shake it off and I can't, so we're both just going to have to live with it from now on."

"I know. I didn't particularly want to be in love with you, either, but I didn't have a choice. I told my daughter that. She'd already worked it out for herself, anyway."

"About you and me? Smart kid!"

"Terrifying. I feel as transparent as a glass of water when she's around. She's desperate to meet you, by the way. She thinks you're a babe."

"Well, she's right, of course. I am."

"Of course you are. Especially with green hair and silver eyes."

"And naked and playing with my tits in the shower, like in the movie?"

"Most especially then," admitted Jon, his body registering enthusiastic agreement. "Only I don't see why you should have to play with your own," he added, circling fingertip once more brushing life into a tiny knot of flesh. "Not when you've got me to do it for you."

"Mmmm," Callum groaned, stretching, his spine arching provocatively. "Is that what you'd like to do, love?"

"You know it is, you revolting little exhibitionist."

"I know I am, darling, but that's why you love me, isn't it? So why don't you just … go right ahead and play?"

In the morning they made tea early, tended to Cobweb and the kittens before it was light, then returned to bed. Shortly after eight they were in the big double–ended bathtub, drowsy, exhausted, soaking up scented bath oil and occasionally smoothing a warm wet hand across one another's flesh.

"I wish it could always be like this," Callum sighed. His arms were resting languidly along the roll–top of the bath; there was definition still in the muscles he had once cultivated with such care, and damp golden fur on his chest and forearms. His face was pink, and a bead of sweat was on his cheek. "Come back to Romania with me, help me finish off the film. There's a couple of scenes you could overdub – a local actor who looked absolutely fantastic in the part, but his English wasn't all that great."

"How can I?" Jon asked him, with a sigh. "I've got to find somebody to fix up the Old Crown. Besides, there are the kittens to look after."

"Well, Tim's coming home, isn't he? Surely they're his responsibility? And maybe he'll take over sorting the house out, too?"

"I'm sure he would if I asked him, but honestly – I don't see why he should, do you? I'm supposed to be the one looking after the place; I think Roy's lost interest, and frankly the house deserves better. I'd like to see it handed over to the new owner in the best possible condition, at least."

"Hmmm," replied Callum, doubtfully. "You don't much like the idea of him selling it, do you?"

"No. But it's his house. He can do whatever he wants with it."

"Never thought of buying it yourself?"

"Thought of it," Jon conceded, with a humourless laugh. "Don't stand a cat's chance in hell of ever being able to afford it unless I sell the house in Leeds first, though, and that's not a possibility at the moment. Justine wants to live there while she's at university, for one thing. And, for another, nobody's ever going to lend me the money to buy it; without Edgar, my career prospects are somewhere in the range between slightly uncertain and absolutely negligible."

"Didn't you say you'd inherited his business, though?"

"Well, yes, part of it – but I have no idea how to run it yet, and I wouldn't want to borrow against it anyway. It's Nigel's livelihood, and Jenny's, as well as mine."

"Well, you could ask Roy to hold on to the house until you're ready to buy it on your own," suggested Callum, "or you could throw in your lot with me and we'll buy it between us. We're going to need somewhere to live, after all."

Jon's eyes snapped fully open. "We are?"

Callum shrugged. His blue gaze was steady on Jon's face. "Easier to be exclusive if we're living under the same roof, isn't it?" he offered, diffidently. "But maybe I'm getting carried away? Neither of us has much of a record with long–term relationships, after all. And I got the impression … you know, before … that you didn't think ours was the sort of thing that could last long enough to make it even worth trying."

"I was wrong about that." It was a quiet admission. "I couldn't understand what on earth you'd want with somebody so much older than you. I thought … 'he's just exploring'. I thought when you'd worked out what it was you wanted in a partner, you'd find someone else and leave me behind. I was happy enough to take the journey with you, but I didn't want to completely lose my heart to you; I always felt it was going to end badly, and I knew that after you … After you, there would never be anyone else. There couldn't be, you see. I wouldn't know where to start."

"Oh love!"

"And the deeper I got, the more I knew it was eventually going to hurt, so I didn't want to think long–term about anything. Besides, while Justine was under age … "

"Point taken. And she really is your daughter, after all."

"I'm not entirely certain about that, even now, but I did at least … you know, with her mother. I have. I can. It's never been what I wanted, though. In the past it was always some sort of idealised, perfect dream boy – until I met you."

"Thank you."

"For what?"

Impulsively Callum hugged him. "For knowing I'm not perfect but loving me anyway, of course. You're one of the few people who's ever seen me for myself – not for the image or the earning potential. In fact, I sometimes think you love me for my faults alone."

Jon considered the suggestion carefully. "Yes," he said. "I think I do. I love you when you're perfect, too, but I love you most of all when you're not."

"Like an old house," smiled Callum, and there was the suspicion of a tear in the corner of his eye. "I know I'm high–maintenance, love, but you've always enjoyed a challenge, haven't you? And I promise, I'll work just as hard at it as you do, this time; I know what I want at last, and it isn't something shiny and new and straight out of the box. It's you, just the way you are – because you want me, just the way I am."

"And you'd really live at the Old Crown?" Jon could still not quite assimilate the outlandish proposition.

"Yes. Why not?"

"It's in the middle of a town, for one thing."

"Right. Handy for the pub."

"That's not the point. The point is, you'd be recognised. People would know where you lived. For God's sake, Callum, you're a star; you can't move outside your own front door without falling over Rossi clones as it is!"

"They're harmless, for the most part. But I'm prepared to risk it if you are."

"You're insane," Jon told him thoughtfully. "Although I suppose we could ask Roy how much he wants for the place without committing ourselves to anything. That's as far as I'm prepared to go, for now."

"Fair enough, love." Callum sank back down into the warm, scented water. "I'm sure I'll talk you round eventually."

"I'm sorry to say," replied Jon, "I have a very strong suspicion that you will."

"Bacon," Callum whispered muzzily, an hour later. Somehow their noble intentions of getting dressed and going downstairs had evaporated with the steam in the bathroom, and they had ended up once more bundled up on the untidy bed ignoring duty – such as it was, in a case like this. There would be no end of awfulness to deal with at the Old Crown eventually, but for now their only option was to watch and wait.

"What?"

"Bacon. Someone's frying bacon. Must be from Tony's cottage, I suppose."

Jon quirked a bleary eye towards the clock on the bedside table – only Roy would ever think of teaming antique ormolu with white nylon fur and Ikea wardrobes. "It's nearly ten," he said. "Tony will have had his breakfast hours ago."

"Well, it's definitely bacon, and it's making me hungry." Callum all but sprang out of his arms and was pulling on his boxers and jeans before Jon had time to react. He had swarmed into his Drama Queen tee–shirt and twitched the curtains aside while Jon was still struggling to assemble his clothes in the right order. "Who do we know who's got a red Mercedes?" he asked, curiously.

"Nobody, as far as I know."

"Well, there's one parked in the yard, brand new, twenty–five thousand quids' worth at a conservative estimate."

Jon was in his jeans and buttoning his shirt when he leaned past Callum to look out. "I don't recognise it," he said. There was mist clinging to the hill behind the farmhouse, and a dusting of white like icing sugar on every exposed surface except the car's. "But it looks as if we've had another frost."

"Is that bad news?"

"Probably. It's all bad news, isn't it, when your house is under water?"

"True. Unless you can get a couple of dozen hunky firemen in revealing uniforms to come and pump it out, I suppose."

"In your dreams, boy," laughed Jon, tidying his shirt–collar absent–mindedly.

"Boy," repeated Callum, in mock indignation. "I'm nearly thirty–five, for heaven's sake; I've got grey hairs!"

"So you have," acknowledged Jon. Some of them were on Callum's chest, and had been discovered during the course of last night and then again quite extensively this morning. "But compared to me … "

"Granddad!" teased Callum, kissing him.

"Whippersnapper," was the affectionate reply. "You'll be the death of me yet. Well, come on, let's get ourselves something to eat before you faint from hunger."

But they had scarcely made it to the top of the stairs when a burly but immaculate figure in jeans, tee–shirt and an apron appeared at the foot of them, frying pan in one hand and spatula in the other, and said mellifluously and with perfect theatrical timing, "Well, if it isn't love's young dream! Come and have breakfast, boys, I'm sure you must be starving after your exertions!"

And Callum and Jon were so thunderstruck at the unexpected apparition that the only thing either of them could think to say in response to that was "*Roy?*"

"Surely you realised Tim would have called me?" Roy asked, pushing heaped plates of food in front of them a few moments later. Jon had a hazy impression of having kissed his former lover on the cheek – and of Callum doing the same, as if they were both dutifully paying their respects to a maiden aunt – but his mind was too scrambled to be processing anything efficiently at the moment. "Anyway, we met up at LAX and flew home together. Interminable stopover in New York, lousy weather delayed us again, diverted to Manchester, hired a car. Ended up staying the night in some dump just off the M6. Crawled into Shapley at first light and went to take a look at the damage. Tim's still paddling through what's left of his house and sorting out his insurance claim, but after I saw your note I decided to leave him to it and come up here."

"And?" Jon was looking up at him anxiously.

"Not good, is it?" Roy shrugged, unaccountably cheerful for a man staring at a considerable financial loss and several months' worth of expensive, time–consuming repairs. "Any of it?"

Jon shook his head. "Did you see anything of the doves?" he asked.

Roy glanced away. "Lots of blood and feathers. Something's had them, I'm afraid. Could be a rat, could be an owl – could be more or less any sort of predator with an empty belly and a bad temper. It looks as if we'll have to restock from scratch in due course." But his tone was that of a man who had always considered doves to be tasteful accessories to an elegant lifestyle rather than living, breathing creatures capable of experiencing emotion.

Callum's hand crept across the table and fastened reassuringly on Jon's fingers, a gesture of comfort which did not go unnoticed by Roy.

"Poor things," Jon said, bleakly. "They must have been absolutely terrified."

"I'm sure it was quick." Callum's grip tightened and held.

Jon was not convinced, but for the sake of a quiet life he loyally concurred.

Roy, who had been pouring tea, sat down and placed his hand familiarly on top of theirs. "So," he said, "may I take it you two are together again at last?"

"You may." It was Callum who spoke, and firmly too.

"I assumed as much, when I heard that you'd walked out on your film in Romania and disappeared off the face of the earth."

"I ... " Callum repeated, numbly. "I did what?"

"It's all over the gossip blogs, dear boy, and the celebrity hacks are having a field day with it. Apparently you stomped and flounced and left them high and dry in the middle of the night, with the film uncompleted and none of the actors paid."

"That's ridiculous. Everybody's been paid – which isn't my job as director, anyway. I simply took a few days off to deal with a personal matter – with the full agreement of the production company, I might add." Callum stopped. "Wait a minute. Did you say I'd left them in the middle of the night?"

"That's the story I was told. Why, is that significant?"

Callum's mouth twisted. "It could be, yes. I did mention to somebody that I was probably going to leave in the middle of the night, but in the end I changed my plans and waited until the morning and flew into Birmingham instead. But I'm starting to see the light at last about something that's been bothering me for years; it's still too early to be sure, but let's just say that the penny's dropped about quite a lot of things in the last day or two – and, if I'm right, I'm going to have to make a few changes from now on."

Roy, obviously putting his own interpretation on the words, bubbled over with enthusiasm. "Oh good! You're going to take the whole magical journey, then, are you? Out and proud, rainbow flags, big fat gay wedding and all the trimmings?"

"Maybe," said Jon, who had taken the hint from Callum's discouraging expression and resisted plying him with questions about his moment of epiphany, whatever it had revealed. "Maybe not. We haven't discussed it."

"Shame. I do hope one of you has at least put the vital question, though?"

"No. It never even crossed our minds."

"We didn't get that far," his love supplied, his cheeky grin restored. "We were too busy. Comfortable bed you've got up there, Roy; I might have to buy it from you some time. We might, I mean to say. And while we're at it – we've been talking, and we'd like to make you an offer for the Old Crown, if you're still planning to sell the place. Hopefully, it'll be an offer you can't refuse. So name your price and we'll pay it, no arguments."

"We will, will we?" Roy laughed out loud. "Jon?"

Jon was looking daggers at Callum, who responded with an apologetic shrug. He knew then that he had been outmanoeuvred, his own innate caution steamrollered once again by Callum's boundless enthusiasm, and he tried very hard to mind about it – but found, very much to his relief, that he could not.

"Yes," he concurred. "Apparently, we will."

"Oh dear. I can see you're a lost cause, the pair of you. Very well, then, in the interests of true love and happy endings – and everything else utterly sick–making and squirm–inducing to the straight population of this country – Arbour Estates is prepared to offer you a special once–in–a–lifetime, queer–as–a–clockwork–orange deal. The place is yours, just as it stands, with every stick of furniture inside it, for the bargain basement price of two hundred and fifty thousand pounds – or, alternatively, two hundred, plus a Mercedes exactly like the one outside. What do you think of that?"

"I think," said Callum, shaking him by the hand, "that you're just the sort of man who ought to be driving a Mercedes, Roy, and there's nothing in the world that would make Pete feel any more of a loser than that."

"I do hope you're right, dear boy," was the sly response. "And, in the meantime, congratulations; the pair of you have bought yourselves a house."

◆

(The attic bedroom at the Old Crown, 2005. The worst after-effects of the flooding have been cleared away, although the room is still far from tidy. JON and CALLUM are comfortably asleep together. The rest is silence.)

◆

The pearl–grey of an early spring morning was hanging above the roof–light when Callum eventually stirred, his face warm and scratchy with stubble against Jon's shoulder. They had given up excitedly counting their consecutive nights together by this time – the total had first reached seven, then fourteen, and then twenty–one, and had become so comfortable with the arrangement that they no longer remembered anything else had ever been the case. It was habit of the most reassuring kind, the kind which gave a structure to their lives; after all their tribulations, they were at long last one another's ever–fixèd mark.

Not that it was an unmixed blessing: Callum was an unruly sleeper who took up more than his share of space in bed and sometimes made his companion wish for a wider mattress. However, the quiet pleasure of settling down beside him night after night outweighed such minor disadvantages; there was more to be grateful for in this relationship than to curse, and Jon accepted it all with a kind of modest pride. He had never felt that he was anybody's chosen partner before; with Rosemary and – even more briefly – with Roy, he had drifted into and out of something he didn't really want but thought he ought to have, and had always felt he was a temporary expedient until something better came along. In Rosemary's case, the 'something better' turned out to be writing; in Roy's, it was Pete. After those two disasters, Jon had reconciled himself to the notion that the romances other people enjoyed were probably never going to come his way; he had become accustomed to living without the privilege of being loved.

Then, all of a sudden, there had been Callum – awkward, stroppy, ridiculously talented, more than a handful in every possible sense – and

Jon had recognised from the beginning that his cause was lost; whether Callum had ever been his or not, he would always have known himself unequivocally to be Callum's.

"Morning, love." Rumbled words soft against his neck. "You smell wonderful." A hand wandered down over Jon's chest and belly and took possession of him simply because it could. "Have we got anything urgent we need to get out of bed for this morning, or can we take our time?" It was a fair question. Their days recently had been filled with plumbers and decorators, with the Conservation Officer, with Roy offering advice, with tabloid journalists wanting yet another story.

"Not really. I'll have to set off about ten to collect Justine from the station, but we've got a couple of hours to spare before that."

"I hope she's forgiven me. I messed things up royally in Bucharest, after all."

"You couldn't help it," was the quiet response. "And I've already forgiven you. I'm sure Justine will, too, when you explain it to her properly."

"You think so? You think there's any possible way I can explain having outed her poor father all over the media without so much as a 'by your leave'?"

"Well, we'll find out soon enough. But she'd hardly be coming to visit if she'd decided to hate you, would she? She knows you're going to be here."

"Good point," conceded Callum. "Only you won't mind if I hide behind you when she arrives, will you?"

Jon rolled his eyes to the ceiling. The attic bedroom was one they hadn't got round to dealing with just yet; it had become an untidy haven from the chaos in the rest of the house as gradually the damage from the flood had been dealt with – the walls dried out slowly with industrial heaters, the wiring replaced, the Rayburn repaired, the kitchen re-installed. Now the house was officially theirs: completion had taken place the day before, with the last paperwork signed and sealed and deposited with the appropriate authorities, and they were ready to receive the first proper visitor to their shared establishment. There had never been any question whom that visitor would be.

For a long, peaceful moment it was all gently sliding hands, caresses intended not to arouse so much as to comfort, mutual appreciation of the simple and undeniable fact of being together. Then, with a reluctant groan, Callum untangled himself from Jon's embrace and headed in the direction of the bathroom. "Sorry, love, there are some things that just can't be postponed."

Jon lay watching him walk away, enjoying the play of muscles under his skin and luxuriating in a sensation of ownership which was a new phenomenon in his life; it was still astonishing to him that he had exclusive rights to Callum's love these days, and Callum had exclusive rights to his. In some respects, this was a goal he had always been striving for but had never imagined he would reach.

The bathroom door opened and closed, the toilet flushed, and moments later an exclamation of mild annoyance reached Jon from beyond his line of sight.

"Bugger!"

"What's the matter?" He was halfway out of bed to investigate even as he spoke.

"Nothing. Bulb's gone on the landing, that's all. Have we got any new ones up here, or will I have to go down to the kitchen?"

"Yes, they're in the cupboard. Hang on a moment."

By the time Jon had retrieved a bulb and stepped out onto the landing, Callum was on tiptoe on the seat of a chair removing the burnt–out one. He handed it to Jon, receiving the replacement from him.

"Thanks, love."

Callum reached above his head to install the bulb, his body stretching sinuously. Jon dropped the discarded one into the bedroom bin and leaned against the door frame to watch him, a smile spreading slowly on his face. It was such an ordinary procedure, turned into a poem by the fluid movements of his lover and the completely unregarded and somehow inevitable fact that they were both gloriously naked.

"What?" Callum had finished installing the bulb, yet remained in position with his hands above his head, looking like a Greek or Roman statue on a plinth.

"You," said Jon. "I'm trying to work out what one of the most famous actors in the country – in the world, in fact – could possibly be doing without a stitch on, standing on a chair unscrewing light bulbs. Any way you look at that, it's fundamentally surreal." He was not unaware, however, that with Callum so far above him, the most immediate view he had was not of the boy's face.

"You're right." Callum, aware of his scrutiny, affected a suggestive little movement of his hips. "*Un*–screwing isn't one of my more obvious talents, is it?"

"Of course not." There was a considered silence. "Would you like me to help you down from there?"

Callum grinned. "Oh yes, I think so. Please. I'm sure I'd never manage without you; I might have to stay up here all day." It was the most transparent falsehood ever to have passed his lips, and both of them knew it for the tease it was.

"Well, I suppose I could just stand and admire you if you did." But carefully Jon placed his hands on Callum's hipbones, let the boy's palms come to rest gently on his shoulders, then took his weight as, by slow degrees, their bodies met and dragged against one another and skin rode sensuously over skin in a long drawn–out pantomime until at long last Callum's feet touched the floor. Even then he was still perched high upon his toes, largely supported by Jon's wiry frame.

"I'm taller than you now," he breathed, reaching in to give and take a delighted kiss.

"You wish!" Jon continued to hold him up with arms which were infinitely stronger than they looked. "Darling boy."

Callum found a moment to toy with Jon's hair. It was long enough for the first suspicion of a curl to have begun to evolve, and Callum had evidenced a fascination for it. "You're going to have to stop calling me that, you know."

"Absolutely not. You can't possibly be a day older than seventeen."

"In which case you'd be a cradle–snatching dirty old man." Another indulgent exchange of kisses followed, and a partial shifting of weight which left Jon with the door frame digging into his spine and Callum wound around him like an eager octopus, all wayward limbs and puckish humour. "So now we know the answer to one of life's great mysteries; how many actors does it take to change a lightbulb?"

"Two, of course," laughed Jon, with what little breath he had to spare. "It takes two actors to do just about anything worth doing; one of them on his own would be no use at all."

"Hmmm." Callum quietened and leaned against him thoughtfully. "You're absolutely right, you know; I'd be useless without you, Jon, and that's a fact."

"You would indeed, and so would I. It's a good job we ended up together, then, isn't it? I'm sure we can be even more useless working as a team."

"Are you suggesting we're nothing but a pair of incompetents, by any chance?"

Jon considered his answer carefully. "Not entirely," he said, at length. "There are occasionally things that we do manage to get almost right, although just at the moment I can't exactly remember what they are."

"I can," responded Callum, and led him back determinedly into the bedroom to remind him.

Three hours later, his body still resonating from the thorough demonstration of Callum's affections which had followed this exchange, Jon collected his daughter from the railway station. Justine was going through an experimental phase with her appearance and had a plum streak in her hair, dark blue lipstick, and wore a necklace which had beads and feathers suspended from it. She jingled discreetly when she moved.

In the car, as they pulled away from the heaviest traffic, she was quick to introduce the subject which was obviously uppermost in her thoughts.

"So – when the Civil Partnership Bill becomes law you and Callum will actually be able to get married, won't you?"

"I suppose we might, in theory," he conceded.

"Great. I could be your bridesmaid or something, couldn't I? Do you have bridesmaids at a gay wedding?"

"I wouldn't know. If you remember, I never got to attend the one I was invited to – I was in hospital over that weekend. But don't get carried away; it's not something we've discussed, and even if we did decide to do it – well, it probably wouldn't be anything spectacular. I'm sure it's just a case of going in and signing a couple of forms or something, not a big romantic theatrical occasion."

"Hah! Lots of luck with that one, Dad. Callum's a movie star – they never do anything quietly!"

"He isn't really," he told her weakly, wishing he'd had the sentiment put on a long–playing record years ago given the number of times he seemed to find himself repeating it, if only to himself – although he supposed that these days he would need to have it transferred to CD or maybe made into an mp3 file.

"Don't be ridiculous; you can't run away from it after what happened in Romania. You're *both* movie stars – and you'd better get used to the idea."

He groaned. That, of course, was the downside of the name recognition he'd been so assiduous in cultivating over the years. He had only wanted to become a bankable commodity and have sufficient income to support his family, but he was a publicly recognisable figure now – and not just through his association with Callum, although that definitely hadn't helped. The headlines in the papers hadn't referred to him as Jon Stapleton, actor; they'd identified him by the name of his most familiar character. ROSSI AND FATHER FERGUS, they'd trumpeted, as though overwhelmed by the surreality of the combination; as though playing *Six Degrees Of Separation* with their fictional avatars.

"You know what?" continued Justine, "I found a poem the other day which would be perfect for somebody to read out at the ceremony. Maybe you could get Uncle Roy to do it; there's no way you're going to get married without having to involve him anyway, so you might as well give him something to do." She was scrabbling in a handbag which bore a remarkable resemblance to Mary Poppins's carpet–bag; her father would not have been astonished to see full–sized items of furniture appearing out of it. What she retrieved, however, was a sheet of paper; as she unfolded it, Jon realised that his daughter had navy–blue fingernails.

"Here we are – it's Keats; 'To a Friend Who Sent Me Some Roses':

As late I rambled in the happy fields,
What time the skylark shakes the tremulous dew
From his lush clover covert; – when anew
Adventurous knights take up their dinted shields;
I saw the sweetest flower wild nature yields,
A fresh–blown musk–rose; 'twas the first that threw
Its sweets upon the summer: graceful it grew
As is the wand that Queen Titania wields.
And, as I feasted on its fragrancy,
I thought the garden–rose it far excelled:
But when, O Wells! thy roses came to me,
My sense with their deliciousness was spelled:
Soft voices had they, that with tender plea
Whispered of peace, and truth, and friendliness unquelled.

Of course, you'd have to change 'Wells'," she added, reaching a breathless conclusion. "It doesn't exactly fit. You could make it 'love' instead … 'But when, O love! thy roses came to me … ' That works, doesn't it? You do call him 'love', I suppose?"

"Yes," said Jon. His hands were unsteady on the wheel, and the thought went through his mind that he should not be driving in this dangerously emotional state. "I do. And you're right, it would be perfect." He was silent for a moment then, concentrating on the road while Justine settled back contentedly into her seat, "Please be as gentle as you can with Callum; he's rather scared of meeting you."

"So he should be," was the wry response. "I'm not going to let him off without a fight, you know – and he absolutely deserves it, for everything he's done."

"He didn't do any of it on purpose," Jon assured her, troubled. "It was just one of those things that happen sometimes – a situation beyond anybody's power to control; I think it's what they call a 'perfect storm'."

"Maybe. But he didn't do much to prevent it, did he?"

"It was actually a bit more complicated than you seem to imagine," came the mild reproof. "By all means have your say, but remember – I'm the one who has to live with him afterwards. Don't damage him too badly, for my sake."

"I promise, Dad, I'll leave him in full working order – only maybe just a little bit dented and scratched. Do we have a deal?"

"We do," he said, silently apologising to the absent Callum. He had no doubt the boy could stand up for himself if he had to, but in the circumstances he didn't think it likely he would try.

The meeting which took place an hour later was circumspect, polite, and unbearably awkward at first. Callum was in chinos, plain black tee–shirt and designer stubble, striving to look relaxed and failing miserably; when he kissed Justine on the cheek she looked faintly astonished, as though trying to suppress a bad attack of temporal dislocation. Despite the amount of warning she had received and the time she had had to get used to the idea, it was apparent she was struggling to process the knowledge that a man she had been watching on screens of various sizes for several years was now here, in this familiar setting, acknowledging his long–term attachment to her father.

"I'm sorry there wasn't time to meet you before I went back to Bucharest," he began. He and she were watching one another carefully out of the corners of their eyes, each trying to get the measure of the other without making it too obvious. "Anyway, I thought I should let your dad break the awful news himself. Just as well we did it that way, as it turned out."

"You were busy," she offered cautiously. It wasn't exactly an olive branch, but as a sliver of olive bark or a small olive twig it would do for now.

Callum met Jon's concerned gaze; there was no way of telling, just yet, whether this was going incredibly badly or unexpectedly well. Justine seemed to have cultivated an enviable poker face, and was giving absolutely nothing away.

"You were flooded and outed all in the same week," she continued.

"And then there was all that strange stuff about you disappearing – those *Planetfall* weirdos swore black was white you'd been kidnapped because you Knew Too Much about something or other."

"I can explain," he offered. "Not the kidnapping story, that's just too strange, but the disappearance thing – I know who started that. It was the same person who was responsible for all that schemozzle at the Athénée Palace – which, if it's okay, is something I'd really like to talk to you about."

There was a distinct relaxation on Justine's side of the table. "I'm listening," she said.

"Good." Some of the strain seemed to evaporate from Callum's voice, and he managed to achieve a slightly less strangulated tone. "Well … after the flood there wasn't a lot we could do here but sit around and wait for the water to go down, so we thought we'd better head back to Romania and wrap up the film quickly while we had the chance – then come back as soon as possible to start sorting out the house. Not to mention buying it."

"We left Roy in charge," her father put in. "It was still his property and he wanted to help. Besides, Callum said it was time he did something to justify his existence."

Justine's mouth curved a fraction. In ordinary circumstances her father might have interpreted that as a smile, but it was obvious she was unwilling to make any concessions until Callum had finished his explanation; she was going to leave him twisting in the wind for as long as she possibly could, and privately Jon was willing to acknowledge that he probably deserved at least a measure of it.

"So, after a couple of days, I went back the same way I'd arrived – Birmingham to Bucharest – and your dad came to London to talk to you and fly out from Heathrow instead. We thought we'd been quite clever, you know; apart from the usual Rossi clones – at the airport in Bucharest, and again at the hotel – nobody seemed to be taking any interest at all. Not until after Jon arrived and we'd settled into our room and we made the mistake of going down to the dining room for a meal, anyway. You need to understand, I'd been living there the whole time I was making the film – the staff all knew me, I had a favourite table and everything; I couldn't see why it had to be different just because your dad was there. In fact I didn't think anyone in Romania would give two hoots about what we were doing together. In hindsight, I must admit that looks pretty stupid."

"You're right, it was incredibly stupid. And it wasn't fair on Dad, either."

"Please!" Jon was quick to protest. "Anyone would think I couldn't speak up for myself!"

"No," replied Callum, "it wasn't fair at all. I had no idea it would escalate the way it did – and, believe me, I've apologised for it since. A lot." The husky laugh which concluded this sentence left no doubt as to the nature of the apology. "But it wasn't just the usual random disaster this time, I'm afraid. This one was quite deliberate."

"If it was deliberate, there's even less excuse for subjecting Dad to all that hassle."

"Justine!"

"Oh, come on, Jon, you know as well as I do that she's right; it was completely unnecessary and I wish it hadn't happened. The thing is, I'm not sure I was thinking clearly at the time – but I'm not trying to weasel out of it or anything."

Justine was watching him cautiously. "So, what's the story?" she asked.

Callum took a breath. "Well, you know Caro, your dad's agent? I gather you're not fond of her?"

Puzzled, Justine frowned. "Not especially. She's okay as an agent, but there was a time when I thought he might be thinking of marrying her and that was totally … " She left the sentence hanging.

"So bad that even I would have to be a better choice?"

There was the suspicion of a thaw in Justine's manner as she turned to Callum. "Frankly, yes. But what has she got to do with you outing my dad?"

"Nothing, directly." Callum glanced over at Jon, receiving a look of sympathy in return. "All right,

I am in blood
Stepp'd in so far that, should I wade no more,

356

Returning were as tedious as go o'er.

I'm telling this in completely the wrong order. What I meant about Caro was that, whatever you think, she's always done her best for Jon – kept him busy, found him stuff he felt comfortable doing and so forth. In other words, she listens to him rather than making him listen to her. Is that fair?"

"As far as it goes," admitted Justine.

"Okay then. My agent was different, I'm afraid. A guy by the name of Lenny. He grabbed me the minute I got out of LAMDA, still wet behind the ears. If I'd been lucky enough to fall into the hands of someone like Caro ... "

"Nobody would ever have heard of you," Jon told him, with a smile. "For all his faults he's made you work hard. Got the very best out of you."

"You get the best out of me," corrected Callum wickedly. "But yes, he steered me into stuff which got my name known – Leichhardt, Rossi, Wild Bill, all the big commercial stuff. What I didn't realise at the time, however, was everything else he was doing to keep my name in the papers. Stuff that doesn't appear in any actor's contract with his agent. Take the thing with Thea, for example: I'm absolutely certain he's the one who tipped off the photographer to be waiting outside Thea's mum's house that time."

"The one who took those pictures of you with Izzy and the baby on the doorstep?"

"That's right. And he encouraged me to be seen all over the place with Izzy. Not that I wouldn't have done that anyway, mind you."

"I thought that was a good idea at the time, too, remember?" Jon pointed out. "I wanted you to be friends."

"True – but you were thinking of mutual support rather than gala premières, love, weren't you? You'd have been happy if we'd sat on the sofa together drinking cocoa and watching *Newsnight*. That wasn't what Lenny had in mind; he wanted us to get our pictures taken as often as possible. You see, Justine, every bit of exposure put my price up a few quid more, and each time Lenny's cut went up accordingly – to say nothing of the presents and backhanders he was taking for

pointing photographers in the right direction. And if that isn't dog–
eat–dog enough for you, there's more."

"Really?" Justine was intrigued now; it was evident in her voice.
"I thought there might be, somehow."

"Yes. Remember Lauren Valenti? You've got one guess who her
agent is."

Justine's eyebrows rose. "The same as yours, by any chance?"

"Give that girl a coconut!" laughed Callum. "That's right."

"So ... she's worth more money if people think she's had an affair
with you?"

"Pretty much. And, as you've gathered, the woman's a total talent
vacuum – so if Lenny's going to turn a profit on her she has to be
notorious rather than famous. You notice she's relaunched herself as a
topless model recently? It's no coincidence people pay her more to sit
still and keep her mouth shut than they ever did to walk about and
talk."

"That's actually impressively sneaky," Justine told him, almost awed.

"It is, isn't it? And I used to think 'sneaky' was a vital quality in an
agent."

"It can be," amended Jon. "In moderation."

"Quite. Unfortunately, 'moderation' isn't in Lenny's vocabulary –
and that was what backfired on me in a big way in Romania." Callum
sipped his coffee thoughtfully before continuing. "I'd told him from
the very beginning that I was probably gay – I wasn't even sure myself,
at that stage. But Lenny was one of only a few people who knew, and
he promised me he'd help me keep it under wraps. That was the reason
I trusted him to manage any stories linking me with women. What I
didn't tell him, then or at any other time, was about my relationship
with Jon. It wasn't only my secret to share, you see? I had your father to
think about, too."

"I do see. Thank you for that."

Awkwardly Callum waved away her thanks. "It wasn't completely
altruistic; I was concerned about what it might do to my earning power
if it ever got out. I've got a mother with dementia and a sister with an
aversion to looking after herself, not to mention an auntie I'd like to

take care of if I can. People depend on me, just like for a long time you and your mum depended on Jon. We both had to keep the money rolling in as much as we could, and that meant staying quiet about things we might have preferred to make known. I'd have been happy to come out of the closet years ago if Jon had been willing to come out alongside me, but he wouldn't consider it while you were still a minor. Better late than never, though, eh, love?" His hand crept across the table and fastened on the backs of Jon's fingers.

"Well, you're out all right now," observed Justine, ignoring their small display of affection completely. "So what was that rugby scrum at the hotel all about?"

"Mostly my fault, like I say. I realised it was Lenny who'd been leaking details of my private life when somebody told me I'd supposedly abandoned the Romanian film in the middle of the night. I'd been intending to go straight to the airport after I called Lenny, but I changed my mind and went back to the editing suite and did a bit more cutting and flew to Birmingham first thing in the morning instead. Before I'd even left Bucharest, however – although I didn't know about it until later – it was all over the internet that I'd stormed off the set and disappeared without a trace. There's only one person that story could possibly have come from. Only one person who hadn't been told that I was actually working through the night."

"Lenny."

"Lenny. And I suspect he realised his gravy train was finally about to hit the buffers, which was why he put everything into one last massive publicity binge. When I got back to Romania I told the hotel staff I had a guest arriving in a couple of days who'd be sharing my suite, then I went back to work and thought no more about it until Jon got there. Only, that evening in the restaurant, I noticed somebody looking at him – a woman at another table – and before we knew where we were she'd come over and told him she was a fan of *Hawker and Duffy* and asked for his autograph. Then, as if things weren't embarrassing enough, we realised people had started to walk deliberately past our table and stare at us. The next thing that happened was that somebody took a picture, and it was downhill all the way from there. So either someone on the hotel staff – or someone on the production company, and heaven knows there are plenty of candidates – must have put the pieces together and phoned Lenny, and he mobilised the troops, hence the flash mob scene in the foyer. He's moved on a long way from sending one dickless photographer; these days it's more like a small army."

Justine was looking from one of them to the other in concern, all pretence of enmity with Callum now discarded. "It sounds ghastly," she said.

"It was. There must have been a hundred people at least, God knows where they came from, and we virtually had to shoulder–charge our way through them to the lifts. That's when I grabbed hold of Jon's hand, to try to rescue him from the mayhem – and that was what got us splashed all over the papers. Honestly, after the Scottish film thing you'd think they'd have worked it out for themselves, wouldn't you, but apparently not. All of a sudden we were headline news, and we decided the only sensible thing to do was make a proper announcement and try to get the whole thing behind us as quickly as we could."

"Hence the panicked phone call in the middle of the night," added Jon. "It wasn't the way we wanted to do it, as you can imagine, but it was out of our hands by then; everybody was going to find out about us sooner or later."

"And a week after being photographed in the dining room at the Athénée Palace in Bucharest," concluded Callum with a sigh, "one of the finest hotels in Europe, we were caught queueing up at Charlie's temporary fish and chip stall in Shapley marketplace – and after that things started to get really strange."

"As if they weren't quite strange enough before," amended Justine.

"Exactly. It didn't take long for the media to get hold of the fact that we were buying the house and planning to live here together; even if it wasn't the solicitors who spilled the beans, there were plenty of others who knew. Mind you, there are a lot of people in the village desperate to make us believe it wasn't them – like Derek Westall, for example – Derek the plumber, Roy's cousin – "

"Everybody in the village is Roy's cousin, or his half–brother, or his auntie," Justine put in. "I know that much about Shapley; it's all utterly incestuous."

"Well," went on Callum, acknowledging her observation, "Derek ran into someone in the New Crown asking questions about us, and apparently told him where to go – and thumped him to make sure he went. What he said, or so I've been told, was 'Callum's one of us now; we take care of our own'. Of course he'd had a drink or two, but it was nice of him to say it."

"He rang up to explain," said Jon, "and he's asked us both to join the Rugby Club, which I'm very much afraid we'll have to do."

"Goodness! It sounds as if the whole town's on your side, doesn't it?"

"We're going to need them," Callum told her, soberly. "Without their support, none of this is ever going to work. We'll need them to close ranks around us and keep the journalists at bay, at least."

"And the Rossi clones as well?"

"Not so much. Most of them seem to have crawled back into the woodwork the moment they found out I was living with another man; considering Rossi's obviously gay you'd have thought they'd be a bit more tolerant, wouldn't you, but I've given up trying to fathom out the way their minds work. And we finished off the last two or three when we suggested they might like to help us with the digging–out." A wicked smile curled across Callum's expressive mouth. "I don't think they wanted to get their pretty red boiler suits dirty. Mind you, that mud did smell absolutely disgusting – and no wonder, there was all sorts of stuff in it. They found a whole dead sheep in the pub car park."

Justine was staring at him from the other side of the table, her adamant expression softened to one of amused tolerance. It was plain Callum had won her over, as indeed all three of them had known would be inevitable from the start; that she had made him work hard for it, however, was just as clear.

"All right," she said, slowly. "You've passed the audition; I'm pleased to tell you, you've got the job."

"The job?" Callum was making a very poor pretence of not understanding her; any outsider seeing him at that moment would have felt he had chosen the wrong profession.

"The job of looking after Dad for the foreseeable future. But remember, mess this up and you'll have me to answer to."

"Believe me, Justine, if I messed it up … " He stopped. "I'm not going to mess it up. If I did, I'd deserve everything you could say or do to me, but it isn't going to happen. There's no way this is ever going wrong again."

"Good," said Justine, unbending towards him at last. "Let's make sure it stays that way, shall we?"

"And Callum, of course, is quaking in his boots after all that?" Three days later, Izzy was sitting with a cup of tea in the kitchen of the Old Crown. Bill had taken Justine and his two boys paintballing and Callum had gone to meet Roy at the theatre. They were intending to walk the stage together and discuss forthcoming productions. Thus, the two old friends were left to adopt familiar poses over elevenses, relaxing and reconciling themselves to the altered circumstances in both their lives.

"In a manner of speaking. They're getting on rather well, in fact. Justine gave us these." He set up a pair of four-inch plastic action figures on the table in front of her. "They're 'for the cake', apparently. If we thought Roy was a demon wedding-planner, we obviously hadn't reckoned on my daughter; she'd have the whole thing plotted down to the last monogrammed napkin if we'd let her!"

"Oh, she's a monster!" Izzy examined the little figures delightedly. "She's even made them top hats! This one's Rossi, the green hair's a bit of a giveaway, but who on earth has she used for you?"

Jon's face twisted in embarrassment. "Nobody on *Earth* at all," he confessed, laughing. "That's Han Solo. I really don't know whether to be amused or horrified by that – Harrison Ford's fifteen years older than me, after all."

"But still devastatingly sexy, you must admit. I think I'd be flattered if I was you. Anyway, Justine's getting on all right with Callum."

"Much to my relief, yes, she is. I think she sees him as a sort of big brother figure or something. They've got very much the same dreadful sense of humour."

"Well, he does behave more like a teenager than a grown adult sometimes," was the good–natured reply. "I must say, it's lovely to spend time with him again. I miss him, you know, in a way; he can be awfully good fun. Obviously I adore Bill and I wouldn't want to change him – but he's quiet, you know, like you. Callum at least knows how to party. Not that I'll be doing very much partying after August." She ran a thoughtful hand over her gently–swelling belly. "I'm probably too old for all this, to be honest; it's such a lottery at my age. You know what they call me at the hospital? An 'elderly primigravida'. That's anybody having their first baby over the age of thirty–five."

The injustice of this description was not lost on Jon. "I suppose Bill's hoping for a daughter, is he, having two boys already?"

"I think so. I couldn't care less what it is, to be honest, as long as it's got the requisite number of arms and legs. They'll tell me what sex it is when I go for my scan, if I want, but I think I'd rather not know. Preserve the mystery a bit."

Jon smiled. He found he was doing that a lot lately, now that the house was beginning to feel like home again despite the amount of work still waiting to be done. The kitchen had mysteriously filled up with roses over the last couple of days. Privately Jon doubted there was a rose of any colour left in the county for anybody else to buy; the whole of Callum's income seemed to have gone on roses lately. The garden, by contrast, looked like a mud–wrestling venue, and they had yet to restock the dovecote; it would be months before the physical scars on the place were healed completely. Nevertheless everything had begun to settle down nicely on the emotional front; the walls of his home had grown up again to shelter him – and Callum, too, this time – and the sensation of belonging here was back, almost as if he had never been away.

"What's happening in Yorkshire?" Izzy asked, as though divining his thoughts. "I know Justine's going to be living in the house while she's at university, but have you got any further with taking hold of the company yet?"

Jon pushed a plate of biscuits in her direction and silently enjoined her to help herself, matching her action with his own.

"Not much. Jenny says there's no urgency: Nigel's lost interest in the projects he and Edgar were working on together. That's why he stepped down from directing *The Merry Wives*. It's a good thing Roy was willing to take it on at short notice, otherwise Bill and I might have ended up stuck with it again."

"I know, and I'd rather have Bill at home with me this year; I'm sure Callum feels the same way about you, too. Any news on casting yet? The last thing I heard, they were trying to get Timothy Spall to play Falstaff."

"That's still up the air, as far as I know. I believe he's interested, but it's doubtful whether he can make himself available. An actor like that is booked up such a long way in advance ... On the other hand, the fallback option is apparently Pete."

"Good grief, really? Do you think he'd do it?"

"In a heartbeat, if Roy asked him. What ego could possibly resist? Not Pete's, that's for sure. And I think he'd make a decent job of it. But I wonder if we're all ready to climb on board the roller coaster of his and Roy's relationship again; they do have a penchant for living their private lives in public, don't they?"

"They do," conceded Izzy. "But you've got your happy ending, luv; maybe they deserve a chance of having theirs, if they possibly can."

"I wouldn't dispute that for a moment. Only I thought they were settled years ago – and so did they, until it all went wrong. I'm just not sure how much stamina the rest of us have for going through the whole performance yet again."

"Well, maybe it won't happen." Izzy leaned back in her chair, stretching luxuriously; she was warm and comfortable and perfectly at her ease. "Maybe Timothy Spall will save the day." But her expression took on an inward character, as if a less optimistic thought had crossed her mind. "Nigel's taken Eddie's death very badly, hasn't he?"

Jon was unwilling to meet her gaze. "He has, I'm afraid. They'd been together a long time. As a matter of fact ... " He stopped, looked up at her in bewilderment, and shrugged. "I'm not completely sure ... "

"Oh?" She leaned forward again, her head tilted. "Was there more to it than we realised, then?"

"I don't know. There may have been, at least on Nigel's side. Last time I spoke to him on the phone, he was very low."

"Hardly surprising in the circumstances; he's not very well himself, of course."

Jon sighed. "It was more than that," he said. "I told him about Callum, and that we'd be looking for projects Treece Associates and Callous Films could work on together in future. What he said was: 'You just don't realise how lucky you are.'"

"Oh!" Izzy turned her face away. "So you think that means he'd loved Eddie all along and never had a chance with him? I must admit, I wondered if there was something like that going on beneath the surface."

"So did I. I never expected to be given the answer."

"Poor old thing! Do you think Jenny knows about it?"

"I can't see how she wouldn't, to be honest; they were more or less a *ménage à trois* for several years towards the end. And we don't know that Eddie didn't love Nigel, do we? On the contrary, I'm sure he did – only maybe not the way Nigel wanted to be loved. But Nige stuck by him anyway. I'm not sure if that's tragic, or one of the sweetest things I've ever heard."

"There's no reason why it can't be both," said Izzy – and, for a long time after that, they were both lost in thought.

"So," said Jon at length. "Are you and Bill thinking of doing the dreaded deed at all?"

"Getting married, do you mean?" Izzy's mouth twisted. "I expect we will, before the baby's born; got to legitimise the poor little bastard somehow. But yes, I do feel like letting Bill make an honest woman of me if he's so inclined. I learned the hard way, Jon: marriage is not about the person you think you can live with, it's about the person you don't think you can live without. I don't know what I'd do without Bill in my life, and that's the truth."

"I know." He was looking down into his cup. "It takes a long time, doesn't it, to work out who that person is?"

"Yes. But when you do, there's never any going back. Like Nigel with Eddie, I suppose, or you with Callum or me with Bill; once you realise who they are, you know you're going to stick with them for life. And thank goodness for that, I say!"

"Indeed. Thank goodness."

She was watching him with an expression of great fondness on her face. "It's the real thing, isn't it, for you and Cal?"

"It is. Even though I've met most of his family now, and he's met mine."

"Goodness! Has he taken you to see his mum?"

"No," Jon admitted, "not yet. He doesn't think she'll understand. He's asked the staff at the home to try to prepare her first, but apparently it's not at all certain she'll know what they're saying."

Izzy reached across the table and patted his hand. "I went a few times," she said. "It was an ordeal, I must admit – and she's had time to get a great deal worse since then. She kept asking if I was Callum's girlfriend – and she wanted to know when Eric was coming to see her. She doesn't seem to realise he's dead. Have you met Ada? I bet she adored you, didn't she?"

"She did seem to, I must admit – but she's a Duffy fan, apparently, so she was prejudiced in my favour already."

"Nothing to do with you being wildly in love with her boy, of course," returned Izzy, laughing. "That would get her on your side for life. She's devoted to Callum and Katy, never having had children of her own."

"Katy was there too. She's living in Ada's house with her children; nobody seems to know where Steve is, he appears to have left her. I was half afraid Callum might offer to have them here with us."

"Now there you have the advantage of me," Izzy told him. "I never actually met Katy."

"I almost wish I hadn't, either," he confessed with a shrug. "She and I didn't exactly click, I'm afraid."

"Well no, I never imagined you would; you're from very different worlds, after all! But how did you get on with Connor? He's a sweetie, isn't he?"

"He's an alien, that's what he is! I don't know the first thing about little boys who play football and build robots out of Lego, although I'm sure I'm not too old to learn. Plus, Callum's only just starting to build a proper relationship with Connor himself and I know how long that takes; it would be a bit much to expect the poor child to assimilate me at the same time, especially as I'm so difficult to explain."

"He'll get used to you; kids are remarkably adaptable that way. But Ada likes you, that's what matters most. You've always been a wow with the older generation, luv; it must be the non–threatening persona – they'd all trust you to look after their pensions and their cats. Even Catherine was smitten, you know. Apparently you remind her of somebody she knew a long time ago; the one she loved and lost, I think."

"Heavens! I'm glad I didn't know that when we worked together."

"You shouldn't know now, so treat it with respect – all right?"

"All right."

The silence which followed was interrupted only by the contented munching of chocolate biscuits. "So, what will you do about the company?" Izzy asked, after a while. "Are you and Jenny going to run it between you?"

"That's the idea, whenever we can find something we want to produce – and assuming we can get our hands on the rights to do it."

"Hmmm. I think Catherine's still got an option on that Flora Sandes thing she used for her one–woman show. Maybe we could pitch that to you some time?"

"Please do. It would make a change from trying to find joint projects to do with Callum: now that we're sharing the same agent, she's been desperately trying to promote us as a couple – as if we were some sort of gay Richard Burton and Elizabeth Taylor or something."

"Crikey!" Izzy's undignified sniggering shook her whole body, and she put her cup down with care to avoid an accident. "Callum quite fancies himself as Burton, doesn't he? With a couple of drinks inside him, he even does the voice."

"I know – whole chunks of dialogue from *Where Eagles Dare*. It's a shame he couldn't do a Welsh accent to save his life."

"Poor love. It's always a shock to him when he runs up against his limitations; he likes to think he can do just about anything. No suitable scripts coming your way, then, at the moment?"

"I've actually found a good one quite recently," Jon informed her. "About a pair of commercial pilots, but it's going to take a bit more developing before we can put it into production. In the meantime, we're looking for something else we can work on together."

"How about *La Cage aux Folles*?" suggested Izzy, impishly.

"Hopefully not something specifically gay," he returned with a sigh. "I don't particularly want to be defined by my sexuality at this late stage in my career."

"You might struggle to escape that," Izzy told him wisely. "All right, then, *Man of La Mancha*. I rather fancy hearing you belt out 'The Impossible Dream'."

"You wouldn't, if you'd ever heard me sing. But a straight version of *Don Quixote*, if you'll pardon the expression, might well be a contender."

"Well, a non–singing version at least. I don't suppose there'll be anything straight about it with you two in the cast! Or how about *Julius Caesar*; Cal would make rather a decent Mark Antony, wouldn't he?"

"Richard Burton again?"

"Why not? Honestly, luv, the world's your oyster isn't it? There's not a thing the pair of you can't do, separately or together, as long as you put your minds to it. Well, maybe one," she added, patting her thickened waist contentedly.

"I wouldn't even put that past Callum," retorted Jon, with mischief in his eyes. "It certainly wouldn't be for want of trying."

"Well, it's not as if you won't be adding to your family by other means, is it? I understand from Karen that you're going to be adopting one of Cobweb's kittens, when things have quietened down a bit – and if you don't watch out, I suspect you may be adding one of my dreadful spotty stepsons to the establishment before too long. Or didn't you notice the way Brendan and Justine were looking at one another earlier?"

"I did. I was rather hoping I'd imagined it."

"Not a chance, I'm afraid. Something's burgeoning in the younger generation, mark my words, and before you know where you are you'll be beating the girls … or the boys, of course … away from Connor with a stick, too. Time doesn't stand still, you know; we all fall victim to it in the end."

"God," he groaned, "you're absolutely remorseless, aren't you?
Bring forth men–children only;
For thy undaunted mettle should compose
Nothing but males."

"Thank you," retorted Izzy cheerfully. "I expect you meant that as a compliment, luv, so that's the way I'm going to take it if you don't mind too much."

Jon relayed the contents of his conversation with Izzy to Callum later that evening. Justine was already in bed, having previously given her father ample opportunity of testing the hypothesis that she might be incubating an attraction towards Brendan Wildman, and the two of them were in the kitchen, slowly tidying up at the end of the day. The novelty of such small domestic chores had not yet worn off, and Callum had even expressed a desire to be taught how to operate the washing machine. Eventually.

"Mark Antony?" he mused. "That's not a bad idea. You'd look great in a toga, and I've definitely got the legs for the skirt. Maybe we ought to mention it to Roy for next year."

"You think he'll still be doing the job this time next year?" It was a notion which had not previously occurred to Jon.

Callum shrugged. "I'd say that pretty much depends on Pete, wouldn't you? Of course, if Tim Spall did suddenly become available … but I don't think he'd be willing to turn down *Harry Potter* for our sake, somehow. Don't blame him, either; I'd definitely do a Potter film if it was offered."

"Wouldn't we all?" sighed Jon. "Unfortunately, I don't suppose it's ever likely to be offered."

"Good thing, in a way; I should imagine Potter fans are even worse than the *Planetfall* lot. They'd be a good bit younger, for a start."

Jon shuddered. "Probably better off staying out of it," he admitted, feelingly. "Although of course the money would be nice."

"Sweetheart ... " Callum's tone was gently admonishing. "I keep telling you, you don't need to worry about money any more. Rosemary's financially independent, Justine's taken care of – and, now that I've wrestled my finances out of Lenny's grasp, I'm a bit better off than I thought I was, even after buying this place and paying for Roy's shiny new 3.5 litre V6 penis–substitute with personalised numberplate. Honestly, if ever a man appeared to be compensating for anything ... "

"That's not exactly fair," returned Jon. "And not exactly necessary, either."

"Which is more about Roy than I ever needed to hear," conceded Callum with a smile. "Although I may say it takes one to know one. But you're right, it was a cheap shot – only the point I'm making is ... we can afford to take things easy for a few months, if we want to. Maybe as much as a year, even. Finish doing the house up, have a holiday ... or we could buy a boat or a racehorse, whatever your little heart desires. How about taking some time to have another bash at the Irving book, for instance? You must be pretty close to finishing it by now."

"I might," came the quiet response. "Although I'm beginning to doubt there'll be a market for it. Most people have forgotten who Irving was, these days. And I must admit I'd like to visit Diana and meet her new friend, if we can find an opportunity to do that. But I actually enjoy working, you know? I wouldn't want to give it up just yet."

"Don't worry, love, I feel the same way; I could no more give it up than you could. There's just something about being somebody else during office hours – 'warriors for the working–day', if you like – and coming home to be who you really are at night. I suppose everybody has to put on a show one way or another, don't they? And everybody's probably just as glad as we are when it finally stops and they get to be themselves again."

"'No man is a hero to his valet'," Jon told him, folding the towel he had been using to dry his hands and turning away from the sink at last.

"The people we're closest to see us as we really are. If they love us anyway, that's a bonus."

"And you never stopped, did you? No matter how badly I treated you, you never stopped loving me. I knew that all along."

"No, I didn't," admitted Jon. "I wouldn't have known how to."

"I've said this before, love – I definitely don't deserve you, but I am going to try to in future. In fact I've been thinking … maybe it's time we got you another watch? Only this time I'll be able to say exactly what I want to say on the back of it. And we can go together, if you like, and you can choose the one you want."

The thought of walking into a jeweller's shop shoulder to shoulder with Callum was a distinctly unnerving one, and for a moment Jon could not imagine how such a scene would play. Then he thought again. All things being equal, the first time they did that would probably not be the last – if Izzy's assertion was to be believed, at least. She had taken Jon's naïf suggestion of a low–key civil partnership ceremony with roughly the same sized pinch of salt Justine had also employed. If it were to happen at all, it would no doubt be accompanied by a fanfare that could be heard from Mars.

"Callum Henley will never sidle unnoticed into any situation," she'd informed him bluntly. "He's an actor to his fingertips, bless him. And it's not just him you're taking on, Jon, it's everybody else he's ever been and everybody he'll ever be in future. Those headlines that talked about Rossi and Father Fergus had it right, you know. In a way, that's exactly what it is … plus the Scottish King and Mr Murdstone, Robin Hood and Lord Darcy, and all the rest of them put together. It's no use pretending those people aren't you, because they are – they just aren't all you are; there's a lot more to both of you than them."

"All right," he replied, after a moment's thought. "Perhaps we can do that in Gostrey when we go to buy the cat stuff. Assuming you're still determined to involve a poor innocent kitten in our ridiculous life, that is?"

"It's not a ridiculous life at all. It's a very nice life." They had emerged from the kitchen by now, and Callum switched the light off as he passed. Their feet were on the stairs and they moved up slowly, side by side, in no particular hurry. Time lay before them in an infinite quantity after all; there was no reason for them ever to be parted unless they chose to – and just at the moment they did not choose.

"And do you still intend to call her 'Bert'?"

"Of course I do. That's her name. It always has been, ever since the first moment I set eyes on her in the bottom of your wardrobe. Cats are like ships, you know: you can't just go changing their names whenever you want to – it's very bad luck."

"It's pretty bad luck on the kitten to be saddled with a name like 'Bert'," observed Jon as they reached the first–floor landing.

"It's even worse luck to be stuck with the pair of us as parents," Callum told him, "but I've no doubt she'll survive it. There are far less pleasant fates for a young kitten, after all." He turned away, took a couple of steps up towards the attic – and then turned back, reaching out his hand to Jon. "Well, are you coming upstairs?"

Jon's fingers tangled in his. "Of course," he grinned.

"'Whereupon'," continued his lover, as they climbed, "'I will show you a chamber with a bed; which bed, because it shall not speak of your pretty encounters, press it to death'!"

"Promises promises," chuckled Jon disbelievingly – but taking his hand and allowing himself to be guided gently towards their bedroom anyway.

Quotations in the Text

Act 1
Scene i
All William Shakespeare: *Macb*th* (aka 'the Scottish play') except

"an attendant lord ... " T.S. Eliot: *The Love Song of J. Alfred Prufrock*

Scene ii
All William Shakespeare: *Macb*th* except

"some must watch ... " William Shakespeare: *Hamlet*

Scene iii
"I go ... " William Shakespeare: *A Midsummer Night's Dream*

"Andante in ... " and "Avete vinto ... " the Italian version of *Monopoly*

"His rash fierce ... " William Shakespeare: *Richard II*

"Your face ... " and subsequent, William Shakespeare: *Macb*th*

Scene iv
"The orchard walls ... " and subsequent, William Shakespeare: *Romeo and Juliet*

"One would as soon ... " Emily Dickinson: *What Soft Cherubic Creatures ...*

"One man in a thousand ... " Rudyard Kipling: *The Thousandth Man*

Act 2
Scene i
"A rat ... " and "Mad as ... " William Shakespeare: *Hamlet*

"Enter Antonio ... " and subsequent, John Webster: *The Duchess of Malfi*

" ... a dinner of herbs ... " *Proverbs* 15:17

Scene ii
" ... the whirligig ... " William Shakespeare: *Twelfth Night*

Scene iii
"As flies ... " William Shakespeare: *King Lear*

Scene iv

"Half a league … " Alfred, Lord Tennyson: *The Charge of the Light Brigade*

Act 3
Scene i

"They fuck you up … " Philip Larkin: *This Be The Verse*

Scene ii

" … the best of times … " Charles Dickens: *A Tale of Two Cities*

"Unto the pure … " *Titus* 1:15

" … the little rift … " Alfred, Lord Tennyson: *Merlin and Vivien*

Scene iii

Scene iv

"Thrice … " William Shakespeare: *Macb*th*

"It is the prettiest … " and "My heart … " William Shakespeare: *Troilus and Cressida*

Scene v

"As late I rambled … " John Keats: *To a Friend Who Sent Me Some Roses*

"I am in blood … " William Shakespeare: *Macb*th*

"Bring forth … " William Shakespeare: *Macb*th*

"Warriors for … " William Shakespeare: *Henry V*

"No man is … " *attrib.* Mme Cornuel

"Whereupon … " William Shakespeare: *Troilus and Cressida*

A note on editions:

The Shakespeare quotations are taken from opensourceshakespeare.org and the edition of *The Duchess of Malfi* used was published by Manchester University Press in 1997. Other quotations obtained from various online sources.

About Adam Fitzroy

Imaginist and purveyor of tall tales Adam Fitzroy is a UK resident who has been successfully spinning male–male romances either part–time or full–time since the 1980s, and has a particular interest in examining the conflicting demands of love and duty.

Manifold Press
- aiming for excellence
in gay fiction.

Acclaimed writers deliver strong
storylines with a variety of
intriguing locations;
whether set in the past,
present or future,
our focus is always on romance.

For a full range of high-quality
plot- and character-driven
ebooks, please visit our website.

www.manifoldpress.co.uk

Image: @GeraldineClark|Bigstockphoto.com

Manifold Press

CPSIA information can be obtained at www.ICGtesting.com
Printed in the USA
LVOW01s1011290714

396549LV00012B/178/P